Jean Girard de Villethierry

The Life of St. John of God

Founder of the Order of Hospitallers

Jean Girard de Villethierry

The Life of St. John of God
Founder of the Order of Hospitallers

ISBN/EAN: 9783337054021

Printed in Europe, USA, Canada, Australia, Japan

Cover: Foto ©Raphael Reischuk / pixelio.de

More available books at **www.hansebooks.com**

The Saints and Servants of God.

SECOND SERIES.

THE LIFE

OF

S. JOHN OF GOD,

FOUNDER OF THE ORDER OF HOSPITALLERS.

"Gaude Maria Virgo, cunctas hæreses sola interemisti in universo mundo."—*Antiph. Ecclesiæ.*

LONDON:

R. WASHBOURNE, 18 PATERNOSTER ROW.

1875.

TO

THE REGULAR CLERGY

OF THE CATHOLIC CHURCH IN ENGLAND,

THE SUCCESSORS AND SPIRITUAL CHILDREN

OF GENERATIONS OF MARTYRS,

WHO,

BY THEIR CHEERFULNESS IN HOLY POVERTY,

THEIR DILIGENCE

IN OBSCURITY AND UNDER OPPRESSION,

THEIR UNEXAMPLED CONFIDENCE

IN THE TRUTHS THEY TAUGHT,

THEIR FORGIVING CHARITY

TOWARDS UNGENEROUS OPPONENTS,

AND THEIR SELF-DENYING KINDNESS TOWARDS THOSE

WHOM THEIR PRAYERS, THEIR SACRIFICES,

AND THEIR SUFFERINGS

RESCUED FROM THE DARKNESS OF ERROR,

HAVE PRESERVED TO THEIR COUNTRY,

TOGETHER WITH THE PRECIOUS EXAMPLE

OF THEIR OWN VIRTUES,

THE UNFAILING LIGHT

OF THE CATHOLIC FAITH,

AND THE HEREDITARY DEVOTION TO THE HOLY SEE,

WHICH DISTINGUISHED

THE PILGRIMS AND SAINTS OF SAXON TIMES,

AND THE PRINCELY BUILDERS

OF OUR NORMAN CHURCHES.

S. WILFRID'S.

TRANSLATION OF S. THOMAS OF CANTERBURY.

MDCCCXLVII.

PREFACE.

THE first life of S. John of God was written by Francesco Castro, Superior of the Hospital of Granada. It was published about thirty years after the death of the Saint, and translated into Latin, French, and Italian, the latter version being by Giovan Francesco Bordini, Priest of the Roman Oratory and Archbishop of Avignon.

Antonio Govea, Bishop of Cyrene and Apostolic Visitor in Persia, published a second Life about 1630: and from these two Jean Girard de Villethierry, Priest of the diocese of Paris, compiled a third, which was rendered into Italian and considerably enlarged by Pietro Cianfogni, Canon of S. Lorenzo and Member of the Academy of Florence, at the request of the *Fate-bene-fratelli*, as the Brothers of the Order of Hospitallers are called in Italy. The following pages are translated from Canon Cianfogni's work, which was published at Florence in 1747.

THE ORATORY, LONDON,
    Feast of S. Scholastica, 1875.

CONTENTS.

BOOK I.

WHICH CONTAINS THE HISTORY OF HIS LIFE TO THE ESTABLISHMENT OF HIS HOSPITAL IN THE CITY OF GRANADA.

BOOK II.

WHICH CONTAINS THE ACCOUNT OF HIS PUBLIC LIFE.

BOOK III.

CONTAINING AN ACCOUNT OF HIS DEATH, OF THE HONOURS PAID TO HIS MEMORY, AND OF THE PRODIGIES WHICH GOD WORKED IN ORDER TO MAKE KNOWN HIS SANCTITY TO MEN.

BOOK I.

WHICH CONTAINS THE HISTORY OF HIS LIFE
TO THE ESTABLISHMENT OF HIS HOSPITAL IN
THE CITY OF GRANADA.

S. JOHN OF GOD,

FOUNDER OF THE ORDER OF HOSPITALLERS.

CHAPTER I.

IN WHICH THE VIRTUES OF S. JOHN OF GOD ARE TREATED OF IN GENERAL.

GOD, Who loves His Church, and provides carefully for all its wants, has always sent men of extraordinary abilities and singular merit to govern, defend, instruct, and edify it, and to give it shining examples of virtue, such as might renew in it that spirit of holiness which is its peculiar characteristic, and ought to distinguish it in the midst of this corrupt world.

Thus at first He raised up the holy apostles who were its fathers, who founded it on a firm rock, and traversed the whole world to shed over it the light of the Gospel; who, forgetting themselves, laboured only to establish the empire of Jesus Christ, having no other desire than that of carrying the glory of His Name to the ends of the earth. He has fostered in her bosom an innumerable number of faithful souls of

1—2

every age and sex, who, full of zeal and fervour, confronted tyrants, despised their threats, and suffered with joy the most horrible persecutions, bearing by their constancy a shining testimony to the truth of the faith, and not fearing to shed their blood to the last drop, thus making it evident that their love was stronger than all the powers of earth, and death itself.

He has also provided for its instruction, for He has always given it pastors and doctors eminent in learning and piety, who, penetrating the most profound mysteries of our religion, have explained them with clearness to all its people, and have continually distributed to them the bread of His Word, while they shone as sacred lights to all in His house.

He has also in all ages appointed certain persons to serve for examples and models to all those who were willing to practise virtue, and for this reason has loaded them with graces and benedictions. Thus He led into the desert the Antonies, the Hilarions, and the Benedicts, that they might become the leaders of all who were willing to sanctify themselves in solitude and separation from the world. He rendered illustrious the Agnes', the Agathas, and the Cecilias, and inspired them with a special love of purity, in order that other virgins might learn from them what their obligations are, and what they ought to do in order to fulfil all the duties of so holy and sublime a state. He willed that S. Francis should render himself illustrious by his poverty, and carry it as far as possible, in order that he might be as it were the master and guide of all those who are poor according to the Gospel. In these last ages He has not failed to raise up many illustrious saints who have imitated the zeal, the courage, the penance, and the holiness of the first

Christians, in order that they might serve to awaken the children of His Church, who were living in fatal lethargy and drowsiness, and whom their example might induce to re-enter the paths of justice. Such was the great Saint whose actions, with the divine assistance, we propose to describe.

He entered the vineyard of the Lord towards the evening only, for he appeared as late as the sixteenth century, but he was made equal to the greater part of the other labourers who were called in the morning, that is to say, in those happy times when Christianity still retained all its fervour; for we shall make it abundantly clear that he was not inferior to them in zeal and charity, and that he imitated all their virtues. In truth he held all the goods of the earth in utter contempt; he neglected the opportunities of acquiring them, and preferred poverty to all the advantages he could hope for in the world.

He imitated the fervour of those penitents of old, so distinguished in our annals, who punished themselves for their sins with such great severity, for what did he not do in order to chastise his body? with what rigour did he not treat himself? and did he not of his own accord, also, impose upon himself heavy penances, heavier perhaps even than those formerly required by the canons for the greatest enormities? He shared in the glory of the most pure virgins, since not only did he refuse to engage himself in marriage, but he took flight as soon as it was proposed to him, and preferred the troubles and fatigues of a poor and laborious life to the repose he might have enjoyed in the house of the rich man who offered him his alliance.

The most famous deserts have scarcely seen solita-

ries more humble and more dead to themselves than
this great Saint, as we shall see when we consider all
that he did in order to make himself appear as nothing,
and to render himself vile and contemptible; and
how much more he laboured to lower himself than
worldly persons to attain to the greatest honours.

We shall see that he was always very submissive to
his directors, and those who had the care of his conscience. He undertook nothing without having consulted them, and was very exact in following all their
orders. He had no other will but theirs, and he
allowed himself to be conducted by them with as
much docility as if he were still in the first years of
childhood.

He did not apply himself to the study of ecclesiastical authors, nor to the discussion of dogmatic theology, because his days were spent in work, and he
could have said with the prophet that from his youth
up he had lived in poverty and toil. For all this he
was not deficient in light, but on the contrary, if we
examine all his proceedings, we shall acknowledge
that he was greatly enlightened in the way of salvation, that he possessed the science of the saints, and
deserves to be ranked with the greatest doctors, because of his perfect knowledge of Jesus crucified,
which is the height of wisdom.

As for his charity, we shall be surprised at it, and
have difficulty in comprehending how a man without
credit or authority could establish a large hospital in
the midst of the city of Granada; how, having neither
possessions nor revenues, he was able to support so
many poor persons; why he did not give way under
the pressure of affairs which poured in upon him from
all sides; and why he was not discouraged in the

midst of so many objects which were revolting and contrary to nature.

We may add also that he merited the crown of martyrdom ; for besides that the holy fathers teach us that penance has the power of making martyrs, we shall see in the following history that in fact he did seek after martyrdom. He traversed several provinces in order to find an opportunity of shedding his blood for the faith of Jesus Christ ; and if executioners and tyrants did not take away his life, this was against his own will, because he eagerly desired it, and had already made the sacrifice of it within himself. Therefore it is reasonable to conclude that God, Who knows our most secret thoughts, accepted the preparation of his heart, and has allotted to him in heaven the same reward as to all His other martyrs.

All these circumstances lead us to say that divine Providence destined him to appear in these latter times, in which the charity of the faithful has grown cold, according to the prediction of Jesus Christ, in order that the example of his virtues might serve to contribute to their conversion and rekindle their fervour.

It is fitting to warn our readers that in these first chapters we shall not give the name of John of God to our Saint, but content ourselves with calling him John, until we have explained what was the occasion which procured him the honour of bearing the illustrious title of John of God. We must also say that we shall not imitate those historians who strive in all things to exalt the character of those whose actions they are describing, by dissembling their weaknesses and defects, and who go out of their way to excuse and justify all that they did, imagining that it is to the honour of great men, and above all of saints, to have done nothing but what is great, distinguished, and perfect ; for such conduct does not appear to us lawful. On the contrary, we believe that sincerity is the first quality required in an historian ; he ought to confine himself strictly to the truth ; and if he conceals or disguises from his readers important facts, under the pretext that they do not contribute to the glory of those in favour of whom he is writing, he no longer deserves credit in other things, and ought to be regarded as a foolish flatterer.

We will, then, simply state events as they happened, and not strive to make John of God appear an impeccable and invulnerable hero. We will praise in him what is really worthy of praise, and find fault with what appears to us to deserve it ; leaving to the judgment of our readers those things which appear doubtful or capable of a different interpretation. By these means we shall endeavour to avoid the reputation of being partial, and too much prejudiced in favour of the subject of our book. We hope that his children, who have induced us to undertake this work, will not be grieved at seeing the actions of their holy father in their natural colours. This itself will be very useful to them, for in it they will study the ways of the Lord ; they will see in it that man can do nothing of himself, and that he is only capable of falling and of going astray, as long as he is not supported by Him Who is all our strength ; they will learn from it how we must rise again when we have fallen ; and they will accustom themselves to praise the mercy of our God, who supports His saints in their wanderings, gives them time to return to themselves, strikes them in kindness and in order to warn them to change their evil habits, and receives them as soon as they return to Him with a contrite and humble heart.

CHAPTER II.

BIRTH OF JOHN.—WONDERS WHICH ACCOMPANIED IT.—HIS EARLY EDUCATION.

JOHN had none of the advantages of birth and fortune, which serve to recommend men to worldly-minded persons; for his family was not one of distinction, and his parents held no high rank in the world. Still we must not suppose them to have belonged to the lowest class, nor say, as some do, that they lived in a state of utter wretchedness and degradation; for one of the first writers of his life expressly mentions that they were of the middle class, and lived honourably. Their property corresponded with their state in life; they were neither too rich nor too poor, and while not exposed to the dangers and temptations which almost always attend excessive poverty, they were also free from the vices and dissipations which are very often a consequence of affluence. It was also remarked that their manners were exceedingly regular, and their conduct exemplary. They took care to occupy themselves with some employment, not only in order to derive profit from it, but also to fill up all their time, and to avoid idleness, which is so contrary to virtue.

The name of John's father was Andrew Ciudad; but we do not know that of his mother, either because she was anxious to live in silence and obscurity, or because historians neglected to ascertain it, not judging it of importance to the glory of her son. They lived in a city of Portugal called Montemor o novo, situated in the archbishopric of Evora. Their piety led them to practise hospitality as much as they could consistently with their means, and to receive into their house pilgrims and travellers, and, above all, ecclesiastics and religious. When they had satisfied this work of charity, so much recommended in Scripture and by the holy fathers, they employed what remained of their money in giving alms, and assisting poor persons who were ashamed to beg.

Towards the end of the fifteenth century our Lord blessed their marriage with happy fruitfulness; for in the year 1495 He gave them a son, who came into the world on the 8th of March, and received at the font the name of John. They received this gift from heaven with all the gratitude they were capable of, and looked upon it as a fresh pledge of the love of God, which obliged them to redouble their zeal, and to serve Him with more fidelity than ever.

We must not omit to mention the prodigies which happened at the birth of this child. Historians declare that at the very moment he first saw the light there appeared on the roof of his parents' house a column of fire, which was seen by every one, and was doubtless a presage of the future. When our Lord Jesus Christ was born, a bright star was sent from heaven, to point out to men that this divine Infant would be the light of the world. When S. Ambrose, still in his infancy, was asleep, a swarm of bees entered his mouth, and lodged in it without doing him any harm, which made his father pronounce that he would one

day be a great orator, and that his speeches would be
as sweet as honey.

William, Abbot of S. Thierry at Reims, relates that
hardly was S. Bernard conceived than his mother had
in her sleep a vision which was destined to make
known to her what would happen to her child; for
she thought she had within her a little white dog,
rather red on the back, which barked continually; in
great alarm she consulted a man of noted piety, who
at that very hour was filled with the spirit of prophecy with which David was animated, when, speaking
of holy preachers, he said to God, " The tongue of thy
dogs shall be red with the blood of thy enemies;" and
seeing her trembling and disturbed, he answered her :
" Fear not, all will be well : you will be mother of an
infant, who as a faithful dog will one day keep the
house of God, and bark loudly in its defence against
the enemies of the faith ; for he will be an excellent
preacher, and, like a good dog, will heal with the
medicine of his tongue the wounds of a great number
of souls."

We know, further, that the mother of S. Dominic
also imagined in a dream that she was carrying within
her a little dog bearing in its mouth a lighted torch,
with which it set fire to the whole earth ; whence
she concluded that the infant she was to bring forth
would be distinguished for holiness, and that by the
example of his life, and the power of his eloquence, he
would kindle the fire of charity in the hearts of men ;
a prediction which, as every one knows, was abundantly fulfilled.

We can then say, since the result has proved it,
that the column of fire which was seen at the birth of
John was not merely a natural meteor, but that it

was created by divine Providence to declare to men
that the heart of this infant would one day be con-
sumed by the ardour of love.

Another remarkable occurrence is also mentioned
by his biographers. The bells of the church of
Nuestra Senora del Obispo, the parish where he was
to be baptized, rang of their own accord in sweet and
pleasing harmony, which surprised the whole city,
and caused different thoughts to spring up in people's
minds. Some were inclined to say that the sound
was caused by an earthquake, but there was no appearance of this, because the same thing had not
happened in the neighbouring churches. Others
feared some trick; but the majority judged that it
was connected with the column of fire mentioned
above, and that these two marvels portended something great respecting the new-born child. One
historian relates that they spoke as the inhabitants
of Judæa did when they heard of the wonders
that accompanied the birth of S. John, the son of
Zachary, "What an one, think ye, shall this child be?
for the hand of the Lord was with him." All these
circumstances raised in some of them a desire to consult a hermit of great reputation, who lived apart
from men, at some distance from the city, on the
mountain of Oca, in order that they might know from
him what he thought of this son of Andrew Ciudad
who was just born. The holy solitary, inspired no
doubt by the Spirit of God, foretold to them very
great things of him, declaring that he would be an
extraordinary man, that his piety would shine forth
on all sides, that his life would be a kind of miracle,
and that the Lord would make use of him to execute
His Will, and to accomplish a work as difficult as it

would be useful. And in order to confirm the truth of his words, and remove from them all suspicion that he was relating visions without foundation, he spoke of the ringing of the bells, which he certainly could not have heard, being too far from the city. He told them that God, by a particular grace, had given him knowledge of it, and confirmed them in the idea that this harmony was supernatural, produced by the angels themselves, and that it was a mark of the joy which these blessed spirits felt. He likewise exhorted them to be very attentive to all that might happen to this child of miracle.

So many wonders rendered John very dear to his father and mother, and greatly strengthened the love of him which nature had implanted in them. Being gifted also with great piety, they reflected that he belonged to God more than to themselves, and they believed it to be one of their chief obligations to use all their efforts to second the designs Providence might have upon him. For this reason they gave their whole attention to bringing him up well. As soon as he was able to speak, they accustomed him to pronounce the Name of God, in order thereby to sanctify, and in some sort to consecrate, his tongue. They lost no time in training him up in all the exercises of piety of which his tender age was capable, and took care that he should be instructed in the rudiments of Christian doctrine. They endeavoured, above all, to give him a good example, and to keep him away from all that might make a bad impression on his mind. They were careful to make him love Jesus Christ, and to teach him early the duty of serving Him from Whom he had his being. They took every precaution to secure him against the shipwreck which children often make, when from want of proper instruction they lose the grace of their baptism before they even know it. Their care was not fruitless, and they had the consolation of seeing that they were not sowing in vain ; for their son profited daily by their instructions. He learned very easily the principal mysteries of our religion, and received without difficulty the feelings of piety which they wished to instil into him. They never found him opposed to their good intentions ; but remarked, on the contrary, that he was inclined of his own accord to virtue, that he did not fall into the ordinary faults of children, but was beyond his years in all things, and showed a disposition which led them to hope everything from him when he should have arrived at a more mature age. This filled them with joy, and induced them to address themselves continually to God, to thank Him for all the mercies He had shown them, and to pray Him to shed His grace and benediction more and more on their son, whom they wished to render perfect only in order that he might be better able to serve and honour Him.

CHAPTER III.

JOHN LEAVES HIS PARENTS' HOUSE.—DEATH OF HIS MOTHER.—HIS FATHER BECOMES A RELIGIOUS.

ALTHOUGH Andrew Ciudad and his wife gave much of their time to the good education of their son, they failed not nevertheless to employ themselves in many other good works. We have already seen that they were in the habit of practising much hospitality. It was in the exercise of this virtue that they met with

a great mortification, and were tried on the point
in which they were most sensible. When their son
was about eight or nine years old, they received into
their house a priest who was on his way to Madrid.
The good reception they gave him, and the courteous
and obliging manner in which they treated him, induced him to delay his departure, and to stay some
days in their house. It was during this time that
John frequently heard him speak of the piety of Madrid, its celebrated churches, and the great number of
learned and holy persons who were living there. There
needed nothing more to make a strong impression on
his innocent heart, and to excite his curiosity. When,
therefore, the priest wished to continue his journey,
John—who was not yet capable of reflecting properly
on what he had been told respecting the deference of
children to their parents, and the dependence upon
them in which they ought to live—allowed himself to
be carried away by the desire he had to follow him,
so that he left his father and mother, and going out of
the house without their knowledge, set off on the road
to Madrid.

Men have judged differently of this event. Some
blamed the ecclesiastic for suffering John to follow
him, and for not opposing him, since no child of so
tender an age can lawfully do anything without
the command or consent of those under whom God
and nature have placed him. Others, on the contrary,
were more reserved in their judgment, and said that
God often conducts His elect by extraordinary ways,
and that in order to sanctify them the more marvellously, He permits some things which, though they
seem contrary to the common course, nevertheless
assist in the execution of His Will. They said, there-

fore, that we must not regard the action of this priest purely in itself, and without any relation to divine Providence, which probably made use of it in order to separate the child from the house of his father and mother, where perhaps he would have been brought up with a delicacy unsuited to the employments for which he was destined.

In like manner many reflections were made on the conduct of the child in leaving his father's house so young. It was said that he imitated Abraham, the father of the faithful, who left his country to go and serve God in a strange land. Others compared him to his great patron S. John Baptist, who lived in the desert almost from his cradle, and who separated himself from his parents and the whole world, in order to prepare himself for his ministry as the Precursor, and to occupy himself solely with Him Who was the expectation of the nations.

Jesus Christ has said, "If any one come to Me, and hate not his father and mother, and wife, and children, and brethren, and sisters, yea and his own life also, he cannot be My disciple;" and some persons, with these words in their mind, maintained that John had put in practice this evangelical maxim, and that, conducted by supernatural light, he had overcome, even at this tender age, the most legitimate affections of nature. We may also remark that since God destined him to be the head of a large order, and the father of innumerable religious, who would leave their families to enter the road to perfection, He wished him to do the same thing in his own infancy, and to separate himself from his parents at an early age, in order that, having been all his life disengaged from the ties of flesh and blood, he might be better able to inspire with the like sentiments all who should submit to his discipline, and might influence them as much by his example as by his precepts.

These are the different aspects under which we may regard the flight of the young Saint, which our readers will judge for themselves. Let us now see how his father and mother bore this separation. Not only were they much surprised, but greatly afflicted at it. They immediately set about obtaining information respecting him, and after the example of the Holy Virgin and S. Joseph, when they had lost Jesus Christ on their return from the Temple, they sought him amongst their kinsfolk, thinking he might be in the house of some one of them. They then made further inquiries, and spared none of the exertions usual on such occasions. His mother especially took extraordinary pains, and imitating Anne, the mother of the young Tobias, often went into the fields and high roads to see if she could not hear some news of her dear son, whom she regarded as the sole object of her hopes, the support of her old age, and the consolation of all her family. When she saw that all her labours were to no purpose, she gave way to grief, and died at the end of twenty days, her life being, as it would seem, really shortened by this event. His father was not less afflicted, but having a stronger mind he was able to moderate his grief; he maintained his self-possession, and his piety led him to raise his mind to God, to adore His judgments, to make Him a willing sacrifice of a son who was no longer in his power, and to consider within himself that he had perhaps been deprived of him only because he had too much attachment to him. Thus he survived his misfortune, and in less than a month found himself deprived both of his son and of his wife. This double privation made him open his eyes to the vanity of earthly things. He then saw clearly the nothingness of all creatures: he was fully persuaded that he ought to attach himself to nothing on earth, and he felt only contempt for the world. He frequently considered within himself that we ought to make all the events of this life serve towards the attainment of our eternal salvation, so as to profit by the visits God vouchsafes us, and to correspond to the designs of His Providence. He was convinced that the Lord had taken two persons dear to him only to set him free, that he might give himself up to His service, and without any delay embrace a more perfect state of life. He therefore broke off all the ties which detained him in the world, and retiring to Lisbon, entered a house of the order of S. Francis, and became a religious. There he began to think seriously of making reparation for the sins of his youth; he passed his days in rigorous penance, and wept bitterly over the least faults he might have committed while in the married state. Entirely forgetting the world, he gave himself up to prayer, and to the contemplation of heavenly things. He entirely renounced his own will, and had no longer any other than that of his superiors. He became a living example of modesty, humility, and charity; and after having persevered in this holy and edifying life for several years, he slept happily in the Lord.

We have thought it better to relate in this part of our history the death of the father and mother of our Saint, that we may not be obliged afterwards to interrupt the thread of our story. We will now describe the different incidents of his life, until he applied himself to waiting upon the sick poor; for it was in this that his vocation properly lay, all other things only serving to conduct and dispose him towards it.

CHAPTER IV.

THE JOURNEY OF JOHN.—THE PRIEST WHO WAS CONDUCTING HIM LEAVES HIM AT OROPESA.—HE ENTERS THE SERVICE OF A CITIZEN OF THAT TOWN.

THE priest who had undertaken to take the young John to Madrid did not accompany him to the end of his journey, but when they reached the city of Oropesa, he separated himself from him, and left him altogether. It would be very difficult to justify his conduct in suffering a child of this age to leave his parents' house, and afterwards abandoning him. Would it not have been more right and just to leave him in the hands of a father and mother who were educating him so piously? Or at least, having withdrawn him from them, would not prudence and charity have obliged him to attend to his education? It is thus that all persons of good sense will reason, for this action certainly appears to be most culpable. But, as we have already observed, divine Providence permitted this priest to induce the child to leave his father's house, because God wished him to be detached from his family, and raised above natural affections from his earliest years; we may even say that God vouchsafed to make use of this indiscretion in order to try him, to teach him not to place confidence in men, and to make him enter upon a poor, austere, and penitent life at an age at which other men are not capable of mortifying themselves. We must, then, represent to ourselves this child, separated from his father and mother, in a strange town, without any one to help him, destitute of knowledge of any kind, and abandoned by all. This appears a hard case; but it is God Himself Who is working in it, and Who wishes to form for Himself a saint, of whom toil, poverty, and humiliation shall be the special characteristics.

The young John was at first relieved by some pious persons, who, compassionating his wretched condition, gave him shelter, and employed him in work proportioned to his age and strength. He afterwards entered the service of Francis Majoral, a man of integrity, who was superintendent of the prisons. It was in his house that John passed a great part of his youth, and inured himself to toil and labour, for he always aimed at doing what was most laborious, and never refused the most burthensome tasks, whenever he could in any way assist his companions and spare them fatigue.

The holy fathers often remark that we sometimes see in the actions of little children certain things by which we can judge beforehand what kind of men they will be in after-life; their reserve, docility, and gentleness are signs that they will afterwards have great gifts of modesty, humility, and patience; and the carefulness with which they correct themselves of their little faults is a clear indication that they will show much zeal and fervour when they have to fight against their passions, and to make amends for their sins. In like manner, the behaviour of John during the first years of his youth was an earnest of his future holiness. Never was there a young man more reserved, more modest, more obedient, and more cir-

cumspect in his words. He was submissive, not only
to his master Francis Majoral, but to all those who
gave him any command. He allowed himself no
exemptions in anything; he suffered with humility
the reproofs which were given him, from whatever
quarter they might come; he was attentive to his
work; he knew how to arrange his time, and employ
it usefully; his words were pure and well chosen; he
avoided giving offence to those with whom he talked;
in a word, though young, he did nothing which
savoured of youth.

As soon as he was fourteen years old, Majoral, who
knew his good qualities, and had tried his exactness
and fidelity in innumerable ways, determined to send
him to a country house which he had near the city, to
take care of his cattle. Not having any will of his
own, he went without any repugnance. He even
regarded it as an advantageous circumstance, since
he hoped to be more separated from the world in
this solitude, and thus to have more time to serve
God.

In fact, he had no sooner arrived there, than he
regulated all his actions in such a manner that his
life was a continued series of good works. He had
appointed hours for prayer in the morning and evening. In the course of the day he further contrived
certain intervals, which he appropriated to this holy
exercise. Everything he saw in the country made
him praise and adore God. He mortified himself in
all things: he watched continually over his senses,
and practised all the good in his power.

His master was greatly edified by his conduct, and
seeing him at the end of some years much further
advanced in goodness than when he had entrusted his

cattle to him, he charged him with the care of watching over the household at his country house, and made him as it were steward of his property. It was in this capacity that John showed his true and solid piety: for, without neglecting his prayers, he devoted himself entirely to his duties: and far from imitating those who imagine that devotion gives them a right to spare themselves, and to live delicately, he laboured more than all the rest; nothing escaped his vigilance; he was everywhere, he had an eye upon all that passed, both within and without the house; he went into the fields in all weathers to give the necessary orders; he allowed no opportunity of benefiting his master to escape him, and by his example he taught all the other servants to be active and diligent in their duties. God blessed his cares and labour, for the property of his master increased under his management; his flocks were multiplied, and prosperity reigned in his house. But what is still more worthy of notice is, that in all his occupations John failed not to procure, in many different ways, the spiritual good of his companions, for he often repeated to them the principal points of the Catechism; he suggested to them good maxims; he selected opportunities to speak to them of God, and did all in his power to gain them to Jesus Christ. Even the people of the neighbourhood came to him, in order to profit by his conversation, to obtain consolation in their troubles, and to ask his advice in the difficulties they met with in their own affairs; and they always went away well satisfied. Thus it was not without reason that we said that God separated him from his father only in order that he might contribute to the instruction and edification of a great number of persons. This was the

way in. which his early youth was spent, and such
were his occupations until he was two-and-twenty
years old.

CHAPTER V.

HIS MASTER WISHES TO GIVE HIM ONE OF HIS DAUGH-
TERS TO WIFE.—HE GOES TO THE WAR IN ORDER
TO AVOID THIS MARRIAGE.

THE wise man says, " Let a wise servant be dear to
thee as thy own soul ;" and it is easy to conceive how
highly Majoral esteemed John, in whom he remarked
so much prudence and piety. He preferred him to all
his other servants, looking upon him as a real treasure,
and thinking himself very fortunate in possessing him.
But the more he knew his good qualities, the more he
feared to lose him in some unforeseen manner. In
order, therefore, to attach him for ever to his interests,
and to take away from him the power of leaving him
and giving his services elsewhere, he thought he could
not do better than offer him one of his daughters in marriage. Any other would have regarded this proposal as
a great piece of good fortune, and would have accepted
it without difficulty, because it was a certain means of
becoming rich, and leading an easy life, as Majoral
was very well off, and able to give his daughter a
considerable dowry. But John thought otherwise,
and such an offer was not capable of shaking his intention, for besides that earthly goods had never
tempted him, and he had always despised them,
he considered with the apostle, that " he that is

with a wife is solicitous for the things of the world, how he may please his wife ; and he is divided :" and on the contrary, that "he that is without a wife, is solicitous for the things that belong to the Lord, how he may please God."

He would not, therefore, hear of this marriage, in order that, being free from the cares and troubles which would have been a necessary consequence of it, he might have his mind more at liberty to attend to prayer and the affairs of his salvation ; and he firmly refused to pledge himself to a state in which his heart would have been divided between God and the world, as it seemed to him to be a very great impediment to the perfection after which he so ardently sighed. As Majoral was not discouraged at first, and continued to speak to him on this subject, hoping to gain him over in time, and to induce him to accept the honour he was urging upon him, John thought it his duty to take means for ridding himself of the tempta- tion, which however proposed nothing to him but what is generally considered lawful and honour- able, and on this account was more likely to sur- prise and get the better of him. He thought, therefore, of leaving a house in which he was treated too kindly. In this he was not deceived, for it is by flight only that we can fight against such temptations. If we listen to language of this kind, we soon give our consent ; whereas, by absolutely refusing to listen, we remain victorious. The holy fathers of the Church have highly praised Joseph for fleeing away, in order to avoid the wicked intentions of his master's wife ; and assuredly they are right, for he is an illustrious example of the zeal we ought to have, and of what we are bound to do in order to preserve our purity. It is this praise which they have given to holy Joseph which makes us request our readers to pay particular attention to the conduct of our Saint; for he renounced an advantageous position and took flight, not to avoid the commission of any crime which might have excited horror, but from the sole love of purity, and with the intention of always living in continence. This proves that he was imbued with good principles, and that he sought only to serve God in the highest state of perfection that was possible to him. If he had had the happiness at that time to meet with a man sufficiently enlightened to give him wholesome advice, and to regulate his zeal, he would no doubt have sought another retreat, in order to live in peace there, and to follow the good movements of his heart. But finding himself alone, and thinking only of separating himself as quickly as he could from a place where he saw that all were striving hard to entangle him in the world, and to detain him by ties which it would not have been in his power to break asunder, he seized the first opportunity that was afforded him of leaving the house of Majoral.

There was at that time war between Francis I., King of France, and the Emperor Charles V. Our history does not require us to enter into the details of the disputes between these two great princes; it is enough to mention that about this time the French laid siege to Fuenterabía, a city situated in Biscay. As soon as the emperor was informed of this, he determined to send relief to it, and ordered the Count of Oropesa to raise soldiers for the expedition. It was amongst these troops that John enlisted, entering as a foot-soldier in the company of a captain called John

Ferruz. This hasty resolution was, as we shall presently see, injurious to him in many respects.

CHAPTER VI.

JOHN RELAXES HIS USUAL PIETY WHEN IN THE ARMY. —THE MISFORTUNES GOD EMPLOYS IN ORDER TO BRING HIM BACK TO HIMSELF.

IT is certain that there is nothing so effectual in cooling down piety as the life which is ordinarily led in war. The tumult of arms almost always disturbs the interior repose of the soul. The bad examples that are seen on all sides have a weakening effect on the strongest, and those who are the most confirmed in virtue: the continual excitement in which they are obliged to live makes them often forget God, and under the pretext that they are far from the tribunals of justice, they think they may do anything. Our new soldier had sad experience of this truth, for scarcely had he reached the camp than he neglected his usual prayers, and no longer took the same care as before to implore the aid of the Blessed Virgin. In a short time the company of other soldiers wrought a change in him ; he began to do as the rest did, and followed the torrent of the corrupt world, so that one of his historians does not hesitate to say that he walked in the broad path of vice, and gave free course to his passions.

We need not go further into this matter. It is sufficient to have spoken of it in general, in order that our readers, when they reflect on it, may humble them selves, may think often of the weakness and frailty of human nature, and consider how important it is to all those who wish to live in virtue to flee from the world, and from all those things which may weaken and be an occasion of scandal to them.

The divine mercy watches continually over the elect, and only suffers them to fall into sins in order that the noble manner in which they rise up from them may serve to edify the faithful, and teach them to do penance. God did not, therefore, suffer John to continue long in the irregular life just mentioned; He soon made him know his fault, and touched him to the quick with wholesome compunction. We will now relate the circumstances of his conversion. The siege of Fuenterabía was prosecuted with much vigour, and the French displayed extraordinary energy. The Spaniards on their side defended it with great courage, and the Count of Oropesa exerted every effort to throw succour into it. It often happened that detachments of the two armies met each other, and according to the chances of war, at one time the French, at another the Spaniards, were the conquerors. One day when the camp of the latter was destitute of provisions, John was ordered to go with a company to collect some, and, that he might make greater haste, a horse was given him, which a little before had been taken from the French. After he had proceeded for some time, and advanced more than a league, he found himself very near the enemies' camp. Then his horse, which was hard-mouthed and badly bridled, recognised the place, and ran off at full speed to its old quarters. John used his utmost endeavours to stop it, but without success, as it only had on a common halter. It carried him off in spite of himself, and, rearing in an extraordinary manner, threw him violently upon the stones.

This fall was so serious that he lost his senses, and was a long time without being able to speak or move ; blood flowed from his mouth and nose for nearly two hours, and, as he received no assistance, he was in danger of death. At last, having returned a little to himself, and seeing the great danger he was in of losing his life, not only from his wounds, but also because he was on the point of falling into the hands of his enemies, he raised himself with difficulty, threw himself on his knees, and looking up to heaven began to call upon the Blessed Virgin. Being hardly able to speak, he uttered this prayer with great fervour, " O holy Mother of God, come to my assistance, and obtain for me by thy prayers that I may be delivered from this danger, and may not fall into the enemies' hands." Scarcely had he pronounced these words than he saw the Queen of Angels, who showed herself to him in order to console him by her presence, and promised to protect and shield him from the violence of his enemies, at the same time bidding him resume his ordinary duties with more fidelity, and remember his promises. Nothing more was needed to cover him with shame, to make him return to a knowledge of himself, and comprehend that his accident was a just punishment for his sins ; he therefore immediately resolved to correct himself and do penance. After he had recovered his strength a little, he began to drag himself as well as he could towards the Spanish camp, leaning on a stick which he fortunately found on the road. His companions seeing him return in so bad a plight, and even wounded, thought he had fallen into the

hands of the French, who had reduced him to that
pitiable state ; but he related his whole adventure to
them, and declared to them the distinguished favour
he had received from the Blessed Virgin. His captain
ordered him to be put to bed, and care to be taken of
him. He was under the doctor's hands for several
days, during which he wept over his irregular life,
many times thanked his sovereign Benefactress, formed
holy resolutions, and promised God to serve Him with
greater fidelity than before.

CHAPTER VII.

OTHER MISFORTUNES OBLIGE HIM TO LEAVE THE ARMY AND RETURN TO OROPESA.

Soon after he had recovered from his fall, God, wishing
to prove him, and to detach him more and more from
the world, permitted another misfortune to happen to
him, which nearly cost him his life. His captain had
made many important captures from the enemy, and
put him in charge of them, commanding him to keep
them carefully. John, through inadvertence, deposited
them in an unsafe place, and consequently robbers
found means to carry them off. When his captain
heard of this, he immediately flew into so violent a
passion as to be entirely beside himself. He accused
John of treachery, and of having had a share in the
robbery ; he treated him with unusual severity, and
even wished to put him to death. Many persons who
knew his innocence interested themselves in his behalf,
but to no purpose, for the captain continued inflexible,
and was fully bent on satisfying his vengeance.

John, therefore, believing it to be impossible to induce him to alter his mind, prepared himself for the worst, and expected nothing more from men. But God, Who had great designs on him, and wished to make use of him hereafter, in order to comfort and preserve the lives of a vast number of unfortunate beings, undertook his defence, and delivered him from this danger in the following manner. A cornet of cavalry, who was a man of good reputation, and had great influence over the mind of the captain, arrived unexpectedly, and some friends failed not to make known to him the misfortune as well as the innocence of our soldier. He was touched at his calamity, and resolved to succour him at all hazards. He spoke, therefore, to the captain, made him understand that matters were not exactly as he imagined, and that John was not guilty of the crime imputed to him. Thus, after some conferences, he obtained his pardon, but on condition that he renounced the profession of arms, and left the camp.

This deliverance, which was as it were miraculous, since it happened contrary to all probability, led John into many edifying reflections. He considered that God, in His excessive goodness, had thus preserved his life, and that this bound him by a new obligation to devote it entirely to His service. He saw, also, how blind men are in running so eagerly after the world, which so ill repays all their toil, and rewards them for the greater part of the time only with misfortune and disgrace, whereas one always enjoys true happiness in the pursuit of virtue. He reflected on these truths when he was leaving the camp, according to the order he had received. But soon afterwards God granted him far greater favours, and illuminated his mind altogether differently. For as he was proceeding along the high road he came to a tree, at the foot of which was a cross. He stopped and prostrated himself with the greatest humility before this adorable sign of our salvation. He thanked our Lord for having delivered him from so many perils, and begged pardon a thousand times for all his sins. His grief and the excess of his contrition caused him to shed torrents of tears. He protested that he would henceforth lead a new life; he acknowledged he had richly deserved from the divine justice much heavier afflictions than those he had already endured; he prayed with much fervour that he might be drawn to Him and detached from all creatures. In short, there passed through his mind an innumerable number of things, which are hidden from men.

For two whole days he continued in transports of this kind, without taking any nourishment or allowing himself any sleep. He then entered into a kind of ecstasy, or mysterious sleep, during which there is no doubt that God made him experience very great consolations. When he returned to himself, he saw at his side three loaves and a vessel of wine. His humility would not allow him to believe that this was a gift from Heaven, because he looked upon himself as quite unworthy of such a favour, and though he was exhausted and oppressed with hunger, he dared not touch this bread and wine, thinking they belonged to some persons in the neighbourhood, and that it was not lawful for him to take them without their permission. Without attending to his wants, he applied himself again to prayer and contemplation. As he was repeating the Lord's Prayer, and uttering the words, "Give us this day our daily bread," he heard a voice saying to him, "John, eat of this bread and drink of this wine, for it is God Himself Who sends them to you, in order to strengthen your weakness, and enable you to pursue your journey." No longer doubting that this was a favour from heaven, he obeyed the voice, ate of the bread and wine, and found his strength immediately renewed. Thus God showed that He took particular care of His servant, and that he was not less dear to Him than many great saints in whose favour He had worked signal miracles; for He treated him as He did Elias and as S. Paul the first hermit, to whom He sent extraordinary assistance, and whom He fed in the midst of the desert.

John having again returned thanks to our Lord for the kindness just shown him, lost no time, but returned as quickly as he could to Oropesa, remembering the agreeable and quiet life he had led there for a long time. Having at last reached the town, he went straight to the house of Francis Majoral, his old master, who received him with much tenderness and cordiality, and having made him relate all his adventures, restored him to his former employment, and entrusted him again with his flocks and property. He acquitted himself of this commission with still greater exactness and vigilance than before his departure. He brought in great gain to his master; he edified all the other servants by his meekness and modesty, and behaved himself in such a manner that Majoral, who still intended to choose him for his son-in-law, and leave him his property, again made him a proposal to that effect. He, on the other hand, showed greater repugnance to it than ever, and was sensibly afflicted at finding that, having run

very great risks whilst in the army, now that he had
come to a place of repose and solitude, he was exposed
to dangers of a more alarming nature ; for the former
threatened only his life, whereas the latter might keep
him from perfection, render him less inclined to virtue,
and attach him to the world. He thought, therefore,
once more of quitting Majoral's house, where he had
lived four years, for he was resolved to do and suffer
anything rather than engage himself in marriage.

CHAPTER VIII.

HE GOES TO FIGHT AGAINST THE TURKS IN GERMANY, AND THEN RETURNS TO MONTEMOR O NOVO.

WHILST agitated by these thoughts, and not knowing
where to find a place of retreat, he heard of the war
which Charles V. was compelled to wage against the
Turks, who were endeavouring to deprive him of the
empire of Germany. He thought this a good opportunity to leave the house of Majoral, who, being an
upright man, could not complain of his doing so for
such a cause. Besides, this war appeared to him a very
holy one, and he regarded it as an occasion of suffering
something for Jesus Christ, and of shedding his blood
in defence of the Church. All this wonderfully animated his courage, and made him forget all he had
suffered at the siege of Fuenterabía, so that he enlisted
in the regiment of Don Ferdinand Alvarez of Toledo,
who was going to the emperor's assistance.

It but too often happens that we are induced by
human and temporal motives to undertake the most

holy things, or that afterwards we become depraved and ruined, even though we may have entered upon them with the best intentions. John avoided these dangers in this war, for, as we have said, he determined to enter it only that he might preserve his purity, and defend the interests of Jesus Christ, and thus, when he arrived in Germany and Hungary, he conducted himself with modesty and discretion. He did not, as before, interrupt his usual prayers; on the contrary, he increased them, and added others, being persuaded that God alone can give success to the arms of the faithful, and overcome the enemies of the Christian name. He was careful to withdraw himself privately as often as he could consistently with his duty, in order to lift up his hands towards heaven after the example of Moses, and to implore the protection of God for all those who were supporting His cause. He attacked the infidels more by his piety than by force of arms, and made it evident on all occasions that he belonged to Jesus Christ, and was worthy to fight under His banner.

But though more pious, he was not less courageous than others, for he was always to be found where the danger was greatest; he never refused to go where the enemy was most numerous, and consequently where there was greater risk, and he fulfilled before the whole imperial army all the duties of a good and noble soldier. He was much esteemed by Don Ferdinand Alvarez, who praised his courage publicly, honoured him with many important employments, and kept him almost always near his person, well knowing that in him he possessed a man capable of undertaking anything, and of executing commissions of the greatest importance. This even brought upon him the envy of the other soldiers, and of some officers, who through jealousy called him the favourite.

It pleased God to bless the arms of the Christians, for they repulsed the infidels, and compelled them to retire from Hungary. By this means the war came to an end, and each one prepared to return to his own country. Don Alvarez embarked with his soldiers in order to avoid the fatigue and difficulty of a long journey by land, and landed at Corunna, where he disbanded his troops.

John finding himself free, felt a desire to visit the place where he was born, in order that he might learn something of his family, of whom he had heard nothing since his departure. He took the road by Santiago in Galicia, in order to visit the tomb of that illustrious apostle, the protector of Spain. He remained there nine days, during which he applied himself to prayer and contemplation, which surprised every one, for it was not common to see in a soldier so much modesty, recollection, and devotedness to God. As soon as he arrived at Montemor, he carefully inquired after his father and mother, of whose death he was ignorant. Having quitted them in his infancy, he had the greatest trouble to describe them; no one recognized him, for they had not seen him since he was eight years old. He therefore spent several days in making inquiries in every quarter of the city, and in asking news respecting his parents. At last he met an old man of venerable aspect, who led an exceedingly holy life, and who was his uncle. He mentioned so many things to him concerning his father and mother, that this good man, recalling to mind and studying his features, recognized him as his nephew.

They spent the rest of the day in asking each other questions. The uncle obliged his nephew to relate all that had happened to him since he left his native place, and John on his part strongly urged his uncle to speak of his father and mother, and tell him what had become of them. After much conversation of this kind the old man at last said to John : " Know, my son, that your mother died a short time after your departure, and that your absence afflicted her so much that every one thought that her days were shortened through grief on account of it. As for your father, seeing himself bereaved at once of his wife and son, he went to Lisbon, entered a monastery of S. Francis, and becoming a monk there. lived a very edifying life, and died a holy death. If you will stay with me, my son, I promise to assist you, to aid you as far as my means will allow, and to treat you as my own son; you will soon prove this, and you will see that my deeds correspond with my words." When John heard that his father and mother were dead, he was filled with the deepest grief and melancholy. He was especially afflicted at the death of his mother ; for believing that he was the cause of it, he attributed it to his own fault, and frequently called himself a parricide. The tears which flowed from his eyes melted his uncle's heart and caused him also to weep, so that they were for some time unable to speak, and their sighs were a dumb language which sufficiently showed what their feelings were. After John had recovered himself a little, he thus answered his uncle's obliging offers : " Since it has pleased the divine Majesty to withdraw my father and mother out of this world into their eternal rest, I cannot, my dear uncle, think of fixing my abode here, but after the example of my father I am going to seek a place where I may serve and adore the Lord far from my native home. It is just that having irritated the divine justice against myself, I should pass the remainder of my days in doing penance. I trust that God in His goodness will show me some favourable occasion for accomplishing this good desire with which He has inspired me. I beg of you, therefore, to give me your blessing, and to recommend me to the Lord, that He may succour and protect me by His holy grace; and on my part I will also pray Him to preserve and reward you for the kindness you have shown me, and the kind reception you have given me in your house." Having pronounced these words, he prostrated himself before his uncle, who embraced him tenderly with many tears, gave him his blessing, and took leave of him in the following words, "Go, my dear nephew, where heaven calls you; I trust that God will bless your intention, and that in consideration of your father and mother's prayers He will fill you with graces and blessings."

This is the way in which he spent the short time he remained at Montemor, and it is thus that Providence wished him to learn the death of those who gave him life, in order to disengage him more and more from the earth, to confirm him in his resolution to devote himself entirely to God, and to lead him, after the example of his father who had so nobly renounced the world, to break all the ties which could retain him in it.

CHAPTER IX.

HE PASSES THROUGH ANDALUSIA IN ORDER TO SEEK
MARTYRDOM IN AFRICA.—HE CONTRIBUTES BY
HIS LABOUR TO SUPPORT A POOR GENTLEMAN
WITH HIS FAMILY IN THE CITY OF CEUTA.

JOHN having no longer any care for earthly things,
sought only how he might please God, and give himself up to Him in the most perfect manner.   He
even thought he should be doing what was pleasing
to His Sovereign Majesty if he crossed over into
Africa, to seek there an opportunity of suffering martyrdom, and shedding his blood for the faith of Jesus
Christ, and with this intention he passed through
Andalusia, on his way to the Straits of Gibraltar.
God, Who destined him to be in after-life the father
and servant of the poor, wished him at this time
to make trial of this charitable employment, and
permitted him, therefore, to be received with much
kindness in a hospital which he fell in with on the
road.   He spent several days there, during which he
performed all kinds of good offices to the poor.   He
attended them, spoke to each of them, gave them
great consolation, and procured them much relief.
He carefully observed the order that was kept in
this house ; and when he remarked any defects which
had crept into it, he mentioned them to the superiors,
who corrected them.   He greatly esteemed the happiness of those who devoted themselves to serving
the living members of Jesus Christ.   He frequently
said that he could not understand how it was that
men, who wished to spend their money properly,

could think of rearing and fattening horses, while so many poor persons were destitute and in want of everything ; he spoke also with so much zeal of the manner in which the sick ought to be treated and assisted, that the superiors clearly saw he had a great inclination for the employment, and would be glad to take part in it. They invited him, therefore, to take up his abode in the hospital, but as he was occupied with the thoughts of martyrdom, and thirsted for it ardently, he rejected the proposal, and continued his journey.

While waiting at Gibraltar for an opportunity to embark for Africa, where he had heard that Christians were being martyred, he met a Portuguese gentleman who had been banished from Portugal for his crimes, and who was going with his wife and four of his daughters to live in exile at Ceuta, one of the nearest cities on the coast of Africa. He joined this unfortunate man and passed the Straits with him.

Hardly had they arrived at Ceuta than the unhealthiness of the climate, joined to grief at his banishment, brought on a severe illness, and the gentleman was soon reduced to want, for money is soon spent under such circumstances, especially at a distance from home and family. His wife and daughters sold the few clothes and jewels they had brought away with them, but this was a slender support, and did not last long, for out of the wreck of their fortune they had been able to save but very little. Thus at the end of some weeks they were without resources, and, to add to their misfortunes, the daughters also fell ill.

These poor people knew not what to do, and

were on the point of giving way to despair, when God inspired them with the thought of having recourse to the companion of their voyage, and of revealing their misery to him. They immediately made known to him the state in which they were, and what they were suffering. He was sensibly afflicted, for his heart was tender and full of compassion; what grieved him more was to be unable to assist them, being himself poor, and having only enough to subsist on from day to day. But of what is charity not capable, and what will it not undertake for a neighbour on extraordinary occasions? He did what no one would have ever ventured to ask him, and what one would hardly believe, were there not certain proofs of it, so much virtue and generosity being required in order to undertake it; for after having sold his clothes and all his little property in order to give his friends the price of them, he determined to labour at the public works and the fortifications of the city, and to employ the pay he earned in assisting them.

He went out very early every day to his work; he loaded himself with very heavy burdens, employed himself in removing earth, and hired himself out to those who were in want of labourers; he lowered himself so as to wait upon the other workmen; he bore with extreme patience the fatigue and heat of the day; he always exerted himself beyond his strength, and neglected no opportunity by which he thought he could gain more money; and when the evening came he gave his earnings to this desolate family. What is still more worthy of remark is, that he grudged himself everything, ate very little, and even refused himself necessaries, in order not to

diminish the small fund he appointed for this alms.
If it sometimes happened that he could not obtain
employment, he was grieved and lamented over it,
not on his own account, since he could say with
the apostle that he knew how to live poorly, and
was no stranger to hunger, but because it rendered
him incapable of assisting those for whose maintenance he had undertaken to provide. This consideration it was that rendered him very vigilant,
and inspired him with greediness after money, but
greediness altogether holy, and very different from
that of people in the world, which deserves only the
name of avarice ; for it was charity alone that prompted
him, and he had no other intention than that of
assisting his neighbour. He spent a considerable
time in this admirable employment, working with
his own hands, according to the command of the
apostle, that he might have wherewithal to succour
his brethren who were in need, and by his example
teaching all Christians that nothing dispenses them
from the obligation of almsgiving, and that they
always have the means of doing so, since even when
they have no money to distribute to the poor, they
can at least work for them, or give them what they
have gained from their labours.

CHAPTER X.

HE LEAVES CEUTA BY ORDER OF HIS CONFESSOR, AND RETURNS TO SPAIN.

THE devil, who is the sworn enemy of virtue, and does all he can to hinder the salvation of men, regarded with extreme impatience the good works of John, and could not endure his charitable exertions on behalf of this poor gentleman. He resolved, therefore, to oppose and put a stop to them; and made use of many artifices in order to attain this object. At one time, transforming himself into an angel of light, he reminded John of the martyrdom he had so much desired, and which he had passed over into Africa to seek; and he represented to him that to remain thus at Ceuta was a kind of apostasy and looking back. On other occasions he endeavoured to catch him unawares by making him see the good he might do among the infidels, and he persuaded him that by going to seek out the Christians who had gone to live with the Moors, and had renounced their faith, he would bring them back into the bosom of the Church. He made use also of the fall of one individual in order to cause him great interior trouble.

In order more fully to understand what follows, it should be known that the city of Ceuta being situated on the coast of Africa, far from the residence of the Kings of Portugal, those who had the superintendence of the fortifications and public works greatly abused their authority. They illtreated the workmen, loaded them with injuries

and blows, kept back their pay, and treated them as
if they were real slaves. This was the reason why
many poor fellows, finding it difficult to return to
Portugal on account of the sea they had to cross,
threw themselves in despair into the arms of the
Moors, and renounced the true religion.

A man with whom John had contracted friendship while at work was one of this number,
which caused him great sorrow. Night and day he
thought over the ruin of the unhappy man; he
wept continually on account of it, and was so
much afflicted that he could neither eat nor drink.
The devil, in order to disturb him still more, put
it into his mind that this man's infidelity would
be imputed to him, that he was the cause of his
damnation, because he had not watched sufficiently
over him, and ought to have taken other precautions in order to keep him to his duty. He sometimes made him believe that he ought to go and
find him amongst this barbarous people, in order
to try to convince him of the extent of his crime,
and to inspire him with sentiments of penance. He
even proposed to him a very dangerous expedient,
which has always been condemned by the Church of
Jesus Christ: which was that, in order the better to
gain over this man, he was to give him to understand
that he wished to imitate him, and to renounce the
Christian religion as the other had done.

All these different thoughts wearied him beyond
measure, and created in him a constant restlessness;
he no longer knew what to do, nor what resolution
to take; he was often seen sorrowful and dejected,
and to judge of the interior of his conscience by what
was seen in his exterior, it was evident he was suffer-

ing great pain, and that his soul was troubled. This is what happened to him during this attack: we do not think it our duty to dissemble it, for not only are these things not culpable in themselves, but they greatly contribute to his glory; for to suffer temptations, to have battles to fight against Satan, is no evil; but to remain firm under these attacks, and courageously to repulse this terrible enemy, is a source of great merit.

We shall see that John acquitted himself with great fidelity; he had recourse to God, he humbled himself in His presence, begging Him to guide him, and to make known to him His holy Will; and because it is written that "the prudent man doth all things with counsel," he applied to a Franciscan friar, who was as pious as he was learned; he confessed his sins to him, and laid open to him all the interior trouble of his heart. He mentioned to him the design he had of going among the infidels to seek martyrdom, or to endeavour to open the eyes of those Christians who had fallen into apostasy. He explained to him the falling away of his friend, the reproach of his conscience on that account, and the dissimulation he had wished to practise in order not to be suspected by him; he concealed from him nothing of all that distressed him and gave him pain. He then experienced the truth of those words of Solomon: "Counsel shall keep thee, and prudence shall preserve thee;" for the good friar instructed him, answered all his difficulties, put an end to his trouble, and restored peace to his soul. He told him that we are never permitted to tempt God, nor to seek danger; that to act in this manner is indiscreet, and to presume upon ourselves; that Jesus Christ has told us, "when they shall persecute you in this city, flee into another;" and therefore that he ought not to go to seek martyrdom amongst the barbarians, but that it was enough for him to be prepared to suffer it when God should point out the time and furnish him with the opportunity.

He made him understand that it was not the office of all to undertake the conversion of those who had made shipwreck of their faith, but that it needed a special vocation, and extraordinary talents, in order to convince such kinds of sinners, and that he ought to be satisfied with praying for them, and lifting his hands up towards heaven, while priests and doctors engaged them in regular discussions. He put to flight the scruples he had on account of the falling away of his friend, by making him see that he had no share in it, and that consequently it would not be imputed to him before God. He several times represented to him that as it never is permitted to any one to lie, it is still less lawful to do so in a matter of faith; that all dissimulation on such occasions is a sin; that, according to the apostle, "with the heart we believe unto justice; but with the mouth confession is made unto salvation," and that he ought to be persuaded that this fiction, upon which he was desirous of acting, in order to ingratiate himself with the apostate, was an artifice of the devil, which would do no good to the unhappy man, and would bring upon himself very great harm. Finally, he explained to him many important truths, in order to console him in his affliction, to strengthen his courage, and to drive away all thoughts which might cause him sadness and disturb his imagination. Seeing also that his dwelling in the city of Ceuta was an occasion of temptation to him on account of the neighbourhood of the infidels, he commanded him to quit it immediately, and to return to Spain, in order to remove him from every kind of danger.

It is easy to understand how much John was afflicted at receiving such an order, for he was obliged to renounce the crown of martyrdom, which had been the principal motive of his journey, and besides this, he could not make up his mind to leave the poor family which stood in need of his labour for their subsistence, and which would have much to suffer as soon as he went away. These considerations kept him in suspense for some time, and made him think he ought to deliberate a little on so important a matter. But when he saw that the Franciscan father continued firm on this point, and maintained that his salvation required him to depart, he hesitated no longer, but renouncing his own judgment, made to God a voluntary sacrifice of his own will, and promised to obey without more delay.

His greatest embarrassment was how to announce this news to the gentleman, for he foresaw that he would be much afflicted at it; he determined, nevertheless, to go and find him immediately. He declared to him that he had wished to remain with him all the time that he was at Ceuta, in order that he might assist him to the best of his humble means, but that the order of his confessor, which he looked upon as that of God Himself, obliged him to depart as soon as possible, that his salvation was concerned in his doing so, and that he could not refuse to obey without making himself guilty of sin. He then exhorted him to trust only in the Providence of God, Who would take care of him and all his family, and Who would not fail to provide him with other means of assistance more solid and secure. Lastly, he promised to remember him in his poor prayers, and often to solicit the divine mercy on his behalf. The gentleman with his wife and daughters burst into tears upon hearing this. John also wept bitterly, threw himself at their feet, in order to take leave of them, and immediately withdrew, that he might no longer witness their lamentations and sighs. As we shall not have an opportunity of speaking again of this gentleman, we may mention here that he soon experienced how effectual was the intercession of John with God, for soon afterwards the King of Portugal, without being asked by any one, recalled him from his banishment, which was to have lasted several years, and reinstated him in all his honours. This cannot but be regarded as a consequence of the promise which the servant of God had made him, to remember him in his prayers.

CHAPTER XI.

JOHN EMBARKS, AND EXPERIENCES A VIOLENT TEMPEST, WHICH IS APPEASED BY HIS PRAYERS.— AT GIBRALTAR HE SELLS DEVOUT PICTURES AND BOOKS.

IT was then from a motive of pure obedience, and with the intention of rendering his salvation more sure, that John set out from Ceuta, and returned to Gibraltar. When the anchor was weighed the sea was calm and the wind favourable, so that a favourable voyage was expected; but as soon as they approached the Straits there arose a furious storm, the wind changed, the sky was darkened, the sea became rough, and the violence of the waves began to carry away the vessel, so that the pilot was no longer master of the rudder. The sailors obliged all the passengers to help in their duty, and they, on their part, used their utmost endeavours to reach the land, that they might get under shelter in some harbour. Seeing, however, that all was to no purpose, they recommended all who were on board to look to themselves, and have recourse to prayer.

John immediately imagined that he was the cause of the tempest, and that the divine justice, irritated by his crimes, was pursuing him like another Jonas. He was even tempted to throw himself into the sea as that prophet did, to appease God by his death, and to save from shipwreck all who were in the same vessel, believing that he was the only guilty person in it. Reflecting, however, on the warning the sailors had given them to pray, he thought he ought to profit by their advice, and immediately began to do so. He poured forth sighs to heaven, he asked God pardon for his sins, he implored His mercy, and addressed Him as the apostles did on a similar occasion, saying, "Lord save us, we perish." He had recourse also to the Blessed Virgin, and calling to mind the protection and all the favours he had already received from her, he prayed her to intercede for them all, and deliver them from their great danger. Hardly had he finished his prayer than the wind ceased, the waves subsided, and the sea became calm as before, so that they all believed themselves indebted to him for their lives, looked upon him as their liberator, and began to consider him an extraordinary man, and one whose prayers were very efficacious.

When they had disembarked at Gibraltar, he prepared himself to go to the church in order to thank God for this great favour ; he exhorted all those who had escaped the danger to do the same, and succeeded in persuading them. The inhabitants were surprised to see so many persons entering the church together, and were curious to ascertain what brought them there. This prayer in common being over, all withdrew to attend to their business and secure lodgings, but John remained a long time in the church, for besides being full of zeal, and already feeling a great attraction to holy places, he remembered the dangerous temptation at Ceuta, from which God had just delivered him, and he wished to return Him solemn thanksgivings. Being prostrate before the crucifix, he prayed with much piety and humility in the following words : "I acknowledge, Lord, that for the just punishment of my sins I fell into the horrible temptation which so nearly caused my destruction. Thou it is Who, by Thine infinite mercy, hast delivered me from it. I promise to serve Thee for the remainder of my days with all the fidelity I am capable of, and I beg of Thee the grace to do so. Cause the light of Thy countenance to shine upon Thy servant ; grant me that interior peace after which I have so long sighed ; show me the way in which Thou wishest me to walk and go to Thee, for it is just that the work of Thy hands should praise Thee, obey Thee, and be entirely submissive to Thy commands."

He was not contented with offering up this prayer once only, but repeated it so often for several days, and accompanied it with so many groans, that it was manifest his soul was penetrated with real sorrow.

He also made a general confession of all his sins, and
omitted none of the duties of a good Christian, in
order to strengthen himself more and more in the grace
of God.

Having no money, he was obliged to work for his subsistence, but as soon as his occupations allowed it, he
went into a church to adore God and offer himself to
His service.   He appeared so modest, so humble, and
so recollected at the foot of the altar, that every one
was edified by him ; floods of tears fell from his eyes ;
prayer often made him forget his work, and his fervour was sometimes so great that he seemed like one
beside himself.   Two things formed the principal subjects of his prayers, his sins and the kind of life he
was to embrace.   With regard to his sins, we may say
that they were always present before him, as was the
case with the royal prophet, that he felt their weight
every day, continually begged pardon of God for them,
and suffered no opportunity to pass of punishing
them by penance.   As for the choice of a state of
life, he thought of it incessantly ; he consulted all
those whom he believed to be learned and enlightened
in the spiritual life ; he considered all the professions
in which he thought he could work out his salvation,
and not finding one which suited the intentions he had
of not engaging himself in the world, and of leading a
quiet life, he often said to God, "Notam fac mihi viam
in qua ambulem, quia ad Te levavi animam meam"—
" Lord, make the way known to me wherein I should
walk ; for I have lifted up my soul to Thee."

Whilst he was in this state of perplexity, the
thought came to him to employ himself in selling
little pictures, and books of devotion ; and he did
not reject it, because it appeared to him an innocent

employment, and also profitable to the salvation of his neighbour, and because he hoped it would give him an opportunity of speaking of virtue to those who dealt with him, and of suggesting to them maxims of piety. He would not, however, proceed further in the matter without consulting his confessor.

Every day he laid by something from what he earned by his labour, and thus in a short time he raised a small fund, which he spent in buying pictures, catechisms, and other little books of piety. He added to these romances and comedies; not that he intended to sell them, or distribute this poison among the public, but only to give a name to his little shop, to attract all sorts of persons to it, and then to speak to them of what concerned their salvation. Thus when young persons came to buy these profane books he dissuaded them, disclosed their poisonous character, and proved to them that they could not in conscience read them; he offered them others which treated of piety, and spoke to them with so much address, that he induced them to buy and read them, and in order the more easily to persuade them to do so he sold them at a very low price, much less than that of other dealers. He acted in the same manner when they asked him for pictures; always recommending them to choose devotional ones, which represented some pious history, or some mystery of our redemption. He employed his skill in making cards, which were much sought after, by means of which little children easily learnt the principles of Christian doctrine: besides this, he spoke to every one with so much sweetness, modesty, and edification, that all were eager to go to him to hear his little exhortations and pious discourses. Thus he reaped much fruit among the people, gained many young scholars to Jesus Christ, and taught them to serve God. Persons more advanced in years listened to him with pleasure, often came to consult him, and always went away much satisfied with him, and resolved to lead better lives than before. It is thus that our Lord began to make known the singular merit of His servant, and insensibly disposed him for another employment of much more importance, in which he would have to deal with all kinds of people, and find a much larger field for the exercise of his charity.

CHAPTER XII.

JESUS CHRIST APPEARS TO JOHN, AND MAKES KNOWN TO HIM THAT HE IS TO SERVE GOD IN THE CITY OF GRANADA.

JOHN's zeal and trade were not restricted to the city of Gibraltar, for he often went into the neighbouring villages and parishes to distribute his books of piety and instruct the inhabitants of the country. This practice was laborious and fatiguing, but he submitted to it willingly, not merely in order to gain temporal profit, for he had nothing but contempt for the goods of this world, but with the view of edifying his brethren, and of teaching them to lead more Christian lives.

One day as he was on his way to a certain spot, where he hoped that, as many people were assembled, he might find an opportunity of extending his business and of speaking much about God, an event happened by which he was made acquainted with the

Will of heaven respecting himself. With a small bundle at his back, containing his wares, he was crossing a field, meditating on the happiness of eternity, when he perceived a fountain issuing from a rock near a tree. The sight of this made him think of taking a little rest, in order that he might be better able afterwards to continue his journey. He accordingly laid aside his fatiguing burden, and sat down near the fountain. But hardly had he done so than he heard a voice calling him, and on turning his head he saw under the tree Jesus Christ full of glory and majesty, holding, as it were, a picture of Granada displayed to view, from the midst of which there arose a cross. The divine Saviour forthwith addressed him in these words: "John of God, Granada shall be thy cross," and directly afterwards disappeared. It is not difficult to imagine his surprise; he was thinking only of pursuing his trade, when he hears the voice of God speaking to him, and declaring to him His Will. He was going into a small town only, and he learns that Providence was calling him to a large and famous city. He was seeking only to rest himself and quench his thirst, when he sees that he must prepare for great trials, and that the cross would be his inheritance.

S. Paul assures us that as soon as God had revealed to him His Son, in order that he might preach Him among the nations, he immediately did so, without condescending to flesh and blood. We may say that John imitated in this the prompt obedience of the great apostle, for from the very moment that Jesus Christ declared to him that he would find his cross at Granada, he no longer thought of earthly things; Gibraltar and his life there were forgotten; he felt within himself a holy impatience to go to this great city, and he had no rest until he had arrived there to obey the commands of divine Providence.

Our readers now see the reason why we said at the commencement of this work that we would not at first give the name of John of God to our Saint; for we ought not to anticipate the designs of heaven, nor pay him the honour which had not been yet granted to him. But now we might call him by this name, since Jesus Christ has spoken and made it known that this name belonged to him; but we shall refrain from doing so for some time longer, that we may imitate his own humility, which did not permit him to adopt it; a name so glorious, that a great bishop afterwards declared to him that if he did not adopt it he would in some measure resist the Will of the Lord.

It is not unprofitable to reflect that it is Jesus Christ Himself Who gave him the name of John of God; this alone would be sufficient to prove his great merit, and complete his panegyric; for what could be more glorious for him than to see that God treated him as He did the most illustrious saints, to whom He has almost always taken care to give names? Thus, He gave that of Abraham to the father of all the faithful; to Jacob that of Israel; to the holy Precursor that of John, and even to His own Son that of Jesus. It is safe, therefore, to conclude that he was a man possessed of no ordinary degree of virtue, that he belonged to God in a special manner, and that there is no need to seek for any other proof of it than the fact that the name itself was given him by our Lord in this wonderful apparition.

CHAPTER XIII.

THE VIRTUES AND QUALITIES OF JOHN OF AVILA.—
JOHN COUNTERFEITS MADNESS IN THE CITY OF
GRANADA.

JOHN was about forty-two years old when he arrived at Granada. He fully expected to meet with crosses, as Jesus Christ had forewarned him; but he knew not as yet what they would be; and this kept him in a holy restlessness, and caused him to offer up frequent prayers: he still, indeed, continued his small trade in books and pictures, to obtain the means of subsistence, but his chief employment was to consult the Will of God, and prepare himself to do all He might be pleased to command him. After the example of the great apostle, he continually said to Him: "Lord, what wilt Thou have me to do?" And he always had on his lips those words of the royal prophet: "My heart is ready, O God, my heart is ready." He thought only of the cross, he desired it with extreme ardour, he spoke about it to every one, and he sought it with no less eagerness than the spouse in the Canticles sought her Well-beloved.

Whilst he was in this state, and these things were occupying his mind, it happened that the feast of S. Sebastian was celebrated at Granada with much solemnity. In the highest part of the city there is a hermitage dedicated to this illustrious martyr, and as John of Avila was to preach, a vast number of people had assembled to hear him; John also went there to join in the public devotion and hear the sermon. As we shall often have hereafter to

speak of this celebrated preacher, and as God willed
to make use of him to guide our Saint and show him
His Will, it will be as well to give a brief account of
his principal virtues, in order that our readers may
become acquainted with the characteristics which
rendered him so distinguished in the Church of Christ.

He did not enter the priesthood until after he had
led a very severe and penitent life, for when still a
layman he fasted nearly every day, he took the discipline very often, and wore a hair shirt, his bed was
nothing but a few faggots of wood, and he observed a
rigid solitude. After his ordination he distributed
all his goods to the poor, reserving for himself one
coat only, which was made of the vilest materials, in
order that his attention might not hereafter be distracted by the administration of his patrimony, which
was very considerable ; he refused all benefices, contenting himself with the dignity of priest, and wishing
to serve the Church gratuitously. He loved poverty
so much that, with the exception of some books, which
were necessary to him in his studies, and vestments
for saying Mass, he refused presents of any kind, and
would never accept them, in order that he might be
able to say to the faithful with the great apostle,
" I seek not the things that are yours, but you."

Not only was he a doctor in theology, but he was
also highly instructed in all the mysteries of the
kingdom of God : he possessed in an eminent degree
the science of the saints, and knew perfectly all the
ways which lead to true life, as may be seen in his admirable works. His zeal was so great and fervent
that he never gave himself any rest, but continually
laboured to gain souls to Jesus Christ ; he neglected
his health, and was prodigal of it on every occasion

when he thought he could be useful to his neighbour.
He had so great a gift of discerning spirits that he
easily knew which were from God and which from
the devil. Thus a nun called Sister Magdalen of the
Cross had become very celebrated throughout all
Spain by her false revelations; he undeceived the
public, and made every one see that her conduct was
full of illusions. On the other hand, when S. Teresa
had been not only persecuted, but accused before the
Inquisition for holding dangerous opinions, and was
sent by the inquisitor to him, he signally justified her.

His learned sermons, together with the example
of his virtues and good life, had so striking an effect,
and contributed to the conversion of so many persons, that he was looked upon as the first preacher of
the age, and was even called the Apostle of Andalusia.
He was consulted by all those who wished to devote
themselves to God and embrace virtue. It is well
known that after having defended S. Teresa, as we
have just mentioned, he kept up a correspondence
with her on spiritual matters, and wrote her several
letters, which are to be found in her works. He was
also very intimate with Father Lewis of Granada,
with whom he very often held communication, and to
whom he imparted his most secret thoughts. Granada
on his part held John in great esteem, admired his
virtues, and having survived him, determined to write
his life, and inform posterity of all the great things
he had remarked in his character.

It was this celebrated man, then, who was pronouncing the panegyric of S. Sebastian when John
went up to the Hermitage. He spoke with so much
force of the happiness of those who suffer for Jesus
Christ, he made the people see so clearly that they

must conform themselves to the pains of this divine
Saviour if they wished to share in His glory, and he
described with so much eloquence the joys and chaste
delights which those enjoy who serve God, that his
words were like burning darts, penetrating the heart
of the servant of God, and lighting it up with the
fire of holy love. From that time John conceived so
great a love of eternal happiness that he could never
more love or think of temporal things. His mind
was more convinced than ever of the obligation all
Christians are under of bearing their crosses, and his
past sins appeared to him so enormous, and caused him
so much grief, that he could no longer contain himself.
He was seen to burst suddenly into tears and utter
deep groans and loud cries, as if he had been a madman. He frequently beat his breast, protested that
he was a very great sinner, and began to cry out in
a loud voice, " Mercy, Lord, mercy !" All who were
present were astonished, not knowing what cause to
assign to such a transport. At one time they said he
must be grievously afflicted at his sins, at another
time that his mind was deranged, and that he was out
of his senses. But what happened afterwards was
still more extraordinary, and confirmed them in the
opinion that he really had become mad : for when he
had gone out of the oratory, he threw himself down in
the middle of the streets, rolled in the mud, tore his
hair and beard, scratched his face until the blood ran,
and dashed his head several times against the walls.

A vast number of people of course gathered round
him, and ridiculed him ; the children ran after him
and made sport of him, seeing his extravagant actions,
and many persons struck him and loaded him with
blows. In this manner he passed through almost

the whole city without showing any astonishment, or uttering any complaint, at all that was done to him. When he reached the house in which he lived, he destroyed all his little stock, for he fiercely tore to pieces with his teeth all the profane books he found in it, and threw them into the street; those that treated of devotion he gave to all who wished for them, without reserving a single one. He did the same with his pictures, and in a short time had distributed them all to the children around him. He did not stop here; he stripped himself of all his clothes on the spot, and gave them to the first poor persons he met. He again began running about the streets of the city, with his head and feet naked, and only a shirt and pair of drawers on his body. He again cried out in the public places, "Mercy, Lord, mercy!" The people again ran after him and heaped upon him greater insults than before; he on the other hand was in nowise moved by them, but showed the utmost patience. In this condition he went to the cathedral, and had scarcely entered than he threw himself on his knees and cried out louder than ever, "Mercy, Lord! pardon this great sinner, who has so many times offended Thee by his crimes." He continued to tear his face, he gave himself heavy blows, he bruised his whole body, and prostrated himself on the earth to implore the mercy of God. Several persons who were in the church began to observe all his actions attentively, and remarking that he did nothing to lead them to suppose him absolutely mad, they said that men ought to suspend their judgment concerning him until they learned the motive which prompted him to act in this manner. Raising him, therefore, from the ground, they consoled him as well as they could, exhorted him to take courage, and to trust in the mercy of God : they thought it well also to take him to the house of John of Avila, that he might examine and judge of him himself. And certainly they could not have acted more wisely, for since God had by means of his sermon touched the heart of John, it was right that he should take charge of him.

CHAPTER XIV.

JOHN OF AVILA, HAVING SPOKEN WITH THE SERVANT OF GOD, UNDERTAKES THE DIRECTION OF HIM, AND PERMITS HIM TO CONTINUE HIS APPARENT MADNESS.

WHEN John was brought into the house of Avila, and the latter had been informed of all that had happened, he was much surprised, and stood as one speechless when he saw a man so disfigured and covered with blood, having on him only a shirt and a pair of drawers, who had been rolling himself in the mud, and making himself the laughing-stock of the whole city : he believed, nevertheless, that he ought not to act hastily, but that it would be well to hear him speak, and to see how all these things had happened, before he formed his opinion of him ; he therefore desired all who were present to withdraw, and allow him to converse with him. As soon as John saw himself alone with him who had so much edified him by his discourses on S. Sebastian's day, he threw himself at his feet with much humility, and explained to him the extraordinary manner in which he had been touched at his sermon ; he made known to him all the feelings with which his heart was being agitated, and the thoughts which had filled his mind ; he gave him a short history of his whole life, acquainted him with his most secret sins, declared his motive for thus counterfeiting madness, and begged him to give him his advice, to tell him what he ought to do to be saved, and to take him under his guidance.

Avila, having heard him speak, immediately saw that he was not out of his mind, but, on the contrary, that he was full of good sense, and animated with very fervent charity ; he nevertheless wished him to remain for some time in his. house, that he might converse often with him, carefully mark his behaviour, and penetrate as much as he could into the secrets of his conscience ; and after having attentively observed him for several days, he was convinced that there was nothing in his assumed folly which deserved to be blamed, because he was led to it by a good motive, and with the intention of mortifying himself. Besides this, he reflected that the ministers of the Church are appointed, not to govern or direct the faithful according to their own will, but to co-operate in their salvation, and assist them to walk in the ways of the Lord, and therefore that they ought not without good reason to dissuade them from things which do not appear wrong in themselves, and for which they perceive they have an attraction, lest they should be resisting, without intending to do so, the designs of Providence.

He considered, also, that all these his actions well became a penitent, and could greatly contribute to humble and lower him in the estimation of men. Wherefore he would not restrain him on this point, but permitted him to follow his own lights, and to continue this kind of public penance. He even went further, for he told him that he took him under his charge, and would assist him with his counsels. He immediately gave him much important advice, and addressed him in the following terms:

"My dear brother John, have confidence in the infinite mercy of God, and rest assured that He will perfect the work He has begun in you, provided that you on your part are careful to persevere in the good resolutions you have formed, that you do not look back, and that, faithfully treading the path He has bidden you to follow, you do not allow yourself to yield to the temptations of the devil. Know that eternal happiness awaits those who, like good and generous soldiers, shall have persevered to the end of their lives in the warfare of Jesus Christ, and that, on the contrary, eternal punishments are prepared for all those who, through want of courage, shall have broken down in the midst of their career, and have turned aside out of the paths of justice. You must expect to undergo many troubles and many temptations, for this is the ordinary lot of those who undertake to fight under the standard of Jesus Christ. Do not fail, then, to come and make known to me the combats you will have to sustain against the devil, and I hope that, the grace of God assisting me, I shall prescribe the necessary remedies for you, and put into your hands powerful weapons which will enable you to repulse all the efforts of the enemy. Go, then, my brother, with God's blessing and mine. I desire that all may turn out for your good, and I venture to say that I promise you that our Lord Jesus Christ will have mercy on you."

These words of Avila wonderfully consoled the servant of God, fortified his zeal, inspired him with new fervour, and induced him to increase his austerities, and to labour more and more to humble and degrade himself. As soon, therefore, as he had left his house, he recommenced his mad actions, he rolled himself in the mud, and covered his face with it. He said several things which could only proceed from one who had entirely lost his mind, and he published in a loud voice all the sins of his past life. "I have sinned against God," said he, "and have broken His commandments a thousand times. Wretch that I am, I deserve to be beaten and ill-treated by every one, and I ought only to be considered as dirt and smoke."

In order that the whole city might know of his mad behaviour, he ran through the streets, and danced and leaped at the corners of the public squares; by doing which he excited the children and the whole populace to follow him, and insult him grossly. Some threw stones at him, others reproached him, and some went so far as to strike him and load him with blows. All this, however, neither disturbed him, nor made any impression on his mind. On the contrary, he rejoiced interiorly at being thus despised, he praised God for it, and esteemed himself the more happy the more injuries and affronts he received, for then he thought he was in some measure conformed to Jesus Christ, Who was mocked and dishonoured in His Passion. Even in his most violent transports many things were remarked in him which showed that he was full of piety, and that he truly loved virtue, for he spoke only words that were good, and that tended to the edification of his neighbour.

He carried on his shoulders a great wooden cross, which he presented to the passers by, inviting them to adore it. If the smallest child said to him, "John, if you love Jesus, kiss the ground," he immediately prostrated himself and kissed it with so much respect and humility that all clearly saw he was full of veneration for this holy Name; and when he declared the sins of his past life to those around him, he did it with signs of sincere contrition, and in terms which fully expressed the great grief he felt for them.

CHAPTER XV.

CONTINUATION OF JOHN'S ASSUMED MADNESS.—HE IS SHUT UP IN THE LUNATIC ASYLUM, WHERE HE IS MUCH ILL-TREATED.—HE CEASES TO COUNTERFEIT AND APPEARS IN HIS NATURAL STATE.

THE servant of God passed several days together in this manner, amid constant agitation, going up and down the city, suffering all manner of insult, lying on the ground, beating himself, and exposing himself to reproaches and ill-treatment from all kinds of persons, all which exhausted him to such a degree that he could no longer move, and fell down in a swoon. Two citizens at last had compassion on his misery, and thought it their duty to succour him. They kept off the people who were around him, took him aside in order to examine him, and perceiving that he could hardly stand on his feet, that his body was all gashed and torn with the blows he had received, or had given himself, and that he was in extreme want of being attended to, they resolved to get him placed in the great hospital where persons who have lost their senses are shut up; and, being kindly received by the governors, they easily obtained for him a place that was vacant, and exerted themselves to have him placed in a private room, in order that he might be more carefully attended to, and that pains might be taken to bring him to his senses.

At first he was treated with gentleness, and many remedies were given him to see if his mind would not recover itself. The keepers soon changed their method when they found that his delirium continued, and that his madness increased. They bound his hands and feet, they stripped him, they beat him with rods, and lacerated his body with a double-knotted cord, in order that the pain might make him return to his senses, and cure him of his frenzy, as very often happens in such cases; but since the desire to suffer something for the love of Jesus Christ, and to expiate his sins, was the true cause of his counterfeit madness, he was far from giving signs of any amendment; on the contrary, he burst out into new sallies of madness, and gave them reason to think that he was becoming worse every day. He even determined to blame those who governed him, and to reproach them with their hardness and cruelty to the poor, in order by this means to draw upon himself more severe punishment. He said, "O, traitors and enemies of all kindness, how comes it that you treat so badly my brothers who are with me in this house of God? Ought you not to have compassion on their misfortunes, and feed them better than you do, since the Catholic kings have so nobly founded this hospital, and endowed it with such large revenues, which ought to be employed in the maintenance and support of the poor?"

Words like these, which were only too true, and which made known the avarice and corrupt practices of the governors, greatly irritated them, and excited them to make him suffer every sort of cruelty. They ordered him to be bound more tightly, to be beaten with rods, and to be punished very rigorously, not on account of his madness, for that was not a crime, but because he had taken the liberty to censure their conduct. We may indeed say that his zeal for sufferings and mortifications had reason to be satisfied on this occasion, for historians inform us that he was put to extraordinary torture, and made to endure the utmost cruelty. What is most remarkable is, that during all this time he exhibited the greatest moderation ; he never showed impatience, nor made any complaint against those who, under the pretext of contributing to his cure, were satisfying their own passions and wreaking their vengeance on him. He sometimes even urged them to increased severity. "Strike," said he, "strike this rebellious flesh, this enemy of virtue, for it is the cause of all my evils. Hitherto I have shown it too great indulgence, and I have cherished it with too much care. It is just that it should now suffer with me, since it participated in my sins." They failed not to obey him, and exercised upon him their rage and fury to the utmost, so that at last he sank under it, and was reduced to the last extremity.

Avila was informed of this, and went immediately to the hospital that he might himself see in what condition John was. He found him very weak, covered all over with wounds, and lying on a wretched mattress. He first of all represented to him many subjects of consolation ; he encouraged him to suffer for Jesus Christ; he told him that if he thought seriously upon the sufferings of that divine Saviour, all that he could himself suffer would appear sweet and easy to be endured; he exhorted him to offer his soul, body, and life to God, and to prepare himself for whatever it might please His sovereign Majesty to require of him; he reminded him that the time had now come for him to put off this voluntary madness, and to resume his senses outwardly, because his penance had lasted long enough, and he must henceforth apply himself to something that might be useful to himself and to his neighbour. Hardly had he departed than John showed himself to be the child of obedience, and willing to submit most implicitly to the order of his spiritual father, for his mind immediately appeared calm and tranquil, no more violent outbursts were seen, and every one found him in his right reason. So sudden a change much surprised the governors of the hospital, and even gave them pleasure, for although they were incensed against him on account of his reproaches to them, they still had noticed in him many good qualities which compelled them to like him in spite of themselves: they ordered great care to be taken of his health, that he should not be allowed to want for anything, and that every attention should be bestowed upon him for the restoration of his strength.

After some weeks he was better, and able to get up and walk about; he began, therefore, to go up and down the infirmaries, and to visit the sick. It would be difficult to express how much he edified them by his spiritual discourses; he spoke with great zeal of the last judgment, when we shall have to give an account of all our actions, of the shortness

and uncertainty of this life, of the obligations we are
under to serve God, and give ourselves up to Him
without any reserve, and of the advantages of sickness and infirmities, which ought to purify us and
make us think of our salvation. Having just experienced the cruelty and barbarity of those who
were appointed to the management of the insane,
he was much moved at seeing the ill-treatment these
poor creatures had to suffer ; he groaned over it, and
was extraordinarily afflicted at it, very often saying
within himself, " When will God grant me the favour
of having a hospital of my own, that I may receive
poor madmen who are estranged in mind, and wait
upon them with all the care and diligence in my
power ?"   He did not stop at words only, but began to
act, and render it manifest to all that he was possessed of solid piety, and knew how to put in practice what he said.   He was very punctual in obeying all who gave him any command.   He waited
on the poor with so much affection that even the
most cowardly were animated by his example.   He
always chose, not only the most difficult employments,
but the most vile and humiliating ; he displayed so
much gentleness and moderation in all his actions
that he had not the slightest ill-will towards those who
had outraged him with so much cruelty.   In short,
he behaved in so humble, so prudent, and so modest
a manner, that all who conversed with him could not
help wondering at the change that had taken place
in him, and said one to another, " Is this he whom
we saw do so many extravagant things?" and they
began to honour and respect him as a man of merit.
In this manner ended his counterfeit madness, which
in the eyes of God was true wisdom, for is it not

wisdom before Him to seek humiliation, to make ourselves vile and contemptible, and to punish our sins ?
And it was only this that John had in view.

CHAPTER XVI.

REFLECTIONS ON THE MADNESS WHICH JOHN MADE USE OF IN ORDER TO DO PENANCE.

IT must be confessed that this conduct of John appears extraordinary, and ought not to be proposed
to ordinary men for imitation ; nevertheless, it does
not follow that it should be condemned, for as St.
Paul says, " Who shall accuse against the elect of
God ?" They are guided by the Holy Spirit, Who is
not tied down to the rules of human wisdom ; all that
He orders is just and reasonable, and one cannot do
wrong in obeying Him. There are particular ways
which He points out to certain souls whom He wishes
to distinguish in an extraordinary manner, and raise
to a high degree of perfection ; others, who are not
under the same conditions, and have not been
favoured with so abundant a share of grace, ought not
to undertake to follow or imitate them, for to do
so would be rashness and presumption ; still, what
the former do is not the less meritorious and praise-
worthy on this account, because of the dispositions
and motives which prompt them. Our readers,
therefore, must not allow themselves to be prejudiced against this conduct of the Saint, nor imagine
that his mode of proceeding cannot be justified
because it does not correspond with their ideas, and
seems to be contrary to the ordinary course of

things ; for who are they that they should dispute with God, and ask Him a reason for His conduct ? Can He not make His servants advance by unusual paths ? and cannot He sanctify them by things which seem to be contrary to our reason ? and indeed when He wished to redeem the world, He used not the means which the prudence of the wise men of the earth would have suggested; on the contrary, He counted as foolishness all the wisdom of men, and by the foolishness of the cross it pleased Him to save those who believed in Him. Thus we ought not to be surprised at His permitting our Saint to do so many things apparently contrary to reason, since His sovereign wisdom required them as his co-operation towards his salvation. Here also we may truly say with the great apostle, that " the foolishness of God is wiser than men, and the weakness of God is stronger than men." These general truths would, without doubt, be sufficient to impose silence on all men, and to prevent them from condemning what seems to be beyond the competence of their limited intellects ; still, it may be useful to show that this conduct of John of God is not without example, and that several great saints have done the same thing.

Every one knows that the wise and holy man, David, fearing that he would be ill-treated at the court of King Achis, led men to believe he had lost his reason, in order that by this means he might save his life : " He changed his countenance before them," says Scripture, " and slipped down between their hands, and he stumbled against the doors of the gate, and his spittle ran down upon his beard. And Achis said to his servants : You saw the man was mad, why have you brought him to me ? Have we need of madmen, that you have brought in this fellow, to play the madman in my presence? shall this fellow come into my house?" (1 Kings xxi. 13, &c.)

Nor is there any one so ignorant as not to know that he made no scruple about dancing and leaping while conducting the ark of the covenant, in order to show his joy; and that when his wife Michol ridiculed him on this account, he thought nothing of her contempt, and protested that he would ever make himself vile and contemptible in the presence of the Lord (2 Kings vi.).

The prophet Isaias did a thing still more surprising by order of God Himself; for he quitted the dress of penance he had been in the habit of wearing; he put off his shoes and the sackcloth with which his loins were girded, and walked thus naked before all Israel. This action was in reality a prophecy of the shame and ignominy which was prepared for, and would be inflicted on, the Egyptians and Ethiopians; because they were to be led into captivity entirely naked, without clothes or shoes, by the King of the Assyrians; but it was not on this account the less extraordinary, nor less opposed to the custom of society (Isa. xx.).

If we pass from the Old to the New Testament, we shall find there also several examples of saints who, with the intention of doing penance and humbling themselves, affected to be mad, and behaved themselves on several occasions as persons who had really lost their senses. When St. Ephrem was informed that he was nominated to a bishopric, and that persons were come to find and ordain him, he made it appear as if his mind was deranged; he allowed his dress to trail in the mud, he walked in a ridiculous manner along the streets, he ate with greediness before every one, and did several other things altogether unworthy of him ; and by this means he avoided the episcopate, for which he thought himself unfit, though every one else judged that his life, his knowledge, and his great talents fitted him for this high dignity ; the deputies, however, who were charged to fetch him, treated him as one who had lost his senses, and went back without him ; which caused him great joy, and enabled him to continue for the rest of his days in the exercise of the functions of the diaconate.

Palladius, in his History, speaks of a holy nun named Isidora, who, through humility, was pleased to pass in the minds of her sisters for one who was silly and possessed by the devil, doing things in their presence which showed she had entirely lost her senses, and by this means drawing down upon herself very great contempt and even very rough treatment. God at last made known her virtue, and manifested her merit to S. Pitirum, who probably was one of St. Antony's disciples. He went to Tabenna, and thence to the convent of these nuns, where he disclosed to them the great wisdom of Isidora and all her good qualities, recommending them to treat her henceforward in a different manner. The good nuns profited by his advice, begged forgiveness of the humble servant of Jesus Christ, and began to respect her and pay her extraordinary honours ; but this was so insupportable to her that she left the convent in order to go and find a place where she might live unknown and despised.

Evagrius, in describing the fasts, austerities, and admirable lives of the solitaries of Palestine, says

that there were several among them who, in order to
overcome vainglory, made it appear as if they had
lost their senses and had become weak-minded. The
annals of the Church furnish several other examples
of saints who have pursued a similar line of conduct; but in order not to make too long a digres-
sion, it will be sufficient to speak of Simeon the
solitary, to whom was given the name "Salo,"
that is, "mad." He was of noble birth, learned,
and very spiritual. By an extraordinary movement
of the Spirit of God he took the resolution to counterfeit madness, in order to humble himself before men.
He appeared in the city of Emesa, where he was sometimes in the habit of going, and there did things
which only a man out of his senses would have done;
he openly entered the taverns, and amused himself
there, eating indifferently with all sorts of persons, and
not refusing any kind of food; if any one happened
to show him any civility and salute him, he flew into
a passion and immediately fled away. One day he
entered a house of bad repute, and was a very long
time shut up there, which was the cause of many
very injurious judgments being passed upon him; and
when he came out again, he pretended to be looking
about on all sides as if to see that he was not
observed; by this means he greatly increased the
suspicions of those who lived in the neighbourhood,
and it was not until some days afterwards that they
discovered that his visit had been one of pure charity
only. He did several other things which apparently
could only proceed from a mind touched with insanity; still he was very wise, and had no object in
view but to degrade himself and render himself con-

temptible. The Church now honours him as a saint, and keeps his feast on the 1st of July.

The illustrious Mgr. Antony de Godeau also mentions in his History of the Church this insanity of S. Simeon Salo, and what he says appears so useful that we quote part of it for the honour and justification of John of God. "I know," he says, "that properly speaking such conduct is not only not good, but even deserving of censure, and I am not astonished at people in the world strongly condemning it and making jokes upon it; but we must consider also that the Spirit of God, Who works in the saints, leads them sometimes to actions which are exceptions to the ordinary rule, and are founded on the foolishness of the cross, which is contrary to all the reasons of human wisdom; the desire of humbling themselves, and lowering themselves before men is sometimes so great in them, that in order to satisfy it, it impels them to methods of acting which appear extravagant; and there are ways of sanctity as far from ordinary ways as heaven is from the earth. The Church honours some other saints who, like Simeon, counterfeited insanity, and by this veneration for them she justifies their mode of life. But these are miracles, not examples, and it is necessary that God, by His Spirit, should give the impulse, and that movements of this nature should be inspired by Him; and before practising them we must consult some very discreet man, who will examine into all the circumstances, the time, the place, and the person, because the devil and a melancholy temperament can easily mislead people in these kinds of extraordinary actions." We see that this great prelate, amongst other things, teaches us that we ought not of ourselves to follow ways which are not of the common order, but that we must be called to them by God, Who works inwardly in our hearts ; and that before embracing them we should have recourse to a person of piety and knowledge, in order to know whether there is not some illusion in what we wish to undertake, and if it is truly God Whom we are seeking.

It is upon these principles that we maintain that this action of John, in counterfeiting madness, was holy and lawful; for he was not led to it of himself; on the contrary, it is evident that it was God Who inspired him with the desire of it, because it was in a church, and at the conclusion of a very edifying sermon, that the thought of it entered his mind. Besides this, we have already shown that all that he did during this voluntary madness tended only to humble and degrade him in the sight of men, and that he made use of it as a veil to conceal and hide his penance, and this undoubtedly can only come from the Spirit of God, to Whom alone it belongs to inspire men with the love of humility and penance. But what is still more important, and what ought entirely to convince our readers, is that in his most violent transports he was always very obedient to Avila ; that it was by his order, or at least with his permission, that he continued to do the things which appeared so contrary to reason ; all his estrangement ceased outwardly, and nothing extraordinary was any longer remarked in him, as soon as this enlightened director advised him to cease acting the part of a madman. This circumstance alone ought to be sufficient to justify his conduct ; for if it be true, as S. Bernard teaches, that self-will spoils the best works, may we not say, on the other hand, that obedience sanctifies all the actions of which it is the principle? and consequently we must conclude that John, who so exactly obeyed this holy priest, was guided by the Spirit of God, and did nothing but what was quite lawful. We have dwelt on this point, because it seemed important to put before our readers the necessary considerations upon it. We now return to our history.

CHAPTER XVII.

JOHN LEAVES THE HOSPITAL OF GRANADA, AND GOES TO FIND AVILA, HIS DIRECTOR, AT MONTILLA.

THE servant of God, after having recovered his strength, and devoted himself for some time to the works of charity we have mentioned, began to think of leaving the hospital in order to go to Montilla, where Avila was at that time discharging the duties of his ministry. At first he met with great opposition, for the managers used their utmost efforts to retain him, as they were greatly edified by his manner of working, and judged him to be a fit person to superintend the poor and the sick. They made him advantageous offers in order to dissuade him from his purpose of leaving them, but he turned a deaf ear to all their proposals ; the desire he had of conferring with his spiritual father, and of consulting him on the plans he had in his mind, made him shut his eyes to all the advantages with which they tempted him ; having therefore taken leave of them, and thanked them for all the kind marks of attention they had shown him, he set out on his journey in a bitterly cold and sharp season, but this his love of penance made him count as nothing. As soon as he arrived at Montilla, he went straight to the house of his director, who received him with every mark of tenderness and charity, and gave him a room in order that he might converse with him without interruption. The holy priest was enraptured and filled with consolation at seeing this poor man, in whom he noticed all the marks of predestination, for he was humble, modest, charitable, patient, mortified, given to prayer, and full of zeal and fervour.

The first days were spent in speaking of what John had done during his counterfeit madness, of all he had suffered, of the thoughts he had had, of the resolutions he had formed, and of the state in which he was. On all these matters Avila gave him advice worthy of his great piety and profound learning. John wished once more to make a general confession, thinking that the lights of him, in whose hands he had placed himself, would serve marvellously to penetrate the recesses of his conscience, and to discover several of his faults, of which he thought he had been hitherto ignorant; he took, therefore, all the time necessary for examining with him all the actions of his past life; he laid before him his doubts and difficulties, he made known to him all his desires and affections, and entreated him not to spare him in anything. Having made this examination he wept over his sins for several days, showing very lively and sincere sorrow for them, and punishing them with the utmost severity; for historians have remarked that he fasted very rigorously, and took only so much food as was necessary to support life; he passed almost whole nights without sleep, and employed them in prayer and in mortifying his body by means of different artifices which the spirit of penance suggested to him. The other austerities that he practised at this time have not come to our knowledge, but we can judge of them by the depth of his contrition, which drew forth from his heart lamentations and sighs, and led him to prostrate himself very often at the foot of the altars, full of a holy anger against himself.

Being thus prepared, he laid open to the physician of his soul all the wounds with which it was covered ; he confessed all his sins to him, and received with much docility whatever he prescribed respecting his spiritual direction, and by this means he acquired great repose of conscience and true interior peace.

We must not omit to mention that his long prayers and continual groanings excited some complaints against him, but this was much to his credit, and serves to show that prayer was very familiar to him. It happened that a bed was placed in his room for another man, who had also come to consult Avila ; and by this means it was discovered in what way he employed himself during the time appropriated to sleep, for his companion declared that he could neither sleep nor rest, because John did nothing but pray and sigh all night, and he requested that he should be ordered to keep silence. But Avila, full of joy at seeing that his house was a house of prayer, and that it served as a temple for this penitent to celebrate the praises of God day and night, was far from giving him any such command ; on the contrary, he thought that he ought to allow his zeal and fervour full play ; he therefore only recommended the other man to profit by his example, and learn from him to weep over his sins.

John had for a long time been desirous of devoting himself entirely to the service of the sick poor. This desire was further increased in him by having resided in several hospitals, and his thoughts were constantly on this subject. He considered, therefore, that he was bound to speak to his director about it, in order that he might not follow his own judgment in so important a matter, nor of himself fix upon a state of life which might have such great consequences. He told him that he felt interiorly drawn towards this holy employment, that he never was more pleased than when he saw the poor and was able to console them ; that he believed that this was the employment God had destined for him, and begged him to give him his advice upon it. Avila strongly approved of his design, exhorted him to persevere in it, told him several things in order to confirm him in it more and more, and gave him to understand that he could not propose to himself anything more useful to his neighbour or more profitable towards his own salvation. He added, nevertheless, that it was not sufficient to consult men on this subject, but that he must speak to God about it, recommend to Him the undertaking, pray Him to manifest His Will, and ask of Him the light necessary to know if this vocation came from heaven. He recommended him also to make a pilgrimage to our Lady of Guadalupe, in order to pray to the Holy Virgin in that very celebrated church, and to beseech her to be his advocate and patron in this matter, in which it was so important for him not to be deceived, or to do anything until he was fully assured of the Will of God.

CHAPTER XVIII.

HE UNDERTAKES A JOURNEY TO OUR LADY OF GUADALUPE.—WHAT HAPPENS TO HIM ON THE WAY.

THE Church of our Lady of Guadalupe is served by the monks of S. Jerome, and people flock thither from all parts to implore the aid of the Blessed Virgin. Miracles are of very frequent occurrence, and there are few persons in Spain who do not go there to make their devotions when they wish to obtain from heaven any particular favour or extraordinary grace. John went thither from a very pure motive, and one worthy of a great saint, for it was to consult God on the choice of a state of life, and to know if He approved of his design of employing himself for the remainder of his days in serving the poor. He waited not until he arrived at this famous church before he began to pray, but during the whole journey he occupied himself with holy things only; he continually raised his mind to God, reciting many devout prayers, and omitting nothing that was necessary for preparing his heart to receive the graces which he hoped to obtain through the intercession of the Blessed Virgin. He added penance to prayer, for he performed this journey on foot in the middle of winter, whilst the ground was covered with ice and snow; he ate very little, indeed we may say that he fasted always, so great was his abstinence. Not having any money he was obliged at first to have recourse to the charity of devout persons, which contributed still more to his humiliation; but in order not to be a burden to any one, and to employ himself while travelling, he determined to collect every day a faggot of bushes

and dead branches, which he found by the way, and
in the evening he sold it in order to buy a little bread
and to pay for his lodging ; if by chance there remained anything over, he did not fail to distribute
it the next day among the poor, and when he lodged
in a hospital, he left there his faggot, or the sum of
money he had obtained for it. In this he imitated
the conduct of S. Hilarion, who did the same thing
when he had no other means of subsistence ; for this
great solitary, not being able to endure the honour
that was everywhere paid to him, often changed his
abode in order to hide himself from men. He even
passed over from the east into the west, and withdrew
into Sicily, where he thought he was unknown, and
dwelt in a desert situated in the middle of that island.
Being destitute of all provisions, he repaired every
day to a field where he collected together wood for a
faggot which his disciples sold in a neighbouring village. They then bought a little bread to live upon
themselves, and to give to those who sometimes came
to visit them.

The journey of John was attended by many other
circumstances which greatly contribute to acquaint us
with his patience, his disinterestedness, his unselfish-
ness, and his other virtues. On one occasion he arrived
so late at a little town called Fuente-Ovejuna, that every
one had already retired to rest. His poverty, which
was manifest from his appearance, was the reason that
no one would trouble himself to open his house to
him, and offer him an asylum. He passed the night
in the public square, but had no difficulty in con-
soling himself for this, when he called to mind how
the most holy Virgin and S. Joseph were refused
admittance into [the inns] at Bethlehem, and how

they retired to a stable, in which the Saviour of the
world was born.

Historians speak in terms of admiration of a miracle
which happened when S. Bernard was writing to his
nephew Robert, to exhort him to return to Clairvaux,
whence he had departed in order to retire to Cluny.
He dictated his letter to one of his disciples outside
the walls of the monastery in an open field, in order
that no one might know of it; and during this time
there came on a great shower of rain, which caused
the monk, who was writing from his dictation, to think
of folding up the paper in order to retire, but the
saint said to him: " It is a work of God, continue to
write, fear not ;" he did not therefore leave off writing
in spite of the storm, and not a single drop of rain fell
on the letter, whence it was seen that the zeal and holiness of Bernard had power to stop the course of nature.
A miracle similar to this was seen in the little town
of Fuente-Ovejuna, for as we have just related, John
passed the night in the streets, and, as it was cold
and the rain was falling, he set fire to the faggot
which he had brought, and had not been able to sell
because it was too late. The elements immediately
showed that they respected his virtue, for the rain,
which was violent, fell neither upon his fire nor on
himself, and thus he received no inconvenience from
it, but warmed himself very comfortably. Many of
the inhabitants, who were looking out of window, were
witnesses of this extraordinary event, which might be
termed a miracle, but instead of profiting by it they
put a malicious interpretation upon it, for they accused
John of being a sorcerer and of practising witchcraft,
and upon this pretext seized upon his person and
treated him with much indignity. They even en-

deavoured to catch him in his words, and for this purpose made a thousand different inquiries of him, and proposed several questions to him, and although he justified himself very well, and proved his innocence very clearly, they insulted him and loaded him with injuries. As soon as it was daylight they thrust him out of their city with ignominy, giving him only a little money and some bread in order to oblige him to quit their territory as soon as possible. It is thus that the sovereign majesty of God, Who generally performs miracles in order to exalt other saints and render them illustrious, made use of prodigies and extraordinary events in order to procure for John contempt and humiliations, because his heart thirsted after them.

The devil, not having been able to vanquish him in this way, attacked him in another, and tried to deceive him by offering him money ; for as he was walking as usual with a load of wood on his shoulders, he met an apparently respectable man who expressed a desire to buy his faggot, and who said to him without any previous bargaining, "My friend, give me your wood, and take this purse of money which I offer you." The servant of God answered with much simplicity that such a sum of money was not suitable for a poor pilgrim like himself, and thanking him, declined to accept it ; and because the man importuned him to receive his money, he was obliged to tell him plainly that he wished for none of it, and that if he forced him to receive it, he would employ it in having Masses said in the church of our Lady of Guadalupe. At these words the devil, who was concealed under this human form, uttered a loud cry, showing by this how much he feared the oblation of the adorable sacrifice, and at the same time the apparition disappeared. This teaches that the evil spirit has power only over those who are cowardly and off their guard, and that on the contrary he flees away from those who resist him, according to the words of the apostle S. James : "Resist the devil and he will fly from you" (S. James iv. 7).

It also proves that we must be indifferent to, and detached from, all earthly things in order to avoid the snares of this enemy of our salvation ; for he makes use of the pretext of necessity in order to tempt those to whom he would not dare openly to propose anything unlawful, and he does all he possibly can to insinuate himself by this means into their minds. He had recourse to this artifice in order to attack S. Antony in his desert, for he caused to be seen in an open field a large silver dish and a lump of gold, hoping that he would feel a desire to make use of it in his need. This great saint, being highly enlightened, took no heed of all this wealth, and proceeded on his way. Half suspecting it to be a snare of Satan, he said to him, " Keep thy gold and silver, and may they perish with thee ;" and he had no sooner uttered these words than the gold and silver vanished like smoke. Even Jesus Christ, during His mortal life, was not free from this temptation, for the devil proposed to Him to change stones into bread in order to satisfy His hunger after His fast of forty days and forty nights ; but the divine Saviour immediately repulsed him, thereby teaching all the faithful to distrust him and not listen to him at all, even in ordinary and indifferent matters, though they should appear necessary to life. We may judge, therefore, from the conduct of John on this occasion that he was

highly enlightened, and unselfish, and that he truly
loved poverty, since he knew how to avoid this subtle
temptation of the devil, and generously refused to
make the profit which was offered him, and seemed
to be quite lawful. But let us follow him on his
journey, and see what happened to him on his arrival
at Guadalupe.

CHAPTER XIX.

HE SPENDS SEVERAL DAYS WITH MUCH DEVOTION AT OUR LADY OF GUADALUPE.—MIRACLES WHICH OCCURRED THERE.

IT would be difficult to express the joy and consolation of the servant of God when he saw from a distance the church of our Lady of Guadalupe; his zeal
was redoubled, his piety became more fervent, and he
felt within himself a holy impatience to arrive there
as soon as possible, in order to worship God and
offer himself to His sovereign majesty, and to pro-
fess to Him at the foot of His altars that he sought
only to obey Him and to execute His Will. The confidence he had in the protection of the Blessed Virgin
further encouraged him, for he hoped to obtain
through her intercession all the graces necessary for
him in order to serve God : the favours he had already received from her seemed to him a certain
token that she would obtain for him still more, and
he promised himself that she would present to her
dear Son his vows and prayers, and would become his
advocate and mediatrix with Him. When he thought

he was on the territory of this church he prostrated himself on the ground with the most profound humility, and kissed it several times, in order to begin adoring the greatness and majesty of Him Who resided in that august basilica. His prostrations and adorations were more frequent as he drew nearer to this celebrated church, and when he reached the entrance, he kissed the threshold and each of the steps, inwardly pronouncing the words of the royal prophet : "Introibimus in tabernaculum ejus, adorabimus in loco ubi steterunt pedes ejus "—"We will go into His tabernacle, we will adore in the place where His feet stood" (Ps. cxxxi. 7).

He then went in front of the high altar to adore the Blessed Sacrament, and to pour forth his heart in the presence of his God. We can easily conceive how fervent were his prayers on this occasion, for since he had so much desired to pray in this holy place, and had endured so much suffering and fatigue in order to reach it, his fervour must then have received additional strength, and he must have been filled with extraordinary transports ; "his heart," we may say with David, must have "grown hot within him, and in his meditation a fire flamed out." Indeed he remained so long before this tabernacle of the great and living God, and his zeal carried him away so far, that when he returned to himself he found he was alone in the church, every one having gone out. Nevertheless, he would not go away until he had made a visit to the chapel of the Blessed Virgin, and he immediately repaired to it.

There heaven was propitious to his vows and prayers, and granted him such great and extraordinary graces that his merit could no longer be concealed, but shone forth on all sides. Antony Govea, Bishop of Cyrene and vicar apostolic in Persia, relates that as John was reciting hymns and canticles in honour of the divine Mother, and was pronouncing those words of the Salve Regina—"Illos tuos misericordes oculos ad nos converte," "Turn then those thine eyes of mercy towards us"—the curtain which concealed her image was suddenly drawn aside in order that he might contemplate and venerate it. This great favour touched his heart to an extraordinary degree, made him shed a flood of tears, and inspired him with new fervour in his prayers, but it was immediately followed by several things which served to humble him and exercise his patience.

The curtain was not drawn aside without making some noise, for God permitted this in order to accomplish the designs of His Providence. The sacristan, who was not far off, immediately ran up, and seeing the image uncovered, thought that the pilgrim had some evil design, and wished to steal the curtain or some of the ornaments of the altar; the condition in which he found him confirmed him in this idea, for he was quite alone, very ill clad, without shoes and stockings. He called him a hypocrite, a robber, and a rogue; he threatened to bring him to justice and have him punished as guilty of sacrilege; in short, he uttered all manner of abuse against him, and treated him as the most abandoned of men. John continued silent all the time, enduring without complaint all this torrent of abuse, and not attempting to justify himself, because he wished to imitate the patience of Jesus Christ in His Passion when He was accused of being a seducer and a blasphemer; and besides this, his humility led him not to reveal the

remarkable favour he had just received; but heaven
soon declared itself in his favour, took his defence in
hand, and made it known to all that he was entirely
innocent of the crime imputed to him, in the following way.

The calmness and moderation which he showed
on this occasion served only to excite the wrath of
the sacristan, who looked upon his silence as an
avowal of his crime, and his patience as an effect of
the inward trouble of his soul, which would not permit him to recover himself. From words he was
about to proceed to blows and violence, and had
already raised his foot to kick him, when the divine
justice punished him and cut short his fury, for he
felt himself suddenly stricken, his leg became helpless
and motionless, as formerly the hand of the impious
Jeroboam when he stretched it forth to punish the
prophet who threatened him in the name of God with
the destruction of his sacrilegious altar. The unhappy man immediately acknowledged his fault, shed
many tears, humbled himself before him whom he
had calumniated, and made many apologies. The
other monks who ran up upon hearing the noise, saw
clearly that there was something supernatural in it,
and said to one another, " Digitus Dei est hic "—
" This is the finger of God." When they learnt all
that had taken place, they recommended him to beg
pardon of God for the rash judgment he had formed,
and for the crime he had committed in attacking an
innocent man, and they induced him to have recourse
to John and beg him to obtain his cure from heaven.
He threw himself therefore at his feet in the presence
of all, again begged his pardon, and entreated him
to intercede in his favour, saying to him as did Je-

roboam to the man of God whom he had offended, " Entreat the face of the Lord thy God, and pray for me that my *foot* may be restored to me " (3 Kings xiii. 6).

John, who was full of charity and accustomed to overcome evil by good, had no difficulty in allowing himself to be persuaded to grant the pardon required of him. He prostrated himself with his face to the earth, he sent forth many sighs to heaven, he besought the Blessed Virgin to protect the poor religious, and to ask his cure of her dear Son, and he did not rise until the other had been effectually cured. Owing to his great humility, John was far from attributing to himself the glory of such a miracle ; on the contrary, he bid the sacristan publish abroad that Mary had been his deliverer, he ordered him to recite before her image a Salve Regina in thanksgiving, and for all rebuke he contented himself with saying to him, " My brother, be more discreet another time."

The Prior and a great number of religious, having been witnesses of this miracle, began to pay him great honours ; they looked upon him as a man who, under a poor and mean exterior, concealed extraordinary merit; they praised him much, and conducted him into their dormitory, esteeming themselves very fortunate in possessing such a guest, and hoping that he would draw down the graces of heaven upon their community. John having just shown so much kindness towards him who had offended him, failed not also to cause it to be seen on this occasion that he was of the number of those whom the Gospel calls humble of heart, for he did all he could to hinder them from treating him with so much respect, and endeavoured to humble and depreciate himself before all the brothers; but the more he strove to lower himself, the more was he honoured in the house, and the care that he took to avoid honours served only to draw down upon him new ones, and to cause him to be esteemed more and more, so that there might have been said of him what S. Jerome said of S. Paula: "Fugiendo gloriam, gloriam merebatur:" "By fleeing from glory he merited it."

In this monastery he remained twenty-two days, during which he gave himself entirely to prayer and contemplation. He was continually seen at the foot of the altars, he diligently attended all the offices, he employed the greater part of the nights in adoring the Blessed Sacrament, he communicated five times, he assisted at all the spiritual conferences which were held, and allowed no opportunity to pass of edifying himself and strengthening his piety. He very frequently recommended to God his great design, that is to say, the desire he had of devoting himself solely to the service of the sick poor. He fervently prayed that His holy Will might be manifested to him, and that he might know if he were destined for this employment. He often conferred respecting it with the Prior, and made known to him all his inward feelings. He failed not also to have recourse to Mary, his loving advocate, going every day to pray before the altar dedicated to her, where he received many very considerable favours.

After he had thus exercised himself in all kinds of good works at this celebrated monastery, and had done all that depended on himself in order to make certain of his vocation, he thought it was time to return to Granada, that he might there receive the cross Jesus Christ had prepared for him. He accordingly took leave of the Prior and all the community. These good monks, grieved at seeing him set out on a journey at this inclement season, gave him a white cloak to protect him from the cold, and made him promise to wear it for the love of them, and not to give it to any one. He protested to them that for his part he would all his life remember all their kindness and charity, and told them that having nothing he could not repay them otherwise than by praying God to be Himself their reward. Still, without thinking of it, he gave them a very great treasure, for he left them the example of his virtues and the good odour of his life. But his humility made him shut his eyes to this, and hindered him from perceiving the great spiritual advantages with which he enriched their monastery.

CHAPTER XX.

HE PASSES THROUGH OROPESA, WHERE HE HEALS A WOMAN BY LICKING HER WOUNDS.—HE GOES TO BAËZA IN ORDER TO CONFER WITH AVILA.

JOHN returned as he went, that is to say, praying as he travelled, fasting, mortifying himself, exciting all whom he met to serve God, and continually thinking of the blessings of eternity. The thought came into his mind of passing through Oropesa, not only in order to see his old friends, but to serve his neighbour according to the different opportunities divine Providence might afford him. He therefore adopted this route, which being already known to him, and not leading him much out of his way, might procure for him many opportunities of doing good and practising virtue.

As soon as he reached the little town, he went to the church according to his custom to say his prayers. Several persons who first recognized him were surprised at seeing him in so poor a condition, imagining that he had made a fortune, since he had been several years in the army. A great number of those with whom he had formerly been acquainted were eager to invite him into their houses, but from different motives ; some from compassion, being touched at the sight of his wretched appearance, others through mere curiosity, and in order that they might learn his different adventures, and the majority that they might laugh at him and turn him into ridicule : he listened to none of them, and without hesitation chose the hospital for his abode, in order that he might serve the sick poor for some time, and exercise himself in an employment to which he believed himself called. He acquitted himself in it with so much care, watchfulness and fervour, that every one was extremely edified, and people began to call him the " Father of the poor."

Amongst all the good works to which he devoted himself during his abode in this town there was one which shone forth pre-eminently, and gained him a very great reputation. He heard that a woman named Anne de la Torre was afflicted with a very dangerous illness and loathsome sores. All the skill of the physicians had been unable to procure her any relief, and the remedies with which they had overwhelmed her had produced no other effect than that of putting her to great pain and of entirely exhausting her property, so that she was very poor and

without any hope of ever being cured. Such an object
as this touched his heart and excited his compassion.
He resolved therefore to go and visit her, in order to
console her under her sufferings, and procure some
alms for her by means of his friends. He conversed
with her on matters of faith and devotion, exhorting
her to suffer patiently, and setting before her the example of a vast number of saints who had spent their
days in sufferings, in order to induce her to sacrifice
willingly to God her body and her whole life; and
he very forcibly represented to her that it was by
His mercy that she was not permitted to receive any
succour from men, in order that she might learn not
to trust in them, and to place her sole confidence in
Him.

But when he was speaking in this manner, he
knew not that he himself was the physician who was
appointed to heal her, and whom God chose to make
use of in order to restore her to perfect health. This
cure, nevertheless, was reserved for him, as the
event proved. For he suddenly felt himself inwardly
drawn to kiss her wounds and wash them with his
tongue; he obeyed this good impulse, and kneeling
down, began several times to lick her sores. His
nature did indeed recoil from it, and caused him to
exhibit some repugnance at the time, but he was determined to surmount it and do it violence in so important a matter, in order to accustom it henceforth
to obey without any contradiction. He went further, for reflecting that Jesus Christ had taken upon
Himself all our wounds, and in His passion had been
compelled to drink vinegar and gall, he made no difficulty about swallowing the matter which issued from
the wounds of the woman, and at the same instant

she found herself perfectly cured and freed from pain.

Such a miracle was soon made known in the town, and everybody spoke of it in terms of astonishment. Several ran to the sick woman's house in order to ascertain the certainty of what was said respecting her cure ; they inquired of her also what the servant of God had done to her, and they were never tired of hearing her relate in what manner he knelt before her to lick her sores and suck out the corrupt mat-ter. Others published everywhere his high virtue, declared that he was a man mighty in his deeds, and scrupled not to compare him to the greatest saints. Some also said that a process ought to be drawn up and an information taken of such a wonderful event, in order to preserve the memory of it ; and all the inhabitants in general began to respect him and pay him great honours. A man less humble than John would, without doubt, have been flattered by all this, but he was greatly afflicted and grieved at it ; he even took an opportunity of hastening his departure on this account, for the esteem and applause which so often gain over and attract the hearts of worldlings, tended only to drive him away from this town, and to induce him to leave it as quickly as possible ; in doing which he imitated the Saviour of the world Who, after having healed the sick and worked miracles, hid Himself, and withdrew into the wilderness in order to avoid the praises and acclamations of the people.

John's humility having driven him out of this city, he went to Baëza, because he had heard that Avila was there, distributing the bread of the word of God, as he had already done in all the neigh-

bouring places. He thought he was bound to
render him an account of his pilgrimage to our
Lady of Guadalupe and of all the graces he had
there received, and besides this, he wished to confer
with him once more on the conduct he ought to pursue in order to accomplish his great design. This
holy priest instructed and consoled him for several days, and decided that it was now time for him to
prepare himself to obey the commands of God and to
follow his vocation ; on taking leave of him he said,
"My brother John, I think it right that you should
return to Granada, whither the Lord has been now
for a long time calling you. He knows your desires
and your intentions, and He will not fail to point out
exactly the course you must pursue in order to serve
Him.   Be careful to regard Him and have Him always
before your eyes in all that you do, and fail not to
act on all occasions as a man who knows that he is
always in the presence of His sovereign Majesty.
When you arrive at Granada, choose a confessor who
possesses the qualities I have pointed out to you ; he
will act as your spiritual father, and you will do
nothing important without his advice ; and if anything extraordinary should happen in which you
think you need my advice, write to me wherever I
may happen to be, and I promise you that with the
assistance of God's grace I will do all in my power to
aid and assist you in whatever way I can."

After so solemn a promise it can not be doubted
that this great man always acted in the capacity of
director of the servant of God ; he had explained to
him all his duties and obligations in the city of
Granada when he saw him the first time ; he had
again conferred with him for several days at Montilla,

as we have mentioned above ; he ended by giving him at Baëza all the advice he deemed necessary for him, and though they were then obliged to part from one another in order to fulfil each his own ministry, the direction was not interrupted on this account, but was continued by means of letters. John wrote from time to time to his spiritual father to render him an account of his conduct and interior feelings, and Avila on his part failed not to write in reply and clear up all his doubts. It is this holy intercourse which gave rise to several letters which these great men wrote at different times; we still have some of those which Avila wrote to John of God, and they will be found in the first book of his Letters. It will not be unprofitable to quote here some passages from them to prove what we have just said, viz., that this holy priest was not only his director for a time, but that he continued to guide him, even when they were separated from each other by the different employments of charity in which they were engaged.

" You have afforded me," he says in one of his letters to him, " great consolation by performing so exactly what we had agreed upon together respecting the obedience you were to show to Father Portillo in the management of the poor. If you always act in this manner, we shall both of us feel satisfied on this point, whereas if you took your own understanding for a guide, I should have reason to fear the deceits of the devil. I entreat you, my brother, in the name of God, to persevere in the same line of conduct, and to show the same obedience until it shall please our Lord that I should go where you are, or you should come where I am, for when we are together I am not much afraid of your doing anything at your own suggestion; but children when absent from their fathers ought to show their deference and obedience to them by not doing anything which might cause them displeasure, but, on the contrary, should act in such a manner that when they see them again they may have cause to rejoice in our Lord. Since He has employed me to take care of you, and has united us in brotherly union by His love, let us act together, and by this means you will find that we shall put to flight and conquer the devil. If you love me and wish to obey me, obey Father Portillo, whom I give you as father in my place. Receive all that he shall say to you as if I said it to you, and do all that he shall recommend you as if I were recommending it to you, until I see you."

Let us see how he explains himself on the same subject in another of his epistles: "I have received your letter. I cannot suffer you to say that you do not deserve that I should recognize you as my son because you are very imperfect, for by the same reasoning I could not deserve to be your father; being still more imperfect than you are, I ought to have a greater contempt for myself than for you, but as our defects do not prevent God from acknowledging that we belong to Him, it is just that we should act in the same manner towards one another, and bear with one another in charity as He bears with us."

CHAPTER XXI.

JOHN TAKES THE ROAD TO GRANADA.—THE DEVIL TEMPTS HIM WHEN ABOUT TO ENTER THE CITY.

WE see in the Acts of the Apostles that S. Paul, being on the point of going to Jerusalem, sent for the priests and elders of the city of Ephesus, and said to them with truly apostolic generosity : " Now behold, being bound in the Spirit I go to Jerusalem, not knowing the things that shall befall me there, save that the Holy Ghost in every city witnesseth to me, saying that bonds and afflictions wait for me at Jerusalem. But I fear none of these things, neither do I count my life more precious than myself, so that I may consummate my course and the ministry of the word which I received from the Lord Jesus, to testify the gospel of the grace of God " (Acts xx. 22).

It seems probable that John conversed with himself in a similar manner when he was going to Granada, for there he expected only afflictions and crosses, and to suffer many things for the glory and service of God. This was not without foundation, for he remembered that Jesus Christ said to him near Gibraltar that Granada should be his cross ; but this shook him not, nor at all diminished his zeal ; on the contrary, it was this cross which was drawing him to Granada ; he went there in the spirit of sacrifice, and with the determination to fulfil the entire Will of His Master. It mattered not what became of him, provided he felt certain that he was obeying Him, and walking in the path He had marked out for him. The advice also which he had just received from Avila, his director, marvellously strengthened his courage, and suffered him not to defer any longer the journey, which he believed to be in accordance with the command of God and of such great importance to his salvation. Thus he set out, and taking the wings of the dove, flew towards Granada, so impatient was he to arrive there as soon as he could.

The devil on his part was not inactive, for being jealous of John's sanctity, he prepared new snares for him, and thought how he might dissuade him from entering the city where he knew God was calling him, and he acted in the following manner in order to gain his object. John having arrived at Granada heard Mass, and immediately went up to the hermitage of the martyrs, which was situated on an eminence near the city, to give thanks to God for all the mercies He had already granted him, and to pray Him to make known at last what was required of him. Whilst descending he, as usual, gathered together a bundle of wood in order to sell it in the city, but the evil spirit suddenly stopped him and tempted him to vainglory, for he inspired him with the thought that if he entered Granada having on him the white cloak which the prior of Guadalupe had given him, and bearing on his shoulders a faggot of wood, the people would think he had again fallen into mental weakness, and that he was still under the influence of his former madness. This made so strong an impression on his mind that he could not resolve to appear in the city in this state. He stopped therefore at the gate called *de los Molinos* which was sufficiently far from any houses, and letting down his load of wood he sold it to a poor woman for some pulse. The devil kept this thought before him the

whole day, considering it a sufficiently great victory
for him to have been able to induce so humble a man
to fear to dishonour himself in the world, or at least
in however small a degree to tarnish his reputation.

It is thus that he still daily tempts the faithful, in-
spiring them with false shame and making them afraid
of undertaking certain things, or declaring themselves
openly on the side of virtue, from fear of attracting
notice and of losing the esteem of persons in the world.
But good Christians ought to rise above these human
considerations and despise the judgment of worldlings, when they have to humble themselves and
labour seriously for their salvation. Our Saint has
given them a good example of this; for, reflecting
carefully on his own conduct, he condemned it and
saw clearly that the shame which had kept him
back was only an artifice of the devil, who, having
ruined himself by his pride, wished to diminish in
him the love of humiliations and make him conceive
some esteem for himself. He accordingly resolved
to fight against him at once, and in order to repulse him, he believed he ought to humble himself, to
degrade himself, and to do immediately what the
enemy had represented to him as little worthy of
him, and as capable of leading people to think that he
was still out of his mind. Going therefore into the
forest, he made a faggot of dead and useless branches
and put it on his shoulders, and in order to confound
Satan, he carried it into the middle of the public
square, in order that all might see him and form of
him what judgment they pleased. At this sight all
the people ran up and surrounded him on all sides.
They remembered having seen him behave like a

madman, and thought he was still under the influence of the same infirmity, which induced several to treat him with great indignity. Some young persons spent the whole day in insulting him, some of them even struck him and covered him with mud, and the most moderate contented themselves with laughing at him and despising him as a mad creature. "What now, John?" they said, "have you become a wood-seller? How did you get on in the hospital with the sick? We don't know what to think of you, you are so fickle, and are every day changing your trade."

This mockery and ill-treatment made no impression whatever on his mind, but the same moderation was always to be observed in him, for not a single hasty word escaped him ; and in order to make full amends for the weakness into which he had fallen, he continued this practice for several days together, and stationed himself every morning in the public square with a faggot on his shoulders, in order to excite the contempt and disgust of the passers-by, and to destroy entirely in his heart all self-love and vainglory. In the evening he sold his bundle of wood in order to get a little bread, and at the commencement of the night he went into the streets and public squares in which the poor lived, that he might distribute amongst them what remained of the price he obtained for it, and when he found a great number of them lying under the porticoes, benumbed with cold, covered with sores, and full of misery, he was sensibly affected at it ; he groaned over it within himself, and ardently desired to be in a condition to succour them and provide for their wants. It is thus that he atoned for the slight fault he might have committed in not rejecting with sufficient promptness this suggestion of the devil, and in listening a little too much to the worldly shame with which he inspired him. The penance he did for it ought to teach Christians that the best way to punish their sins is to perform works which are contrary to the faults they have committed; to humble themselves when they have been carried away by pride, to fast when they have fallen into intemperance, to give alms and distribute their property to the poor when they have usurped that of their neighbour, or have wished to enrich themselves inordinately. But this they hardly ever do; they make satisfactions which have no relation to the sins they have committed, and do not combat their ruling passions; whence it happens that they always remain the same, and after having frequently done penance, they are neither more mortified nor more holy.

CHAPTER XXII.

HE HAS A VISION IN WHICH IT IS MADE KNOWN TO HIM THAT HE WILL PASS THE REMAINDER OF HIS LIFE IN LABOUR AND TOIL.—HE HIRES A HOUSE IN WHICH TO LODGE THE POOR.

AFTER John had resisted the devil as we have just mentioned, and had overcome the temptation employed to surprise him, he applied himself to prayer in order to fortify himself more and more against these kinds of attacks, and went often into the churches to consult God respecting his state, and to ask Him to accomplish at last His holy Will in him.

His prayers were not ineffectual, for soon afterwards
our Lord opened to him a vast career in which there
were a thousand opportunities for signalizing his zeal,
exercising charity, and practising patience. He willed
also to give him some foreshadowing of it, and to make
him see by some visible sign what that was to which
He destined him.

One day, as John was on his knees before the crucifix in our Lady's church, he had a vision during
which it seemed to him that there were no doors
to the church, or at least that they were closed,
and that the Blessed Virgin, descending from the
altar with S. John the Evangelist, came and placed
on his head the crown of thorns of Jesus Christ,
and that she said to him: "John, it is by thorns,
by labours, and by sufferings that you must gain
the crown which my Son has prepared for you."
John was immediately filled with great contrition
for his past sins, and cried out, "O my adorable
Saviour, since Thou deignest to honour me, wretch
that I am, with so particular a favour, I promise
Thee from the bottom of my heart that henceforth
thorns shall be all my joy, and that I will have no
other employment than that of imitating Thy sufferings." As soon as he had uttered these words the
vision disappeared, and the doors of the church
appeared to him open. We should have known
nothing of this favour, which he received in private,
had he not himself declared it to Brothers Melchior
and Dominic, for whilst conversing with them simply
and familiarly respecting all that had happened to
him in the course of his life, he spoke of this event,
and told them that he always bore it very attentively
in mind, and looked upon it as a warning from God,

Who wished to show him that the cross and sufferings were his lot.

Our readers must not imagine that he was wrong in taking heed of this vision, or in believing in it, for besides that he felt the effects of it upon his body and mind, we know that God has often employed visions of this kind in order to make known His Will to His most faithful servants. It was in a mysterious dream that the angel revealed to S. Joseph the Incarnation of the Word, and commanded him on the part of God to flee into Egypt, and afterwards to depart thence in order to return into Judæa.

John was continually occupied with this vision, and thinking it over in his mind without exactly knowing what was the meaning of it, nor what were the pains and sufferings which it announced to him. Still his heart hungered and thirsted ardently after the cross, he sought it everywhere, sighing after it, and expecting it with holy impatience; yet still it came not; and this it was that afflicted him and filled his soul with bitterness, for as the wise man says, "Hope that is deferred afflicteth the soul" (Prov. xiii. 12). God at last listened to his prayers, and showed favour to his desires, by giving him to understand what the cross was which He had prepared for him, for as he was walking along the streets he perceived a house with a notice on it in these words: "This house to let in lodgings for the poor." All his troubles ceased immediately, he was no longer restless, his mind became calm, and he had a firm conviction that God gave him this opportunity of serving the poor, that he ought no longer to seek after any other cross, and that this was the true interpretation of the words which Jesus Christ addressed to him near Gibraltar : "John of God, Granada shall be thy cross." He therefore deliberated no longer on what he ought to do, but thought only of the measures he should take in order to hire the house, and provide shelter in it for the poor, of whom there were a very great number in Granada, and who suffered greatly, when sick, from want of attention and assistance.

But there was one great difficulty, for he was himself very poor ; he lived only on what he could obtain for the small quantity of wood which he sold every day, he was without credit in the world, and there was every probability that the proprietors of the house would not listen to him when he presented himself to take it. Nevertheless, he did not consider all these obstacles, which would have been only too likely to discourage a less zealous man than he was. He shut his eyes to his own weakness, and trusting only in the favour and protection of Him for Whose glory he was acting, he took some steps towards bargaining for the price of this house, and by a marvel which we cannot rate too highly it was given to him for what he offered, without inquiry whether he was able to pay the rent.

This was the commencement of the hospital of Granada, which in a short time became so celebrated. It was a poor man who first projected it, without having any money in hand to provide for the expense ; he took upon himself what seemed to be entirely beyond his strength, he consulted not the rules of prudence, and allowed himself to be carried away by the fervour of his zeal ; nevertheless his undertaking was fortunate, and succeeded completely, as we shall see in the course of this work. By this we perceive that it was in accordance with the command of God, and that to Him must be given all the glory of it; for the more feeble the secondary causes are, the more does His sovereign power shine forth and manifest itself, and the less probability there is in anything, the more are we bound to acknowledge that it was His Providence which guided it and caused it to succeed.

BOOK II.

WHICH CONTAINS THE ACCOUNT OF HIS PUBLIC LIFE.

CHAPTER I.

HITHERTO we have considered John simply as a private individual; we have spoken of his birth and education, and described the troubles he experienced in his youth; we have related · the different favours which he received from God on several occasions, and shown ,that heaven often interested itself in his preservation, and performed prodigies in order to protect him. Now we come to the time when he enters upon his public life, when we shall see him mount the stage on which his virtue will shine with great brilliancy. He will no longer labour in secret, but his actions will be exposed to the sight of all the faithful. His fervour will signalize itself on all occasions; his charity will be universal and will be extended to all men; he will be the father and protector of the poor; he will lay the foundations of a great order; he will apply himself to the conversion of sinners; he will protect widows and orphans; he will be the preacher of almsgiving; he will treat with the great without neglecting the little; he will be known to princes and sovereigns; he will be found at their courts, which he will edify by his discourses, and

still more by his conduct; he will give the Church
an example of the most eminent virtues; he will be
a great penitent, and will practise austerities which
shall make even those blush who think they are leading an austere and penitential life; he will teach all
Christians to what a height they ought to carry the
love of their neighbour, and enable them to see that
it is not impossible to be at once men of prayer, and
employed in outward works of mercy for the good
and benefit of their brethren. He will verify in himself that celebrated saying of the holy fathers, that
one can be a martyr in the midst of the peace of the
Church, because his mortifications will be so great and
so extraordinary that we shall be justified in calling
them with S. Jerome a long martyrdom. In short he
will be a light which will shine over the whole city of
Granada, and rouse the courage of all its inhabitants
by his zeal; and he will labour with all his might to
kindle in their hearts the divine fire of charity. This
is the substance of what we have to relate in this
second book: we must now resume the thread of our
narrative.

As soon as John had made sure of a house, he thought
about providing it with the furniture which was
absolutely necessary, and without losing any time
he went all over the city, seeking out the sick, the
crippled, the infirm, and the poor of every sort in
order to fill his hospital. The greater part of those
who saw him acting in this manner blamed him,
accused him of indiscretion, and looked upon him as
a rash schemer, who was taking upon himself a thing
that was utterly impossible. They represented to
him that having neither property nor revenues, he
ought not to burden himself with so great a number

of poor persons ; that it was tempting God, and presumptuous ; that he ought to regard the enterprise he had formed as an artifice of the devil, who wished to deceive him under the veil of charity ; that this virtue ought to be regulated by prudence, and that a wise man should not take upon himself any employment or ministry unless divine Providence placed him in a condition to succeed in them and fulfil all their duties.

Those who spoke in this way judged only according to outward appearances ; they imagined that John was merely acting according to his own lights in this important matter, and they were not aware that he had taken the advice of the celebrated Avila, and of many other highly enlightened persons, and that he was only following the orders of that Providence which they themselves objected to him. Thus all their arguments, though specious and apparently just, made no impression on his mind, and he contented himself with answering them that in truth he was poor and without any property ; that he could do nothing of himself, and that his own weakness was well known to him ; that he knew the foundation of a hospital to be infinitely beyond his power, but that Jesus Christ was sufficiently powerful to sustain and strengthen him ; that the poor of whom he was taking care were His children and His members, and that He was well able to support them ; His Providence was the revenue and patrimony of those who had nothing on earth, and who received no aid from men, and He did not abandon those servants who trusted in His goodness and mercy ; and that as he had commenced this work in His Name and for His glory, he was resolved not to give it up until God had given him undoubted marks of His Will, and had made it known to him that He did not approve of his enterprise.

His firmness astonished those who had taken upon themselves to remonstrate with him. His faith covered them with confusion, and the ardour of his charity brought them to their senses, and led them to wish to take part in the foundation he was preparing; they accordingly began by placing some money at his disposal, to provide for the most pressing wants of his poor. Their example induced the other inhabitants to make him presents. One of the royal chaplains sent him three hundred and twelve reals, which were employed in purchasing beds; several pious persons clubbed together and gave him sufficient to provide other articles of furniture, and by this means his house was in a short time furnished with all that was necessary for the exercise of hospitality. Not only did the poor not want for anything in this house, but they were very well taken care of; all their troubles were sympathized with, much kindness and gentleness was shown them, every kind of remedy was supplied to them, all their wants were anticipated, and they were treated with so much care in the new hospital, that others who enjoyed good health had reason to envy them, for even the rich were not better treated in their own houses.

He was not satisfied with succouring the poor in their bodily sicknesses and with giving them remedies, but he endeavoured above all to procure the salvation of their souls and to reconcile them with God. For this purpose, when he received them into his house, he first gave them spiritual advice, and as soon as he had washed their feet and presented to them a wooden cross to kiss, he recommended them to put their consciences in order, and prepare themselves for receiving the sacraments, addressing them in these or similar words : " My dear brothers, you ought to give infinite thanks to God for that He has waited so long a time for you to do penance. Examine carefully what are the sins you have committed, because I am going to bring you a charitable physician who will endeavour to heal your souls. Do not be troubled about what concerns your bodies, for everything shall be supplied to you, and we will not spare the remedies. Hope in God, rely on His goodness and mercy, and you will see that, very far from abandoning you, He will provide for all your wants, and will bestow on you favours of every sort." He then caused a confessor to be brought to them, and exhorted them to disclose to him all their most secret sins, and to lay open for his judgment all the diseases under which their souls laboured. He took care that they should frequently receive familiar instructions. He procured them visits from spiritual persons, who taught them the use they ought to make of their sicknesses, and he omitted nothing that could in any way edify them and contribute towards their eternal salvation. When people saw that he had such good intentions, they exerted themselves in seconding his zeal : priests came of their own accord and offered to work in his hospital, and although there was already a large number of poor in in it, there was no lack of evangelical labourers who were willing to employ themselves in assisting them, in helping them to die well, or in instructing them to serve God and do real and true penance.

CHAPTER II.

HIS CONDUCT IN HIS HOSPITAL.

S. JEROME, speaking of the extensive alms of S. Paula in the beginning of her widowhood, assures us that she fed all the sick, going through every part of Rome to seek them, and thinking she suffered a great loss when any one else assisted and fed a poor person. We may say the same of John of God; his tenderness for the sick was so great that he wished to have them all in his hospital and to serve them with his own hands; for this reason he was not satisfied with admitting them when they asked for beds, but went himself to find them; he made inquiries in order to ascertain where they were, and allowed himself no rest until he had brought them into his house. If any one escaped his care and diligence he was grieved, and considered he had suffered a real loss. *Damnum putabat si quisquam debilis et esuriens cibo sustentaretur alterius.* By this he showed how far removed he was from the ordinary habits of men, who are very glad not to be so exactly informed of the necessities of their brethren, and take good care not to anticipate their wants, nor to be curious in endeavouring to find out what they stand in need of; thinking they have satisfied all the duties of charity when they have distributed some trifling alms to the poor who follow after and importune them.

John's extraordinary ardour in filling his hospital with the poor, did not prevent him from being very exact in providing everything they wanted; he caused them to sleep in separate beds lest they should catch each other's diseases; he placed in a separate ward those who had dangerous fevers; he left a sufficient space between each bed to allow of their being cleaned, being persuaded that cleanliness contributes greatly to the healing of the sick; he gave them food at certain fixed hours; he knew the proper time for dressing their wounds, in doing which he was entirely guided by the direction of the surgeon; he was with them at all times of the day, and never did they call him without his immediately appearing at their side; and they received what they stood in need of almost always from his own hands.

At that time there were very few persons who took the trouble to assist him and second his zeal. Thus it was necessary for him to give orders for everything, to be constantly moving about to satisfy all the wants of his patients, and to occupy himself with a thousand different things; nevertheless, everything was done at the proper time and place, and the poor were waited upon and assisted with the greatest regularity. This surprised every one, for people could not understand how one man could fulfil so many difficult employments, and bear up against so much fatigue. But what cannot charity do? It assumes different shapes, just as does the grace from which it flows; it is discouraged at nothing; it endures everything; it strengthens those who act under its influence, and makes them surmount all the difficulties which would perplex and dishearten those who were prompted only by human views. Accordingly, we see John always consistent with himself; nothing disturbed or distressed him, and never did he complain of anything; on the contrary, there was seen in his countenance a certain liveliness which showed the interior joy of his soul. His fervour increased every day, and considering the manner in which he acted on all occasions, we should conclude that an invisible hand was ever guiding and supporting him.

After having worked in this manner all the day, he used to go out about nightfall to beg alms for his poor; he walked through the streets with a basket at his back and a kettle to hold broth on each arm; neither wind, rain, nor other inclemencies of weather stopped him from making his usual round. When he wished to ask alms for the sick, he cried out in a loud voice at the corners of the cross-roads, " Do good to yourselves, my brothers, do good to yourselves."* These words were full of hidden meaning, and showed that he was acquainted with the truths of Scripture, which assures us that " a merciful man doth good to his own soul"—" benefacit animæ suæ vir misericors." People were at first surprised at hearing such words uttered in the darkness of the night, and some were thus led to look out of their windows, or to open the doors of their houses, in order more easily to distinguish him who cried out in this manner, and when they saw that it was the same man who a short time since had been shut up in the hospital as a lunatic, they despised him, took no heed of what he said, and supposed he had again fallen into his former insanity, so that at first he collected but very little alms.

Nevertheless, he was not discouraged, and God sent him other aid for the support of his poor; he was also very glad to see himself thus despised, and

* Hence was derived the name of *Fate-bene-fratelli*, by which the brothers of his order are known in Italy.

secretly rejoiced in his heart that the charity he was practising towards his brethren exposed him to fresh humiliations. He always went out at the same hour to beg alms, and ceased not to say as usual, " Do good to yourselves, brethren, do good to yourselves." As his voice was touching and moved people to sympathy, many felt themselves at last interiorly affected at hearing him thus cry out, and desired to converse with him. They soon found out that he spoke very sensibly, and that all that he said inclined them only to give alms and show their charity. But they were surprised at seeing him in so poor a condition, so emaciated, pale, and worn out by his great austerities and continual labours. All this disposed them to take pity on him, and inspired them with the thought of assisting him, and of contributing to the support of his poor. Accordingly they began to offer him considerable alms; some gave him money, others bread and the scraps from their tables, others poultry and provisions suitable for a hospital.

When his basket and two kettles were full, he returned with joy to his poor, reckoning as nothing the load he was carrying, which would have been too much for any other man, because the charity which animated him rendered it light and easy. On entering he used to say to them : " May God preserve you, my brothers; pray to the Lord for your benefactors ;" and at the same time he caused what he had brought to be warmed up again, and distributed to them according to their wants. He then always reminded them to give thanks to God and offer up their prayers for their benefactors, and after this he passed a great part of the night in working in the infirmaries and other parts of the house. Not only did people give him alms, but many piously disposed persons went to visit his hospital, and were much edified at all they saw in it; the poor were suitably provided for, well waited upon, instructed with the greatest care, and consoled with so much kindness and charity that their evils appeared to them light and easy to be borne. All this greatly served to make his house known, and to attract to it all kinds of persons, great and small, noblemen and gentlemen, rich and poor.

CHAPTER III.

THE ARCHBISHOP OF GRANADA BECOMES PROTECTOR OF JOHN'S HOSPITAL.—THE RECOMPENSE OF A WIDOW'S ALMS.

THE archiepiscopal see of Granada was at that time occupied by Don Pedro Guerrero, a personage as much celebrated for his learning as for his piety and other eminent qualities. He governed his diocese with much vigilance, entering into the detail of everything that took place in it, and fulfilling very carefully all the duties of a good pastor; above all, he made a good use of his temporal means by most liberally sharing them with the poor. We might add in his praise, that he was highly esteemed at the Council of Trent, in which he nobly supported the interests of the Church and of religion; but we must leave to his biographers the task of celebrating his merits. What we have said is sufficient to give our readers a favourable idea of him, and to make them understand that it was highly honourable to

John of God to have had to deal with so great an archbishop, and to have merited his good-will.

As soon as this prelate heard of the new establishment that the servant of God had formed for the benefit of the poor, he thought it his duty to take cognizance of it, and to examine how it was carried on. Accordingly he went to the hospital, observed the order which was kept there, saw the manner in which the sick were treated, and inquired into the instructions which were given them and all the spiritual aids that were provided for them. He interrogated John on several important points, and asked him what had induced him to take upon himself the care of so many poor, how he intended to provide for their subsistence, what were the principles he thought of acting on for the future, and where he expected to obtain sufficient means to enable him to carry on such an undertaking. The father of the poor answered him with much humility, and very candidly made known to him all the thoughts of his heart. He said he had devoted himself to the service of the poor because he believed Jesus Christ demanded it of him, and that this was the state of life He wished him to be in ; he also carefully related him the signs by which He had manifested His Will to him. He confessed that he had no revenues wherewith to support so many poor, but that he trusted in the Providence of God, which does not abandon its own ; he moreover promised to do nothing of himself, but always to follow the advice which wise and prudent persons might give him.

The archbishop, being fully satisfied with his answers, highly extolled his zeal and charity, exhorted him to persevere, publicly approved of his establishment, promised him his protection, and caused considerable sums to be given him to defray the expenses of his hospital. The people followed the example of their pastor, and went in crowds to see the new house; they admired the propriety with which everything was conducted; they considered the poor happy in having found such a father, and conceived a high esteem for John's virtue and charity, so that when he went out to beg, he was no longer repulsed as before, or exposed to public ridicule; on the contrary, he was praised and honoured, people came out of their houses to salute him, to recommend themselves to his prayers, and to give him considerable alms; and he, in order to thank those who gave him anything, said in an humble and grateful manner: "You know not now the good you are doing yourselves, but God will make you see it when He pays you back your alms." He wished by this to show that those who distribute their money to the poor, far from losing it, entrust it to God Himself, that they put it out at interest in His hands, and that they ought to rest assured that He will pay it back to them with interest in heaven; this, also, is what the wise man says, "He that hath mercy on the poor, lendeth to the Lord; and He will repay him" (Prov. xix. 17).

It sometimes happens that God does not wait for the next life to reward those who give alms, but allows them even in this world to reap the fruit of their charities. The whole city of Granada saw a remarkable instance of this in the person of Anne Fusteros, who even in this life received a reward for all that she gave to the servant of God. She was very fond of the poor, and practised literally the advice

which the holy Tobias gave his son: "According to thy
ability be merciful. If thou have much, give abundantly; if thou have little, take care even so to bestow
willingly a little; for thus thou storest up to thyself
a good reward for the day of necessity" (Tob. iv.
8). She was very careful in giving alms to John's
hospital, more or less according as her means allowed, and as she did not possess much, she often
deprived herself of some necessary of life in order to
give something to the poor. One day, not having
anything to give, she could not continue her usual
alms; still she was unwilling entirely to interrupt her
charity, and remembering the widow who is praised
in the Gospel for having in her want taken two small
pieces in order to make an offering of them to the
poor, she believed that Jesus Christ would also be
pleased if she offered to His members the little that
still remained to her, and having only a small quantity of salt, she sent it to John with as much joy as if
it had been something very considerable. This action
was so meritorious before God that He willed to
reward it immediately, not only by filling this woman
with graces and blessings, but by visibly assisting one
of her children, and by causing all that she had given
to the hospital of Granada to be paid back again to
him; for she had a son who was at that time bearing
arms in Italy under Charles V. It happened that the
troop to which he belonged was disbanded, and it
was necessary for him to think of returning into Spain;
money failed him on the road, and he was compelled
to beg the assistance and charity of the faithful. It
was then that the alms of his mother began to bear
fruit, for there was usually given to him every day
the same alms that she offered to John's poor, and

salt was offered to him the same day that she gave
some to the servant of God. It was not long before
the news of this marvel was spread all over the city
of Granada, for the soldier, arriving there soon afterwards, spoke to his mother and several persons of
the alms and bounty he had received, and they discovered that he had every day received the same
things that his mother had given to John's hospital.
This made people more eager than ever to go to
visit the poor, and to contribute towards their support, all being firmly persuaded that to deny oneself in order to give alms is to sow in a fertile field,
from which fruits are reaped in abundance, not only
in heaven, but often on earth also.

CHAPTER IV.

JOHN HIRES A NEW HOUSE FOR HIS POOR.—THE ANGEL RAPHAEL COMES TO SERVE THEM.

THE approbation which the Archbishop of Granada
had given to John's new establishment, and the
story of the woman's alms, rendered his hospital very
celebrated, and the poor flocked to it from all parts,
hoping to find in it the assistance they stood in need
of; besides this, his charity attracted them still more,
for he received them so kindly, treated them so well,
and attended them with so much care, that they were
almost glad to be ill, and looked upon their sickness
as a fortunate thing for them. Thus the house he had
at first taken was soon found to be too small, and he
was obliged to hire another still larger and more

commodious in order that he might be able to admit
all who presented themselves. He himself laboured
in the removal of the property. He carried in his
arms several sick persons who were unable to walk,
and so took them from the old to the new house ; he
caused the beds and all the other furniture to be
brought into it, and in a very short time he was
able to practise hospitality there. He made excellent
regulations for it, having a separate room for those
who were dangerously ill, another for cripples, and a
third for those who had only ordinary fevers ; he also
appointed a part for pilgrims and strangers to sleep in
who had no place to go to, and by this means it was
easy for him to show charity to all kinds of persons,
and he was no longer compelled to send away any
of those who implored his aid.

He was almost alone in the new house, as he
had also been in the one he had just left, and as he
had not a sufficient number of persons to fulfil the
different offices, the angels of Paradise often came to
his assistance, and esteemed themselves happy in being
able to serve the poor, and share with him so noble an
employment. He perceived one evening that there
was a scarcity of water in the hospital, and that there
was not sufficient for the night, so he immediately left
what he was engaged in, and without further delay
took up the pitchers and other vessels, and went to
the fountain, which was at a considerable distance.
In his absence the Angel Raphael, whose name tells
how much he loves to comfort the poor, taking upon
himself a visible form, performed several kind offices
to the poor, and assisted them in such a manner that
they clearly saw he was not an ordinary man. Upon
John's return, he learnt what had happened, and

immediately concluded that it was this holy angel who
had come to visit his hospital and had waited upon
his patients ; for a little time before he had promised
to assist him in his ministry.

Another day, as he was thinking within himself
that he had not bread enough for the supper of his
poor, he saw a comely young man enter the infirmary, dressed almost in the same manner as himself,
and carrying a basketful of bread. This gave him
much joy, and caused him to bless divine Providence, which never abandons its own, but always
watches over them and provides for all their wants.
Whilst he was making these reflections, the young
man came near to where he was, and said to him,
" John, we have one and the same office ; take this
bread which heaven sends you to supply your want,"
and in a moment afterwards he disappeared ; whilst
all were persuaded that it was the same Angel Raphael who had provided for the sustenance of the poor.

What happened a short time afterwards appears
no less wonderful, and serves still more to show us
how great an interest this blessed spirit took in all
that regarded the servant of God. He was returning one evening very heavily laden with what he had
obtained by begging in the city for his patients, when
he met in the street a poor man, very weak, and exposed to all the accidents of a dark and dreary night.
John had compassion on him, and like the Samari-
tan in the Gospel, he immediately put this poor man
on his shoulders in order to take him to his hospital ;
but as he had more zeal than strength, and his body
was much weakened by his fasts, austerities, and continual labours, he soon fell to the ground, not being
able to support the double burden with which he was

loaded, for he did not put down the provisions he was carrying when he took the sick man on his shoulders. He then loudly reproached his body, accusing it of cowardice and effeminacy ; he threatened to subdue it, to ill-treat it, and to make it suffer for its laziness ; meanwhile, one who seemed to be a gentleman accosted him, offering to assist and conduct him to his house, and said to him, "My good man, you are unreasonable in blaming your body; why have you loaded it too much? give me your hand and lean on me." The servant of God, taking him for what he appeared, very humbly thanked him, saying, "My brother, I have to deal with an ass which is well fed, but will not work ; however, blessed be God, I hope I shall tame it and bring it to its duty; and since charity induces you to assist me, permit me to ask you your name in order that I may show you my gratitude on all occasions." The holy angel was pleased at last to make himself known, and replied to the father of the poor before several persons who were witnesses of their conversation: "John, I am the Angel Raphael. God has entrusted to me the care of your person, and of all those who shall serve the poor with you. I keep account of all your actions and of all the alms that are given you, and I am charged to protect and preserve all those who shall favour the undertaking you have commenced for the benefit of the poor." Our readers must not be astonished at the frequent apparitions of the angel in favour of John and his patients, nor must they doubt their reality under pretext that the same thing does not ordinarily happen in these latter ages, for the hand of God is not shortened, and He is always equally powerful when He wishes to honour and reward His faithful servants. The holy patriarchs often received similar visits in their time; the same S. Raphael guided the young Tobias on his journey; another angel led S. Peter out of prison; and the heavenly powers have often assumed the likeness of men in order to serve and help the faithful. Hence we ought not to be surprised at seeing John receive the same graces as were bestowed on the patriarchs and the greatest saints, whose faith and virtues he so closely imitated, as we shall see hereafter; besides which, he was undertaking a great and difficult thing, and one which had need of being accredited in the world by some shining testimony in order that it might succeed. Thus, then, it was as it were necessary that he should have such apparitions at the commencement of his hospital, in order to attract the inhabitants of Granada to it, and induce them to support it by their alms.

—

CHAPTER V.

JOHN RECEIVES JESUS CHRIST INTO HIS HOSPITAL UNDER THE FORM OF A POOR MAN.

THESE favours and acts of kindness from the Angel Raphael without doubt served greatly to bring the new house into esteem, but it was looked upon very differently when it was known that Jesus Christ Himself had honoured it with His presence. For the servant of God, on another occasion, carried on his shoulders a poor sick man to his hospital, and as he was preparing to wash his feet, according to his custom, before he placed him in a bed, he perceived on them the marks of wounds. Being much surprised at this, he raised his eyes, and then his surprise was still greater, for he saw his countenance shining all over with light, and he discovered that he was washing the feet of Jesus Christ Himself, so that he was on the point of fainting away. But the divine Saviour encouraged him, saying, "John, My faithful servant, do not be alarmed, but return to yourself. If I visit you to-day, it is in order to show you how pleasing to Me are all your actions, and the care that you take of My poor. I consider as done to Myself all that you do to My members. I receive all the kind offices you show them and all the assistance you procure for them. I count all the steps you take for their benefit, and all the words you utter in order to excite men to pity their misery, and I will not fail to reward you for them. Persevere as you have begun, preserve always your first fervour, and never relax any of your exercises if you wish to obtain the crown which I have prepared for you."

With these words our Blessed Lord disappeared, and John no longer saw any one, but the infirmary was filled with so great a light that the poor patients thought it had taken fire and was about to be reduced to ashes. Those who had still some strength left got out of their beds intending to make their escape, and others, seized with fear, began to cry out, "Fire! fire! the hospital is on fire!" The servant of God ran up to them and reassured them as well as he could, giving them to understand that the fire they had seen was not intended to consume their bodies nor to destroy the hospital, but to inflame their hearts and to excite in them the ardour of charity, and he recommended them to thank Jesus Christ for His good-will towards them in coming to visit them under the form of a poor man.

The holy fathers have greatly exalted the happiness of Abraham, who, thinking he was showing hospitality to pilgrims only, had the glory of receiving into his house angels from Paradise, or even, as some say, the God of heaven and earth, Who was pleased to take human form in order to confer on him this honour. We may say that the father of the poor was not inferior in this point to the great patriarch; he imitated his fervour in going after the poor in order to find them out and bring them into his house; he generally even carried them on his shoulders, took care of them and provided for all their wants, and used to wait upon them himself, in order to become in a more especial manner like' to the Father of the faithful. He also received a similar reward, for when he thought that he was stooping down to wash the feet of an ordinary man, he discovered that it was before Jesus Christ Himself that he was humbling himself; he saw Him full of glory, he heard Him speak, and had the consolation of learning from His own mouth that his undertaking was very pleasing to Him, and that He approved of the services which he rendered to His members.

As soon as the news of this miracle had spread throughout the city, persons ran from all parts to John's hospital; they questioned his poor, who bore witness to what they had seen; they congratulated him on this favour which had been granted to him as a singular grace, saying [that his establishment was the work of heaven, and that it was the duty of all to contribute towards it. Thus physicians offered to attend all his sick gratuitously, apothecaries promised to supply him with medicines, and to wait as long as might be necessary before they received any payment for them; the rich undertook to give him alms, those that were poorer gave him their word that they would labour to the best of their power for the benefit of the sick, and several begged to be admitted into his house to wait upon the poor. Thus it pleased God to manifest the virtue and merit of His servant, and to render his hospital celebrated, in order that it might be a lasting monument of his charity.

CHAPTER VI.

THE BISHOP OF TUY COMMANDS HIM TO TAKE THE NAME OF JOHN OF GOD, GIVES HIM A PARTICULAR HABIT, AND ENJOINS HIM TO WEAR IT.

THE lovers of the world ordinarily give their whole attention to observing its fashions and customs in order to conform to them. As soon as anything new appears, they are taken with it, and immediately wish to adopt it; they are constantly changing their dresses, and are always striving to have more splendid ones. Those, on the contrary, who make profession of piety fly from pomp and show; they seek after what is simple and modest; they dispense from day to day with some of their ornaments; they show by their exterior deportment that they love not the world; they seek not to please it, and are never more happy than when they share in the poverty of Jesus Christ, and bear some mark of it in their own persons.

John being entirely dead to the world, desired not to please it, or to have its approbation; nay, so far from this, we have seen that he did several extraordinary things, which were calculated only to bring down its contempt upon him. Never was any man more averse from all that could savour of luxury and vanity, and throughout the whole course of his life he was utterly indifferent to a vast number of things which others would have deemed lawful and compatible with his condition and fortune. It might be said that his zeal went a little too far on this subject, especially after he had established his hospital, and had become the father, as it were, of all the poor ; for he appeared in public with clothes so ragged and worn that several persons were scandalized. They thought that this rendered him too contemptible, and prevented their having intercourse with him ; others attributed it to his negligence and indolence, which hindered him from taking reasonable care of his person ; even those who judged of it rightly, because they were persuaded it proceeded from his humility and great love of poverty, failed not, nevertheless, to say that virtue ought to be regulated, and that it should not prevent us from aiming at a certain propriety, and from observing a decent moderation, which is midway between excessive neatness and negligence that offends those with whom we have to deal.

These different arguments in nowise shook him, nor induced him to change his manner of life, for he always continued to wear very ragged clothes, and if by chance he met in the streets a poor man still worse clad than himself, he immediately took his clothes and gave him his own, so that he seldom returned from the city without being very badly dressed. Having one day entered in this state the palace of Don Se- bastian Ramirez de Fuenleal, Bishop of Tuy and

President of the Royal Court of Granada, in order to pay him a visit, that prelate was much surprised at it, and could not refrain from forming in his own mind an unfavourable judgment on such conduct, but with wise and prudent moderation he dissembled it at first, in order to understand his visitor's dispositions better; he received John very kindly, welcomed him cordially, and spoke to him with singular freedom and openness. After some conversation he questioned him on several circumstances in his life, asked him his surname, and what was his native country and his family.

John was greatly embarrassed, for on the one hand he did not wish to divulge the surname he had received from heaven, and on the other he had a scruple of concealing anything from the prelate. He hesitated for some time within himself, not knowing what course to take. But at last he followed the movements of his humility, and without speaking of the rest, contented himself with saying that the name of John had been given him at the font of baptism. The bishop, not being satisfied with his answer, continued to press him further, and told him that he wished absolutely to know his surname. Thus, notwithstanding all his modesty and reserve, he was obliged to speak out, and to explain himself fully on this point. He related to the bishop, therefore, all that had passed in the vision which he saw near Gibraltar, and owned that Jesus Christ, whilst announcing to him that Granada should be his cross, had given him the name of " John of God."

The prelate, having listened to this recital very attentively, immediately made him a short exhortation, telling him in a very touching way that he ought not to conceal the favour which Jesus Christ had granted him, but on the contrary, that he ought to make it known, and that his humility was ill-timed ; that there were certain graces which it was good not to speak of, but that this one was too important to be concealed, because it clearly proved that he had been sent by God to found his hospital ; that Scripture tells us that we must not disclose the secrets of princes, and on the contrary, that we are bound to publish the works and wonders of God, and therefore he ordered him to speak openly of this vision, and henceforth to take the name of John of God.

He did not stop here, but spoke to him also respecting the manner in which he was dressed, and represented to him in strong terms that although it is absolutely necessary to humble oneself, and to fly from vanity, there is nevertheless a certain outward propriety to which we ought to pay attention ; that clothes were not intended merely to cover our bodies and protect them from the severity of the weather, but also to distinguish the states and conditions of men ; that soldiers, merchants, and workmen have a particular dress of their own ; that magistrates had also chosen such as was suitable for themselves, and that consequently those who give themselves up to God and renounce the world ought in like manner to have one which would show that they no longer belonged to the world ; that all the congregations of the Church were distinguished from each other, not by their rules and constitutions only, but also by a holy dress which is peculiar to each ; that he ought to consider the great advantage of being clad differently from people in the world, because a dress of this kind continually reminds those who wear it to separate themselves more and more from the spirit, fashions, and customs of the world ; that it restrains them on many occasions, and hinders them from following their passions and from giving themselves up to excess. That the holy fathers say that a monk's habit compels him to despise the world and to separate himself from it, and that vice and irregularities ought never to insinuate themselves into the heart of him who is clothed in it. Consequently that he ought to leave off wearing a secular dress, and take one which would show that he no longer belonged to the world, but was dedicated to God; that this would tend greatly to preserve him in a holy and irreproachable life, would also give him greater credit and authority when he spoke on behalf of the poor, and would serve to procure him help, for many persons, seeing him thus clad in the livery of Jesus Christ, would willingly join him and labour with him in his hospital, and that by this means he would soon see himself the father of a great number of persons who, after his example, would devote themselves to the service of the sick poor.

Having thus spoken, he sent immediately to buy some stuff, marked out the form and shape of a habit, and had it made without delay. He then clothed John in it, enjoining him to wear it for the rest of his life, and to give it to all who should join him and place themselves under his direction. John was very faithful in obeying him, for he never quitted it, and at his death left it to his children, who have since continued to wear it, and do so at the present time. Thus we may truly say that it was this great bishop who gave him a habit and a name : a habit, because he made him put off his secular dress, and clothed him in the regular habit which has since been worn by all those who belong to his order ; and a name, because he made him see that he would be in some measure ungrateful for the grace of Jesus Christ, if he did not take the name of John of God, since his divine Saviour had so named him.

These two things contribute greatly to the glory of John, for we see that he was so humble as not to dare to take the name Jesus Christ had given him, but thought himself utterly unworthy of it, and it was necessary for this prelate to oblige him to do so, and to make him understand that this humility would be injurious to him, if he did not yield to the orders of divine Providence. His life also was so pure and so holy, and he showed so great an estrangement from the world, that this bishop thought he ought to give him a dress different from that of people in the world, and that it was proper to clothe him in the habit of a religious, though he was not one yet, nor had taken any vows. Too many persons are found at the present day who, under a holy habit, lead an entirely secular life, and by their corrupt manners dishonour the sanctity of their profession ; but John of God led the life of a real religious when he was merely a secular, and was judged worthy to be conse- crated to Jesus Christ when he was engaged only in waiting on the poor, and least of all things thought of establishing a new order in the Church.

CHAPTER VII.

JOHN OF GOD RECONCILES TWO MEN WHO BORE
DEADLY HATRED TOWARDS EACH OTHER, AND
ADMITS THEM INTO HIS HOSPITAL TO SERVE THE
POOR.

THE first establishment of our Saint's hospital had
something extraordinary about it; it was also attended by a miracle, as what we have hitherto said
sufficiently proves. We will now add that God
willed also that there should be a prodigy in the
manner in which he became united to the two first
disciples who offered themselves to him to serve his
poor. These were two men named Antony Martin
and Peter Velasco, who were both much talked about.
The former accused the latter of having killed his
brother, and had come expressly to Granada in order
to follow up his action against him in the criminal
court of justice. He was in the prime of life and
of an ardent disposition, and moreover had powerful
friends and great interest with the judges, so that he
urged on his cause with great animosity, and aimed
at nothing less than having Peter Velasco condemned
to death; and meanwhile he had him strictly confined
in prison. Whilst he was thus proceeding against a
guilty man, he became one himself, for he gave himself up to debauchery; he indulged his passions,
and obtained from some infamous traffic large profits,
which he spent in feeding his luxury and vanity.
In the midst of these excesses he failed not to give
alms; he showed friendship to John of God, often
going to his hospital and leaving there something for
the poor. This was perhaps the real cause of his

conversion, and drew down the graces and mercies of heaven upon him, for Scripture assures us that alms protect those who offer them, and often deliver them from the bonds of their sins. The wise man says, "Shut up alms in the heart of the poor, and it shall obtain help for thee against all evil. Better than the shield of the mighty and better than the spear, it shall fight for thee against thy enemy" (Eccl. xxix. 15, 16, 17).

As the hatred and enmity of these two men gave great scandal, several persons undertook to reconcile them; men of learning interfered, and all who had any reputation for piety endeavoured to do so, but in vain, for their animosity seemed to be so great that it was impossible to overcome it. John of God, out of respect and from humility, suffered others to act first, believing them all more capable than himself of succeeding in such an undertaking; but when he saw them all discouraged and despairing of being able to attain their object, his charity no longer permitted him to rest, and he thought himself obliged to make some attempt to procure so important and desirable a reconciliation. He began by praying, professing before God that he expected nothing from himself, but hoped for everything from His goodness and mercy; he entreated Him to bless his design, and promised to give Him all the glory of the conversion. He then set out immediately to obtain Velasco's pardon of Martin. Meeting him in the public square, he presented to him a crucifix which he drew from his sleeve; he threw himself at his feet, and addressed him in the following terms :—"My brother, if you desire Jesus Christ to pardon you, you must pardon your enemy, and if you wish to oblige Him to forget your sins, you ought yourself to forget the injury that has been done you. Consider that, though God is infinitely merciful, still He will not have mercy on those who do not show it to their neighbour. If your enemy has caused the death of your brother, know that our Lord has died for you and for me ; and if the voice of your brother's blood leads you to revenge his death, it is much more just that the voice of our Saviour's Blood should oblige you to forgive the offence that has been committed against you. Be persuaded, then, that if you wish still to detain Peter Velasco in prison, and if you show yourself inexorable to the prayers that are made to you in his behalf, the justice of God will also be inexorable towards you, and will condemn you to eternal torments."

These words, uttered in a voice full of resolution and charity, penetrated so deeply into the heart of Antony Martin, and made so strong an impression on his mind, that, bursting into tears, he threw himself on the ground before the servant of God, and returned him this noble and Christian answer : " My brother, although I have hitherto regarded Peter Velasco as my most deadly enemy, I declare to you that I am ready to become friends with him, and that I will show him the utmost tenderness and affection for the future. I most heartily beg of you to pray to God for my soul's life with as much zeal and fervour as you have prayed to me for that of my enemy. Not only do I grant all that you desire of me, but I give myself to you, I entreat you to assist me with your advice, and to permit me to serve the poor under your direction. I will now take you to the prison in order that I may embrace Velasco in your presence, and effect his liberation as soon as possible, and do you for your part take me to your hospital, in order that I may consecrate myself to God's service and that of the poor. If your words have had so much influence over my mind, and if they have thus compelled me to pardon my enemy, how much more will the example of your actions be capable of confirming me in my present good intentions and of making me persevere in them."

John of God, delighted at hearing him speak thus, embraced him tenderly, and shedding over him tears of joy, encouraged him in the resolution he had taken, and publicly acknowledged that it was the right hand of the Most High which had brought about this change in his heart. They went together to the prison to visit Velasco, whose life in it was a hundred times worse than death, for he was in fear every hour lest they should come to conduct him to the scaffold. His fears were redoubled when he perceived Antony Martin, because he thought he had come to hasten his execution, and to be himself a witness of his punishment, but the servant of God appearing at the same time encouraged him, told him he had nothing to fear, and explained to him that Martin had no intention either of insulting him or of contributing to his death, but, on the contrary, that he wished to be reconciled to him, and pardoned him. Martin then coming forward, declared that he had forgotten all their differences, that he wished to live on good terms with him, and asked for his friendship, and that on his part he would strive to show himself worthy of it. Velasco replied in the most humble language, giving him to understand that the death of Martin's brother was due rather to accident than to ill-will. He entreated Martin to pardon him, and assured him that he would henceforth acknowledge that he owed his life to his clemency. This interview ended with great marks of real union and sincere reconciliation ; they gave each other the kiss of peace, and took an oath never more to separate from each other, or violate the friendship they had contracted. They then both declared to the servant of God that they put themselves under his direction, and that they wished to live with him in his hospital.

Although Martin had signed the paper for Velasco's liberation on the spot, still some days were required for the necessary legal proceedings which had to be gone through before he could be set at liberty. John of God therefore returned to his poor, taking Martin with him, and as soon as all was prepared they went to the prison and took out Velasco, who followed them to the hospital.

This undoubtedly was a triumph for John of God, for what could be more glorious for him than to have effected a reconciliation which appeared impossible to the most influential and learned persons in the city? Every one applauded him when they saw him between these two men, who, after having lived so long at enmity with each other, and made so much noise in the world, now appeared to have but one heart and one soul. They spoke everywhere of Peter Velasco's happiness in having found so powerful a protector, who had thus vigorously undertaken his defence and caused him to be set at liberty. They could not comprehend how Antony Martin had in a moment become so humble, so gentle, and so modest, for he had always passed for a man who was violent, proud, and full of vanity. They said that John of God had a particular gift for obtaining influence over men's minds, and regarded him as a truly apostolic preacher, who had the secret of touching and softening hearts. They spoke of him in the highest terms, calling him the father and liberator both of Antony Martin and Peter Velasco.

When he had introduced both of them into his hospital, he diligently set about instructing them in their duties and obligations; he spoke to them of the enormity of the crimes to which they had abandoned themselves, of the scandal they had brought upon the whole city, and of the obligation they were under of doing penance. He recommended them to go into retreat for some days, to examine at greater leisure all the steps of their past life, to penetrate into their most secret feelings, and to discover the infinite number of irregularities into which they had fallen, while living in the world, without even being aware of them. He then persuaded them to make a general confession, and after having tried them for some time, and fully ascertained the reality of their conversion, he gave each of them a habit similar to the one he had received from the hands of the illustrious Bishop of Tuy, and permitted them to wait on his poor, and to be employed in the different occupations of his hospital. We shall see in the course of this history what great progress they made in virtue under his guidance : it is sufficient for the present to say that having been great sinners, they became great penitents ; and having scandalized all Granada by their disorderly conduct, they edified it by their holy and exemplary lives; and after having been the ministers of Satan, they became most faithful ministers of Jesus Christ.

These were the first spoils which our Saint gained from the devil; he carried off from him two men in the possession of whom he thought he was secure, and whom he regarded as two agents of his empire. Several learned and distinguished persons had long tried to effect their conversion, as we have already said, and had not been able to succeed; but, though no scholar, and only following the movements of the charity which burned in his heart, John had no sooner spoken to them than he caused them to enter into themselves, obliged them to change their lives, and gave them back to Jesus Christ. This ought to teach us that not always do those who have great lights and extraordinary talents, bring forth most fruit in the Church and convert most sinners, because even when they shine much outwardly, and are held in great esteem, they are often dry, lukewarm, and destitute of grace before God; and, on the contrary, that plain men, and those who are not much spoken of in the world, have much more unction, speak with greater effect of the truths of salvation, and are more capable of instilling them into the hearts of those whom they instruct; and that Jesus Christ often prefers employing them to effect great conversions, in order that the power of His grace may be the more conspicuous, and that the wise and learned may have no cause to boast of their learning and wisdom.

CHAPTER VIII.

THE CHARITY OF JOHN OF GOD CAUSES HIM TO ASSIST ALL WHO HAVE RECOURSE TO HIM, AND GO TO HIS HOSPITAL.

ONE of the most essential conditions of charity is that it should be universal, not restricted to certain persons, but extended generally to all who are in want and necessity. This is also evident, for it proceeds from God, Who is charity itself, and consequently it ought to imitate His conduct and be like Him in all things. He sheds His goodness over all men; He makes His sun to rise, and His rain to fall upon them all, and bestows on them all a thousand favours. Our Saint was fully convinced of this truth, for he was devoted to the service of all; there were no unfortunate persons on whom he would not have compassion, and whom he was not ready to assist. His hospital was open to all those who sought admission into it; in one part were seen persons wasted away by burning fevers, in another the wounded, the help-less, and the paralytic; those who were covered with sores and afflicted with diseases still more loath-some were admitted into it; none were refused ad-mittance; no question was asked of those who asked for beds whether they came from the country or the city; they had only to speak and they were listened to. In short it was sufficient to be ill, and to labour under any ailment in order to obtain admission into this holy house, and to be well taken care of in it. Besides the infirmaries, the servant of God had provided a distinct part for those who were mad and had lost their senses; he took extra-

ordinary care of them, and used his utmost endeavours to restore to them the use of their reason. If
it happened that little children were laid at the door
of his hospital, he willingly took charge of them, and
had them fed and brought up with much kindness;
he endeavoured to procure for them a Christian education, and omitted nothing that lay in his power to
make up for the guilt and inhumanity of the parents
who had so cruelly abandoned them.

The report of so many good works and of such ex-
traördinary charity soon reached the neighbouring provinces, so that in a short time John of God became the
refuge of all the unfortunate, and people began to apply
to him from all quarters. Persons of every descrip-
tion were seen to enter his hospital; widows and
orphans, the poor who were ashamed to beg, old men no
longer capable of working, who, not having been
idle in their youth, were on this account the more
worthy of assistance; labourers whom the hail and
storms had ruined; merchants who had become bank-
rupt, and whom rich misers allowed to starve because
they would not pay them their debts; persons, lastly,
who were unable to bear the expense of the lawsuits
that were instituted against them, or who were themselves obliged to go to law in order to claim property
which was unjustly withheld from them. He received all with an open countenance, and showed that
he took part in their troubles. He consoled them,
and exhorted them to be patient, advising them
to make a holy use of their misfortunes, to endure
them in a spirit of penance, and to offer them to the
divine Majesty in expiation of their sins. He then
procured for them all the assistance he could : to some
he promised a monthly or yearly pension for their

subsistence; others he supplied with grain to sow in their land; to others he gave ready money to pay their creditors, stuff to make clothes of, and articles of furniture for their use.

If there were any who stood in need of credit with judges like the one described in the Gospel, who only administered justice after repeated importunities, he recommended them to persons in power, who took their causes in hand and pleaded for them. If he discovered any who were suffering and being ruined because they were not paid, he sought for friends to speak to their debtors and compel them to satisfy their demands. In a word, he joyfully undertook whatever he thought tended to the consolation of those who applied to him and begged his assistance; every one looked upon him as the father of the poor, the refuge of the unfortunate, the protector of the weak and of all who were oppressed; it was remarked also that by a particular effect of divine Providence, which shed its blessing on all his works, and multiplied, so to speak, in his hands the benefits of which he was only the dispenser, no one ever went away from him without having received some assistance, or without being satisfied with his charity, and greatly consoled.

As the number of pilgrims, travellers, and poor persons who came every evening to ask a lodging of him was so great that his hospital could not contain them all, he was obliged to hire another house close by in order to accommodate them : he prepared a large hall on the ground-floor for them to sleep in, some on mattresses, others on counterpanes or mats, according to their wants and condition; and there was ample room in it for two hundred persons.

He also appointed another part for women, who were thus well provided for. This establishment was of the greatest service, for besides that the poor were well treated in it, care was taken that instructions should be given them, and that they should be taught the things of God; moreover, they were not in danger of committing the sins into which people of this class often fall when they are obliged to pass the night in the streets. Hence, he wished them all to come to lodge in his asylum, and when he saw that they did not do so, he went himself to seek them in the streets, and dragged them into it almost by force, in order to prevent the disorders to which he feared they might give themselves up. His great maxim was that we must give alms to all who come, and that we ought never to refuse those who ask in the name of God. He never turned away any who came to him in his hospital, but always granted them whatever they desired of him, when it was in his power to do so.

Some of his friends, who had not so much zeal and charity as he had, often blamed his conduct; they accused him of want of discretion and of excessive liberality; they represented to him that he ought to use discernment, in order to find out the poor who deserve assistance, because there are some who are utterly undeserving of any kindness. They came sometimes to tell him privately, "Here is a man begging alms of you who is in no need of them." He simply replied to them, "This good man does not deceive me; it is for him to consider what he is doing, for as far as I am concerned, I only give him alms in the name of God." Accordingly he always continued to assist all who had recourse to his charity, without troubling himself to examine whether they really were in want.

In this he imitated S. John the Almoner, who was one of the most celebrated bishops who have governed the Church of Alexandria. In the time of this holy patriarch the Persians invaded Syria, which they entirely devastated, carrying away with them a great number of the inhabitants into slavery. Those who escaped their hands fled to this holy man as to a sure refuge, and begged of him to receive them, which he did gladly. He ordered the hospitals to be opened to all who were sick, and took from his treasury as much money as was necessary to give alms to all who asked it. Some who came to be relieved were richly dressed : and his almoners being indignant at this went and told him of it, but he answered them in a severe tone, looking sternly at them, although he was naturally gentle and of a cheerful countenance, "If you wish to be the dispensers and almoners of the humble John, or rather of Jesus Christ, obey with simplicity what is commanded you in the words, 'Give to every one that asketh you.' (Luc vi. 30). If you inquire so carefully into the wants of those who apply to you, know that God wishes not for such inquisitive ministers, nor does His servant John. If what you give belonged to me, and were my property, I should not blame you for sparing it, but as it belongs to God alone, He wishes us to obey Him exactly in the distribution of His property. If your want of faith makes you fear lest my revenue should not suffice to give to so many poor, I do not share in your incredulity, and since it has pleased God to appoint me the unworthy dispenser of His benefits, though all the people in the world were to assemble at Alexandria and ask alms of me, they could not exhaust His infinite treasures, nor those of His Church."

We have repeated at length these noble words of the great bishop, in order that our readers may see that John of God's piety was really enlightened, and founded on the maxims of the holy fathers, who teach that we must not always be exact in examining the necessities of the poor to whom we wish to give alms, lest we should run the risk of refusing those who are really in want; Jesus Christ is sometimes hidden under the appearances of these poor persons whom we will not listen to, and God considers our intention in giving alms, not the qualifications of those on whom we bestow them: *Deus, non cui detur, sed quo animo detur, attendit.*

CHAPTER IX.

THE SERVANT OF GOD SUCCOURS A GREAT NUMBER OF THE POOR WHO ARE ASHAMED TO BEG.

THE holy doctors of the Church, while speaking of alms, say that it is not enough to succour the poor who make known their wants and who are in the habit of exaggerating their misfortunes, but that we must seek out those who have not the courage to own their poverty. Charity obliges us to anticipate their wants and spare them the shame of asking, and the prophet wishes to teach this truth when he says: *"Beatus qui intelligit super egenum et pauperem"*—"Blessed is he that understandeth concerning the needy and the poor." John of God was very careful in performing this part of his duty; for he was not satisfied with waiting upon the sick in his hospital, and with assisting those who informed him of their misfortunes, but went himself into every quarter of the city of Granada in order to find out poor persons who were ashamed to beg. He entered the houses of widows and orphans, and under the pretext of paying them a visit, he noticed how they lived, and what they were in want of. He had always confidential persons whom he employed to make these holy discoveries, wishing them to go about everywhere, not from curiosity, nor in order to amass wealth, but in order to mix with the poor and learn their wants, and as soon as he was informed of any families or citizens who were in want of anything, he immediately took care to succour them. He himself bought for them bread, meat, fish, wood, and everything that was necessary for them : he provided them with beds, blankets, linen, and other articles of this kind, without waiting for them to make known the subject of their poverty.

Knowing that idleness is the mother of all vices, the enemy and destroyer of virtue, as S. Bernard says, he procured employment for those whom he supported. He employed the married and unmarried women in spinning and sewing; he gave the men labour proportioned to their strength and dispositions, and he sought to accustom even little children to work, in order that they might early contract the habit of it, and be entirely formed to it when they should arrive at a more advanced age. Thus he performed a two-fold act of charity towards these poor persons, for at the same time that he furnished them with the means of living, he protected them by employments of this kind from falling into many sins which they might have committed had they remained idle. In order also to animate them still more to labour and to render them more diligent, he offered rewards to those who made the greatest progress and had soonest finished their tasks ; and he did all this with so much kindness and address, and in so captivating a manner, that all loved him, were delighted to see him, and obeyed him with joy. He carried his charity still further, for he endeavoured to teach them how to work in a Christian manner, and not as pagans, or as irrational animals. Hence he used to make familiar exhortations in places where they were assembled ; he induced them to recite prayers at certain hours ; he often spoke to them of virtue ; he read good books to them ; he recommended them to raise up their minds to God while their hands were employed in work ; and he represented to them that they were bound to perform all their actions in the name of the Lord and for His glory.

He had also a marvellous zeal for doing good to religious houses of monks and nuns; he eagerly sought out opportunities of serving them and procuring them some benefit, and he was never better pleased than when he could get information of their wants, in order that he might provide against them as soon as possible. He regarded all who withdrew into the cloister as persons who have no other employment than that of praising and blessing the God of heaven and earth, of offering to Him prayers for the whole Church, and of drawing down upon the people His graces and mercies ; and this was the reason he so ardently strove to assist them. He thought it a great happiness to contribute to the maintenance of persons

who think no longer of the world, except it be to lament
the disorders and sins which are committed in it.
His humility inspired him with the thought that, not
being himself in a condition to pray and spend all his
time in contemplating the blessings of eternity, he
ought at least to contribute something towards the
support of those who are dedicated to this holy practice, and he hoped that by labouring and employing
himself for them in outward ministrations he would
share in their prayers, in their meditations, and in all
their good works.　Assuredly he was not deceived, for
when we are not in a condition to pray, to meditate,
to fast, or to mortify ourselves, we fail not to have the
merit of these good works, provided that we have the
desire to practise them, and are united in charity with
those who really do practise them ; wherefore the royal
prophet said to God : " Lord, I am a partaker with
all them that fear Thee, and that keep Thy commandments " (Ps. cxviii. 63).

Lastly, being filled with universal charity, and
apparently born for the good of all, John of God maintained in the city several poor scholars : he provided
them with books, paper, and all that they required to
pursue their studies ; he sent them bread and other
provisions ; he induced pious persons to assist them and
give them money ; and in order to be certain that they
made a proper use of the charity that was shown them,
he watched carefully over them, and observed how they
behaved, and if they led regular and truly Christian
lives.　What we cannot sufficiently admire is that all
these different employments hindered him not from
paying every necessary attention to his hospital ; for
before going out he gave orders for everything ; he
marked out in particular what was to be done during

his absence, and as soon as he returned he visited all the sick one after the other; he comforted them, waited upon them himself, asked them if they were satisfied and had been well attended to, and then, without considering whether he was fatigued, he returned into the city to beg for them until a late hour of the night. It was thus that his charity led him to sacrifice his time, his strength, his health, and his life itself for his neighbour. He took no rest, but was always at work; wherever any good might be done, he was sure to be there; every moment of his life was consecrated to the service of his brethren; he took upon himself all that was difficult and mortifying in his hospital, leaving to others the easiest and least painful employments; he always had a thousand things on hand; he gave himself up entirely to the humblest person who applied to him; he looked upon himself as the father of all the poor, he thought only of them, he laboured only for them, and, forgetting himself on all occasions, he sought only to relieve them and to enable them to live in peace and comfort.

CHAPTER X.

HOW SIMON OF AVILA, WHO CALUMNIATED JOHN OF GOD, WAS MIRACULOUSLY CONVERTED AND BECAME HIS DISCIPLE.

S. John Chrysostom well says that great virtue must have many enemies; and this is evident, for as the world is full of wicked and sensual men, a great number are always to be found who blame, decry, and persecute those who leave the broad way and follow after justice. Some, through envy, try artfully to obscure the brilliancy of their glory and to tarnish their reputation; others, in order to justify in some measure their own wicked conduct, accuse them of similar evil habits; others, out of pure malice, censure in them what is most lawful, seeking to make their best actions pass for crimes, and by this means bring down upon themselves the curse pronounced by the prophet Isaias against those who call good evil, and light darkness.

John of God experienced from the very commencement of his hospital these different kinds of abuse; for all the care which he took of the poor, and the exertions he made on their behalf, were imputed to his madness, and were looked upon as a continuation of the extravagances he had already committed. People accused him of putting to an improper use the alms which were given him, and of converting them to his own profit; they called him a hypocrite, saying that all he was doing was only to make himself esteemed in the world; and whereas S. Bernard says that when we cannot excuse an action we must at least justify the intention of it, these men, on the contrary, strove to have it believed that he had evil intentions in all the good works he performed. Simon of Avila, a citizen of Granada, was one of the most violent against him, and allowed no opportunity to escape of slandering his person. He followed him everywhere in order to learn all his proceedings, and to cast suspicion upon them; he sent persons into every quarter of the city to speak ill of him on all occasions; he marked all the houses he frequented, and failed not to say publicly that irregularities were committed in them; he endeavoured especially to cast odium upon his intercourse with the widows and orphans whom he assisted ; in short, it is enough to say that this man was one of those who, contrary to the prohibition of Scripture, are constantly studying to find out and discover, if possible, some wickedness in the house of the just. The Lord regarded him from heaven, and had great designs upon him, for He willed to make him one of His most illustrious servants ; at first He overlooked his errors, gave him ample opportunities for coming to himself, and waited long for his repentance ; but seeing that he continued inflexible, and that his malice increased every day, He at last determined to confound him, by punishing him openly, and employing prodigies to make him enter into Himself.

The servant of God having gone into a house to visit and console a widow whom he supported with her four children, Simon of Avila was informed of it by his emissaries, and resolved to go near where this house was situated, with the intention of spreading calumnies as usual, and of observing more closely what took place in it. He even approached the widow's room to find John, and to have it in his power to publish afterwards that he had surprised him in unlawful intercourse with her. As he was at the top of the stairs, and was about to knock at the door, he perceived, as King Baltassar did, a writing on the wall, which not merely held out threats to him, but contained all the sins, even the most secret, of his past life, and set them before his eyes. This astonished him beyond measure, and greatly troubled his conscience, causing several thoughts of despair to arise in his mind, and reducing him to such a state that he knew not what to do, or what course to pursue. This was not all; for historians add that, raising his eyes upwards, he saw above his head a gleaming sword ready to pierce and destroy him. This sight completed his confusion, and made him lose his senses, so that he fell down backwards from the top to the bottom of the stairs.

At the noise of his fall John of God and the widow ran immediately to see what was the matter, and were much surprised at finding him on the floor at the foot of the staircase motionless, speechless, and apparently deprived of life. They immediately endeavoured to assist him, shook him, lifted him up, called him, threw wine over him, carried him out into the fresh air, and left nothing undone which they thought might recover him, but all to no purpose, for he did not return to his senses. Then John, relying on the goodness of God, and hoping everything from His mercy, prayed to Him fervently for this man, who was his declared enemy; he breathed many prayers to heaven, and thrice pronounced the sacred words, Jesus and Mary, making the sign of the cross over him each time. At that moment Simon began to open his eyes, and shook off the kind of lethargy into which he had fallen. Many persons worthy of credit, whom this accident had attracted to the spot, and who witnessed the prodigy, have made depositions respecting it, so that we cannot doubt it, unless we would refuse belief to the most strongly authenticated facts.

When the unhappy man saw that he had been assisted and delivered from so great a danger by him whom he had shamelessly calumniated, and persecuted on every occasion, he blushed at his own iniquity, acknowledged his fault, conceived a sincere repentance for all the slanders he had uttered against John, and immediately retracted them, making him many apologies. He did not stop here, but wishing to make amends for his fault in a still more striking manner, and to labour earnestly in the work of his salvation, he, a few days afterwards, went to find John in his hospital, again publicly asked for forgiveness, and entreated him to admit him into the number of his brethren, and to permit him to serve the poor under his direction. The servant of God, seeing him contrite and in excellent dispositions, willingly received him into his small community and gave him the habit; and this good brother lived in it for the rest of his days with so much piety, humility, and fervour that the Church has since appointed commissioners to compile the process of his beatification.

From this and other instances already mentioned our readers cannot fail to see that our Lord worked miracles in order to give companions to our Saint, and to associate with him men full of zeal and fervour, who might share with him the toil and labour of his ministry : and this proves beyond a doubt that the establishment of his hospital was properly speaking the work of God's Providence, since after having laid the first foundations of it, He took care to provide for its continuance by calling to it subjects capable of serving it and discharging all its offices. We also know that it is the same Providence which has given so happy an increase to his order, and has willed that it should spread in all parts of the world, and be established even beyond the seas, in order that it may serve as a refuge to the poor and afflicted; for it has always possessed persons of singular merit, who have governed it with prudence and wisdom, and have had an ardent zeal for God's glory, rendering themselves conspicuous by their great charity, and giving themselves up entirely to the service of their neighbour and the relief of the sick poor.   Hence all who belong to the family of this great Saint, cannot but consider themselves the co-adjutors of Providence, and feel persuaded that God has appointed them to execute His designs, and convey His benefits to the p or.   Therefore, without neglecting anything on their side, they ought to trust in God for all that regards the poor, the care of whom He has confided to them ; they should have a firm confidence that He will not fail to provide for them and furnish them with everything that may be necessary ; and above all, they should be careful to give Him all the glory of the good they may do, because ministers and stewards ought to refer everything to him who employs them, and enables them to work.

CHAPTER XI.

OF THE CARE JOHN OF GOD TAKES OF SEVERAL YOUNG WOMEN.

THE wise man, who says to God: "Lord, give me neither beggary nor riches," gives us to understand that these two things are equally dangerous, when we know not how to make a good use of them, and do not take charity for our guide ; for riches very often lead to luxury, debauchery, and many other grievous excesses ; while poverty is, to a great number of persons, an occasion of falling and of scandal ; and we every day see many commit acts of injustice and lose their souls from the mere apprehension of being in want of the necessary means of living, or even of comforts. Our Saint being fully aware of these truths, was seized with fear whenever he heard of young women without money or means of supporting themselves, dreading lest they should too easily listen to the poisonous language of those who, under the pretext of taking care of and assisting them, might lead them into sin, as is very often the case. Hence he generally anticipated their wants, and undertook to support them, in order that they might not be exposed to temptations of this kind. It will suffice to relate one or two examples, in order that our readers may have a good idea of his charity.

He learnt one day that a young lady had been for a long time in the city of Granada, carrying on a very important law-suit, and that owing to the tediousness of the formalities of justice, her means were all exhausted, so that she began to be in want of everything. He had no hesitation as to what he ought to do on this occasion: he immediately went to find her out, in order to learn her condition from herself, and finding it to be true that this law-suit had reduced her to great poverty, he promised her aid of every kind until her case was decided, and sent her all that she stood in need of. Not having any relations in the city to keep an eye upon her, he watched over her himself, often visiting her to see if she behaved in a proper manner, if she employed her time well and worked as he had enjoined her. Notwithstanding all his precautions, a young man used to visit her, to pay attentions to her, and to strive to ingratiate himself with her by insidious conversation and a thousand different artifices. It happened once that he was with her when the servant of God came as usual, but he took care to hide himself as soon as he heard the knock at the door of her room, so that when the Saint entered he had no suspicion of his presence : still he perceived that the young lady was more gaily and carefully dressed than usual, and that her manner was worldly and affected. This raised suspicions in his mind, and made him fear she was engaged in something unlawful. He therefore spoke to her very forcibly against ostentation and vanity; he told her that a Christian woman ought to be modest in her dress, in her looks, and in her outward deportment; that she is not allowed to wear worldly ornaments, because she ought not to try to please people of the world, but is bound to be holy in mind and body, as the Apostle says; and that she ought to keep herself chaste and pure for her lawful Spouse, Jesus Christ. He then represented to her that God sees everything, that He knows our most secret actions, and reads our hearts and consciences, and at the Day of Judgment will demand an account of all that we shall have disguised and dissembled from men. Lastly, he exhorted her to behave in a manner becoming her condition, and not to sully the brightness of her purity by giving way in the smallest particular, or by familiarity with persons of the other sex.

His exhortation produced a good effect on her mind and heart, for she immediately acknowledged her fault, put off the ornaments she had prized, and resumed her usual dress; she repented of having listened to those who were endeavouring to weaken and surprise her, and she lived with the greatest circumspection during the whole of the law-suit, and of her residence at Granada. The young man also profited by John's words, which he heard from his hiding place. He conceived on the spot a deep sorrow for having entertained the thought of injuring this young lady, and asked her pardon as soon as the servant of God had gone away; he declared to her that he was anxious to reform his life and to do penance; and in order to show that he was really converted, and that his heart was touched with sincere contrition, he told her he was going to find John of God, in order to take his advice and submit to whatever he might order him to do. He kept his word, for without any delay he went to the hospital, where he confessed his sin to the father of the poor, testifying great sorrow for it; and he asked him what he ought to do in order to appease the anger of God, which his crimes had aroused. He listened with respect to all that John said to him, and faithfully put it in practice; he became a model of wisdom, modesty, and discretion, and edified all by his good life and irreproachable conduct.

Divine Providence, a short time afterwards, furnished John of God with another opportunity of exhibiting the great care he took to prevent everything that might prove dangerous to young women. He was told, very late one evening, that a little girl, newly born, had been left in the public square; he immediately ran thither, and having found her entirely without covering, he wrapped her up in his cloak, and the next day had her taken to a village three miles from Granada. He went there himself, and placed her in the hands of a respectable person to be brought up; he visited her twice a week during all the time of her infancy; he paid all her expenses regularly, and gave her a Christian education.   Reflecting also that when grown up she would have no means of supporting herself, and that her poverty might give occasion to some attempt upon her, he was anxious to save her from such a temptation.   He therefore allotted to her fifty ducats, which he put out to interest, so that she might be sure of having a certain sum to provide for her dowry.   She was afterwards married to Francis Olivarez, and lived esteemed by all, as became a good mother of a family.

These two stories show us that his charity was exact, watchful, and liberal, for he neglected not the smallest matter, and nothing escaped his care.   He waited not for the mischief to be done before he remedied it, but always anticipated it, foreseeing it at a distance, and stifling it even before ·its birth. No difficulty disheartened him, and he grudged no expense when the glory of God and the salvation of his neighbour were concerned.

CHAPTER XII.

THE SERVANT OF GOD GOES INTO PUBLIC PLACES IN
ORDER TO PREVENT THE SINS WHICH WERE COM-
MITTED THERE, AND TO LABOUR FOR THE CONVER-
SION OF DISSOLUTE WOMEN.

NOT only did John of God watch over the conduct
of young women, and keep from them all the temptations which he thought might attack them; but
his charity induced him to procure the conversion
of those women whom he knew to be engaged in a
criminal life. He could not see without shedding
tears, and without having his heart pierced with a
lively sorrow, these unhappy creatures laying snares
for the youth of the city; he could not endure to
behold them abusing the advantages they had received from nature, in order to offend the very God
of nature, or to see them abandon to sin their bodies
which were destined to be the temples of the Holy
Spirit. Hence he felt himself inwardly urged to make
them open their eyes, to induce them to abandon this
criminal course of life, and to inspire them with
feelings of repentance.

This was an undertaking of the greatest importance, requiring much zeal and prudence, and suitable
only to a person firmly established in virtue and above
all suspicion. Accordingly he did not attempt it without having first sought advice; he consulted Avila, his
spiritual father, on the subject, laying open to him
the impulses of his heart, and begging him to tell him
if he ought to listen to and follow them. This holy

priest, knowing him perfectly, and being acquainted with his interior feelings, readily gave him permission to treat with these poor women, in order that he might draw them out of their irregular courses. But he gave him at the same time very important advice, which we will quote here, because from it we see that this great director was full of wisdom and prudence, and that John of God implicitly obeyed him.

He warned him in one of his letters to be always on his guard, and to be very reserved in the conversations he might have with such persons, and likewise with all married or unmarried women. "I exhort you," he says, "to have as little intercourse as possible with women, because they are, as it were, a snare which the devil lays for the destruction of God's servants. You know into what sin the sight of a woman made David fall, and how a love for women perverted the mind of his son Solomon, and led him to such an excess of impiety and madness as to set up idols in the very temple of God ; we, therefore, being much weaker than they were, cannot derive too great lessons of fear from such dangerous falls. Their example ought to render us wise ; and you must not deceive yourself by saying that only the desire of procuring their salvation leads you to converse with them, since if we do not take great care, good intentions may lead us into many dangers, for God does not wish us to seek the good of souls at the expense of our own salvation." He says again in another letter, " Take care lest the women whom you are endeavouring to lead to the service of God do not bring upon you much trouble and expense. I should think it would be better for you to try to get them married as soon as possible, or placed out in service with some ladies, for otherwise they may incur the danger of ruin."

Fortified, therefore, with the permission and advice of this holy priest, without whose consent he did nothing of importance, he followed the drawing of his zeal, and omitted no opportunity of labouring in this good work. He very often went near the houses of abandoned women, and when he saw any persons intending to enter them, he immediately spoke to them, begged them not to do so, and represented to them that the frequenting these public places was very sinful, and drew upon them a great many very terrible chastisements. When he saw that his entreaties were ineffectual, he threatened them with God's judgments and the eternal pains of hell. His remonstrances generally produced a good effect, for many profited by them, saw the evil of their own conduct, and resolved to renounce all iniquity for ever. On such occasions he returned home full of joy and gladness, and gave thanks to God for having blessed his words, and made them penetrate into the hearts of these sinners. But on other occasions his exhortations were ill received, and drew down upon him very harsh treatment; for some were so violent as to load him with abuse, and to strike him as if he were impertinent or mad. We need not say that, he suffered all this with the greatest patience and even with joy, for our readers can well imagine that the charity which gave him strength and courage to speak on such occasions, inspired him also with much gentleness and patience to suffer the outrages of these insolent persons; nay, the moderation and humility which he displayed on those occasions had often more effect than his words, for they converted and brought back into the right way those who had been deaf to his remonstrances.

The following is a notable instance of this. As he was passing one day through a part of the city in which there were some suspicious houses, he saw in the street a young man of quality, named John de la Torre, speaking with two women who did not bear a good character. Being grieved and pained at this, he accosted him in a civil and respectful manner, "My brother, though I have nothing now to say against these women, and though I should be glad to think you have no evil intentions, permit me nevertheless to tell you that the long conversations you are holding with them in the street fail not to bring discredit both on you and them, and to give occasion for evil to be spoken of you; hence I recommend you to speak no longer publicly with them, to abstain henceforth from these conversations with persons of the other sex, and never to do anything which may violate the fidelity you owe to our Lord Jesus Christ, and scandalize your neighbour."

These wise and Christian words failed not to displease the mind of this young man, who was blinded by the violence of his passions, so that he answered John only with insult and blasphemy, and even had the insolence to give him a box on the ear. John of God, feeling himself struck, remembered the gospel precept, and immediately offered him the other cheek, saying, "Strike, my brother, strike. I willingly consent to be ill-treated, provided that you refrain from your sinful and scandalous actions;" and at the same time he threw himself at his feet to show that he had no bitterness

against him, and to induce him by this means seriously to consider what he had done. At this sight
the two women took flight, and hurried off as quickly
as they could, feeling utterly confused at what had
happened on their account. The neighbours, attracted
by the noise, quickly ran to the spot, and sharply rebuked the rash man for daring to strike John of God,
whom they so highly esteemed, and whom they regarded as the protector of the whole city. The
young man remained completely confounded, and seeing that what he had done was censured by all, he
threw himself at the feet of the father of the poor,
and humbly begged his pardon. John, on his part,
redoubled his acts of humiliation, by humbling himself still more, so that it was necessary to compel him
to receive the satisfaction which was offered him.
Thus the quarrel ended with mutual demonstrations
of friendship; the scandal was put an end to, and the
servant of God was loaded with praises by all who
were present on the occasion.

But it did not satisfy his zeal only to dissuade
some from committing sin; he undertook to destroy
the evil in its very origin, and to fight against those
monsters of wickedness who enchant men's minds and
bring destruction on their bodies. He went, therefore, even into the houses of these wicked women,
and represented to them the enormity of their
crimes; he exhorted them to give up their course
of life, and showed them what they ought to do
as penance for their sins. He was not content
with speaking thus in general terms; he took each of
them aside privately, and made them sit down; then
drawing a crucifix from his sleeve, and kneeling
down, he repeated aloud with an humble and contrite

heart all the sins of his past life; he beat his breast like the publican in the gospel, and shed torrents of tears; he sighed deeply, and begged for mercy from God, promising amendment for the future; he also read the Passion of our Lord Jesus Christ, and testified so much grief that he often touched the hardness of their hearts and drew tears from them.

As soon as he saw any one of them beginning to be touched, he urged her more strongly, addressing her in the following manner: "Consider, my sister, how much you have cost God, and what He has suffered for you, and be not the cause of your own destruction. Reflect that as He has promised the just a crown and an eternal reward, so He has also prepared eternal punishment for impenitent sinners. Do not then provoke His wrath any more by your crimes, for fear He should abandon you for ever, and hurl you to the bottom of hell. Quit your present mode of life; weep for your sins; punish them with holy severity, and then trust in the goodness and charity of our Lord, and I promise you that He will accept your repentance and will show you mercy."

Some he found who declared that they were very willing to renounce sin and to lead good lives, but that they had no means of supporting themselves, and were encumbered with debts. He told them immediately that they ought to trust in God, Who would take care of them and enlighten their minds, and make them know what He required of them, and that He was able to provide for all their temporal wants. He represented to them that there was only one thing absolutely necessary, which is to praise and serve God; and that they ought to be indifferent to everything else, and ready to die a thousand times rather than offend Him henceforth in

the least thing. He also deprived them of this pretext, for he had recourse to ladies of piety with whom
he was acquainted ; he explained to them that there
was a good work to be done, that he was engaged in
succouring some souls which were groaning under
the tyranny of the devil, and that he had need of
money to pay the debts of certain women who
wished to be converted. He almost always found
prompt assistance in the charity of these ladies, and
seldom left them without their having given him
all that he asked. And if it chanced that they
could not immediately furnish the sums necessary
to pay the creditors of these women, he treated with
them himself, giving them a note of hand by which
he bound himself to satisfy them at the earliest
opportunity.

Having thus freed them from their debts, he
brought them to his hospital, and had them placed
in a separate infirmary, where care was taken of
them, and where they found many others who had
formerly been engaged in the same iniquitous course
of life with themselves. They saw some there
whose heads were covered with cancer, and who had
already lost several bones ; others were covered with
scars and sores, others unable to move ; some had
lost limbs which had been eaten away by corruption,
and all were so revolting that they could not be
looked upon without horror. These objects made
them see the disastrous consequences of their sin,
which so ill repays those who have obeyed it and been
its slaves. This, moreover, led them to reflect upon
themselves, and to consider that they were bound to
do very severe penance for the sins to which they had
abandoned themselves, since they saw that the divine

justice laid so heavy a hand on other persons who
were not more guilty than themselves, and punished
them so severely and frightfully. Those who served
them often said to them with S. Paul, " What fruit
therefore had you then in those things of which you
are now ashamed? for the end of them is death "
(Rom. vi. 21). They failed not also to address
them in the other words of the same apostle, "As
you have yielded your members to serve uncleanness
and iniquity unto iniquity, so now yield your members
to serve justice unto sanctification " (Ibid., 19).

This is only a part of what John of God did in order
to withdraw these women from the slavery of the devil
under which they were labouring. We shall see in
the following chapter the care he took of them in
order to protect them from relapsing, and to make
them persevere in the new life which they embraced.

CHAPTER XIII.

CONTINUATION OF THE SAME SUBJECT. THE SAINT
PROVIDES FOR THE SUBSISTENCE OF THE WO-
MEN WHOM HE HAD CONVERTED, IN ORDER TO
PREVENT THEIR RELAPSING INTO THEIR OLD
HABITS.

AFTER these converts had been for some time
attended to in the hospital, and had sufficiently
recovered their health, they were taken into particular
houses appointed for this purpose; for Juan Fer_
nandez, a man who was commended for his piety, and
much esteemed by all Granada, uniting with the

servant of God in these exercises of charity, devoted
his time as well as his money towards their further-
ance, and had hired several houses in the city for the
accommodation of those who had been saved from
ruin. Whilst in them, they were thoroughly instructed, and the enormity of their sins was forcibly
represented to them ; they were told of the obligation
they were under of satisfying the divine justice, and
of passing the remainder of their lives in austerities
and penance ; there also others were enabled to judge if
their conversion was real and sincere, and when fully
assured of it, considered what it was best for them to do.
If they showed an inclination for a life of celibacy, and
by strict continence to make amends for their past
disorderly lives, they were placed in the convent of
penitent women, and supplied with everything necessary for them, or they were placed under the charge
of some pious ladies who took care of them and
watched over their conduct.

But if it was remarked that they had an inclination
for marriage, John of God was the first to obtain suitable matches for them, knowing that all have not the
same gift, and that heaven can be reached by different
ways ; by means of his friends he procured dowries
for them ; he used his utmost endeavours to establish
them respectably in the world ; he even made journeys
to the Court for their benefit, and there collected considerable sums, which he distributed amongst them, so
that he married sixteen of them in one month ; and,
what is still more, he formed their minds to piety
in such a manner that they became good mothers, and
edified the Church as much by their prudent conduct as they had before scandalized it by their
irregularities.

We must here mention what he did privately for some of these unfortunate creatures, for it will serve to show our readers how far his charity went. One Friday he placed himself, as usual, near some of their public haunts, and found there four women who, hearing him speak of God and of virtue, said that they were determined to be converted and to change their lives, but added that they could not break off their present course of life, until they had gone to Toledo, which was their native place, to settle their affairs and dispose of their property, but that as soon as they returned they would listen to their consciences and would put into practice the resolution they had made. He many times blessed God for this, and, not to suffer their good dispositions to grow cold, or to give them time to change their minds, he offered to have them sent immediately to Toledo, and to defray their expenses on the road; wherefore, hiring four horses, he gave one to each, and the next day he took the same road himself, but on foot, and accompanied only by Brother Simon of Avila.

It is plain that he only acted on this occasion from motives of charity, and that he had no other object in view than that of serving these women as much as he could, and of smoothing the way for them in order to facilitate their conversion. But they did not correspond with his good intentions; three of them turned out to be only hypocrites, or if we are willing to think them sincere when they spoke about being converted, we must at least say that they were unfaithful to grace, and that they did not persevere; for, on the very first evening, one of them left her companions, repented of having repented, and, according to all appearance, returned to her former habits, and the other two disappeared when they reached Toledo and were no more seen. Thus the servant of God met only the fourth in that city, and had the mortification to see himself deprived of almost all the spoils which he had expected to gain over from the devil. Still he consoled himself by calling to mind the history of the shepherd in the gospel, who returned to his house full of joy, though bearing only one sheep on his shoulders.

Brother Simon Avila did not bear this misfortune so well, but expressed to John of God the resentment he felt at their deceitfulness; he even somewhat indignantly told him that he had been too credulous and had trusted their word too readily. Our Saint, on the other hand, listened to him with the utmost patience, and contented himself with making him the following answer, which showed the tranquillity of his soul and his submission to all the dispositions of God: " My brother," said he, with his usual simplicity; " if you had gone and bought four baskets of fish at the market of Morillo, and if three of them were spoilt on the road, would you not console yourself for your loss by seeing that the fourth was in good condition? Let us now do so, and since out of these four women whom we thought we had converted, there remains to us only one who gives signs of piety, we ought to be rejoiced and glorify God for it. Let us return to Granada with her, and be sure that if she can remain faithful to our Lord, our journey has not been in vain." It turned out as he desired; for this woman went back with him to Granada, and was very obedient to him. He married her afterwards to a respectable man in the city. who greatly prized her. She on her part brought up her family wisely, was highly esteemed by her neighbours, and impressed all with a favourable opinion of her character. Thus he thought himself only too well repaid for all his troubles, and for his journey to Toledo, for he well knew that there is nothing more important or more precious than the conversion of a single soul, and that it is preferable to the conquest of the whole world.

CHAPTER XIV.

THE CONVERSION OF A GENTLEMAN NAMED DON FERNANDO, WHICH WAS REGARDED AS THE EFFECT OF JOHN'S PRAYERS AND SANCTITY.

JOHN OF GOD'S reputation for charity and good works spreading on all sides, not in the city of Granada only, but throughout all Spain, a young man of quality, wishing himself to behold his good deeds and make trial of them, came to see him for that purpose. He was called Don Fernando, and was a gentleman by birth, very rich, and about twenty nine years old. He thought of marrying, and was paying court to a young lady who was his equal in birth and virtue, but not in fortune. He could not, however, make up his mind to proceed further in so important a matter without consulting some disinterested and prudent man, and casting his eyes on John of God, he determined to have an interview with him; but before doing so he wished to make trial of his piety and charity. As he knew that John generally began to go round begging very late in the evening, he feigned himself to be poor, and stopping him one night in the street, accosted him in the following terms : "My brother, your charity being known to all Spain, I take the liberty of addressing myself to you in order to beg your assistance. I am by birth a gentleman, but my fortune is not equal to my birth, for I am suffering such dreadful poverty that I fear it will lead me to the brink of despair. I appeal, therefore, to you, the father of the poor, for assistance in the wretched state to which I am reduced. And though I am fully persuaded of your great charity, nevertheless I could not venture to promise myself that you can give me all the money which I stand in need of, for I am in want of two hundred ducats to pay my debts and restore my affairs a little, and this is too large a sum to ask of you."

John of God, by no means suspecting any trick in this speech, had no sooner heard him speak than his heart was moved with compassion. He exhorted him to be patient, to trust in the goodness of God, and to rely on His Providence. He promised to do all he could to procure him prompt assistance, and told him to meet him the next day at the same place and hour. As soon as they had parted, he thought over the means he ought to take to procure this sum; he spoke about it to his friends; he went about begging from some rich persons, and made such great exertions that it was all collected by the time appointed for meeting him. He was first at the appointed meeting-place, so great was his ardour in this good work. Seeing the gentleman coming at a distance, he advanced towards him with a cheerful countenance, saying : "I bring you the two hundred ducats you stand in need of." Don Fernando was filled with astonishment, and hardly able to believe what he heard, so extraordinary did this action appear to him. He immediately prostrated himself before him in order to kiss his feet, and exclaimed in the words of the Queen of Saba, when she had seen the wisdom and magnificence of Solomon : " The word is true which I heard in my own country; I did not believe them that told me, till I came myself and saw with my own eyes, and have found that the half had not been told me ; thy wisdom and thy works exceed the word which I heard." He then told him he was not poor, and that he had only pretended to be so in order to try him ; that his name was Fernando, and that very far from standing in need of alms, he was himself able to bestow them, and that he had brought him two hundred ducats for his poor. Lastly he entreated John to pray for him, and to ask our Lord to make it known to him if it was His Will that he should engage himself in marriage.

The servant of God received his alms with the deepest gratitude, praised his charity, and, according to his usual custom, said : " My brother, you will one day know the good you are doing yourself, when our Lord, by His infinite mercy, shall reward you by filling you with His graces, and I pray that this may be done very soon." He added nothing more, contenting himself with offering up his prayers for him in particular, and with recommending to God the affair of his marriage. The effects of his intercession were soon seen ; for Providence caused it to be clearly understood that this young man ought not to think of marriage, and that he was called to a higher state of perfection.

As, some days afterwards, he was going on horseback, according to the custom of the country, in front of the house of the lady whom he wished to marry, his horse, which was strong and powerful, stopped short suddenly and would not move. He urged it on with the spur, but to no purpose, for the animal, though not in the habit of starting, reared on its hind legs, and kept going backwards. And this not without good reason, seeing that God then made a prodigy appear, somewhat like that which frightened Balaam's ass when he was going on in the way which the Lord had not pointed out to him; for this young man the next moment perceived a gulf in the middle of the street, from which there issued a thick black smoke, which made him believe, as he afterwards declared, that it was the mouth of hell; and raising his eyes upwards to commend himself to God, he saw several angels showing him the gate of heaven wide open, and saying to him: "Come and enter."

This was more than sufficient to convince him that God, in consideration of the prayers of His faithful servant, had sent him this vision in order to show him that he must not marry, but endeavour to reach heaven by a different way. He therefore immediately went to the hospital of John of God, to lay before him what had taken place, and ask his advice as to what he ought to do. The father of the poor, having listened attentively to him, explained to him with much judgment many circumstances in this prodigy. Still, being unwilling to decide respecting his vocation, and knowing, moreover, that his own director Avila was at that time in Granada, he recommended the young man to go to him and to submit implicitly to his decision. Don Fernando obeyed, and that same day consulted Avila on the state of life he ought to embrace. This great man gave up to him all the time he wished, made him repeat the history of his whole life, conversed often with him, examined all his inclinations, and tried him in different ways. Having ascertained that he had all the talents necessary for serving the Church, he decided in favour of the ecclesiastical state, and recommended him to resume his studies, to make himself learned in the Scriptures and the holy Fathers, and to instruct himself in all those things which a man ought to know who is destined to be the salt of the earth and the light of the world. He followed exactly all the advice of this holy priest, and in the end became an imitator of him in the duties of the priesthood; for he distributed all his money amongst hospitals, and led so poor a life, that he was called the poor priest. Neither would he accept any benefice, but gave himself up with so much zeal to the preaching of the gospel and the conversion of sinners, that his memory is still revered all over Spain, and steps have been taken in order to procure his canonization.

CHAPTER XV.

JOHN OF GOD, NOT CONTENT WITH ASSISTING THE POOR HIMSELF, PERSUADES OTHERS ALSO TO SHOW CHARITY TOWARDS THEM.

THE celebrated Avila, of whom we have just spoken, says in the instructions he has left us on the manner of leading a Christian life, that when we cannot assist those who have recourse to us in their wants, we ought to refer them to persons who are in a condition to help them. Our Saint being his disciple and spiritual son, failed not to observe this rule. For even when he had no money, and was overburdened with poor, he nevertheless did not send away without assistance any of those who implored his aid and recommended themselves to him; neither did he neglect any of the good works which divine Providence gave him an opportunity of performing, but went and begged rich and influential persons to supply for his own want of means ; and his words were generally accompanied with such force and persuasion, that he almost always induced them' to second his good intentions. The whole city of Granada witnessed this on several occasions, as the following facts abundantly prove.

As he was one day walking in the city, he saw the body of a man entirely uncovered, and yet no one looked at it or thought of burying it. He was the more grieved, because he was far from his hospital, and was not himself able to do all that he would have wished. Nevertheless he could not make up his mind to continue his journey without having set right this matter, which was one entirely of charity. He remembered that he knew a rich man in that quarter of the city, and he immediately thought that he should please him much by giving him the opportunity of performing this good work, which is so much recommended in the Holy Scriptures, as in the case of the holy old man Tobias. He went therefore and proposed to him that he should have this body interred, but found that he was of the number of those who are rich for the world, that is, for purposes of display or gain, but who declare themselves to be poor and of limited means as soon as they are asked to give alms and comfort the poor, for he answered that he had no money, and could not at that time afford the expense.

John took his leave, surprised at such hardness of heart, and withdrew without saying anything more; then, having reflected a short time on what he ought to do, his charity suggested an expedient to him, which he determined immediately to put into practice. He went up to the body, and laying it on his shoulders, carried it to the door of this avaricious man's house, and then going up into his room, said to him with holy frankness: "My brother, I have civilly begged you to give burial to a poor man, neglected by every one, and I asked this charity of you in the Name of God, but you did not deign to listen to me. Nevertheless, this man is your brother in Jesus Christ, as well as mine, and you have a particular obligation to do him this good office, for he has died in your neighbourhood, and God has permitted it to be so, in order that you may have an opportunity of performing this good work; but you neglect it and keep your money in your purse, not considering that it was given you, not for yourself only, but also that you might give part of it to your neighbour. Think then on what you ought to do, and prepare to pay the last duties to this dead man. I have brought his body to your door, and will not take it away, in order that it may stand up as a witness against you at the day of the last judgment. I cite you before the sovereign tribunal of Jesus Christ, and will myself be your accuser there if you persist in your want of humanity. This is all that I have to say to you." These words astonished the rich man, and nearly aroused his anger, for he was not in the habit of receiving rebukes of this kind; nevertheless, he dissembled his indignation, and did what the servant of God desired him, either being touched with salutary repentance, or because he feared to dishonour himself in the eyes of the world, by refusing burial to a body which was laid at his door; accordingly he opened his purse, and gave all that was required to bury the dead man respectably, and procure prayers for him.

On another occasion, when John of God was returning from a village whither he had gone out of charity, he perceived in the fields some little children who seemed to be almost entirely naked, their clothes being very thin and all in rags. He immediately conceived a desire to assist them, and to give them dresses and other clothes, but he had no money about him, and he saw no means of obtaining any soon enough to satisfy this pressing want. Hence he resolved to have recourse to the charity of others; and this he did readily, for he was persuaded that to solicit the rich in behalf of the poor is a charitable work, which belongs especially to those who, though not provided with the goods of fortune, nevertheless have credit and friends. He therefore took these little children to the house of a merchant's wife, whom he knew; he begged her to take care of them, to have compassion on them, and to respect in them the infancy of Jesus Christ. She listened to him with much pleasure, and immediately sent to buy some clothes for them, so that he had the consolation of conducting them to the house of their parents, well-clad, and provided with all they needed.

To the two instances mentioned above, we must add a third, which is still more striking, and will show clearly that this holy man had a peculiar gift for inducing all kinds of persons to bestow alms, even those who were most attached to the goods of the earth. We can easily understand that a new hospital, open to every one, and without any fixed and certain income, was often in want of many things, and even reduced to great extremities. It happened, then, one day, that there were no provisions and no money to buy any, and yet it was necessary to feed the poor, and to support them as usual, without taking into account all the other out-of-door charities, which could not be neglected without making many families suffer greatly, and exposing them even to despair. In this extremity John of God applied to two of his friends, hoping to obtain assistance from them, but they paid no attention to anything that he could say, and had no idea of retrenching any of their superfluities in favour of the poor. Giving up all hopes of receiving anything from this quarter, he thought of a rich merchant of Geneva, named Piola, whom he knew intimately, and from whom he had already received alms on different occasions. Calling on him about mid-day, he found him at dinner with his wife. After some compliments he made known the object of his visit, begging Piola to lend him thirty ducats to relieve the urgent necessities of his poor. The merchant's wife, who was greatly attached to his interests, hearirg that he wanted to borrow money for them, rose up from the table in great anger, making a sign to her husband not to listen to this proposal. He had no need to be reminded by his wife, for he had as much disinclination to it as she had. Nevertheless, he did not break off the conversation with so much incivility, but continuing to speak to John of God, he said : "My brother, I am engaged in business ; I buy and sell every day, and consequently cannot part with my money. It is necessary to keep up my credit, and to satisfy those with whom I have to deal : and even though I had not present need of it, I would not lend it you unless you had good security to give me."

The father of the poor, on hearing these words, answered him with an air full of confidence : "My brother, I will give you a very good one for it," and at the same time drawing out a crucifix which he was in the habit of carrying in his sleeve, he added, " Here is my security ; do you wish for a better than this?" The merchant looking at the crucifix, saw bright rays of light issuing from all parts of the image of Jesus Christ which was attached to it. This frightened him, and brought him to acknowledge his fault. Accordingly he threw himself at John's feet ; he immediately counted out to him the thirty ducats he asked for, and would not receive from him any note or security. His conversion was still more complete, for his wife dying at the end of six months, he separated himself entirely from the world, and after having arranged his affairs, went to find our Saint ; then placing in his hands an inventory of all his property, he made it all over to him irrevocably, and begged him to admit him to serve the poor among his brothers. John gave him a favourable reception, being delighted at seeing him in such good dispositions. He put him into retreat and tried him for some time, after which he gave him a habit like his own, and admitted him as one of his brothers. John then divided all the money he had brought into two equal portions, one of which was distributed amongst the poor of the city who were ashamed to beg, and the other kept as a fund for the support of the sick in the hospital. This good brother, after having lived under his direction in a very edifying manner, and made great advance in piety, ended his career happily, and his holy life was crowned by a death precious in the sight of God.

It may be well to remark before concluding this chapter that when our Saint told the merchant that Jesus Christ would be security for the money which he wished to borrow for the poor, he spoke only according to the words of the wise man, who assures us that "he that hath mercy on the poor lendeth to the Lord, and he will repay him" (Prov. xix. 17); commenting upon which S. Augustine says, "God has no need of your money, but the poor have need of it. You give it to the poor and God receives it. The poor would be glad to pay you back what you lend them, but they have nothing to give. They cannot show their gratitude otherwise than by praying for you; and when they do so, it is as if they said to God, 'Lord, they have lent me money, be Surety for me.' If then the poor cannot pay back what you have lent them, consider that they have God Himself for their Surety." This maxim is of great importance in the Christian life, and as John of God found it useful in turning the heart of this unfeeling rich man, all the faithful ought often to reflect upon it, in order that they may be more and more persuaded that in giving alms they do not lose their money, but put it out to interest; it is to God that they lend it; He receives it by the hands of the poor, and He is Surety for it, and on some future day will repay it amply.

CHAPTER XVI.

DIVINE PROVIDENCE WATCHES OVER JOHN OF GOD.

NOTHING gives greater glory to our Saint than what we have to relate in this chapter; for on the one hand we see that his charity was so great and extraordinary that he hesitated not to expose himself to imminent danger of death for his brethren; and on the other how divine Providence interfered to preserve his life. Thus we shall be obliged to describe a kind of opposition between God and His creature. John, following the ardour of his zeal, runs after death, and God, through His goodness, wills that he should live and remain still on earth. John confronts a thousand dangers by which he risks his life, and God performs prodigies and miracles to prevent him from dying. John undertakes things for the good of his neighbour which are beyond the ordinary obligations of charity, and God overrules the course of nature in his favour, and commands the elements to stop and spare him. But this opposition is soon at an end, because the Will of God, which is a sovereign law, cannot but be accomplished, and John is perfectly obedient to it; having no fear to die, he refuses not to live, and says with the great apostle, "To me, to live is Christ, and to die is gain" (Phil. i. 21). The two following stories will explain to the reader what we have just said.

Besides the hospital which John of God had established in Granada, there was another of royal foundation, which was governed by the principal inhabitants of the city. These governors did not make a good

use of the property belonging to this house, but
wasted it on foolish and useless matters ; one day they
invited several of their friends, and spared nothing
on the occasion, without considering if it were right
o waste the property of the poor in such feasts.
But God could not suffer this profanation, and took
such vengeance for it, as clearly showed how greatly
such an excess had provoked His justice, for as the
stewards and cooks were employed in preparing the
dishes, a chimney took fire, and the flames soon extended to the neighbouring parts ; and because it was
not put out at once, the fire spread quickly, the
rooms and sleeping apartments were in danger, and
there was every appearance that the whole of this
great hospital would be reduced to ashes. The
report of the accident was not long in spreading
through the city; the alarm-bell was rung, and
every one ran to see what was the matter. Things,
however, were already in such a state that no
one dared to hope that any part of this celebrated
house would be saved. It was useless for the governors to give orders, no one would execute them ; the
masons and other workmen stood almost inactive,
fearing to expose their lives, so desperate did everything appear to be ; and what was still more to be
lamented, and drew tears from all the bystanders, the
poor patients lying in their beds were about to be de-
voured by the flames without there being any possi-
bility of assisting them, for the fire already raged in
the passages of the infirmary.

John of God being informed of this disastrous event,
immediately repaired to the spot, and seeing that the
sick patients were left to themselves and on the
point of being burned alive, he did not hesitate a single

instant, but devoting his own life in order to save that of his brethren, he rushed through the flames, and reached the door which opened into the wards. Upon entering he found almost all the patients already half dead, either on account of the smoke which was suffocating them, or because the fright added to their sickness reduced them to the last extremity. He lost no time, but carrying away all the weakest he put them in a place farther removed from the fire, and then returned to throw out of the windows the mattresses, straw beds, counterpanes, and other furniture which might serve as fuel to the fire. To have done this only would undoubtedly have been a great thing, and sufficient to gain him immortal glory, but soon afterwards he performed a still greater action. As the flames were continually increasing, and the wood-work of the attics had already caught fire, some cannon had been brought up, and were going to fire upon this building in order to beat it down, to hinder by this means the flames from spreading any further, and so to try to save the rest of the hospital, but John of God made a signal from a window that they were not to fire upon it. He immediately got up on the ridge of the roof, cut away the rafters, and threw down some small beams which were half burnt. He thus did more work than a great number of workmen could have done in so short a time, and extinguished the fire.

He was more than two hours on the top of this building without being noticed by any one, for only vast volumes of flame and smoke were to be seen on all sides, and it was thought that he had perished. Tears and sighs were heard; some said that more care ought to have been taken of so great a man, and that the fervour of his zeal ought to have been restrained ; others declared that in losing him they had lost more than if the whole hospital had been entirely ruined. The poor mourned, saying that they had no longer a father and protector ; all, in short, wept over the death of such a man, and were truly inconsolable. But the joy was universal when he appeared again after having done all that we have described. There arose a shout of joy, and people ran to salute him, to congratulate him, and to thank him in the name of the whole city ; to all which he answered with his usual modesty that he had done nothing, and that to God alone the glory of all that had happened was to be given. Many had the curiosity to look at him carefully to see if he were not wounded, and if they could not find on him some traces of the fire ; he was, however, quite well, and without any serious injury ; it was remarked that only his eye-brows and eye-lids were burnt, which showed to what danger he had exposed himself. Divine Providence also willed that he should keep this mark for the remainder of his days, that it might be a public monument of the extent of his charity, and of the respect the flames had for him.

It would be difficult for us to conceive how much respect and veneration this heroic act gained him from all the people. They called him a worker of miracles, and a man sent from God. The inhabitants of Granada who formerly had called him a madman, were the first to proclaim his merit and celebrate his praise. They compared him to the children in the furnace of Babylon, who walked in the midst of the flames without being hurt by them, and they said of him, as was said of S. Laurence, that the material fire could not abate his charity, and that it had far less strength than that which burnt within his heart: *Segnior fuit qui foris ussit, quam qui intus accendit.*

There was another incident which, though not so striking, was nevertheless a certain proof of the visible protection which heaven afforded him. One winter the River Xenil overflowed its banks to an unusual degree, doing much damage, and carrying away with it entire houses and much wood. The majority of the inhabitants went to its banks from curiosity in order to see the ravages it was committing; but John of God, thinking only of his sick patients, went thither out of pure charity, and with the sole intention of working for them; for he thought he ought not to neglect to collect the wood which was floating on the surface of the water, and which being lost to the owners, as almost always happens on such occasions, belonged naturally to the poor, and would be of great use to his hospital. He therefore took some of his household with him, and set about gathering this wood together. There being a great quantity in the middle of the river, he determined upon going over in a boat to a kind of small island, which was very deep in the water, and from which he expected to be able to collect much. As soon as they saw him getting on it, the people cried out to him that he was exposing himself to evident danger of perishing, and this was true, for this apparent island was nothing but a heap of sand, which had by chance stopped there, and which might at any moment be carried away by the violence of the waves which beat against it. All this, however, did not disturb him nor hinder him from persevering in his purpose;

he only replied to those who gave him this advice, " I fear nothing, for I am sure that God and my poor will protect me."

He continued therefore gathering together the wood, and with such success that he collected nearly two hundred loads of it, which he caused to be conveyed to his hospital, and then he went away. What astonished every one was that he had hardly left the island before the waters carried it away, loosening the sand, which did not really form a solid body. The people accordingly acknowledged that God had only caused it to remain there for the father of the poor, and for as long a time as was necessary for him to obtain his provision of wood. This circumstance caused them to speak loudly in his praise. They proclaimed aloud that he knew how to make the elements obey him, and that God daily performed miracles in his behalf; they acknowledged that he was all-powerful, and he had only to wish for a thing, and it immediately took place. They no longer pronounced his name without adding to it some epithet of praise ; they called him incomparable, the protector of the poor, and the refuge of all the unfortunate. These two events were well known, and needed no other attestation than their public notoriety. Nevertheless, the censor of the city and all the chief inhabitants failed not to make a juridical deposition respecting them in view of his beatification, so that we may say that the account of these two events is as certain as the events themselves appear wonderful and extraordinary.

CHAPTER XVII.

JOHN OF GOD TRANSFERS HIS HOSPITAL TO A NEW
HOUSE BY ORDER OF HIS ARCHBISHOP, AND GOES
TO BEG IN THE COUNTRY, IN ORDER THAT HE
MIGHT HAVE WHEREWITH TO PAY THE DEBTS HE
HAD CONTRACTED FOR THE SUPPORT OF HIS POOR.

WE have already mentioned that the great number of
poor who came to our Saint had obliged him to leave
the first house in which he had established his hospital, and to take a larger one, in order that he might
be able to receive all who begged his assistance. We
must now add that this house also was found to be
too small for his zeal and all his good works; for as
a fire gains more strength in proportion as more fuel
is heaped upon it, so his charity increased every day
at the sight of his neighbours' misery : poor persons
were brought to him from all parts, and he refused
admittance to none; he even anticipated them; he
went to find them out, he carried them on his
shoulders into his infirmaries, as we have already mentioned, and he was never more pleased than when he
saw himself surrounded by a crowd of distressed persons, and had difficulty in finding rooms and beds to
put them into. Don Pedro Guerrero, Archbishop of
Granada, loved him very tenderly; he had on several occasions given him public marks of his esteem,
and often contributed towards the support of his sick
patients by his alms; when, therefore, he was informed that the house in which the hospital then was
did not suffice to hold a fourth part of the poor who

flocked to it from all sides, he thought it his duty
as pastor to supply this deficiency, and procure him a
larger house, which should in some measure correspond
with the extent of his charity. He first conferred
about the matter with the principal men of the city,
and then convened a general assembly of all the inhabitants, to whom he explained that the hospital of
John of God was open to every one ; that all kinds
of sick persons were received in it, pilgrims, travellers,
and strangers, and that it might be said to have
become a public asylum and place of refuge for all
the afflicted ; and accordingly he suggested that
the public ought to take an interest in its support. It was evident that the present house was not
capable of holding a fourth part of those who applied
there ; every day showed this, and it very often
happened that persons could not even get into the infirmaries, so many were there already, and John of
God knew not what to do. All these considerations,
the archbishop said, induced him to think it would
be proper to transfer his hospital into a larger building, in order that he might satisfy his zeal, and attend
to those who came to consult him, or to beg assistance
in their misfortunes. The whole assembly were of the
same opinion as the wise and zealous prelate, and
they resolved as soon as possible to commence this
work which so nearly concerned the glory of God
and the comfort of the poor.

It happened that a very large house, formerly occupied by some nuns, was at that time vacant and for
sale. Its advantageous situation in the Via Gomelly
made them think of establishing John of God's hospital there, and it was determined to see and purchase it. The archbishop was not one of those pastors

who preach up alms and recommend them to the faithful without taking the trouble to give any themselves, but he set the example to his people on this occasion, and was the first to contribute towards the purchase of it, for he gave as much as five hundred crowns to be employed in it; rich persons also gave very considerable sums, and every one gladly contributed what he could afford towards so good a work, so that in a short time the house was fully paid for, and John of God transported his poor into it.

In the upper part of the house infirmaries for the sick were prepared, in which he provided at least two hundred beds, and the rooms of the lower part were destined to receive pilgrims and poor beggars who had nowhere to go. The order which he established in this house was admirable, and surprised every one. As soon as the dawn began to appear he came out of his cell, and standing on a spot from which all who were in the house might hear him, he cried out in a loud voice, " My brothers, let us praise God and give Him thanks, for the birds of the air take care to praise and bless Him by their singing and chirping," and immediately afterwards he went down to the rooms of the pilgrims and the other poor to whom he had given shelter; he offered up some morning prayer for them, and exhorted them to conduct themselves holily during the day and to avoid occasions of sin. If there were any amongst them who were not sufficiently instructed in Christian doctrine, the sacristan of the chapel, which was in the house, catechised them, and in the meantime he went up into the infirmaries of the sick to say the same prayers for them, and to explain to them the principal mysteries of religion.

Then Mass was celebrated, at which he assisted with all his brothers. The proper time was fixed for waiting upon the sick; each brother had his office, and all was done without noise or confusion, and whether he was there or not, the same rule was always observed, because Brother Antony Martin did exactly the same as himself. John gave him all authority for maintaining the discipline of the house whilst he was engaged in those important matters which he was obliged to transact out of doors.

The great number of sick and of pilgrims whom he received into his house, the poor who were ashamed to beg, and whom he supported in the city, and all the other works of piety which he performed, obliged him to go to great expense, and he had often no money to go on with, for what he obtained by begging and from his small income was not sufficient, so that he was obliged to take many things on credit from the dealers in provisions; and on some days he borrowed as much as three or four hundred ducats, in order that he might be able to assist all those of whom he was the father and protector. By borrowing so frequently he at last made himself many creditors, whom to all appearance he could never pay: this pained him greatly, for he knew that justice ought to go before charity, and that he must pay his debts before he gave alms.

The devil, being jealous of all the good which he saw him doing, did all he could to oppose it, neglecting nothing which he thought might thwart his designs, and making use of the present occasion to endeavour to ruin his hospital, and induce him to interrupt the course of his charities. He excited some persons, therefore, to say to him that there was imprudence and indiscretion in giving so much alms, whilst he had so great a number of creditors whom he could not pay; that it was not lawful for him to put whole families to inconvenience, nor to ruin those who had lent him money, under pretext of assisting the poor; that he ought to moderate his zeal, and not undertake more than his means allowed of, and that he would do well to discontinue his charities and sell his house in order to pay his debts. There were even some who went still further, offering to take the whole care of his hospital on themselves, to support it at their own expense, and to satisfy all his creditors. These reasons, which seemed plausible, together with these apparently advantageous offers, at first produced some impression on his mind, disquieted him, and threw him into a state of indecision; for on the one hand his creditors were very urgent, and it pained him much to see them suffer, and on the other, he could not resolve to abandon his poor, to leave the care of his sick, and renounce his hospital, because he thought it was his vocation, and the work that God required of him.

In this perplexity he had recourse to his spiritual father Avila, and wrote to inform him of the condition in which he was. He carefully informed him of all the debts he had contracted in order to bestow his usual charities. He mentioned to him the advice which had been given him to leave the care of his poor and of his hospital, as well as the promise some private persons had made him to take it upon themselves, and he begged him to say what determination he ought to come to. This great man did not take long to deliberate on the advice he ought to give him, for he immediately saw that all this was nothing but an artifice of the evil spirit, who wished to diminish his zeal, to weaken his courage, and to thwart all his good works.

He therefore answered him in the following terms : " Whosoever, in order to detach you from the employment in which you are engaged and to give you another, has offered to pay your debts, must be a devil who has taken a human form in order to deceive you by making you believe that you could, without offending God, leave that to which you have been called ; for S. Paul says, ' Let each one remain in the state to which God calls him.' Thus, if He should wish any one to act as a servant, and instead of obeying Him he should, through false humility, prefer to keep swine, he would commit a sin, and have to give an account of all the good he might have done in the employment which God had appointed for him. Hence, if a creature all resplendent with light, and calling himself an angel of God, should wish to withdraw you from your ordinary duties, tell him he is a devil, and that nothing shall induce you to quit the path in which God has placed you, because the Gospel teaches us that he only who has persevered to the end shall be saved. Read this text often, and may God watch over you and preserve you from all evil !"

Instructed and strengthened by this answer, John turned a deaf ear to all that was said to induce him to resign the government of his hospital, and began to think of the means he was to take to pay his creditors. As up to the present time he had obtained much assistance from the inhabitants of Granada, he was unwilling to be a burden to them on the present occasion, or to ask of them any extraordinary alms. Accordingly, he determined to go into the country to beg, and went through all Andalusia, having left to Brother Martin the management of his charities. God visibly blessed his undertaking, for in the course of his journey he found many pious persons who gave him considerable sums, and paid him great honours. Amongst others the Duke and Duchess of Sessa received him very honourably in their castle, were delighted in conversing with him on many pious subjects, and paid a good part of his debts. They further contracted a particular friendship with him, took great interest in his poor, and besides their accustomed charities to him on certain days, failed not every year at the feast of Easter to send him clothes, shirts, and shoes for his poor, and for the rest of their lives were the firmest supporters of his hospital. As soon as he returned to Granada, he began to distribute to his creditors all the money he had collected, and expressed much gratitude to them for the favour they had done him in being willing to wait so long a time until they were paid what was due to them. By this means he found himself in a condition to continue his charities in greater peace and tranquillity, and he saw by experience that God forsakes not those who trust in Him, and who labour only for His glory.

CHAPTER XVIII.

THE ARCHBISHOP OF GRANADA ADVISES JOHN OF GOD TO GO TO THE COURT OF SPAIN IN ORDER THERE TO OBTAIN SOME ASSISTANCE FOR HIS POOR.

DON PEDRO GUERRERO, Archbishop of Granada, was the father and protector of all the poor in his diocese, and especially of those who were the most afflicted and in the greatest want. It was natural, therefore, that John of God should give him an account of what he had done during his journey into Andalusia, and of the alms he had collected there; and accordingly he did not fail to do so, but went to his palace in order to relate to him all that had occurred. When the prelate heard that the alms he had collected were not sufficient to clear all his debts, he recommended him to go to the Spanish Court, in the hope that he would there meet with prompt assistance and liberal charity. A man of the world would have regarded the advice of the bishop as a command, would have joyfully submitted to it, and, without any deliberation, would have entered upon the journey, which would give him the opportunity of seeing and conversing with the great. But our Saint was not so hasty; he was unwilling to commence a journey to Court before he had written to Avila, in order to know if he thought it advisable, and had no objection to urge against it.

This wise director had no wish to oppose the plan, seeing that it was authorized by the bishop, and tended only to the comfort of the poor. He only cautioned his spiritual son to conduct himself with great reserve and circumspection at Court, which for many is a place of relaxation and corruption, and to keep himself in the fear and presence of God. In his answer to John he said : "I approve of your going to Court, if you think it advisable, in order to avoid getting into debt, to ask for aid from the Council of Castille ; but take care, there as elsewhere, to strive above all to serve our Lord, in order that you may one day possess the glory for which He has created you, and that He may ever be your support and strength."

As soon as John of God received his answer, he prepared in good earnest for the journey, and set out with one of his brethren, whom he chose as a witness of all his actions, and as his counsellor in the important matters he would have to transact. He was greatly respected wherever he went, and his reputation was so great and so well established, that as soon as he arrived at any city the people contended who should entertain him, a vast number coming and offering him their houses ; many even used something like violence to drag him to their houses, reckoning it to be a great honour to entertain him. But he always refused these invitations in places where there was a hospital, and infinitely preferred lodging with the poor than with the rich, because in the apartments of the latter he saw only objects which offended his eyes, and which breathed luxury and vanity, whereas amongst the poor everything pleased him and suited his inclinations. As he met in these hospitals as many friends as there were poor persons, and always found opportunities of working and employing himself usefully, he did not hasten his departure from them. He even remained so long in that of Toledo, that his companion was annoyed at it, and took occasion to tell him that he was staying there too long a time; but he only replied: "My son, by the mercy of God we are not useless here; moreover, you know that I do not stop in any city without our Lord's furnishing us immediately with some opportunity for exercising charity towards the poor. Take courage therefore, and do not be annoyed when the good and advantage of our neighbour is concerned."

There were many persons who, when informed of the object of his journey, gave him much alms whilst he was still on the road. But these he did not keep long, for when poor persons came to him on the road and represented their wants to him, he could not refuse them and leave them unrelieved. Thus he distributed to them all the money which had been given him for his hospital in Granada, at which his companion again feeling vexed, was induced sometimes to say: "My father, you are forgetting the object of your journey;" to which our Saint made the following judicious reply: "My son, to give at the place where we are, or to give at Granada, is always to give for God, and there is no doubt that our Lord has sent us here to perform works of charity, since He causes us to find poor persons here." Thus he continued always to distribute liberally to all who were in any want the alms he had received for Granada.

As soon as he arrived at Valladolid, where the Court then was, Maria de Mendoza, widow of the Grand-Commander Francis de Los Cobos, made many attempts to have the honour of receiving him into her house, and fearing lest some one else might carry off from her such a guest, she used all her influence with their Majesties, that he might be ordered to lodge in her palace. We need not stop to describe the good reception she gave him, for we may easily imagine that a lady of her rank, who employed all her fortune in bestowing alms and charity, would not fail to receive well the father of the poor. Not only did she take great care of him personally, but she often gave him considerable sums to be disposed of as he thought best, and to form a fund for Granada. Nevertheless, he kept none of them for his hospital, but distributed at Valladolid all that he received from her liberality, because he was not in the habit of keeping money so long as he saw poor persons, and there always was a very great number of them round him, his charity attracting them from all parts.

Spain was at that time governed by Don Philip II., who had not the title of king, but was called Prince of Castille, because his father, the Emperor Charles V., was still living, and had not yet given the Crown up to him, as he afterwards did in 1555, at an assembly held at Brussels. The Conde de Tendilla and some other lords having spoken to him about John of God, whom they had known at Granada, he expressed a wish to see him, and ordered him to be brought to him without fail the next day. As soon as the father of the poor had been introduced into his palace, and had come into his presence, he fell on his knees and made him the following compliment, which was worthy of his Christian simplicity: "My lord, when I speak to any one, I am in the habit of calling him my brother in Jesus Christ; as for you, you are my lord and my prince, and will shortly be my king: by what name do you command me to call you?" "Brother

John," replied Don Philip, " it shall be as you please."
" I will call you then, good Prince," continued the
Saint. " May it please God to make the beginning of
your reign happy, to fill you with prosperity, and to
give you the grace to have a happy life as well as a
happy death, that you may one day come to enjoy
eternal life."

These words, which came from the bottom of his
heart, were so pleasing to the Prince, that he
stooped down to raise him up, and taking him
by the hand, made him enter his cabinet, where he
gave him so long an audience that the whole Court
were astonished at it, and on dismissing him he
ordered a considerable sum to be paid to him for
his poor. He was then taken to the apartments of
the Infantas, the Prince's sisters, who also received
him very kindly, spoke to him about his hospital,
and required him to give them a short history of all
his works ; they desired him to visit them often, and
their liberality to him corresponded with their piety
and birth. He frequently returned to the palace as
he had been ordered, and was always admitted to
an audience with these illustrious princesses, who took
pleasure in hearing him speak, and showed that they
were edified by him. Their maids of honour, after
their example, greatly esteemed his virtue, conversed
with him on subjects of piety, asked his advice, and
often gave him money, and, when they had none,
sent him their jewels, that he might sell them and
apply the money to the support of his poor. But he
kept nothing out of all this money for his hospital;
he distributed at Valladolid all he received, so that
after a long abode at Court he had not collected
any funds for Granada, and it did not seem as if he

could do so at all, since charity deprived him of all that was given to him.

Doña Maria Mendoza and several lords, having been told that he always acted in this manner, thought it better not to give him any more ready money, but to adopt some other means to enable him to pay his debts. They therefore placed their alms in the hands of some bankers, and drew up letters of credit, payable at Granada, which they gave him, and by this means checked his liberality, and enabled him to assist the poor of his hospital, and satisfy his creditors. It is necessary to frighten and threaten the rich men of the world, in order to compel them to bestow alms, but with John of God they were obliged to make use of artifice in order to hinder him from giving; charity requiring them to close his hands at Valladolid, in order to open them when he should arrive at Granada. This is the way in which he spent the nine months that he remained at Court; he came there from motives of charity, he abode there for the interests of charity, he was wholly employed in matters of charity, and he departed out of charity, because the poor of his hospital were in want of him, and were expecting him with impatience.

When he arrived at Granada, after so long an absence, a universal joy spread through the whole city. The rich were delighted to see him, since they regarded him as the common father and protector of all the citizens. The sick thought that his presence would restore them to health. The poor who were ashamed to beg, hoped to receive fresh assistance from his kindness. The families whom he supported were consoled, and their misfortunes appeared as nothing after his return; and all the inhabitants in general praised God for their happiness in possessing him, and for the opportunity they were about to have of being again edified by the example of his virtues.

CHAPTER XIX.

ON HIS SPIRIT OF PRAYER.

FROM the beginning of this book to the present chapter, we have described all that our Saint did for the establishment of his hospital, and have related many of his actions which were very striking, and drew upon him the eyes of the inhabitants not of Granada only, but of all Spain. We must now say something of his principal virtues, and then relate different circumstances referring to the same subject, in order that our readers may remember them with greater facility, and may often reflect on them and be edified by them. We will begin by his gift of prayer, because it is worthy of great admiration ; and in order to comprehend it, we must remember that the holy Fathers teach us that the employments of Martha and Mary are seldom united in the same person. When after Martha's example we devote ourselves to an active life, we are not always much disposed to contemplation with Mary ; outward things to which we apply ourselves are as dust which troubles the interior eye of the soul, and hinders us from perceiving the unspeakable beauties of God ; and the constant activity and agitation of body almost always deprive us of that spirit of peace and tranquillity which is necessary for meditating on the truths of salvation.

Thus it would seem that there could be **no probability** that John of God would have the spirit **of** prayer in any great degree; for we have seen that he always led an active life, undertook very great works for the service of his neighbour, had a vast quantity of affairs on hand, and hardly ever kept any time to himself, especially after the commencement of his hospital. Nevertheless all bear him witness that he always made much prayer, and that all his occupations did not interrupt his spiritual exercises, nor diminish the fervour of his meditations. When he went to the war early in life, he was already in the habit of saying the Rosary of the Blessed Virgin every day, and the Pater and Ave twenty-four times, and this without reckoning the prayers which he said every evening and morning like the rest of the faithful. Having learnt from the royal prophet that " unless the Lord build the house, they labour in vain that build it; unless the Lord keep the city, he watcheth in vain that keepeth it ;" he never did anything of importance without having long recommended it to God in his own prayers, and engaged other pious persons also to pray for the same thing. This was the reason that he almost always succeeded in all that he undertook ; for God generally blesses the undertakings which are referred to Him, and which are not acted upon until after His Will has been consulted, and the aid of His grace implored. He had long been in the habit of worshipping God in all creatures; all that took place in the universe furnished him subjects for meditation, and the very smallest things led him to make very useful and spiritual reflections. Father Avila, and all who knew him intimately, have assured us that he always kept himself in the presence of God, and that nothing could make him lose sight of it, so that he could say with David : " I set the Lord always before my sight" (Ps. xv. 8).

This sight and presence of God inspired him with great fervour in all his actions, and caused him often to cry out : " God sees us, my brothers ; the servant, who knows that his master is looking at him, does his work well." On many occasions a great trembling was remarked in him, and at the same time these words proceeded from his mouth : "Lord, I am an abominable sinner," from which every one saw that he had a very exalted idea of the holiness, greatness, and sovereign majesty of God, and that he thought himself quite unworthy to appear before Him. He also often prostrated himself on the earth, and uttered words which were not always distinctly heard, but which were so many acts of adoration, and the outpourings of his heart. If whilst walking in the streets he met some object which offended his eyes, and which he thought was contrary to decency, he immediately held out the crucifix which he always carried in his sleeve, and said in a loud voice : "Learn Christian virtue and modesty, from the Wounds of Jesus Christ."

When he went into the city, he failed not to enter all the churches which he found open, in order to adore the Blessed Sacrament, and sometimes he remained a very long time there without thinking of it, having fallen into an ecstasy ; and when he returned to himself, he would say on departing : " My Master, we do not lose time in remaining with you." The prophet said to God : "I prevented the dawning of the day, and cried, because in Thy words I very much hoped. My eyes to Thee have prevented the morning, that

I might meditate on Thy words" (Ps. cxviii. 147-8). Our Saint practised this with great care. He always rose very early in order to have time for his prayers and spiritual reading, in which he generally employed more than an hour before applying himself to external occupations; and because he was fully employed during the whole day, and had not so much time for contemplation as he could have wished, he made up for these losses in the night, and stole from sleep all the time that he could, in order to give it to prayer and meditation, on which subject we have some remarkable facts to relate.

Doña Eleanora Guevara was always very fond of him, and even when he was only a private individual used to give him alms, and often afforded him shelter in her house. She showed the same kindness after he had established his hospital, and as she could no longer speak and converse with him on pious subjects because he was always engaged, she invited him sometimes to take supper at her house, in order that she might at least converse with him during the meal. The four daughters of this lady were still alive when the juridical informations were drawn up by order of the Holy See, and they deposed that as soon as he left the table he went into their mother's private chapel, and that he generally spent the whole night there in prayer; they added that they were well assured of what they said, because they went at different hours to look through the chinks of the door, and always found him on his knees, and often heard him groan and sigh deeply in his prayers.

A person named Luke, a man of great probity, and licentiate in Theology, declared before the judges who were appointed to hear the witnesses, that his

grandfather on certain occasions used in like manner
to receive our Saint into his house, and that when he
had retired to the bedroom prepared for him, they
heard a sound of many little bells in the house. The
same thing happening several times, they had the curiosity to search all over the house to discover whence
this proceeded. After having visited every part,
they came near his apartment, and some one looking through a hole into his bedroom, perceived that
his lamp was still alight, and that he was praying
very quietly on his knees. They waited there some
time in order to see how long his prayer lasted, and
after the lapse of more than an hour they were surprised at seeing him suddenly rise up, fasten some
little bells to his legs, and walk quickly up and down
his room. They concluded that he did this in order
to awaken himself and keep off sleep, for after a few
turns he immediately fell on his knees again and continued to pray as before.

This circumstance alone is more than sufficient to
show us how great was his ardour for prayer. He
worked the whole day for his poor, undergoing extraordinary fatigue, and when night came on, instead of
taking rest, he gave himself up to this exercise, and
because nature often gave way, and the outward man
yielded to sleep, he used violence against himself, as
did formerly those holy solitaries of whom S. John
Climacus speaks, who stood up all night, and were ingenious in tormenting themselves, in order that they
might be better able to keep awake. He reproached
his body, saying to himself: "It is not fitting that
those who ought to serve God should spend their time
in sleep; and after having employed all the means
which his zeal suggested on such occasions, he at last

had recourse to those little bells we have just mentioned, because their shrill sound awoke him better, and kept sleep from him a long time. We may add that people in the world who are fond of soft beds, and who take sleeping draughts in order to procure sweeter and more peaceful repose, have cause to blush at their own effeminacy when they reflect on the manner in which John of God acted.

His prayers were not only very frequent, but so fervent that on many occasions they made him shed floods of tears ; the sighs which he uttered were heard at a distance, and he was often found in transports and raptures. There have even been witnesses who affirmed that they had seen rays of light issuing from his mouth and reaching up to heaven whilst he was praying, which was a sign that his prayers were very pleasing to God, and that as precious incense they ascended to the foot of His adorable Throne. It is certain that he had a very great love for the Church, and that he was very careful to intercede for her before God. He continually recommended her wants to Him, he prayed Him to send her worthy labourers, to animate her ministers with His Spirit, to clothe them with justice, as the royal prophet had formerly so much desired, and to give them all the talents necessary for labouring with fruit in His harvest.

Lastly, well knowing that gratitude is one of the principal duties of Christian justice, he failed not himself to pray, and to make all his sick do the same every day, for all those who supported and protected his hospital, or served it in any manner whatsoever. He drew down upon them the graces and blessings of heaven, and in return for the temporal blessings which he received from their liberality, he obtained for them as far as he was able the enjoyment of the unspeakable benefits of the next life, and entreated the Lord to admit them into His eternal mansions.

After attentively considering all that has been said, our readers will agree with us that John of God perfectly fulfilled the employments of Martha and Mary, difficult as the union of the two must always be; and consequently they will confess that he had an extraordinary gift of grace; that he was one of those great souls who are always ready for all kinds of good works, and that he may serve as a model not only to those who are devoted to hospitality and the service of the poor, but also to solitaries and contemplatives, since he had the zeal and care of the former, together with the repose and calmness of the latter, and was able to be actively employed without distraction, and to pray without neglecting any of the kind offices which charity constrained him to perform for his neighbour.

CHAPTER XX.

ON THE OBSTACLES WHICH THE DEVIL RAISED AGAINST HIS PRAYERS.

It is not necessary to stop to explain the force and effect of the prayers which the faithful offer to God, for it is a thing perfectly well known. Jesus Christ has said to them: "Ask and it shall be given you, seek and you shall find, knock and it shall be opened to you; for every one that asketh receiveth, and he that seeketh findeth, and to him that knocketh it shall be opened" (S. Matt. vii. 8). He has further promised them: "If two of you shall consent upon earth concerning anything whatsoever they shall ask, it shall be done to them by My Father who is in heaven." And the Apostle S. James declares that the continual prayer of a just man availeth much ; and in order to prove it he relates the example of Elias, who by praying stopped the rain or made it fall upon the earth, according as he judged it conducive to the glory of God, and to the benefit or punishment of the people. The devil, who is aware of these truths from experience, and knows that on an infinite number of occasions he could do nothing against those who have the spirit of prayer, and often implore the divine mercy, employed, therefore, all kinds of artifices, and made extraordinary efforts to disturb and impede our Saint's prayers. If he happened to be late at night in church before the Blessed Sacrament, he would blow out the lamp, or upset the oil and make a great noise in order to distract and frighten him. He appeared to him under hideous forms, as that of an owl and of other animals of this kind, and he offered him many other insults. But John despised all this; he drove away these spectres by making the sign of the cross, and often said to the evil spirit, " Thou wishest to turn me away from prayer, and, in order to revenge myself on thee, I will pray longer than usual."

Brother Dominic Benedict, whose cell was near his, heard him on one occasion about midnight speaking in a loud voice, and disputing vehemently as if he were fighting against some one. He immediately ran to his aid and found him on his knees, greatly fatigued and exhausted, and crying out in a loud voice, " Jesus, deliver me from Satan ; Jesus assist me." This good brother, surprised at what he saw, went to a window to call some one, and there he immediately saw a hideous monster breathing fire from its mouth and nostrils, at which he was still more frightened. He made a noise therefore to awaken the brothers, and when they came he said, "Do you not see the devil on this window?" but they saw nothing, because this infernal spirit had already departed and quitted the field. Still they knew that something very unusual must have happened, because the servant of God was all beaten and bruised, and they were obliged to make him keep his bed for eight days. During all this time he would not say anything about what had happened to him; they only remarked that on making the sign of the cross, he said in a low tone to himself, "Thinkest thou, traitor, that I am a man to give up what I have once undertaken?"

A short time afterwards, as he was praying in his cell at midnight, the devil appeared to him under the form of a beautiful woman. He immediately rose up and said to this pretended woman in a tone of indignation, "By what means did you enter in, seeing that the door of my room and those of the hospital are shut?" "I can enter wherever I please without doors," she replied. "You must then be a devil," returned the Saint, "otherwise you could not have entered here." And at the same time he went to the door to feel with his hand if it were not well closed, and on turning round again there was nothing more to be seen. He immediately went to his sick, and bursting into tears, said, "My brothers, why do you not pray to our Lord for me, that He may protect and defend me?"

Another night he was heard to cry out, "Jesus, Son of the great and living God, come to my assistance." The brothers, aroused by the noise, immediately went to his cell, and saw him on his knees before an image which represented the mystery of the Annunciation, and holding a crucifix in his hands. They asked him what was the matter, to which he replied, that whilst he was praying he was caught up by his body, lifted up in the air, and then let fall upon the floor; and in fact they discovered that he was wounded and required to be attended to.

It is thus that the devil, fearing his prayers, employed every expedient to resist them, because they destroyed his empire. At one time he took the form of a woman in order to deceive him, and at another he used violence and ill-treatment, as I have just related. But the servant of God continued firm and fearless; the more he saw himself persecuted by this infernal spirit, the more he redoubled his prayers, and like the blind man at Jericho, the more they endeavoured to make him hold his peace, the louder he raised his voice, crying out, " Jesus, Son of David, have mercy on me." Speaking on this subject I should add, in order not to return to it again, that on several other occasions Satan treated him very roughly, as if to punish him and take revenge for all the good actions he performed, for he hates those who love virtue and follow after it with all their heart. Going one evening out of the infirmary by a door which opened upon some stairs, he felt some one pushing violently against him without being able to see any one near him, and he rolled down to the bottom of the stairs, crying out, " Jesus, be with me," and the brothers coming up found him stretched on the ground and almost motionless.

I have already several times mentioned that he generally went out to beg in the night, because he had other occupations during the day. Once he met a

14—2

man in the middle of the street who said to him :
" Give me alms."   To whom he replied : " In whose
name do you ask them ?" the man made no answer
and disappeared, but he appeared again a little further
on and said to John, " Why do you not give me alms ?"
The father of the poor replied, " Unless you ask them
of me in the name of God I cannot give to you."   At
these words the pretended poor man gave him a
severe blow in the stomach, and he saw him no
more from that time, which made him think it was a
devil whom God's Name alone had compelled to flee
away.   I will relate another insult which this evil
spirit offered him one evening as he was returning
laden with what he had collected by begging in the
city.   He took the form of a pig, and running between
his legs he threw him violently down, and immediately
disappeared.   Some persons, coming to his assistance,
raised him up and carried him to his hospital, where
he was put into a bed, because his body was bruised
in several places.   They had great difficulty in learning how this accident happened to him, for he simply
said, " That wicked one wishes to overcome me, but
with the grace of our Lord I will conquer him.   He
tries hard to frighten me, but I hope soon to make him
fear me."   And so it happened, for from this time Satan
dared no more to attack him or show himself to him.

Those who read this history will perhaps be astonished at seeing our Saint so often exposed to the illusions of the devil, because they experience none of
these things themselves, and are not liable to them,
however much they pray and practise virtue.   We
would have such persons reflect that this perhaps
may arise from their prayers and good works being so
feeble and imperfect that the devil, being in nowise

inconvenienced or molested by them, does not give himself the trouble to disturb them. Let them read the lives of the ancient solitaries, and they will there see that the devil, after endeavouring in vain to overcome them by his ordinary temptations, did afterwards attack them in the same way. He strove by open violence to drive away S. Anthony from an old castle to which he had retired in order to flee from the world and lead a mortified and penitent life. He often appeared to him to combat him, and compel him to quit it, and sometimes he beat the saint so cruelly that he could no longer stand on his feet, and was obliged to say his prayers lying on the ground. He frequently appeared to S. Pacomius under different forms in order to seduce him, and he caused many other saints to see horrible spectres to hinder them from praying. If, then, this enemy of our salvation no longer employs artifice and violence against the faithful of our age the reason is evident; it is that he despises them, not thinking it worth while to turn their attention from their prayers at which they are already so careless, and he has a thousand other means of keeping them from virtue, and of destroying godliness in their hearts. If they showed more zeal and more fervour he would fear them, and would use every effort to shake and vanquish them, but finding them so feeble and languid, he overthrows them without difficulty, and there is no occasion for him to prepare for them the severe struggles which are only required against courageous souls far advanced in the path of perfection.

CHAPTER XXI.

ON HIS PENANCE AND AUSTERITIES.

To say that John of God had devoted himself to the service of the sick poor, and had taken the charge of a large hospital, is as much as to say in a few words that he led a very austere and penitent life, for what state of life can we conceive harder and more severe than that in which the mind meets with nothing but mournful objects, in which the senses are continually mortified, and the body wearied out by constant fatigue, in which we have always the image of death before our eyes, whilst we cannot be certain of a moment's peace, but are burthened with a thousand different cares, and in which we have need of total self-renunciation in order to give up our whole time to others, and to satisfy their wants ?   Thus, were I to stop here and not add anything more, we should be compelled to admit that he was very austere, and that he did very severe penance. But the writers who have described his actions have pointed out to us many circumstances from which we learn the particular mortifications he practised from the time of the establishment of his hospital, and these we must relate to our readers.

In general he did not allow more than one hour in the night to sleep, devoting the rest to prayer and labour. When speaking on this subject he used to say that lazy and sleepy minds were of no use to God, and that we must always watch and pray, because we know not at what hour the Lord will come. A mat spread on the earth served him for a bed, a stone for a pillow, and a ragged cloak for a counterpane ; and fearing to be too comfortable on such a bed he often went to take his hour's sleep in a small carriage which had formerly been used by a lame patient, and which was under a staircase in a very narrow and inconvenient place, so that, while he was in it, he was in a very painful and forced position. I should thus be justified in comparing him to the most austere of the ancient solitaries who were so sparing in their sleep, fearing to devote too much time to it, that to avoid such a misfortune, they used to lie on the ground, and in places where they found most mortification. S. Hilarion, for example, made himself a cell so small and so narrow that S. Jerome says it was more like a tomb than a chamber.

John of God always went bareheaded in all weather, even in rain or snow. He shaved his hair as well as his beard in order to prevent its protecting him, however slightly, from the inclemency of the weather. He wore no shirt ; all his clothes consisted of a dress of coarse cloth, which he had received from the hands of the Bishop of Tuy, and a pair of drawers, worn wrong side out. He never wore shoes or stockings, either in winter or summer. Like the penitents of old he always travelled on foot, never riding on horseback, or in any vehicle, even when he was most fatigued and in the most unfavourable weather; owing to this he very often suffered greatly, for on many occasions his legs were bruised and his feet wounded, and on his return from Valladolid whither he had gone in order to beg for his poor, it was remarked that the skin on his head, face, and neck had entirely peeled off, owing to the excessive heat of the journey ; great cracks were seen on his legs and feet, and the

weight of his clothes had wearied him so much that
he was quite exhausted, and could hardly move any
further.   He never warmed himself even in the
severest winters, because he looked upon cold and
heat and other inconveniences of this kind as part of
our penance, and he thought we ought to endure
them willingly in order that this satisfaction which
the divine justice has imposed on us may become an
occasion of merit to us ; and when it happened that
persons of importance, whom he dared not resist,
compelled him to approach the fire to warm himself a
little, their kindness only served to increase his suffering, for the heat gave him very great pain, and it was
a real punishment for him thus to pass from great
cold to great heat.   But he did not complain of it,
because he took a pleasure in suffering, and it was a
matter of indifference to him whether he mortified and
crucified his flesh by the cold or by the heat.

He was so temperate in his diet that it could almost
be said of him as of his holy patron, that he hardly ate
or drank, for in general he took nothing but onions,
and of these so few that it was a matter of astonishment how he could live and endure such great
fatigue.

If on some occasions charity obliged him to go and
dine in the houses of those who were kind benefactors
to his poor, he ate only of one dish, always choosing
the smallest portion and the worst meat, which he even
covered with ashes, in order that whilst partaking of
unusual dishes, his penance might not be interrupted.
And as he always thought of his poor, he used to ask
permission of those who entertained him to take to
them the delicacies which were set before him, being
delighted to procure for them any gratification, whilst

he employed severity and rigour only against himself. To the fasts enjoined by the Church, he added many others of his own, and being filled with the zeal and fervour of the Christians of the first ages, he fasted also after their manner, taking only one meal, and that towards evening. All Fridays being devoted to the remembrance of the Passion of Jesus Christ, he felt that the best way to honour this great mystery is to crucify oneself, and he therefore greatly increased his austerities on these days, usually fasting on bread and water. Not content with subduing his flesh by such severe abstinence and fasts, he afflicted it by frequent disciplines, severely scourging himself with thick knotted cords. He once burnt his body so much with hot bricks that it was necessary to dress his wounds for several days before he could be cured. Thus he could generally say with the great Apostle S. Paul that he carried on his body the marks of the Lord Jesus. Moreover, notwithstanding that he was much enfeebled by so many fasts, vigils, and mortifications, he failed not to fatigue himself and to labour incessantly; he went out begging as usual, and discharged all the duties of his hospital ; and when he had not strength to perform some good work which was laborious, he immediately laid the blame on his body, which he loudly reproached, as if it had been in fault.

Having already related a striking instance of this, there is no occasion for us to repeat it. We must not be astonished at his employing such severity against himself, for he was the disciple of the celebrated Avila, and had been instructed in his school. See how this great man speaks on this subject : " When the body," says he, " performs its ordinary work negligently, under pretext of being tired, and of being in want of some rest, instead of giving way to indolence, redouble your courage and efforts by confidence in God, and tell this lazy one to do what it is bound to do." Accordingly he had no consideration for his body; he overburdened it on all occasions, and regarded it as an untamed animal which we must compel to work without ever listening to its complaints or heeding its pretended wants. Hence, when his friends represented to him that it was his duty to take more care of himself, to keep himself for his poor, and to spare his strength in order that he might serve his neighbour longer; that he found in his hospital only too many occasions for self-mortification, without seeking after others; that to be constantly waiting on the sick was a sufficiently great penance, and that God did not require of him to overburden himself, and thus to throw away his life; to such persons he answered with zeal and modesty—" S. Paul, after having preached the gospel, and undergone all the labours of his apostolical ministry, failed not to chastise his body and to bring it into subjection by a very rude and austere penance; and S. Nicholas of Tolentino, after having subdued and macerated his flesh by innumerable austerities and mortifications, feared nevertheless to appear before the tribunal of Jesus Christ; consequently I, who am an abominable sinner, who have been guilty of so many sins, ought not to confine my penance to the government of my poor only, but to punish and chastise myself in many other ways, in order to satisfy the justice of God, and to avert His wrath in a miserable eternity."

The violence and fervour of John's charity rendered him deaf to all that persons could bring forward in order to induce him to moderate his penance,

and it suggested to him additional reasons to show
that he ought not to spare himself, and that he
could not do enough to expiate his sins. Christians
of our day seem to think very differently. They are
but too ready to listen to what is said to them to dissuade them from doing penance, and they remonstrate
against those who speak to them of the necessity of
mortifying themselves, and of doing violence to themselves in order to enter the kingdom of heaven; in this
it is easy to see that they do not imitate the saints,
but are pursuing a different path from that which
they followed when they were on earth.

CHAPTER XXII.

ON HIS PATIENCE UNDER INJURIES, AND HIS GENTLENESS.

As S. Paul has said that charity is patient and kind,
does not take offence, and beareth all things, it is
certain that a man so charitable as our Saint must
be also very patient and gentle. Every one knows
that patience and gentleness always accompany
penance, and that all who are truly sorry for their
sins are also very gentle and very patient. The history of David furnishes us with a striking instance of
this; as soon as he discovered his guilt, he declared
that he listened to those who calumniated him no
more than if he had been deaf, and that he opened
not his mouth to complain, any more than if he had
been dumb. We have another example of it in the

patience and meekness of John of God, combined with the great austerity of life described in the preceding chapter. We have already spoken of all the pains he took to try to convert dissolute women and girls. Many of them corresponded to his good intentions, and were really converted. But there were some who not only refused to listen to the good advice he gave them, but loaded him with injuries, saying that he had bad motives, and accusing him of wishing to allure them in order to satisfy his own passions. He listened to all these slanders without being disturbed by them; he showed no anger against them, nor treated them less kindly than before; and when some persons rebuked these unhappy creatures, and wished to prevent them from calumniating him, he, in his humility, said: "Let them alone, say nothing to them, and do not deprive me of this crown; they know me very well, they know who I am, and treat me as I deserve."

One of these women, even after she had been converted and had forsaken her evil habits, afforded him an opportunity for displaying his patience in the presence of a great number of persons. After having rescued her from the state of perdition in which she was, he had married her to a very respectable man, had taken her debts upon himself, and always continued to assist her. She one day went to his hospital to beg of him some clothes which she said she stood in need of. Not being able to satisfy her request immediately, he made excuses to her, begging her to return the next day. This delay, though very short, made her exceedingly angry, and she broke out into violent expressions against him, calling him rogue, hypocrite, and impostor. He, on the contrary, showed a most admirable moderation, for he suffered her to say all that her malice suggested, he spoke to her with angelic meekness, and in order literally to obey the precept of Jesus Christ, which orders us to do good to those who hate and persecute us, he gave her a very considerable alms, and from his ardent zeal for humiliations, he promised to give her as much more if she would go and repeat the same abuse of him in the public squares. His patience and gentleness made such an impression on the mind of this passionate woman that, reflecting on her own behaviour, she acknowledged her fault, and repented very sincerely of it: and on the day on which the Saint was buried, she appeared in the streets along which the procession was to pass, and walked with the other women whom he had converted; she accused herself publicly of the sins she had committed, declared that it was he who had freed her from the slavery of the devil, and that she owed her salvation to him ; she bestowed great praise on him, and spoke of his virtues in so touching and pathetic a manner, that many persons shed tears at hearing her, and conceived a particular esteem for her.

A short time afterwards he met by chance a wicked beggar, who, by his insolent conduct, afforded him the means of obtaining a great triumph, for to subdue our anger, not to feel resentment amid the greatest insults, and sincerely to pardon the grossest injuries, is no slight victory. This wretched man was standing with many others at the door of a gentleman of Grenada, named Anthony Zavan, and seeing our Saint, he ran up to him with the rest to beg alms of him. They all received some ; but this fellow, who regarded begging as a good trade, and as a means of subsisting without any trouble or labour, was not easily satisfied with the alms given him, unless they were somewhat considerable; so he flew into a passion with John of God because he had given to him, as to all the rest, only a real. He called him a hypocrite, a false religious, a rogue, a stealer of alms, and even had the audacity to slap him on the face. This outrage would doubtless have induced the servant of God to give him a fresh alms, even larger than the first, for he was always in the habit of overcoming evil by good; but when the other beggars began to rebuke the insolent fellow, and the servants of Anthony Zavan were running up to seize and punish him, as he deserved, he ran away, and John of God, having already pardoned him, interceded for him, and prevented their following him.

He behaved with the same kindness to a young man who, having stolen a horse from the hospital, tried to escape with his booty; but in vain, for, by the special dispensation of God, after having several times lost his way, he found himself the next morning, at break of day, before the gate of the hospital, where the horse was recognized and he was arrested. He would have been delivered up into the hands of justice, had it not been for the interference of John of God, who, after strongly representing to him the enormity of his crime, gave him an alms, and saved him in order that he might have time to recollect himself and satisfy the divine justice by good and salutary penance.

On another occasion, the tranquillity of his soul was again displayed; for having entered the house of the Holy Inquisition to beg, a page, wishing to insult him, pushed him into a basin of water, which was in the middle of the court. He exhibited no emotion at this, but got out of it with the same calmness as if he were leaving his cell or some place of rest ; and so far from making any complaint about it, he thanked him, and prevented his being punished for his insolence.

Lastly, he gave a great proof of his gentleness and patience, when a frantic fellow attempted to take away his life. It happened in the following way : A man who did not seek to serve God, but only to obtain shelter from want and a livelihood in the community, offered himself one day to be received among the brothers ; John of God tried him for some time, ascertained his intentions as far as he was able, and put to him all the questions necessary for making sure of his vocation ; but after having considered everything before God, he decided that he was not called to this state. He told him this in a very civil manner, and recommended him to go back to his home. The wretched man, seeing himself disappointed in his expectation, pretended to obey him and to be going away ; but suddenly turning round, he took a large stone, which he carried in his pocket on purpose, threw it into John's face with all his might, covered him all over with blood, and nearly killed him on the spot. The brothers and all who were in the Infirmary laying hold of him, wished to have him punished ; but the Saint would not suffer this, saying the man had done this only under the first impulse of anger, and without premeditation ; that he himself had, perhaps, spoken too roughly to him, and had not been sufficiently cordial to him ; that if any one deserved punishment it was himself, who had committed so many sins, whereas this man had fallen only through frailty, and because he followed the first movement of his anger.   Thus he saved him from the punishment he deserved, and threw the blame of the assault on himself.

He was often told that some really zealous and virtuous persons found fault with what he did for the good of his neighbour : on such occasions he was still more careful to humble himself, and to strive after greater patience, that he might edify them at least by his silence and modesty.   And if he thought himself obliged to speak to them in reply, he did not try to justify himself, but only advised them not to be so ready to find fault with him without taking the trouble to discover if he really were in the wrong, because by doing so they themselves were committing a considerable fault.   He often merely said to them : " Patience, my brothers, patience ; the surgeon who is impatient never performs a good cure ; there is a time to be silent and a time to speak ; do you make use of your eyes and let us act. The dumb language of our actions will speak for us, and what you see will force you to retract your words."   This happened very often, for many of those who had been too forward in blaming him, afterwards loudly praised him, justified his conduct, and everywhere proclaimed his wisdom and virtues.   Thus his example teaches us that a legitimate and powerful means of repelling calumny is to hold our peace, to practise great patience, to continue quietly doing our duty, and by the holiness of our lives oblige slanderers to retract their words and acknowledge that they were mistaken.

Though my readers see that he was so gentle, so

patient, and so calm under the grossest injuries and the most unworthy treatment, still they must not suppose that he had a heart of stone or of bronze, that he was entirely insensible and suffered nothing from all that was done against him; for this would be forming a false idea of his virtue, and trying to make him resemble those imaginary stoic philosophers who were represented as not having any passions, and as not feeling pain even when they were made to endure the most horrible tortures. He was subject to the same defects that other men are, had the same passions, and was not less sensible than they are of injuries and affronts; but he had learnt to restrain himself, and to overcome all his natural weaknesses; with the assistance of grace he checked the impetuosity of his passions, and his moderation and gentleness made him dissemble the injuries which were painful to human nature.

Thus his patience was not an effect of his insensibility, but of his charity, of his love for his neighbour, and of the severity with which he treated himself; and therefore we may apply to him what S. Bernard said respecting the courage and generosity which the holy martyrs displayed when placed upon wheels and other instruments of torture : " Neque hoc facit stupor, sed amor, submittitur sensus, non amittitur ; nec deest dolor, sed superatur, sed contemnitur ;" " This is not stupidity, but love ; the senses are subdued, not lost ; pain is not absent, but conquered and despised." But there is no need to search the holy Fathers for maxims to make my readers understand on what his patience was founded, for we have only to hear him speak himself on this subject. He happened one day to be in that part of the city of Granada in which the

Moors dwelt. These unbelievers assailed him with innumerable insults and injuries; one still more violent than the others, had the impiety to say: "Wretched being, show us that thy Christ ever performed miracles." To this he immediately replied: "Assuredly it is no small miracle of His grace that I am able to refrain from doing anything unworthy of the Christian name, with the sole design of pleasing Him and observing His law, whilst you are irritating me in so many different ways;" showing by this that he did in reality feel the injuries and insults that were offered him, but that in order to obey Christ he suppressed what he felt, and that, from fear of dishonouring His Holy Name, he observed strict silence, and thought not of revenge.

CHAPTER XXIII.

ON HIS CONFIDENCE IN THE GOODNESS AND PROVIDENCE OF GOD.

If we carefully examine the Saint's conduct under different circumstances, we shall see that he always had an especial confidence in the Providence of God. When only twenty-two years old, he left Majoral's house, who, as we have related, offered him his daughter in marriage and an advantageous settlement considering his condition and rank, and preferred leading a poor and laborious life to engaging himself in the world, trusting that the Divine Providence would never forsake him. Some years afterwards also he refused the proposals of his uncle who promised to make him heir of all his property, and he left Montemor-o-novo, his native country, to go wherever Providence might call him, having no other design than that of following God, and accomplishing His holy will. The different journeys and pilgrimages which he hesitated not to undertake, though he had no money, prove that he relied alone on Providence, and trusted in it.

We will relate a circumstance which took place at the beginning of his conversion, and is a further proof of his great confidence in the goodness of God. Whilst living in the house of Don Michael Avis Vanegas, a very rich gentleman of Granada, he happened one day not to have any money or food for several poor persons who came to beg some. He immediately went to his host's kitchen, and, finding no one there, he took all that was being prepared for the dinner of the family, and distributed it amongst these poor people. Humanly speaking, and according to the ordinary practice of the world, he exposed himself by doing so to be ill-treated, and to be driven away from the house, and, indeed, the cook, seeing what was done, had already begun to cry out loudly against him. But the desire he had to give alms and to succour the unfortunate led him to transgress ordinary rules; he trusted that God would provide a dinner for Don Michael by some other means, and He did so, for a little before mid-day great presents were sent to him, which appeased his anger and amply recompensed him for the dishes which John of God had distributed among the poor.

But it was in the establishment of his hospital that his confidence in God appeared most strikingly: for though poor, and without any means of support in

the world, he undertook the care of many poor and
sick persons. The expenses which such an undertaking brought with it, in no wise alarmed him ; he
was not afraid to take in hand a matter which seemed
to be beyond the power of a rich man, because he
reckoned upon the treasures of Providence to enable
a house to subsist, which was founded only upon it,
and which had no other resources. The result
justified his expectation, for his hospital increased
day by day ; the poor flocked to it from all parts ;
a vast number of unhappy persons fled to it
as to a sure refuge, and nevertheless he was always
able to support his different charities, and God
failed not to send him extraordinary assistance when
his wants were the most pressing. It is very true
that sometimes He allowed a considerable time to
elapse before He assisted him, and on certain occasions permitted him to suffer a little. But this was
to try his faith, and to cause the great confidence
he had in the goodness of God to be known to all ;
for so far from being disquieted or showing any distrust on such occasions, his confidence only increased,
and as S. Paul says of Abraham, he hoped against
all hope ; and he did not do so in vain, for God
Himself furnished him with means of supporting his
hospital.

I will relate a striking instance of this. One day,
seeing that he had no bread for his poor, and that
the dinner hour was drawing near, he took his
basket and left the house with a calm and cheerful
countenance, as if he knew where to obtain all the
bread he stood in need of, so certain was he in his own
mind that Divine Providence had some in store for
him, and would enable him to find some when it was

necessary for the support of his sick patients. And, such was in reality the case, for he had scarcely passed along one street in order to go and beg when he met a man of beautiful aspect, who gave him much more than he had need of, and it was thought to have been an angel who had assumed a human form, because the next moment he vanished; and this bread had so extraordinary a taste, that every one declared he had never before eaten any so good.

It was this firm confidence in the Providence of God which rendered him so liberal, and often induced him to distribute to the first poor man whom he met the alms which had been given him for his hospital.

One day as he was returning from the city loaded with bread for the dinner of his poor, he was followed by a number of labourers and artizans, who, on account of the rain and bad weather, had not been able to find employment. They told him they were famished with hunger, and would, in all probability, not taste anything that day, because they had no money, and could not expect to earn any. This affected him so much, that he distributed to them all the bread he was carrying, and gave them twelve reals besides. Any other person would perhaps have said that, being entrusted with the care of all the poor of his hospital, he ought to think of them first, and that he had no right to give to others what was intended for them. But he was not in the habit of reasoning in this manner; he could not keep anything so long as he knew that his brethren were in want, and when he had no longer anything to give, he had recourse to Divine Providence, which showered down its gifts upon him with a liberal hand.

We must also add that God sometimes worked visible miracles on his behalf, in order to confirm his zeal, and reward him for thus confiding in His goodness and providence. The two following anecdotes will show this. As he was one evening returning to his hospital with bread, fowls, and other things of this kind which he had begged in the city, the devil, never tired of persecuting him, threw him down on the ground with his load. Those who witnessed his fall saw two bright lights come down from heaven to afford him light, and two young men raise him up, put back into the basket all that had fallen out of it, conduct him as far as his hospital gate and then disappear, which made it clear that God protected him and watched over his preservation.

On another occasion, having learnt very late on Christmas Eve that there was no firewood to boil the broth for the sick, he immediately went out with some of his brothers to cut some on a mountain from which he was in the habit of getting it. He spent several hours in this fatiguing employment, so that the night was already far advanced when he was ready to return ; and the darkness being so great that he could not see his way, it was very much to be feared he would fall down some precipice. But Divine Providence, in which he always trusted, immediately came to his aid, for all who were with him saw two torches which constantly preceded him, guiding him along the most safe and easy paths, and not leaving him until he again reached his poor, for whom he had been working. This wonderful event was soon made known, not in the hospital only, but also in the city, and greatly added to his renown. It was everywhere said that this prodigy was a proof of his sanctity and

of his great merit, and that he must be a favourite of
heaven, since such extraordinary things were performed in his behalf. He nevertheless thought only of
humbling himself, and told all who spoke to him of
the event that they ought to regard it as an effect of
the protection God afforded his poor. He even derived
edification from the circumstance of the time at which
it happened, and recommended his patients to adore
Jesus Christ, Who, having been born on that day in
order to be the light of the world, had not refused to
give light and guidance to those who were toiling for
their benefit.

CHAPTER XXIV.

ON HIS LOVE OF POVERTY, HIS HUMILITY, AND HIS DISCERNMENT IN SPIRITUAL MATTERS.

A MAN who despised riches and all the conveniences
of life, who never kept any out of all the alms which
were placed in his hand, who, forgetting himself, was
ever thinking how he could do good to others; one
who, after the example of S. Paul, endured hunger,
thirst, fasting, cold, and nakedness, at the same time
that by his cares and constant labours he was delivering
others from them, such a man must, indeed, have had
a great love of poverty. Now John of God acted
in this manner. He would not hear of a marriage
or of an advantageous settlement in the world. He
refused the offer his uncle made him of all his property.
He always laboured for others, and never for himself.
Without appropriating anything to himself, he distributed the riches of a vast number of persons who

placed them at his disposal. He enriched whole families, and always lived in want of all things. Lastly, he refused himself even necessaries, whilst he was very liberal towards the poor, and granted them all that they could desire ; consequently it is just to conclude that he was full of love for poverty.

The manner in which he always acted proves also that he was very humble ; for he never sought to exalt or bring himself into notice. The lowest and most fatiguing employments were always those which he strove after. Although he had it in his power to rise in the world by his industry, and by the assistance he could have obtained from his relations and friends, he delighted in being unknown and forgotten by men. He was more eager for humiliation and contempt than ambitious men are for honours and dignities, and we can truly say that he literally fulfilled those words of S. Paul, "Do not mind high things, but consent to the humble." At the beginning of his conversion, that is to say when he gave himself in good earnest to God, he showed that he was truly humble at heart, and had nothing but contempt for himself ; for being one day in a church, a taper was given him in order that with several others he might follow the Blessed Sacrament, which was to be carried to a sick person. He did so, but with much confusion, and with a deep feeling of his own vileness, and as soon as he returned to the church, he said to the sacristan upon giving him back his taper, "My brother, you were mistaken in offering this to me ; so great a sinner as I am is not worthy of such an honour, and does not deserve to approach so near to so holy and tremendous a mystery." And he carefully avoided being thus employed again, and for some time afterwards always left the church when he saw that such a ceremony was about to be performed.

As words and conversations serve to make known a man's feelings and inward desires, Jesus Christ assuring us that the mouth speaks from the abundance of the heart, we can again say that John of God was very humble and devoid of self, for he never spoke of himself but in terms which showed that he looked upon himself as the last of all men ; he called himself on all occasions an abominable sinner, and of his own accord he published all that he knew to be capable of lessening the good opinion men had of him. If it happened that something was said in his praise, he took care to add to it circumstances which tended to show that he did not deserve the praises that were given him ; and every time that he succeeded in any undertaking or performed any remarkable action, he failed not to give all the glory of it to God, and to declare that he had hardly any part in it, being only a weak instrument which it pleased His Sovereign Majesty to make use of. We need not here repeat what we related at the conclusion of the preceding chapter respecting the two lights which God sent to guide him on Christmas Eve ; but we must beg our readers to recal to their memory what we said in the first book, of the acts of folly and extravagance which he strove to exhibit before the whole city of Granada, for in them we have a convincing proof of his profound humility. He feared not to expose himself to public ridicule, to pass for a madman, and to have the finger of scorn pointed at him, which is one of the greatest sacrifices we can make to the divine Majesty. Numbers of persons are found ready to offer Him their riches and even their bodies, but where are those to be found who willingly consent to be deprived of the honour and reputation they enjoy in the world, and who divest themselves of them in order to live in contempt and abjection? This may be regarded as a masterpiece of humility, for John of God could not have done more in order to express in his own person the foolishness of the Cross of Jesus Christ, which has saved the world, and confounded the false wisdom which reigned on earth.

Although he was not instructed in the sciences, nor formed in the schools, on account of all his journeys and his laborious kind of life, we may nevertheless say that he had great lights and knowledge, for to know Jesus, and Jesus crucified, is no mean science, and S. Paul boasted of having no other. Now the whole course of his life makes us clearly see that he had this knowledge perfectly, and had made very great progress in it, because all his actions were nothing but a continual imitation of the Cross of this Divine Saviour. It is scarcely necessary to say more on this subject, but as special proofs of his discernment in spiritual matters are to be found in some of his letters, we are sure our readers will not be sorry to see an abridgment of some of them.

Writing to the Duchess of Sesa, he speaks to her with much clearness on Faith, Hope, and Charity; he gives her accurate definitions of these three virtues; he wisely tells her that we owe charity to our own souls first, and then to our neighbour; and he points out to her that the duty we owe to our souls consists principally in cleansing and sanctifying them, which is agreeable to what S. Peter says, " Animas vestras castificantes "—" Purifying your souls in the obedience of charity." He explains to her also the four cardinal virtues, and describes their effects and properties. "Prudence," says he, "teaches us to conduct ourselves in all things with wisdom, and to follow the advice of the ancients, and of those who have had more experience than we have. Justice consists in giving to every one that which belongs to him, to God that which is God's, and to the world that which is the world's. Temperance teaches us to observe due moderation in eating and drinking, in our dress and in all that concerns the body. Fortitude renders us generous and constant in the service of God; enables us to be as joyful under labours, tribulations, and sickness, as in prosperity and health, and to thank God equally in both states."

He recommended her so to distribute her time as to devote a part of it to prayer, a part to work, and the rest to the necessities of the body. With respect to prayer, he advises her, as soon as she awakes in the morning, to give thanks to Jesus Christ for all the benefits and favours she is continually receiving from Him; to thank Him particularly for having formed her in His own image, and called her to a knowledge of the true Faith; to beg His pardon not only for her own sins, but also for all those which men commit against Him, and to offer up her prayers for all the world. He wishes her to work with her hands, to employ her time in some fitting and useful occupation, in order that she might avoid idleness, which is the parent of all vices, and that she might say with S. Paul, that she ate not her bread without earning it. Speaking of the necessities of the body, he tells her to take care of herself in order that she might serve God, as we feed an animal which we wish to make use of. Lastly, he recommends her continually to bear in mind three things : death which no one can avoid, which destroys all that is beautiful in this world, and permits us to carry away with us nothing but a poor winding-sheet; hell, where we shall have to endure eternal punishment for pleasures which last only for a moment, if we do not take care to do penance for them, whilst we are still on earth ; and Paradise, where God has prepared for us a glory and happiness so great and so extraordinary that eye has not seen nor ear heard, nor the heart of man ever conceived anything like to it.

We have another letter which he wrote to the same Duchess, in which he recommends her to pray whilst going to bed at night, to make acts of faith before going to sleep, and to say the Credo, the Pater, Ave, and Salve Regina. He tells her she was bound to take care that all her servants said prayers every day. He points out to her that we ought always to watch, because we have to fight all day against the world, the devil, and our own flesh, and because we know not at what hour the Lord will call us to Himself. He goes still further, for he tells her to watch even in her sleep, in order to avoid being surprised by the evil spirit, and he reminds her that the heart of a Christian ought never to sleep ; in which he only follows the thought of the spouse in the Canticles, who says, " I sleep, and my heart watcheth." He recommends her to meditate often on all the circumstances in the Life and Passion of Jesus Christ, in order to find in them instruction and consolation under the sufferings and tribulations to which she would be exposed. Lastly, he briefly lays before her the principles which are found in Scripture and in the holy Fathers respecting alms; he tells her that they wipe away sins as water extinguishes fire; that they give us the means of practising a holy usury with God, since He gives us back much more in heaven than we lend Him on earth; and that, properly speaking, they are only a kind of restitution which we make to Jesus Christ, because the goods which we distribute amongst the poor, who are His members, belong to Him, and have been given us by His liberal hand.

We could dwell still longer on some of his other letters, in which we see that he was deeply instructed in the truths of our religion, and well able to strengthen the piety of those who placed confidence in him. But this would lead me too far; what we have said is sufficient to show my readers that he had in reality great lights, and that if he had studied the sciences, he would have made great progress in them; but he had made the Cross, the Sufferings, the Passion and Love of Jesus Christ his only study, and these were sufficient for his own edification, and for the consolation of his patients and his poor.

CHAPTER XXV.

ON THE KNOWLEDGE HE HAD OF FUTURE EVENTS, AND OF THE SECRETS OF CONSCIENCES.

ALTHOUGH a man may be very holy and virtuous without being able to penetrate into the future, and into the secrets of consciences, still we will write a chapter to show that John of God had received this gift and prerogative from heaven, because it adds much to his glory, and gives us a high idea of his merit. Speaking first of the knowledge he had of future events, we have an incontestable proof of it in his letters. He wrote one to the Duchess of Sesa, to assure her that God would bless her marriage by the birth of children, which she asked of Him, and it was believed he had had a revelation of it, for all the circumstances he had foretold came exactly to pass.

On another occasion he made a similar promise to a lady of quality; for when he was at Toledo, Eleonora de Mendoza, the wife of Don Alvarez, earnestly recommended herself to his prayers, and entreated him to ask children from God for her; he promised her he would do so, and as a pledge for the performance of his word he left her his walking-stick. His prediction proved true, for at the time he mentioned this good lady had the consolation of seeing herself a mother. He not only foretold the birth of children, but he foresaw their dispositions and the kind of lives they would lead, of which he warned their parents. Thus happening one day to be begging in Granada, at the house of Maria Suarez, he saw her little daughter; placing his hand on her head, he looked at her a long time, and delivered an opinion respecting her very similar to that which S. Germain of Auxerre formed respecting S. Geneviève when he saw her as he was going into England, for he announced to her mother that she would one day be a great servant of God, and would possess eminent piety, and he told her it was her duty to give her a good education in order to co-operate with the designs of God on her. His prophecy was afterwards fulfilled, for this young lady made daily fresh progress in vir-

tue, and arrived at so high a degree of perfection, that
her directors judged her worthy to communicate every
day, and after long perseverance she died in the
odour of sanctity.

On other occasions he made known to fathers the
destinies of their children. When the Caballero de la
Vega was conversing with him on the state of his
family, and acquainting him with the measures he
wished to take in order to educate his two sons for the
highest posts at court, he gave him to understand that
Divine Providence destined one of them for the Church,
and that the other would live in the world. Whilst
waiting for the alms he was in the habit of receiving
at the house of Don Jago de Agrega, he began to
sketch a sword on the wall, and when asked why he
did so, he answered that he wished to show that God
would reward Don Jago for his alms, by leaving in the
hands of his sons and nephews the sword of Justice,
which they would bear with as much honour and reputation as he had. All this took place afterwards,
and it was then seen that he had the gift of prophecy.

Whilst lying sick in one of the infirmaries of his
hospital, he learnt by revelation that a young lad who
slept in a room higher up than his own was near his
end and would soon breathe his last; he therefore informed an infirmarian of it, telling him to place a
blessed candle in his hands, and this had no sooner
been done than the lad died. On another occasion,
when visiting his patients, he found one whom no one
thought to be in danger of death; but God made
known to him that his sickness was very dangerous,
and that he would soon die; he therefore declared
aloud that he ought to have extreme unction given

him; but the sick man, not thinking himself in such great danger, would not receive it; nevertheless he died a moment afterwards, and God declared by evident proofs that he was punished in the other world in the flames of purgatory for having neglected to follow the advice of the father of the poor.

Having been informed of the death of others, we may well believe that the time of his own was not concealed from him. Accordingly we have been assured on trustworthy authority that several times during his life-time he said he should die between a Friday and a Saturday, and we shall see in the next book that he was not deceived. He also foretold that his Order would in a short time make great progress in the world, and that it would spread on all sides to the benefit and comfort of the poor; so that we cannot doubt that he had a knowledge of future events on several occasions. We have also certain proofs that God often revealed to him the secret thoughts of persons, and discovered to him the whole of their consciences, as in the following instances. Being one day in his hospital, at the bedside of a sick man who had been for eight days in a kind of agony, he perceived that he still had some intelligence left, and therefore said, " Unhappy man, why will you not confess your sin? Do you not see the devil waiting to cast your soul down into hell?" The man, surprised at hearing him speak in this manner, asked how he came to know that he had not confessed his sins. " I know it," replied John of God, "and in order to leave no doubt of it on your mind, I say that you have two wives, and besides this, that you are contaminated by a crime still more horrible, of which you were ashamed to accuse yourself to a priest. I warn you to reflect on your state, to confess as soon as possible all your crimes, which are already known to God, and to strive without any delay to save your soul, which is on the point of perishing for ever." These words greatly astonished the dying man, who thought his life was known to no one, and he immediately asked for a priest, to whom he made an exact confession of his sins. He then died with many signs of true contrition.

On another occasion a woman in his hospital fell into despair, and was continually calling upon persons to drag her along the streets and across the square called Vivarambla. John, hearing her shouting in the middle of the night, and fearing lest it might disturb his other patients, went up and asked what was the matter with her that she cried out in this manner. "I want them," she replied, "to drag me into the place called Vivarambla." The servant of God then said, "If you had driven the devil from your heart, and had confessed the sinful state in which you have lived ten years, you would not have such a strange desire, but would be at rest." She then owned she had lived in sin for ten years, and that during all that time she had not approached the Sacrament of penance. He instructed her how to make a good confession, and exhorted her to beg pardon of God for all her sins; he spoke much to her of the goodness with which He receives sinners who return to Him, begging His mercy with a contrite and humble heart, and placed her in the hands of a confessor. All her excitement immediately subsided—she received the grace of reconciliation and died peaceably.

The servant of God whilst walking one day in the city, saw two young men talking together. Our Lord made known to him that they had already conceived in their heart the detestable sin which once drew fire from heaven on the five cities, and that they were about to commit it. He immediately accosted them, and spoke so forcibly on the enormity of the sin they were meditating, that they detested it themselves and resolved to do real and true penance for it. Lastly, a short time before his death he was warned in a revelation, that a poor weaver was on the point of hanging himself in despair; though he was very ill he went in great haste, and found him in a field under a tree apart from the rest, to which he had already attached a rope. He sternly rebuked him, and represented to him the heinousness of the sin he was on the point of committing, and, seeing that he was only reduced to this extremity because he had no means of supporting his wife and children, he promised to assist him and to recommend him to devout persons, who would not fail to befriend him, thus saving his life, and restoring him to his family. From all these circumstances we may conclude that he had that gift of prophecy and of discernment of the secrets of consciences which is granted only to extraordinary saints, whom God wishes to distinguish and render illustrious in His Church.

CHAPTER XXVI.

ON HIS LOVE OF GOD.

ALL that we have hitherto related will suffice to convince our readers of the great love our Saint had for God. Indeed all his actions bore that character, and all his words breathed the love of God, of which his entire disinterestedness and detachment from all earthly goods was the consequence. The love of God is the soul and life of all Christian virtues, and without it there is nothing good in man. His mortified and penitent life, his continual prayer, his many labours. for the benefit of his neighbours, his entire confidence in the goodness and providence of God, were all derived from this source. But we will give some instances, which will be so many additional proofs of his great love of God. Every time that he heard His holy Name pronounced he prostrated himself on the ground, and, after kissing it, said with wonderful fervour, "I adore Thee, my Lord and my all." Judging from his outward appearance we should say he was continually occupied with God, that he always adored Him in his heart, and that he tenderly loved Him. All who looked. at him were edified by his deportment, which inspired respect and devotion at the same time. He always carried a crucifix in his sleeve, as we have frequently mentioned ; he kissed it very often with extraordinary devotion, and he also made those kiss it who spoke to him, saying, "Kiss the image of the adorable Jesus: remember that the blood which flows from His wounds is the only remedy for your sins ; pray Him to apply the merit of it to you, and do not abuse His goodness by committing fresh sins."

The royal prophet has said " My soul thirsteth after the living God : when shall I come and appear before the face of God ? My tears have been my bread day and night ; whilst it is said to me daily,—Where is thy God ?"—Ps. xli. 2, 3. It was the same with our Saint, who had an ardent desire to be united with his God, to whom he said, with the spouse in the Canticles, "Draw me : we will run after Thee, to the odour of Thy

ointments."—Cant. i. 3. He complained to Him of the
length of his exile and pilgrimage, often crying out,
"How lovely are Thy tabernacles, O Lord of Hosts : my
soul longeth and fainteth for the courts of the Lord, my
heart and my flesh have rejoiced in the living God."—
Ps. lxxxiii. 2, 3. He grieved, and his soul lived in continual bitterness because he saw himself detained on
earth.

When he read the Passion of Jesus Christ in St. John's
Gospel, he could not contain himself, but shed such
floods of tears, and uttered such deep sighs that it was
easy to see that his heart was penetrated with a lively
sorrow for the sufferings of his Divine Master, and that
he could say with the great apostle " *Christo confixus sum
cruci.*"—"I am crucified with Christ." He was even often
obliged to leave off reading, for the fervour of his zeal
caused him to utter the following words, full of spiritual unction : "Is it possible that the Son of God should
endure such great pains for us, and that we should
show so little gratitude for them ? He longed to die
for us, and we refuse to die to ourselves, and to renounce our evil habits. Oh, how horrible and frightful a monster is sin. I detest it with my whole heart,
and would gladly suffer death to keep men from it."

Whilst working in his hospital or walking in the
streets, certain transports were remarked in him, and
he was heard to utter broken sentences and devout
aspirations of his soul towards heaven, making it
evident that his heart was an ardent furnace, in which
the fire of charity was continually burning, and that
this was the cause of those sentences which he uttered,
without thinking of them ; and thus in spite of himself
he manifested those inward feelings which he would
have wished to conceal entirely from men.

As we always feel a lively sorrow whenever outrages are committed against those whom we love greatly, it was impossible for our Saint not to be much pained every time that God, Whom he so ardently loved, was offended. Accordingly his biographer relates that he was inconsolable when he saw sins committed in his presence. Whilst returning one day from the city, with a basket of provisions on his shoulders, which he had begged for his poor, he pushed unawares against a gentleman, who turned round in anger, because his dress was a little splashed by the mud. John of God immediately apologized to him for it, but he was offended at being called "brother," and would not accept his apologies, but abused him in violent and blasphemous language, and gave him a severe blow. The holy man immediately began to weep and groan, not because he had been ill-treated, but because God had been offended, and His holy Name dishonoured, and he exclaimed, "O my Lord, I am the cause of this blasphemy! Strike me, my brother, strike me; I am very willing to bear the penalty of your crime." The gentleman hearing him speak in this manner, asked who he was, and, being told it was John of God, he repented of his passionate behaviour, and within an hour afterwards went to the hospital to beg his pardon, and to offer him an alms of fifty ducats. All these circumstances clearly shew that John bore a mortal hatred against sin, and consequently that he had a very great love of God.

CHAPTER XXVII.

ON HIS LOVE FOR THE POOR.

IT is almost needless to speak in this chapter of the love our Saint had for the poor, for his whole life is one continued proof of it. He laboured only for them ; on them he bestowed all his cares and gave himself entirely up to their service. He boasted of being their agent and advocate, he solicited the great on their behalf, he laid before them their distresses, wrote letters to induce them to bestow alms, he went to seek them in their palaces, and even at Court, to compel them to assist the poor, not allowing himself any rest whenever there was an opportunity of procuring them aid and doing them any good office. These words which he often uttered, are sufficient to show how greatly he loved them : "Oh, my God and my all," he used to say, " if I see Thee not in the poor, I will no longer look down on the earth, but will raise my eyes continually upwards to heaven, in order that by the light of faith I may contemplate Thee dwelling in the midst of Thy glory."

We have already seen that his charity induced him on several occasions to exchange clothes with beggars whom he met in the streets, and that one of the reasons why the Bishop of Tuy ordered him to dress in a different manner from the people in the world, was that he might no longer be able to deprive himself of his clothes in order to give them to the poor. We have seen that he never refused alms to those who asked it of him in the Name of God, and that to appear to labour under any distress was sufficient to obtain prompt assistance from him. We have also seen that during his visit to Valladolid he distributed at once to all who spoke to him of their misfortunes the money that was given him for his hospital at Granada, so that people found it necessary to give him letters of exchange only, in order to stop the flow of his liberality.

We will now relate further proofs of his love for the poor. Don Enriquez de Ribera, Marquis of Tarifa, was staying for some time at Granada, on matters of importance. John of God went to his house one evening to beg alms, and found him at play with other lords. He took advantage of this circumstance to speak to him of his poor, sayin that as he was playing, no doubt he had more money than he needed, and consequently that both he and all the company present had it in their power to bestow alms and give him something for his hospital which was in want. This skilful appeal made such an impression on the minds of the Marquis and the other gentlemen present that they all contributed to make up a purse of twenty-five ducats, and put it into his hands.

After his departure they spoke much about him and his charity, and the Marquis said he should like to try him to see what use he made of the alms that were given him. Accordingly he disguised himself, and changed his clothes from fear of being recognized, and the night being dark, posted himself where he knew John of God would pass whilst making his usual rounds. As soon as he saw him, he said: " Brother John, I am a gentleman, and have been staying a long time in this city in order to put an end to a law-suit which is of great importance to me, and I am now reduced to such want that I know not what to do. I fear lest poverty should compel me to commit some act of injustice and so offend God. Hence, having heard of the great liberality you shew towards all, I determined to seek you, in order to obtain relief from your compassion." John of God, who sought out the poor, and took long journeys to find them out, in order to relieve them, was not a man to reject a person whom he believed to be really in want, and whom Providence seemed to have sent to him. He consoled him in the best manner he could, promised to remember him, and to procure him assistance, and " whilst waiting," said he, " until I can do something more for you, accept these twenty-five ducats which have just been placed at my disposal," giving them in the purse in which he had received them. The Marquis, filled with admiration of such generosity, immediately returned to the other lords who were expecting him. He related to them what had passed, and shewed them the purse which the servant of God had returned to him. They were all much surprised, and gave great praise to the father of the poor : they regarded him as a man of extraordinary merit, and said that he must have great confidence in the Providence of God, since, though he had a large number of poor persons to support, he nevertheless was willing to give to one man so considerable a sum, which would have been very useful to him for his hospital. The Marquis, being very liberal, would not suffer this act to pass unrewarded, nor would he deprive the poor of the twenty-five ducats which had been given them. Accordingly the next day he went to the hospital, and after the customary salutations, smiled and said to the servant of God : " What, Brother John, they tell me you were robbed last night, and that your purse was taken from you. Tell me the whole truth, I should like to know how it happened?" When John of God assured him he had not been robbed, the Marquis interrupted him adding, "You cannot deny what I say, since the stolen property is in my hands, and I am myself the robber. Take back again your purse and the twenty-five ducats, and in addition here are one hundred and fifty dollars in gold of which I make you a present. Do not forget, if you please, to come every day to my house, for I have given orders to my steward to deliver to you every day, so long as I shall be in Granada, one hundred and fifty loaves, four sheep, and eight fowls for the dinner of your poor."

One night John of God found lying on the ground in the public square a poor person, who was so much deformed that he was more like a monster than a man. Any other person would have been frightened and have gone away, but John so loved the poor that, in whatever condition they might be, they always attracted his notice. Going up to him, therefore, he asked him if he wished to go to his hospital. The poor man answered that he did, only that he must be carried there, because he could not move, whereupon John immediately took him on his shoulders, and began to walk; but he did not go far without giving way under the burden, which was too much for his strength, so that he was obliged to stop to wipe the sweat off his brow, and to take breath. Before resuming his burden, he cried aloud in the spirit of prayer: "May the name of Jesus be my strength and protection." At these words this poor person uttered a loud cry and disappeared. This was enough to shew him that it was the devil who had assumed this hideous form in order to deceive him, and to inspire him with aversion for the poor, so as to deter him from carrying them thus upon his back. But the Spirit of Evil deceived himself, and made a mistake on this occasion, for nothing that had at all the appearance of poverty could disgust or discourage John. On the contrary this had great charms for him, and his charity made him close his eyes to all that was most opposed to his natural feelings every time that it was necessary to assist those who appeared to be forsaken and destitute of all support.

We could relate many other incidents of this kind, but there is no need to dwell on such proofs, since we have so noble and remarkable a one in the foundation of his hospital, for this holy house will be a lasting monument of his love for the poor. He wished to bring them into one place in order that he might be always with them, that he might see them at all hours, talk to them, console them, and shew them every possible care and attention. As we have already said, he took into his hospital every sick person without rejecting any. Pilgrims and strangers were also welcome, and he gave alms to a vast number of poor persons who were ashamed to beg. These different charities involved him in great expense, and, having hardly any income at all, he was often obliged to borrow. It sometimes happened that he was so deeply in debt that he was afraid to shew himself in public for fear of meeting his creditors, as he informs us in one of his letters, the originals of which are preserved in the Royal Hospital at Madrid. Still this did not diminish his zeal, for he always kept up the number of his charities without discontinuing any, because his love for the poor was unbounded.

What we have to relate in the next book will more fully convince our readers of his love for the poor; for they will see that this great Saint, even in the midst of accumulated maladies which finally caused his death, could never forget them, and that he recommended them to his archbishop and to all who honoured him with a visit. He specified to his dear brother Martin all that he was to do for their comfort, he gave them his blessing, and to the end of his days he preserved the tenderness of a father for them, and consecrated to their service the last moments of his life.

BOOK III.

CONTAINING AN ACCOUNT OF HIS DEATH, OF THE
HONOURS PAID TO HIS MEMORY, AND OF THE
PRODIGIES WHICH GOD WORKED IN ORDER TO
MAKE KNOWN HIS SANCTITY TO MEN.

CHAPTER I.

THE BEGINNING OF HIS ILLNESS.

JOHN OF GOD was by nature strong and robust, and of
a good constitution, so that to all appearance he was
likely to live a long time; but his strength soon left him,
and the infirmities of old age came upon him prema-
turely; his powers forsook him by degrees, so that
he was almost unable to do anything, at a time when
it was expected he would have laboured more than
ever for the poor, who regarded him as their father
and protector. This was no wonder, for his many austerities, fasts, vigils, journeys, and laborious attendance
on the sick were more than sufficient to enfeeble the
strongest body, and to destroy the most robust health.
It is even a matter of astonishment that he should
have lived fifty-five years, and that he did not die
soon after the establishment of his hospital.

Though he had become very weak, and no longer possessed the same strength as when in the vigour of life, he
nevertheless continued to perform his usual duties;
he went out begging, kept vigils, and employed himself both in and out of the house. He paid no attention to his own infirmities; his zeal came to the
assistance of his weak and failing nature, and his
charity compelled him to do things which no one
would have dared to have required of him, because
they appeared to be infinitely above human strength.
But at last he was obliged to give way; and, his body

being no longer able to endure the fatigue to which his courage every day exposed it, he was forced to take a little rest, to keep his bed for some days, and to have recourse to remedies.

Not being in the habit of sparing himself, or of heeding his own sufferings, he did not take the time that was necessary for the re-establishment of his health. An event happened which obliged him to go out sooner than perhaps he would have done, for he was told that the river Xenil had overflowed its banks and was carrying away much wood. He would not allow this opportunity of benefiting his poor to be lost. He therefore left his bed without considering that he was still an invalid, and, taking with him one of his brothers and a youth who served in the hospital, he went to the river-side to collect as much as he could of the wood which would have been dispersed and lost in the fields. Whilst engaged in this laborious work, he perceived that the boy whom he had brought to work with him had gone too far and was being carried away by the stream. His ardent charity gave him no time to deliberate; but he immediately threw himself into the water with his clothes on, and began to swim in order to save the boy's life, but he could not reach him, for he was already very far off, and the waves were rapidly overwhelming him. The grief he felt at this terrible accident, the cold he suffered in the water, and all the fatigue he underwent on this occasion weakened him very much, and greatly increased his illness, so that he had the utmost difficulty in reaching his hospital, where he arrived hardly able to stand. He passed the night in great suffering, the death of this poor boy constantly recurring to his mind, and his pain being intense. When it was day he wished to get up, though his brothers did all they could to prevent him; and, telling one of them to accompany him, he went off to the houses of all those to whom he thought he owed anything, in order to reckon with them and write down in a book all the sums for which he might be indebted to them. On his return he had another account-book brought out in which all the furniture of the hospital was noted down: he heard it read out, signed every page, and put his hand to it in order to certify its authenticity. There was still another book, containing the regulations to be observed in his hospital, and some constitutions, pointing out what the brothers were obliged to do during the day, and the different employments they were to be engaged in, which he also signed, and then he delivered these three books into the hands of Antony Martin in the presence of all the brothers, in order that they might know the debts with which he was encumbered, and that they might be careful during his illness to conduct themselves as if he were always with them, and had his eye upon them in all their occupations. This done, he returned to his bed, feeling very weak and ill. But hardly had he done so when he was told that the archbishop wanted him and required his presence. Anyone else would have excused himself on account of the state in which he was; but he did not think of his health where obedience to the commands of his superiors was concerned, and he felt certain that he could not employ it better than in sacrificing it to obedience. He therefore got up immediately and went, though with much pain, to the archbishop's palace. Being brought into the prelate's sitting-room, he threw himself on the floor to beg his blessing, and remained on his knees as usual while listening to what he said to him, though he repeatedly made him a sign to rise.

The archbishop was induced to send for John of God, because he had been told by some persons who were unacquainted with the manner in which matters were conducted in the hospital, and who perhaps were acting under the influence of ill-will, that he received into it poor persons who were quite undeserving, that he relieved families in the city who were able to gain their own livelihood, that he also supported women of bad character, who turned him into ridicule, and made a bad use of the good he was doing for them. He thought it was his duty to enquire into all these matters, and to speak to the servant of God about them ; accordingly, he related to him all that he had heard, and represented to him that he ought not to receive into his hospital persons of bad character who might give scandal; the alms of the faithful, he said, were not intended to maintain sinners in their evil habits ; he ought to take care not to encourage them in idleness by bestowing alms on them ; and he might find plenty of really poor persons without wasting his time in taking charge of common vagabonds; in regard to the dissolute women whom he supported, he ought to be careful lest he should be only affording them the means of continuing their evil courses, and though it was a very meritorious work to labour for their conversion, yet that there was also harm in encouraging their wickedness in however slight a degree.

John of God, after listening respectfully to all his re-monstrances, made the following wise and discreet answer: "My most illustrious prelate and superior, when it shall please you to visit the hospital you will not find in it the abuses and disorders persons have told you of, and you will acknowledge that I alone ought to be driven out of it. God has placed me in it to labour for the comforting of the neglected poor, and the conversion of sinners who are groaning under the tyranny of the devil. If I received into it the good only, our infirmaries would soon be empty, and I should have no sinners to convert. I know that I do not perform my duty as I ought, nor correspond to the grace of my vocation, and therefore I must tell your excellency that I am not worthy of such an office, that I am a fraudulent consumer of the bread of the poor, and deserve to be driven out of this holy house." The archbishop hearing John of God speak in this manner tenderly embraced him and said: "My brother and most dear son in Jesus Christ I am perfectly satisfied with what you tell me. Some persons wished to calumniate you to me, but I am fully persuaded of the sincerity of your intentions, and of your admirable conduct. Return to your hospital and follow up the good inspirations which God sends you. I invest you with all the authority which my position gives me over your house, being confident that you will only use it for the glory of God and the good of the poor, and I promise never more to listen to what may be said against you."

The servant of God having heartily thanked the prelate, immediately returned to his hospital, being in great pain owing to his illness. After his return he seemed so tranquil and collected, and such serenity shone in his countenance, that no one would have perceived that he had been justifying himself against his calumniators. In fact his humility and patience were so great that injuries and calumnies in no way disturbed him, because his heart loved God alone, sought only to do His Will, and was entirely disengaged from all temporal concerns.

CHAPTER II.

CONTINUATION OF HIS ILLNESS. BY AN ORDER FROM THE ARCHBISHOP HE IS REMOVED INTO THE HOUSE OF DONA ANNA OSSORIO, IN ORDER THAT GREATER ATTENTION MAY BE PAID TO HIM.

As soon as he reached the hospital he went to bed. in order to recover from the fatigue he had gone through, and to obtain relief from his pain, which was very great. He saw clearly from what was going on within him, that the time was drawing near when the Divine Majesty had determined to take him out of this world, at which he was greatly rejoiced, and he pronounced in the depths of his heart those words of the royal prophet, " Lætatus sum in hic quæ dicta sunt mihi, In domum Domini ibimus—I was glad when they said unto me, We will go into the house of the Lord." Still he would not tell his brothers of the presentiment he had of his approaching death, for fear of grieving them, but only assembled them around his bed, in order that he might have the consolation of conversing with them. When they had all come into his cell, he turned himself towards them, and ex-pressed the greatest kindness and love for them, he exhorted them to peace and union, recommended his poor to them, upon whom he begged them to bestow every possible attention. He told them to obey An-tony Martin as they had obeyed himself, and he an-nounced to them that he appointed him to occupy his place during his illness, and also to be his successor in case it should please God to call him to Himself. With tears in his eyes he begged their pardon for the bad example he had given them, and for all the faults he had committed in their presence ; he protested that if it pleased our Lord to restore him his health, he would strive with all his might to correct himself, and that he hoped by the grace of God they would then see a marked change in him. His brothers could not hear such tender and touching words without tears ; they begged his pardon for the want of docility they had shown in not following all the lessons he had given them, and they all promised to employ the remainder of their days in the service of the poor, and never to abandon them. They entreated him to intercede with God for them, and to obtain for them the graces they stood in need of, that they might duly perform the functions of their ministry. They then withdrew, fearing lest their sighs and tears might affect him too much.

His illness did not at all abate his zeal and activity in the cause of the poor. Not being able to go into the city himself to beg for them, he sent notes and letters to persons of his acquaintance, and to all those who were in the habit of giving him alms, requesting them not to discontinue their contributions, or forget his hospital. God blessed his endeavours, and the amount of alms collected was not diminished ; on the contrary, the nobles and citizens no sooner heard of his illness than they offered to assist his poor, and supply them with all kinds of provisions with greater generosity than ever. Thus he had the satisfaction of seeing everything going on as usual, notwithstanding his own weak state of health ; and, being filled with joy at this, he adored the Divine Providence which always protects those who trust it, and is able to succour them when there appears to be least hope for them. Doña Anna Ossorio, the wife of Don Garzia of Pisa, and a person of great merit, had been in the habit of sharing in the good works of the servant of God, and when she heard of his illness she immediately gave up every other occupation to go and visit him, for she felt sure that, though very attentive in waiting upon other sick people, very indulgent towards them, and ready to do anything for their comfort, yet that he would deprive himself of everything, would deny himself the smallest comforts, and treat himself with the greatest rigour. Such indeed was the case, for she found him in his cell, dressed in his usual manner, lying on some boards, with only a mat for a mattress, a torn cloak for a counterpane, and for a pillow the basket in which he was in the habit of collecting alms. Besides this, she saw him surrounded by a number of poor persons, who pained him by the sight of their sufferings, and increased his illness by their groans and importunate cries.

Hence, she saw the necessity of removing him from the hospital, for so long as he remained there it would be impossible for him to have any rest, distracted as he would be by the cares of its management, and unable to obtain such remedies as were necessary for his restoration to health. But knowing his character she felt certain that he would never leave his poor unless compelled to do so, and therefore she immediately took measures to secure the object she had in view. She sent to Don Pedro Guerrers, Archbishop of Granada, to inform him of the Saint's condition, representing to him the impossibility of his being properly attended to so long as he remained in the hospital amongst the poor, and begging permission to remove him into her own house, where greater attention might be paid him. The prelate knew our Saint's character too well to suppose that he would ever be induced to leave his hospital without an express command to that effect, and he therefore immediately issued a written order commanding him to obey Doña Anna in all things as he would himself, and to do all that the physicians required of him.

Whilst the order was being prepared at the archbishop's palace, Doña Anna sent away from the Saint the poor that were crowding round him, and ordered a carriage to be in readiness to convey him away. In order to induce him to move, she reminded him that he never would obtain any rest in his hospital, for that new distractions would constantly arise, and, the poor being always about him, he would have no peace, and therefore that it was his duty to consent to be removed to her house, where he might in a short time regain his health and strength, and then resume his usual occupations. He showed, however, by his answer, how much he was pained by the proposal of deserting his poor. "What, my sister," said he, "shall I desert the poor whom God has placed under my charge, and for whose sake He permits me still to live? The very thought of such a thing fills me with horror. I thank you for your kindness, but, believe me, if I accepted it I should be acting very wrongly. If this sickness is to end in my death, what better place can I wish to die in than this hospital? and, if my health is to be restored, where shall I regain it more profitably than in the house of God? I know your piety, my good sister, and the devotion and good order of your household, so that your house is truly a house of prayer, and it is this which makes me think myself unworthy of being taken into it. Do not, therefore, urge me any longer to accept your offer. If you did but know how miserable a sinner I am, you would think me utterly undeserving your compassion."

The lady, seeing that her entreaties were unavailing, showed him the archbishop's order which had just arrived, and at the same time told him that everything was prepared for his removal. Then he no longer resisted, but, entirely resigning his own will, he only said: "The Son of God obeyed His Father unto death, even unto the death of the cross, and His most unworthy servant John of God shall to the last moment of his life by his own blind obedience adore and honour that of his Redeemer. Only allow me, madam, to call together my brothers, that I may tell them what they are to do in my absence." As soon as they were assembled around him, he expressed to them his grief at leaving them, and told them that nothing but obedience to the archbishop's express command could induce him to make such a sacrifice; he then gave them his blessing, and exhorted them to persevere in their obedience, to observe the rules he had given to them, and to acknowledge Antony Martin as their superior. He astonished them all by the firm tone of voice in which he spoke, and then leaving his cell he went to prostrate himself before the Blessed Sacrament, to offer his body, soul and life to the sovereign Lord of heaven and earth. He was so long at prayer that they were obliged to interrupt him in order to put him into the carriage which was waiting. The poor showed their grief at the departure of their benefactor from the hospital by their tears and sighs. Those who had more strength than

the rest got out of their beds and ran after him, in
order to stop the carriage and prevent him from
leaving them. Many of them, like the disciples of
S. Martin, going down on their knees, said : "Dear
Father, why do you abandon us? under whose care will
you leave us? and what will become of us when you
are gone?" Some in their beds called upon them not
to take John of God from them ; whilst others, unable
to make themselves heard, watched him as he was
departing, and with tears in their eyes stretched out
their arms towards him.

The servant of God, seeing all their grief,
sighed deeply, and looking up towards heaven
said to them : " God knows, my children, that
I had a great desire to end my days amongst you ; but,
since He wishes me to die without the consolation of
having you around me, His holy Will be done." Then
giving them all his blessing, he said : " Remain in
peace, my children ; and, if we are no longer to see
each other, at least pray to our Lord for me."

At these words they all again began to weep, and to
speak to him in so touching a manner that he could
no longer refrain from shedding tears ; his heart was
filled with such grief that he nearly fainted away.
It was necessary to take him into the open air and
sprinkle wine over his face in order to recover him ;
as soon as he had a little returned to himself Doña
Ossorio ordered the carriage to move on, lest his
affliction might bring on another fainting fit.

There were fresh difficulties in the streets, for the
crowd of people was so great that it was impossible to
proceed ; all had left their houses to come out to see him.
Nothing was heard but sighs and lamentations. Some
regretted the loss of so great a man ; others were

anxious to see him; many recommended themselves to his prayers, and all desired to get his blessing and bid him a last farewell. It was necessary therefore to send for a body of guards to make a way through the crowd and to keep off the throng, and even then it was with great difficulty that they reached Doña Ossorio's house, on account of the frequent and unexpected obstructions, which were the marks of the love and veneration the people had for him. We may truly say he went forth from his hospital amid public acclamation, and to his death as it were to his triumph; and such in reality it was for him, for he left this earth, which is a place of misery and exile, and was about to enter the heavenly Sion, there to reign for ever and receive a crown of everlasting glory.

CHAPTER III.

WHAT TOOK PLACE DURING THE FIRST DAYS THAT JOHN OF GOD PASSED IN DOÑA OSSORIO'S HOUSE.

THERE was grief in the whole city of Granada when the illness of John of God was publicly known. Every one wept for him as if he were already dead; he was the sole topic of conversation; people spoke of his wonderful charity, and compared him to the most distinguished saints; they related all that he had done for the poor; they declared that the establishing of his hospital alone was a sufficient proof of his extraordinary merit, and they called him the father and protector of all the afflicted. Consequently as soon as they heard that his life was in danger, they all gave themselves up to grief, fearing that they were about to lose him. The inhabitants went in crowds to Doña Ossorio's house to visit him, to console him, and to offer him their services. So many went to see him that he had not a moment to himself, and his state became much worse. When, however, an attempt was made to prevent people from disturbing him, they said he was their father, and they had a right to see and speak to him; they even broke open the door, and went up into his bed-room in spite of all opposition. Guards, therefore, were placed around the house in order to forbid entrance and keep the people off.

In the meantime the Municipal Council met, and, wishing to show him every mark of honour, nominated deputies to express to him the great affliction of the whole city on account of his illness. The deputies immediately set out, and entering his room told him that they had come to assure him of the heart-felt sorrow of all the citizens at his illness; they declared that all were anxious to console him, and that all the city possessed was at his disposal; they proceeded to say that they had witnessed his charity to their poor, and that they were commissioned to thank him for it, that they would never forget his virtues, and the good example he had set them, and that they begged him to remember them when he was in heaven. John of God replied: "I am a miserable sinner; you have seen my acts of indiscretion and folly, and the scandal of my transports has reached you. It is true that the goodness of God has made use of me to comfort your poor; but it is through your alms that I have been able to do so. If I have the happiness of possessing God in heaven, I promise never to forget your charity. I recommend to your care my hospital, and all my brothers who have been united with me in the management of it." He could say no more because of his tears and sighs.

The deputies also wept and begged his blessing both for themselves and the whole city. At first he made some difficulty about granting what they asked, saying that he was only a sinner, and that it did not belong to him to bless others : as he was making these excuses, he saw the archbishop entering his room, whereupon he said, "Here is our excellent pastor and common father ; we will all receive a blessing from him." The prelate, going up to him, ordered him to grant this consolation to them and the whole city, saying : "Isaac, Jacob and the other patriarchs, when on their deathbeds, did not refuse to bless their children : all the inhabitants of Granada are your children ; bless them therefore before you depart from them, and by this show that you love them with the same tenderness as the poor in your hospital."

After speaking thus he went into another room in order to give John an opportunity of finishing his conference with the deputies. In the meantime he inquired of the physicians what their opinion was respecting his illness. They declared him to be in a dangerous state, because his body was much wasted,—his fasts, austerities, and excessive labours having exhausted his strength and ruined his constitution. Returning therefore soon afterwards to his bedside, he spoke a long while to him in private ; he recommended him to think seriously of his condition and to search into his conscience ; he explained to him many very edify ing truths respecting the future life and the unspeakable happiness which the elect enjoy in heaven ; he exhorted him to patience under his sufferings, and constant submission to the decrees of Divine Providence ; he did not conceal from him that his sickness was dangerous, believing as he did that the knowledge of his approaching death would be a source of rejoicing to him, and that he frequently repeated to himself those words of the apostle, " I desire to be dissolved and to be with Christ ;" before leaving him, therefore, he told him to prepare for confession, and that he would come the next morning to give him the Sacraments.

This visit filled John of God with consolation and joy ; he was delighted to think that his archbishop should wish to attend him, and enter into the details of his life and conscience ; moreover, he hoped to derive much benefit from his spiritual discernment and knowledge. His mind was also full of those heavenly truths upon which he had been conversing, and the more he thought of them the more delight he felt. But what gave him the greatest joy was to see himself on the eve of completing his pilgrimage, and of entering the holy Sion. He looked upon himself as a captive whose fetters would soon be broken, as a traveller who was on the point of entering again his native country, and as a child about to throw himself into his father's arms. The thought of death, far from causing him any alarm, was the source of pure joy to him. He continually blessed God for His goodness in bringing it upon him, and for giving him a place in the mansions of heaven,—saying, " Rejoice, O my soul, for thou shalt soon satisfy thy thirst in a torrent of delights ; thou shalt see thy Beloved face to face, and shalt reap the fruits of thy labours." His only grief was that his last hour was so long delayed, and that he was still absent from the harbour after which he had so long been sighing.

As his poor and his beloved disciples were ever in his thoughts, he begged them to send brother Antony Martin, that he might make known to him his last wishes. As soon as he had arrived, John of God pointed out very clearly all that he would have to do for the perfect establishment of the order of which he had laid the foundation. He gave him all the instructions he believed to be necessary for the government of the hospital and the good of the poor. He told him that the Angel Raphael had revealed to him the day and hour of his death, but he forbade him to mention it before his decease. He assured him that the same angel, S. John the Evangelist, and the Blessed Virgin would always protect their order and their hospitals, and accordingly that their assistance ought often to be invoked. He foretold to him the troubles and difficulties he would himself meet with, and also that all his labours would terminate successfully. He exhorted him not to be discouraged at the difficulties which would be thrown in his way, to be always faithful to God, and to watch diligently over his brethren and his poor. He ordered him to write out immediately a memorandum of his debts, and to bring it to him very early the next morning, before the archbishop arrived. Lastly, he promised to pray for him, and often to make mention of him to God, so soon as, through the Divine mercy, he should have the happiness of enjoying His Sovereign Majesty in heaven.

Whilst he was speaking to Antony Martin, Doña Ossorio had an altar fitted up in his room according to the archbishop's order; it was decked with the richest ornaments from the prelate's chapel, and everything was made ready for the decent performance of the ceremony on the following day. This having been done, the sick man began now to live only for heaven, and already to taste the joys of eternity ; and, wishing to devote to God the last moments of his life, he desired to be left alone as much as possible. His pious hostess, willing to please him, faithfully acceded to his request, leaving with him one person only, who she knew would not in any way disturb him ; and it is through this person that we are acquainted with some of the graces and favours which he received that night—for instance, that the Angel Raphael and many other saints visited him, spoke to him, comforted him, and revealed many very important things to him.

CHAPTER IV.

THE ARCHBISHOP ADMINISTERS THE SACRAMENTS TO HIM.

BROTHER ANTONY MARTIN, with his heart full of obedience and affection towards John of God, thought of him the whole night, and repaired to his room very early in the morning as he had been commanded. Seeing, however, that he was in a state of great recollection, he dared not speak to him for fear of interrupting it : he therefore merely presented to him the list of the debts in silence.

Very soon afterwards arrived the archbishop, who, like a good shepherd, attended to all the wants of his flock, and would not suffer one of his most beloved sheep to leave this world without having given him with his own hand

the bread of angels, and fortified him with the salutary
and life-giving remedies which Jesus Christ has instituted in His Church. He first of all knelt down
before the altar which had been prepared, and prayed
there a considerable time; then he went up to the
sick man and asked him how he had spent the night;
what thoughts had occupied his mind, and if he were
prepared to make his confession. After having heard
his confession, he celebrated Mass, and gave him the
holy Viaticum, and then immediately afterwards
administered the Sacrament of Extreme Unction to
him in the presence of many persons. The ceremony
was very beautiful and edifying, for the prelate did
everything with great devotion and dignity; his exhortations were very touching; any one hearing him
speak would at once see that he was one of those in
whom the Word of God dwells abundantly, as S.
Paul says, and on whose hearts the truths they declare are firmly impressed.

The sick man on his part displayed all the virtues
to be expected in a dying person; he gave signs of
the deepest humility, protesting that he was unworthy
of the graces and mercies he was receiving; he publicly begged God's pardon for all the faults he had
committed, making a kind of accusation and amends
for them in presence of the bystanders. He answered
in a clear and distinct voice to all the archbishop's
questions, as well as to the prayers. He received the
body of Jesus Christ with so much fervour and zeal,
that all who were in the room blushed for shame,
thinking they had never approached this august
Sacrament with the requisite disposition. He showed
great submission to the Will of God, declaring that
he was willing to live or to die as it might please

Him. In short he spoke and acted in so Christian and devout a manner that all his words and actions were so many lessons to teach men to die well.

When all had gone out, the archbishop began to converse with John of God in private, and to urge him to tell him without disguise all that was passing within him, and if he had anything still upon his mind, that he might set it right, and restore him to perfect peace, as far as lay in his power. John of God, being a true child of obedience, and not in the habit of concealing anything from the anointed of the Lord, acknowledged that the Angel Raphael had come the night before to visit him, and to assure him that God was about to show mercy to him by withdrawing him from the world; that the Blessed Virgin had also honoured him with her presence, and had promised him that the Angel Raphael and S. John the Evangelist, who were with her at the time, should be the protectors of his order and of his poor. He then went on to say that so many graces and favours did not nevertheless prevent his having some anxiety, and that three things caused him uneasiness. The first was his cowardice and negligence in the service of God after having received from Him so many graces and mercies. The second was his leaving without assistance and support the poor of his hospital, the families in the city whom he was in the habit of relieving, and the abandoned women whom he had converted. The third was his not being able to pay all the debts he had been obliged to contract for the support of his poor and sick. The archbishop replied in the following manner : " My dear son, you do well to acknowledge that you have not served God as you ought to have done, and to be vexed at your cowardice and want of zeal ; but you ought to trust in the goodness and mercy of our Lord Jesus Christ, Who died for you, Who has washed and cleansed you in His Blood, and by the infinite merits of His Passion and dolours will supply for all your weaknesses and imperfections. Be not, therefore, afraid on account of your past life, for the charity of God will cover your faults and imperfections, and will grant you pardon for them. As for your poor and all whom you have been in the habit of assisting, do not be uneasy about them. I adopt them as my children, and will take care of them ; and, even though you had not spoken to me about them, I should not have abandoned them, since my duty obliges me to support them. Neither ought your debts to trouble you, for I give you my word that I will pay them, and your creditors shall lose nothing. Be not therefore disturbed, but patiently await the moment which will put an end to your labours and conflicts. Think only of your salvation : pray for me, and rest assured that I will fulfil the promises I have made you."

After having spoken thus to him, the archbishop gave him his blessing, and taking from him the list of his debts, went immediately to the hospital to give orders, and to confirm Antony Martin as superior of the brothers and of the poor. In fact he gave him power over all, commanding them to obey him as they would do himself, and publicly promising to continue his protection to the house, provided the rules and regulations of John of God were observed in it.

CHAPTER V.

HIS DEATH.

BEING thus fortified with the sacraments of the Church, and no longer having anything on his mind to disturb him after what the archbishop had said and promised to him, the sick man felt a holy impatience to complete the sacrifice of himself. His thoughts and words were of God only, and he anxiously awaited the time when he should be united with Him in a blessed eternity: he already saw with the eyes of faith the happiness of the next life; and, impatient to enter the heavenly Jerusalem, he could hardly be persuaded to allow any relief to be given to his bodily sufferings, or to take the remedies which were offered him, since he regarded all such things as useless for one who thought that he was near his end, and who no longer looked upon himself as belonging to this world.

He sometimes even complained of the kindness and attention shown him; he often refused what was given him, saying it was far too good for a poor miserable sinner like himself, who ought to be treated in a plainer and simpler manner, and his hostess was obliged to make him take what the physicians ordered by reminding him of the obedience the archbishop had laid upon him, when placing him under her care. Still he was pained at seeing so much done for him, and once when Doña Anna had brought him some broth, and told him to be very obedient and to do all that they required of him, he could not refrain from saying: "My good sister, you offer me this restorative, whereas the Jews gave our Lord Jesus

Christ nothing but gall to drink.   Consider what you
are doing, I entreat you ; so abominable a sinner as I
am ought not to be attended to with so much care ;
nevertheless, I thank you for your charity."   We see
by this how differently he thought from worldly-
minded persons, who imagine that when ill they may
with safe consciences allow their bodies every kind of
indulgence, as if they were not bound to mortify
themselves even during their sicknesses, that they
may appease the justice of God and present themselves
before His Throne at least as penitents, if they cannot
appear there as just and perfect.

Feeling that his strength was fast leaving him, and
that the end of his pilgrimage was at hand, he was
very glad to speak once more to Antony Martin and
his other brothers.   He first of all conversed with
each one in private, giving him the advice he thought
most suitable for him, and pointing out what he ought
to do for his own sanctification and the service of the
poor ; then, calling them all together, he spoke in the
following manner : " My brothers and dear children,
you see that I am about to depart this life.   If you
remember observing in me carelessness and negligence
in the service of God, want of zeal for His glory, and
unfaithfulness to my vocation, do not you give way to
the same faults, but be more diligent in performing
your duty.   Love the poor tenderly, regarding them
as your masters, and yourselves as their servants.   I
entreat you to obey cheerfully him whom I have
appointed to govern the hospital and to hold my
place in it.   Above all things be very careful to execute all the commands of our most illustrious prelate,
remembering that he stands to you in the place of
God, and is the depository of His power and authority.

Apply to him in all your necessities as to your Superior ; place confidence in his fatherly kindness, and respect him as your archbishop ; I am sure his charity will induce him to perform all that he has promised me. Receive my blessing for yourselves and for our poor. I beseech the divine Majesty to fill you with graces and to sanctify you more and more. Farewell, then, my dear children ; I look forward to the happiness of seeing you all in eternity, and I commend myself to your prayers."

The brothers were filled with grief, and could only answer by their tears and sighs. Being unable to speak, they showed by their gestures their readiness to do all he commanded them, and then returned to their ordinary duties in the hospital. The sick man, having thus bid them farewell, gave himself up entirely to prayer and to preparation for eternity. Those who were in his room heard his deep sighs, and the words full of fire and charity which he constantly repeated. Being entirely disengaged from all earthly things, he was inflamed with an ardent desire of heaven, and already ascended thither in spirit. He constantly repeated aloud verses of the psalms, and other pious ejaculations. As he was lying on his bed earnestly looking upwards into heaven it was evident that his soul waited only for the command of the Sovereign Lord of life and death to go and repose in His bosom. We may compare him to the great S. Martin, who, as Sulpicius Severus tells us, prayed continually with his eyes and hands lifted upwards towards heaven.

Sometime afterwards he begged Doña Anna Ossorio to read to him the Passion of our Lord Jesus Christ according to S. John, so that he might employ the remainder of his life in meditating on the last actions of our divine Saviour, and learn from Him how to suffer; that he might unite his own suffering with his, and beg of Him the grace of a happy death. The recital of the Passion produced an extraordinary effect upon him; his pale and exhausted countenance suddenly resumed its original freshness, and became so animated as to be more beautiful than ever. It was concluded from this that great things were passing within him. The recital of his Master's sufferings seemed to kindle his zeal; each circumstance in His Passion excited his love; the joy and tranquillity of his soul were diffused even over his body, giving to it in some sort a fresh vigour.

When Doña Anna had finished reading, he spoke to her and to all who were present. He represented to them the necessity we are under of suffering with Jesus Christ if we wish to share in His glory, and that our sole employment ought to be to fulfil in ourselves what is wanting of our Saviour's Passion. He exhorted them with so much firmness to love of suffering that they were all surprised, being at a loss to comprehend how a man who seemed to be at the point of death could still give such exhortations; but they had no reason to be astonished, for every time that he thought or spoke of the Cross his zeal was stirred up and received new strength.

As soon as he had finished speaking, he fell into a kind of ecstacy, which lasted a considerable time. When he returned to himself, he requested to be left alone in his room, that he might take a little rest. His request was immediately complied with, all thinking that he really desired to go to sleep. But it was not this rest that he sought for; he wished to be entirely alone with God, to converse with his Creator only, to open his heart freely to his divine Master, and to be able to give free vent to the tears which his love caused him to shed. And indeed through the doors and partitions they could hear him weeping bitterly, sighing and speaking in a voice interrupted by sobs; they heard him at one time call God to his aid, offer himself to Him, and protest that he submitted with all his heart to His holy Will; at another beg pardon for his sins, most tenderly implore His mercy, and offer his body as a victim of expiation to appease the justice of God, begging Him to burst asunder his bonds and admit him into his eternal rest.

Having spent some time in this edifying manner, as soon as he saw that the hour and moment of his death was at hand (for, as we have said above, he had a revelation of it beforehand) he rose from his bed, put on the habit of his order, and, taking in his hands the crucifix he used to carry in his sleeve, went and threw himself on his knees before the altar on which the archbishop had celebrated the holy Mass. There he shed floods of tears, made acts of contrition and of the love of God, and most humbly adored the Author of his being; then pronouncing in a clear and distinct voice, heard by those who were near him, the words, "*Jesus, Jesus, into Thy hands I commend my soul,*" he immediately expired and went to receive the reward of his labours.

At the same instant a great noise was heard; the room in which he was was shaken, and it seemed as if a great number of people were going out of it. Doña Anna, therefore, and those who were with her attempted

to enter; but, finding the door closed, they dared not
open it.   Some time afterwards they went again to the
door, and not hearing him either move or speak, thought
they ought to interrupt his sleep, which was beginning
to be too long for one who was so ill.   Accordingly
they pushed open the door, and upon entering the
room were greatly surprised to find the sick man on
his knees before the altar, holding his crucifix in his
hands.   They thought at first that he was praying,
and was in some rapture, for his body was in a posture of devotion, and his face appeared very calm and
beautiful.   Most of them, therefore, wished to retire
for fear of interrupting him ; however, some priests
and religious went up to look at him more closely,
and, not hearing him breathe, they touched and called
him, but in vain, for they found his body stiff, and
saw that he had passed to a better life.

He came into the world in 1495, and quitted it in
1550 on the 8th of March at midnight, between Friday
and Saturday, thus dying when exactly fifty-five
years old, for he was born also on the 8th of March.
The first forty-two years of his life were spent in
travelling about, in making pilgrimages, and in very
fatiguing employments, and the last thirteen were
dedicated entirely to the service of the poor, as we
have shown.   Judging from the strength of his body,
he would have lived much longer; but his fasts, vigils,
mortifications, and constant labours had shortened
his days, and therefore we may say that his death
was truly precious—for what can be more noble and
more pleasing in the sight of God than to sacrifice
one's life to Him by the labours of penance?

As he had ardently loved prayer in his life, he had
the happiness to die praying ; and it is very remark-

able that his body after its separation from the soul still remained in the posture of prayer, and may be said in some measure to have continued in prayer ; for S. Paul, the first hermit, having also died on his knees, S. Jerome maintains that the posture itself was a prayer before God : " *Cadaver Sancti Deum, cui omnia vivunt, officioso gestu precabatur :* The saint's body by its very attitude continued to pray to God, to Whom all things live." Hence we may say that few saints have died in a more edifying manner, or in one that more nearly resembles the condition of the blessed in heaven, who are for ever praising and adoring the Sovereign Majesty of God.

CHAPTER VI.

HIS FUNERAL.

JESUS says in the Gospel that "whosoever shall humble himself shall be exalted"; our readers will therefore naturally expect that John of God's memory should be greatly honoured, inasmuch as his whole life was one of humiliation and forgetfulness of self. Accordingly we see that God rewarded the humility of His servant by permitting extraordinary honours to be paid to him. God had begun to exalt him in his life-time, especially after the foundation of his hospital; and we have seen in the second book how highly he was esteemed in Granada, in all the provinces, and even at the court of Spain. But all this appeared as nothing when compared with what took place afterwards, so that we may say without hesitation that no man has been more honoured after his death than he was. We read in history of funerals more remarkable for concourse of people, for the presence of great personages, or for outward splendour; but in none of them shall we find more respect, love and sorrow, in which consist the only true honour we can pay to the dead, everything else being mere ceremonious pomp.

The archbishop, informed of his death very early in the morning, went immediately to pay him the last duties; he found his body in the same posture in which he had died, *i.e.*, on its knees before the altar, and what greatly surprised him was that there proceeded from it a very sweet odour which filled both the room and the whole house. Having said some prayers for the repose of his soul, he ordered two more altars to be fitted up in the room, so that Mass might be immediately said for him on three altars, then, having offered up the first sacrifice himself, he returned to his palace, to allow time to prepare for the interment.

We must not omit to mention that when the archbishop entered the room in which the body was, a prodigy took place like to that which happened at his birth, namely, that all the bells of the city rang of their own accord so solemn and mournful a peal, that it was clear that heaven itself was interested in his death. By this signal all the inhabitants knew they had lost their father and protector, and nothing but tears and sighs was heard throughout the whole city; the streets resounded with the lamentations of the widows and orphans whom he maintained, and the rest of the poor expressed a lively sorrow, declaring that they had no longer any one to supply their wants; the sick in the hospital were inconsolable, thinking they would be turned out of it; even the rich declared that Granada would henceforth suffer severely, since he was dead on whom the public relied for charity.

Nothing but the sight of the body would satisfy the people; they flocked from all parts to Doña Ossorio's house, and so great was the crowd that it was necessary to double the number of guards round the house to prevent confusion and disorder. The tears and devotional feelings of those who beheld the body were alike excited, for it was placed on a platform in a kneeling posture, as he had died. Not the common people only, but the great, the rich and all the different corporations of the city came to sprinkle him with holy water and pray for him; in fact, no one kept away.

At first it was doubtful where he would be buried, the chapel in the hospital not being adapted for that purpose; Doña Ossorio, however, declared that he ought to be buried in her vault in the church of the Minims. These good fathers also used their utmost endeavours to obtain so great a favour, and it was at last granted to them. The Marquis of Tarifa, the Marquis of Senalvo, Don Pedro de Bobadiglla, and Don Juan de Guevaro, four distinguished noblemen, esteemed it a singular privilege to be allowed to carry the body down from the room, and place it on a raised platform in front of the house.

As the procession was on the point of starting, there arose amongst the religious orders a contest which reflected great honour on the deceased, for they all wished to have the privilege of carrying his coffin. The friars of S. Francis alleged strong reasons in support of their claim, saying that S. John of God had always imitated the poverty and penance of their holy father, that many of their order had confessed and directed him on different occasions, and that his father had forsaken the world, and ended his days amongst them. The Minims contended that the privilege belonged to them, since they were to celebrate the office, and receive the body into their church. Neither did the other orders lack arguments to prove the justice of their claims ; and the archbishop settled the dispute by ordering them to carry it by turns, the friars of S. Francis taking the lead.

They left the house about nine o'clock in the morning, but did not reach the church of the Minims until noon on account of the numbers of people who thronged the streets and prevented them from advancing. The procession was arranged as follows. The poor who were able to come out of the hospital went first with Antony Martin and the other brothers, and after them came the girls and married women whom he had placed in safety, each with a lighted candle in her hand ; they wept aloud and publicly proclaimed the charitable acts of the Saint. Next followed all the confraternities of the city with their crosses and banners, then the religious communities according to the order of their seniority ; lastly the clergy of the city, the chapter of the cathedral, and the archbishop in his pontifical robes. Twenty-four chief men of the city were placed round the body, which was followed by the president and all the officers of the royal chancery of Granada, the other magistrates of the city and a vast number of persons of quality.

During the ceremony the bells of the cathedral, of the parish churches, and of all the monasteries tolled continually, thereby proving how universal was the mourning for his death in the whole city, and how anxious the citizens were to pay honour to his memory. Not the faithful only but even the Moors lamented his death. They blessed him in their own language, and proclaimed his virtues and all his good works, so that not only those of the household of the faith, but even strangers and the greatest enemies of the Church bore honourable testimony to him.

When they arrived at the small square before the Church of the Minims, commonly called Our Lady of Victory, they were obliged to stop on account of the vast number of persons who had assembled there to honour the servant of God. Some asked to see him once more, others wished to touch his bier with their rosaries, medals, and prayer-books, and many desired to have something that had belonged to him, which they might keep as a precious relic ; some even were on the point of carrying off the pall which covered his body, and dividing it amongst themselves, so that each might keep a piece of it in his family. When the populace were kept back, and their zeal restrained a little, the procession entered the church, where the bier was placed on a rich catafalque prepared for the occasion. The Father General of the Minims sang the Mass, and another religious of the same order preached the funeral sermon. The body was left for nine days in the church before its interment, and a different preacher pronounced his panegyric each day ; and for the rest of the year every preacher spoke of him in terms of admiration, and always proposed to his audience some one of his virtues for imitation. These are some of the honours which God caused to be paid him at the time, as the crown of his humility.

CHAPTER VII.

HIS VIRTUE IS ACKNOWLEDGED AND PROCLAIMED BY ALL AFTER HIS DEATH.

HOWEVER virtuous a man may be in his life, he is never praised or honoured by all; there are always persons who, through envy, interest, or some other motive, speak against his conduct, and find fault with his best actions; but, as soon as he has paid the debt of nature, and is no longer in the world, they then commonly begin to be more just in their judgment of him—they acknowledge his good qualities, and the voice of slander is silenced.

This happened to our Saint, who, notwithstanding his admirable and exemplary life, was frequently despised and condemned on different occasions. For instance, many inhabitants of Granada continually ridiculed him, and looked upon him as a man of no value on account of his former acts of madness. Some also at Valladolid had considered him prodigal and foolish because he gave away all that he received, without keeping anything for his hospital. He was in like manner despised at Toledo, when on his way to court; but after his death all praised him, even those who had abused and spoken against him. In these three great cities especially, extraordinary honours were paid him: the inhabitants loudly proclaimed his praises, and published glowing accounts of his principal virtues; they called him the father of the poor, the support of the weak, the comforter of the afflicted, and *the* Saint. They said he had imitated the Apostles, since, having nothing of his own, he had made many rich, or at least provided them with a comfortable subsistence; they magnified his almsgiving and all his actions; indeed, no one spoke of him, or mentioned his name, except with the greatest veneration.

We will relate a circumstance which shows clearly that at his death a very great change took place in many persons' minds, and that those who had despised him most were now the first to honour him. The Marchioness of Guzman having given birth to a daughter, was anxious that John of God should stand as its godfather, and proposed the same to her husband, Don Diego, begging that he might be sent for from Granada. The marquis at first violently resisted the proposal, declaring that he should dishonour his daughter by giving her such a godfather, and injure himself by contracting affinity with one who was so poor and of such mean extraction; nor would he give his consent to it until after much importunity from his wife. No sooner, however, had he heard of the death of John than he declared he thought himself much honoured by the favour; he spoke of it to every one, telling all his friends he thought his daughter would gain more glory from the holiness and merit of her godfather than from the nobility of her birth.

If those who had opposed and derided him respected him so much after his death, and paid him these great honours, we must not be surprised if those who loved and esteemed him in his lifetime should have spoken so highly in his praise. Don Guerrero, Archbishop of Granada, who was so intimately connected with, and had so perfect a knowledge of him, was in the habit of calling him, when alive, "the hidden man;" but, after his death, "the humble man exalted ;" he was never tired of speaking in praise of him, often saying that the greatest happiness of Granada was to possess his relics, and to have him for protector.   The holy priest, John of Avila, his director in the spiritual life, and the confidant of the secrets of his conscience, never preached without mentioning his great merit and perfection ; he used to propose him to his audience as a model for their imitation, and often warned those who had despised him as a madman to do penance and beg his pardon for having done so.   Cardinal Don Pedro Deza, having been long President of the High Chancery of Granada, had an accurate knowledge of the graces and gifts God had bestowed on John ; he used to call him "the wonderful man," and to speak of him as a prodigy of charity.   Being at Rome when the tidings of his death reached him, he mentioned all his good works to the Pope and the Cardinals, who were impressed with so high an idea of his sanctity that they determined to appoint commissioners at once to inquire into the principal circumstances of his life.

That our Saint's merit was acknowledged everywhere, even at court, is further evident from what a lady of high rank said to the brothers of his hospital. The good religious had drawn up an account of his most remarkable actions, and shown it to several of their friends, and amongst others to Doña Sancha de Toledo, lady of honour to one of the royal princesses. She was much astonished at its brevity, and could not refrain from saying, " How is it, my brothers, that you have collected together so little of the life of so wonderful a man ?   If any one had come to me, I would have given him memoranda sufficient to make up a thick volume.   It is not right to conceal the wonders

God worked in him, nor to place a candle under a
bushel. Gratitude obliges you to make known to all
the great deeds of your holy father, and to put aside
the veil under which, out of humility, he wished to
conceal all his virtues from the knowledge of
men."

Lastly, no one could help being persuaded of his
sanctity, for he was spoken of, not only by devout
persons, but in every rank of society ; the most celebrated orators wrote panegyrics upon him ; all the
religious orders strove to honour him and make known
his good works; and lastly, poets made him the subject
of their verses, describing in glowing words the great
things he had done for the good of his neighbour.
Of these, Lopez de Vega was one of the most successful. He wrote the life of John in verse, and re-
corded faithfully the principal events of it, describing
in such strong and affecting terms the exhortations he
was in the habit of making to persons of evil life to
induce them to forsake their wicked ways, that on
one occasion a depraved woman of Segovia who heard
them read, immediately began to reflect seriously on
the life she was leading ; she detested her wickedness,
and was converted in a very edifying manner ; so that
it was believed, not without reason, that when she was
listening to the poet's words, John of God interceded
for her, and gained her the grace of repentance.

CHAPTER VIII.

THE PERFUME WHICH ROSE FROM HIS BODY, ON ACCOUNT OF WHICH THE ARCHBISHOP OF GRANADA CONVERTS THE ROOM IN WHICH HE DIED INTO A CHAPEL. A CHURCH IS ALSO BUILT OVER THE SPOT ON WHICH HE WAS BORN.

As our bodies are temples of the Holy Ghost, as the Apostle assures us, they are on that account worthy of respect and honour; and we see that in the case of persons eminent for their sanctity, God often works miracles to show that He wishes especial respect and veneration to be paid their relics.

From what has been said in the first two books, we see that our Saint was gifted with an eminent degree of virtue, and that on many important occasions his members, under the guidance of the Holy Spirit, were instrumental in performing miracles. Our Lord also warned the faithful by signs and prodigies to honour his body, and to regard it as something holy and deserving of veneration, for He rendered it incorrupt for a long time, and caused a very sweet smell to proceed from it.

The incorruptibility of his body was manifested on the occasion of the translation of his relics; but we will here say something respecting the wonderful perfume proceeding from his body. The whole house was filled with it, so that all who entered perceived it. The first persons who noticed it were Doña Ossorio, the priests, the religious, and others who were present at his death. The Archbishop of Granada also perceived it when he came to sprinkle him with holy

water, and, from the depositions made by order of the
Holy See, we find that a great number of persons bore
witness to it as to an undoubted fact. The same perfume always remained with the body, for when sub-
sequently extraordinary lights were seen in Doña
Ossorio's chapel, and on this account an opening had
been made in the vault, the odour immediately spread
all over the church. It was perceived also again when
another coffin was about to be let down into the vault;
and when the archbishop heard of this, he ordered
the coffin to be taken elsewhere, and forbade that any
one henceforward should be buried near the body of
our Saint, wishing thereby to show how much it
ought to be respected. Not only did the odour accompany the body, but it remained for nine consecutive
days in the room where he died, so that it was perceived and looked upon as a sure mark of sanctity by
the judges of the city, who came with the archbishop's
deputies to make an inventory of the things that belonged to him, which they wished to preserve as
relics.

This prodigy made Doña Anna Ossorio desire to
convert the room into a chapel, since it did not appear
to her right to apply to a profane use a place which
had been sanctified by so precious a death. The archbishop, when informed of her design, highly approved
of it, and granted her full permission to carry out her
wish; and the chapel became afterwards very famous,
through the numerous miracles which God worked in
it on behalf of those who invoked our Saint.

What seemed to be most surprising of all was, that the
odour was renewed every week, and lasted from Friday
at midnight until the following Saturday evening, of
which we have many clear proofs. It will be suffi-

cient to relate what Doña Ursula Romos deposed on oath respecting it, as follows :—Going one Saturday evening to visit Mary, the daughter of Anna Ossorio, who esteemed John of God so highly, she happened to find the family at prayers in their private chapel. Upon reaching the chapel door she smelt a very fragrant odour, and enquiring what it was that smelt so sweetly, Mary replied—"My dear lady, do good works, and you will yourself send forth an odour like that which you are wondering at. Do you not know that this oratory was the room in which S. John of God died? Though it is now more than fifty years since his death, the odour you speak of is still renewed by him, but it is on Saturdays chiefly that we perceive it, because on that day he departed this life." Ursula was much surprised at hearing this, and wished to make proof herself what Mary told her ; accordingly, she communicated the following Thursday, fasted the next day, and went to the chapel on Saturday morning. Hardly had she entered when she smelt the same odour, and, being filled with consolation and joy, she prayed a long time, to adore and thank God for His infinite mercy. Then she went to Mary, and told her she had really smelt the same fragrant smell as on the preceding Saturday, when Mary answered—"This which seems to you so surprising a favour is a common thing with us ; we enjoy it every Saturday."

We must also mention here that the Canon Basil de Torrès, Secretary to Cardinal Don Pedro Deza, declared that he had frequently smelt a fragrant odour proceeding from the bed on which John of God died. Philip Gomez also said that when our Saint had entered his house on one occasion on account of the badness of the weather, and his clothes had been placed near the fire to dry, there came from them a very fragrant smell.

Just as this miraculous perfume induced Doña Anna Ossorio and the Archbishop of Granada to convert the room in which John of God died into a chapel ; so similar prodigies which happened at Montemor Novo were the reason why a church was built over the spot where he was born. The country people often went to the house which had belonged to his father, to pray and implore his assistance, and obtained there many remarkable favours ; the blind recovered their sight, the sick were healed, and the afflicted received sensible consolation. Some of them even carried away small quantities of the earth on which the blessed child had trodden, and wore it wrapped up in small pieces of linen round their necks, and making use of it in sickness, derived much benefit from it. All these circumstances seemed to be so many voices proclaiming that God wished to be honoured on this spot, and that the holy man ought to be venerated there in a special manner. No one, however, took any steps in the matter; the house remained in the same condition, and only a few sick persons there secretly invoked one, who they saw had so much power from God. At last the Providence of God openly declared His Will that a church should be built there by the following circumstance.

In the year 1607, Brother John Lopez, a disciple of our Saint, went with a companion from Castille to Montemor Novo to see if they could not found a hospital there for the public benefit. They took up their abode in the house of their blessed father, spending their time in prayer and retreat. Many persons of the city came nevertheless to see them, and consult them on matters regarding their salvation. One day as they were speaking to a young man of the noble actions of the servant of God, a stone detached itself from a wall, which seemed in a good state of repair, and fell down at their feet without doing them any harm. Thinking the house was in a dangerous state, they left it immediately, and no sooner had they done so than it fell in, though it seemed as if it would have lasted much longer. The people immediately declared that this was a sign from heaven by which it was made known to all the inhabitants of the city that they ought to build a church on that very spot, to glorify God and thank Him for the graces with which He had enriched the servant of God.

This was soon done. Don Alexandro de Braga, Archbishop of Evora, ordered a solemn procession through the whole of the city on the day on which the first stone of the new church was laid. He also gave considerable sums of money towards the expences of it. The citizens and great proprietors in the neighbourhood very liberally opened their purses ; and all took pleasure in contributing something towards the sacred edifice, so that it was soon completed.

It was not long before the devotion of the people rendered this holy temple very famous, not in Portugal only, but throughout all Spain. Pilgrims and sick persons flocked to it from all parts, great miracles were wrought at the intercession of the Saint, and many of the faithful were cured in it, some by applying small bags of the earth to the affected parts of their bodies, others by rubbing themselves with oil from the lamp before the altar, and others by merely offering up prayers and performing their devotions there.

Persons still continue to come from a great distance ;

great and small, rich and poor, priests, religious, and laymen go thither to beg of God through the intercession of John, all the graces and mercies they stand in need of for their salvation, and seldom does any one go away without having obtained all that he asks for, provided he prays in a proper manner; for S. James the Apostle says many ask and receive not, because they ask amiss.

Thus we see that John of God was a very illustrious saint of the church of Jesus Christ, since he has sanctified the place of his birth as well as that of his death, our Lord wishing churches to be built on both those spots, an honour which has been granted to very few other saints; for though men have wished to perpetuate the memory of some saints by erecting temples to them in the places where they died, yet it is rare to find any whose birth and death have both been honoured by the erection of new churches.

CHAPTER IX.

BEATIFICATION AND CANONIZATION OF S. JOHN OF GOD.

THE miracles which have been related in the foregoing chapters, and innumerable others which are contained in the processes drawn up by order of the sovereign pontiffs, the petitions of the Emperor Ferdinand II., of Philip IV., King of Spain, and of Elizabeth of France his wife, and of many other Christian princes, the ardent desires of all nations who looked upon John of God as a saint to whom they had already frequently prayed to, together with the earnest solicitations of the religious of his order, all these determined Pope Urban VIII. to issue a bull on the 21st of September, 1630, by which he announced that before proceeding to our Saint's solemn canonization, he should be placed in the rank of the Blessed, and that his Office might be publicly recited. The Saint's beatification was accordingly celebrated at Rome with all possible magnificence in the church of S. John Calibita. Twenty-six cardinals were present on the first day of the ceremony, and Father Nicholas Riccardi of the order of S. Dominic, master of the Sacred Palace, preached a very eloquent sermon in honour of the blessed servant of God. The feast was kept up for the whole octave by an extraordinary number of people, and never was there seen more zeal and fervour than were displayed on this occasion.

All that I have hitherto related ought to be sufficient even in the opinion of the most scrupulous to make the blessed John of God declared a saint. For if to canonize a person it be necessary for him to have led an exemplary life and to have been employed in labours of penance, I have shown that he lived in so holy and edifying a manner as to excite the admiration of the greatest men of his time, and I have spoken at great length of his astonishing and incredible penances. If miracles are required, I have related so many that I am afraid I have wearied my readers, who in general are not pleased with descriptions of this nature. If witnesses be demanded, there are four hundred and sixty who have deposed to his sanctity in the processes of the informations drawn up by order of the Holy See ; and I can further add that, although the canonization of S. John of God was desired and petitioned for by all the inhabitants not only of Granada but of Spain and Portugal, the sovereign pontiffs avoided precipitation by taking time for mature deliberation, and allowing nine and forty years to elapse after his beatification without canonizing him. During this interval God performed fresh miracles through his intercession and by means of his relics, of which the Pope makes mention in the bull of his canonization. The devotion of the people to him, very far from diminishing, was daily increasing. His feast was celebrated with great splendour in the churches of his order, and the faithful flocked thither in crowds to venerate and pray to him, as one of the greatest saints.

Pope Innocent XI., of glorious memory, considering all these circumstances, was induced to make further inquiry into them. He examined the depositions of the miracles performed after his beatification. He prayed, and invoked the light of the Holy Spirit; he performed many good works, several times offered up the holy sacrifice of the altar, and omitted nothing which he thought might enable him to know the Will of God. At last after taking every precaution and frequently consulting the cardinals, one day whilst saying Mass he felt himself interiorly moved to canonize the blessed John of God, and he immediately had a bull drawn up to that effect. This was issued on the 13th of June, 1679, but the solemnity did not take place for some years on account of the continued ill-health of Pope Innocent XI., but it was performed by Pope Alexander VIII. on the 16th of October, 1690. Four other saints were canonized at the same time: namely, S. Laurence Giustiniani, Patriarch of Venice; S. John Capistran, Minor Observantine; S. John of S. Facundo, Augustinian; and S. Paschal Baylon, of the order of S. Francis.

CHAPTER X.

ON THE VIRTUE AND RARE GIFTS OF THE VENERABLE SERVANT OF GOD, ANTONY MARTIN, THE DISCIPLE AND SUCCESSOR OF S. JOHN OF GOD.

As the wise man assures us, virtuous children are the glory and crown of their fathers, we cannot better finish the life of S. John of God than by speaking of the piety and perfections of those who were his first disciples, and who possessed a great abundance of his spirit; for we shall thus contribute to his glory, and shew how perfect he was himself. We shall also see how much his order increased, and how holy must have been the union of his brothers, since God in after years bestowed so many blessings upon them.

It will be remembered that in his last illness John appointed Antony Martin to be his successor, and besought all his brothers to obey him as himself; we will begin therefore with him, for it is evident that he was well instructed in all the maxims of the Saint, and very exact in following them. Though born in a humble rank of life, he had received a very good education, and from his earliest infancy every means had been adopted by his father to instil virtue into his mind. It is true that he did not profit by them at first, and that when young, he was led considerably astray by the violence of his passions; but God mercifully raised up a charitable hand, which plucked away the thorns and brambles of sin by which the surface of his heart was covered, and rendered him like to that good ground mentioned in the Gospel which yielded fruit a hundred-fold.

We need not here repeat what it was that induced him to give himself to God, as it has been already related in the seventh chapter of the second book : we have only to speak now of the wonderful deeds of his subsequent life. From the time that S. John of God admitted him into his hospital to serve the poor, he embraced a mode of life which would appear almost incredible if we had not before our eyes the example of his holy father. He wore no stockings, shoes, or sandals ; he went with his head always bare ; his subsistence was only bread and water, and of this he took so small a quantity that people wondered how he could live, looking upon his fasts as something beyond the strength of nature, and rather to be admired than imitated. Remembering that he had formerly indulged his body with pleasures, he allowed it no rest, but was continually punishing it. Not satisfied with the austerities already mentioned, he added many others to them. He wore hair-cloth to the day of his death, without ever putting it off, though engaged in the active and laborious service of the poor. Those who have made trial of this kind of mortification know how insupportable it is when accompanied with continual and violent exercise ; but besides this, he every day disciplined himself very severely, and then immediately put his hair-cloth on again, thus undoubtedly giving himself very acute pain.

He slept on the ground, using an old mat for a mattress, and a stone for a pillow. We can easily imagine that he could take but little rest on such a bed ; and it was known that he slept very little, that he spent almost the whole night in prayer, weeping for his sins, and contemplating the sovereign greatness of God.

As for the poor, he loved them so tenderly that he was never tired of waiting upon them. He used to call them his creditors ; and since charity is a debt which we can never fully pay, and which, as S. Augustine says, is always pressing upon us—"*Semper redditur et semper debetur*—is always being paid, and always due," he thought he could never do enough for them. His diligence in serving them astonished all ; he was everywhere, discharging all the offices of the house, working in doors and out of doors, and choosing the most laborious and fatiguing occupations. To see him so actively engaged, one would have said he was the only person in the hospital of Granada, or that other brothers were only there to witness his toils and labours.

He had a special gift of ingratiating himself with the poor patients : after conversing with them for a short time only he inspired them with contrition, gained their hearts to God, and persuaded them of the necessity of renouncing all the false maxims of the world, if they wished to enter the narrow path of the Gospel. He always spoke so kindly and gently to them that they felt comforted as soon as they saw him ; they thought lightly of their ailments after they had made them known to him, and they bore their sufferings patiently, when they saw him near them and endeavouring to comfort them.

After the example of his holy father, he never refused to receive any of the poor who came to the hospital ; and such numbers of them were admitted that the ordinary alms which he received were not sufficient for their maintenance. He was therefore compelled to borrow large sums, and to contract debts on all sides, and thus he became surrounded by creditors whom he had no means of satisfying. Remembering that S. John of God on such occasions had obtained from the Spanish court great assistance, by means of which he was enabled to pay his debts, he determined to go thither, trusting that Divine Providence would bless his journey, and touch the hearts of the great in favour of the poor, whose cause he advocated. His success fully answered his expectations, for he collected a considerable sum, each member of the court willingly contributing towards paying debts which had been contracted for charitable purposes, and for the support of the members of Jesus Christ. Don Philip, who was a very pious prince, and the Infanta Juana, his sister, were the first to bestow upon him their royal bounty; and knowing that the hospital at Granada was the cause of great glory to God and of benefit to the poor, they determined to establish one at Madrid also. He was ordered therefore to go quickly and pay his debts at Granada, and to return to Madrid as soon as possible, there to lay the foundations of a new hospital.

As soon as he arrived at Granada he distributed to all his creditors the money that had been given him, and provided for the most pressing wants of the hospital, which he entreated his brothers to take great care of, keeping up the strict order their blessed father had established in it; and he informed them that Don Philip had ordered him to return as soon as possible to Madrid, to found another hospital there.

He would not, however, set out without having previously obtained permission from his archbishop, Don Pedro Guerrero, who was greatly attached to their community, and protected it on all occasions. This great prelate was far from opposing an undertaking which he knew would prove so beneficial to all the poor of the great city, but immediately gave him his blessing, and recommended him not to delay his departure any longer.

The good religious therefore left Granada by the command of his archbishop and of his prince, to go and exercise his zeal for the poor in the capital of the kingdom. Don Philip, who was impatient to put his pious design into execution, no sooner heard that he had returned to Madrid than he caused the foundations to be laid, and in the course of a very short time the present magnificent building was erected. The poor were received into it, hospitality was practised with great regularity, and such excellent arrangements were made by Antony Martin, that all might have fancied themselves at Granada, in the house which John of God had himself founded.

This work being successfully accomplished, God, who had destined his servant to bring it to perfection, did not long withhold from him the reward and crown of his virtues. He took him to Himself in the year 1553, at the age of fifty-three. He was universally regretted, and was buried with much honour, for all the lords of the court attended, to show their great sorrow at his death. His body was laid in the principal chapel of the Franciscan Convent at Madrid, where it remained for more than forty years, after which time it was solemnly translated into the church of his hospital as a precious relic.

Thus we see what kind of a person the first disciple and successor of S. John of God was ; he lived only three years after his holy father, but during that short period he did great things. He maintained and confirmed the good order his holy father had established in the hospital of Granada ; he kept up the practice of the same charities ; and he walked exactly in his steps, perfectly imitating him in all things. Divine Providence opened to him towards the end of his life a new career, which seemed to need a man full of strength and vigour ; and he obeyed with joy, though already worn out by toil and much enfeebled by his excessive austerities. He went cheerfully to Madrid, and his fervour was in nowise abated by the trouble and fatigue which a new establishment always causes. Living as he did for God alone, and having a great desire to be freed from this mortal body that he might enjoy the sight of His Sovereign Majesty, he was delighted at meeting with opportunities of pain and labour which might shorten his days and the sooner end his pilgrimage; and it was this which urged him to undertake so willingly whatever was most difficult and contrary to nature. Thus we may say that from the time of his conversion he was always admirable at Granada, at Madrid, in his hospital, or at court. He laboured incessantly, was industrious in mortifying himself, indefatigable in the discharge of his duty, and entirely resigned to the Will of God. In short, he followed exactly the example of S. John of God, and was a worthy son of so great a father.

CHAPTER XI.

OF THE HOLINESS OF THE VENERABLE SERVANT OF GOD, PETER THE SINNER.

OUR readers will be much edified by a short history of the life and actions of Peter the Sinner; for in them we shall see great love of poverty, truly evangelical simplicity, ardent love of God and of his neighbour, the most profound humility and most austere penance.

He was a native of Andalusia, but the precise place of his birth and education is not known. It is certain, however, that from a very early age he gave signs of great piety and practised much mortification; for we are told that he employed himself in very laborious occupations, such as drawing water for the inhabitants of the town of Jaen and other places in the neighbourhood, and in serving them in every way that he could. He also refused all offers of presents or alms, endeavouring to live on his labour only, and on what he gained by the sweat of his brow, that he might be able to say with the Apostle he ate no man's bread fraudulently. As he was very sparing in his diet, he always had something out of his wages to give in alms to the poor.

After working all day he withdrew in the evening to some place where he spent almost the whole night in prayer, having no other bed than the bare ground. His whole exterior breathed the spirit of penance; he was clothed like the poor in coarse woollen stuff; he endured every kind of hardship without complaining or giving any signs of pain; he went bare-foot in all seasons of the year, and it was only in his old age that his superiors obliged him to wear shoes.

As no one knew his family, he took great care to conceal his surname, that he might remain more unknown to the world, and that his parentage might not be discovered ; but this very precaution is a presumption that he was descended from some noble family and that through humility he wished to conceal the knowledge of it from men. In order to make himself appear still more vile and contemptible in the eyes of the world he called himself Peter the Sinner, and further, he imposed on himself all the penances and humiliations which are due to sin, living during his whole life as a great sinner, who was touched with true contrition.

After living some time in the town of Jaen, the love of retreat induced him to withdraw to a hermitage on a lofty mountain in the territory of Malaga. There he spent several years in prayer and the contemplation of heavenly things ; and to avoid the tediousness which is so much to be dieaded in a solitary life, he used to add manual labour to his prayer, making wooden spoons, baskets, and similar things, which he sold for his support.

Doubtless he received from our Lord in this holy retreat many very special graces and extraordinary favours, but they did not come to the knowledge of men, because he spoke very little about himself, and generally observed silence, except when charity obliged him to speak. When however he was obliged to go into the neighbouring towns, he seemed to be all on fire with the love of God, and he spoke with such zeal and unction of His greatness and goodness that it was clear he enjoyed great familiarity with Him, and that his heart was deeply penetrated with the truths he expounded.

Whilst living thus in his hermitage, the thought of going to Rome to venerate the tombs of the holy apostles came into his mind; nor did he discourage it, because he hoped to find in that pilgrimage many opportunities of self-mortification and penance. He performed the journey like a true penitent, walking always barefoot and with head uncovered; he endured most patiently the rain, the cold, the burning heat of the sun and all the inclemencies of the seasons; he was often in want of the necessaries of life, and suffered all the hardships which usually accompany poverty.

He visited the holy places of Rome with great devotion, kissing and bedewing with his tears the happy soil which had been so many times dyed with the blood of martyrs; on several occasions he gave striking marks of his solid piety, and all were edified by his holy life. During his abode in that great and famous city, divine Providence made use of him for the conversion of a Jew, with whom he had several interviews. The holy man brought him to see clearly that his religion was false and deceitful, since it obliged him to observe a law which had been abolished, made him live in the expectation of many prophecies which had been fulfilled, and required him continually to pray for the coming of the Messias, Who had already visited His people, and saved men by the shedding of His Blood. His words, seconded by the interior grace of God, made such an impression on the mind of the Jew that he asked for baptism and embraced Christianity.

The servant of God, when about to leave Rome

to return to his native country, saw reason to fear that the company of the other Jews, of whom there were many in the city, might prove injurious to his convert, and that these unbelievers would make him return to the Synagogue ; he therefore took him away, that he might keep watch over his conduct.

As soon as he reached Spain, he went straight to Seville and like another Jonas at Nineveh appeared in the streets barefooted, with a cord round his body and in a ragged cloak, that he might do public penance before all. Then he cried out in a loud voice warning the inhabitants to do penance likewise, and his words were so moving that many were converted on the spot and entirely renounced the world. He continued for several days to speak of God and preach penance in the public squares, and our Lord bestowed such benediction on his words that very many of the citizens placed themselves under his direction. This success induced him to found a hospital for the benefit of pilgrims, and those who on account of their poverty could not obtain a lodging elsewhere; he put his design into execution without any delay, and was thus enabled to find useful employment for those who had given themselves up to him.

His confidence in God's Providence was so great that when he went into the streets, he did not beg for his poor, but merely addressed an exhortation to those whom he met, and by this means he gained more alms than if he had actually asked for them. The great number of poor and sick who came to him from all parts soon obliged him to enlarge his hospital. He built a new infirmary, and arranged a place apart for the sick, while the pilgrims slept as before in the lower rooms, on beds laid out on large planks, and hence the house was called the Hospital of the Planks.

He was not one of those who forget prayer and lose the habit of it as soon as they begin to be engaged in active duties ; on the contrary, he felt himself drawn to it, and desired to give himself entirely up to it, while the recollection of the sweetness he had enjoyed in his hermitage made him continually sigh after solitude. He very often warned his brothers not to give themselves up entirely to outward occupations, but always to reserve for prayer a considerable part of their heart and their time. In order to render them more spiritual, and to prevent their effectually losing the spirit of prayer through too much outward activity, he often withdrew them from the hospital, taking them to a mountain called Ronda, where they spent some time in contemplation. Then he would send them back to serve the poor, while others came, who in their turn gave themselves up to prayer and meditation on holy things. By this means he practised them successively in the lives of Martha and Mary, taking care that the cares of the one did not make them lose the love of the quiet and recollection of the other.

He himself remained almost always on this mountain, only going down into the city to obey the calls of charity and to benefit his neighbour. His humility often prevented his appearing in public, for being well known, every one showed him great marks of honour and respect, which were insupportable and extremely painful to him. The pain he felt on these occasions became at length so great that he determined never to enter the city again. He accordingly recommended the hospital to the care of Peter the Sinner the younger, a man of eminent piety and much esteemed by all the people of Seville, and setting off for Granada went to the hospital of John of God, to serve the religious and do all that they required of him.

In changing his place of abode he did not change his habits of life, but lived in the same manner, as at Seville. With his head and feet always bare, a crucifix in his hand, wearing a long plain dress, he used to go into the streets and exhort the people, making them shed many tears, and bringing them to repentance; he then retired to a mountain to pray in quiet, and occupy himself in manual labour. After some time many of his friends represented to him that it would be much better for him to remain always in the hospital of John of God, and even to put on the habit of his order, as he was already far advanced in years, being nearly seventy years old, and his strength was no longer equal to such excessive fatigue and to the rough and painful life which he led on the mountain. They added that it would be very advantageous for him to live in a regular community, because he would be no longer his own master there, for he would have a superior whom he would be obliged to obey, and that this would be very meritorious for him in the sight of God. They had another reason also for advising him in this manner, but they concealed it from him for fear of grieving him and wounding his humility; it was that if he lived always in the hospital, his example, his charity, and his counsel would be of great use to the brothers and patients. They hoped also that all the inhabitants of the city would be able to derive greater benefit from his admirable instructions.

He yielded willingly to their advice, for the obedience they spoke of, which would be indispensable in a regular community, made a great impression on his mind.   He accordingly offered himself to the religious of S. John of God, and begged them to admit him into their society and give him their habit; they received him very gladly, thinking themselves fortunate in being able to possess a man of such merit, whose reputation stood so high in the world.   His friends were not wrong in supposing that he would be of great service to the hospital, for he procured much alms for it by his exhortations, and by the edifying and at the same time engaging and effectual manner in which he addressed the rich, and informed them of the wants of the poor.

From the time that he began to live in this holy house, he regularly rose at midnight, went secretly to the church and prostrating himself in prayer remained there generally until the morning. After meditation he used to sing with great fervour hymns and canticles before the Blessed Sacrament, often saying in the transport of his zeal, "Who shall separate me from the love of the Crucified? I am sure neither the devil, nor any creature of this world shall be able to do so."

All who found him praying thus in the church, were much moved at seeing him so absorbed in God and so full of fervour, and his example induced the most tepid to pray and pass a part of the night with him at the foot of the altar.

As soon as the day began to dawn, and he knew it was about the hour at which the labourers would be going to their work, he hastened to the public squares, and getting upon a table knelt down and read aloud the Christian Doctrine, that all who did not know it might learn it by hearing it frequently repeated. For the rest of the day he went about the streets with a crucifix in his hand, and collecting together the beggars and all whom he found doing nothing in different parts of the city, he made them very beautiful and spiritual exhortations, from which all classes of persons might derive profit.

His great devotion to the Blessed Sacrament, caused him to redouble his zeal when the festival of Corpus Christi drew near ; he was seen in transports of joy, and his whole demeanour showed the tender and affectionate piety of his soul. He generally walked in front of the solemn procession in which this august Sacrament is annually exposed to the adoration of the people, he used to sing hymns all the way, making profound reverences from time to time, prostrating himself on the ground, and thus giving public proof of the fervour of his love and of his great veneration for this adorable mystery.

In all this there was nothing affected, for his biographers tell us that his mind was so wrapt up in God that he no longer thought of creatures, or regarded them in what he did ; but that he acted as if there were only God and himself in the world, that he was so inebriated with divine love as hardly to give a thought to things of this earth, and that hence he sometimes prayed and worked in public places just as if he were shut up in his cell, without perceiving that a great many people were looking at him.

No doubt this was very extraordinary, and anyone attempting to imitate him in this, would probably be guilty of vanity and hypocrisy, or at least of indiscretion, but this holy man could not be suspected of these sins, and all who saw him thus pray, sing, and prostrate himself in the streets and in the churches, were fully aware of his great piety and of the uprightness of his intention ; they looked upon him with wonder, as a man entirely transported in God, and at the sight of his great fervour they burst into tears, and accused themselves of tepidity and cowardice.

He was once selected by the superior of the hospital of Granada to go to Madrid and speak to the king of Spain on a matter of importance. This commission embarrassed him greatly, for he was very old and infirm, and could not perform so long a journey without much inconvenience. He had moreover a great aversion to the court and to all worldly matters ; but he did not allow this to be seen, for he considered that he had entered the community to be no longer his own master, but to live and die under obedience. He therefore set out immediately, and as if he had a presentiment that this would be his last work, he mortified himself unusually on the way, that he might end his days in the exercise of penance ; for he ate very little, took no care of his health, and hardly ever rode on the ass which the superior had given him in consideration of his age. At Madrid he went to lodge in the hospital of his blessed father, and accounted himself a stranger who was unworthy to eat with the religious ; he did not enter their refectory, but contented himself with some morsels of hard bread which he carried in his basket.

Hardly had he begun to treat of the business on which he had been sent, when he was attacked by a violent fever, from which he suffered for several days. He clearly saw that this illness would cause his death, and was therefore anxious to leave the city, and be

as far as possible from the court and all worldly
society, that he might escape all importunity. Accordingly he went to Mondigiar, to the house of the
Count and Countess of Tondilla, who were very
pious and very fond of all John of God's order. When
he entered their house he told them frankly, "I have
come here to die." They received him in the kindest
manner, and took every possible care of him. During
his whole illness nothing but joy and delight were
depicted on his countenance; so far from complaining
or showing any signs of impatience in his great sufferings, he did nothing but praise and bless God, Who was
so soon to take him to Himself. He sang hymns and
canticles, and told everyone that it was time for him
to go and take his place at the nuptials of the Lamb.

His sickness increased daily, and it was thought
well to give him the last sacraments, which he received with all the piety and edification to be expected
from one so perfect in all Christian virtues. He
passed his last night with the count and countess,
who wished to watch by him themselves, that they
might profit by his example and conversation. When
he felt his end approaching he redoubled his hymns
and canticles, like the swan of fable, which never
sings more melodiously than when about to die. He
often cried out, "Gather, gather these flowers," alluding to what the spouse says in the Canticle of Canticles, "Flowers have appeared in our land;" and in
truth he was on the point of entering the land of the
living, where he was to gather, not the flowers only,
but the fruits of all his good works. On repeating
the same words several times with a countenance full
of interior joy, he gave up his soul into the hands of
his Creator.

His death was deeply lamented by all. The Count caused his funeral to be celebrated in a manner worthy of his great merit, and immediately sent his holy body with great pomp to the religious of S. John of God at Granada, who would have been much grieved to lose so precious a treasure. Sufficient tokens of his sanctity had been given during his lifetime, and God vouchsafed to give additional proofs of it after his death, for though it took more than fifteen days to transport his body from Madrid to Granada during very hot weather, yet when they came to bury him it was found at his burial to be wholly incorrupt.

———

CHAPTER XII.

OF THE WONDERFUL LIFE OF THE VENERABLE SERVANT OF GOD, JOHN THE SINNER.

THIS good religious enjoyed so high a reputation, and did such great things in the order of our Saint, that we cannot refrain from relating the principal events of his life. Chronological order would require us to place it after that of Sebastian Arias, since he lived after him, but we prefer to speak of him next to Peter the Sinner, whose humility he imitated by taking his surname.

He was born on the 6th of March in the year 1546 at Carmona, a city of Andalusia. His parents were of noble birth and great piety, his mother in particular being a lady of eminent virtues. In the married state she performed all the good works which her condition permitted, and after she became a widow she withdrew into her son's hospital, of which we shall speak presently, and there served the poor for many years and ended her days happily.

Before his birth, she practised vigorous mortifications, and fasted three times a week, so that he may be said to have been conceived in fasting, and born in the arms of penance. His life corresponded with his birth, for he followed his mother's example, and became a very great penitent. God made known his future sanctity when he was still in the cradle, for like another S. Nicholas he fasted three times a week and refused to take nourishment on the days on which his mother was in the habit of fasting. Having acquired this holy habit so early, he always adhered to it, never failing to fast three times a week, and eating on those days nothing but vegetables badly dressed. When arrived at years of maturity, he increased his austerities greatly, for, not being satisfied with his three fasts a week, and wishing to imitate the ancients he determined to keep three lents every year, the first from All Saints to Christmas, the second from the Epiphany to the Purification, and the third that kept by the universal Church before Easter; and during these three Lents he took food only every three days. His other austerities corresponded with his fasts; in imitation of S. John of God, he always went bare-headed and bare-foot, wore hair-cloth, and slept on the ground, using a mattress very seldom.

After his father's death he went to the city of Xeres de la Frontera to take care of the poor prisoners, of whom there was a great number. He went about begging for them, he urged on their causes, and rendered them every kind of assistance. The judges and all the inhabitants were much edified at seeing his kind and charitable behaviour towards these miserable creatures, and gave him a room in the prison, that he might be nearer them and able to see and speak to them at all hours.

Being in prayer one night, he had a vision in which Jesus Christ appeared to him under the form of a poor man covered with sores, who said to him, " John take care of the poor, and I will accept your charity as done to Myself." By this he understood that he was called to serve the sick poor ; accordingly he left the prison, and with the assistance of some rich friends, laid the first foundations of the hospital of S. Sebastian. He made up a few beds, and took in some sick persons on whom he bestowed so much care and attention, that the chief persons of the city who were convinced of the great advantages of his establishment, gave him large alms, and in a short time several companions joined him in the service of the poor.

As he had a great desire of perfection, he thought seriously on the means he ought to take to attain it, and not finding any more suitable than the religious life, in which the evangelical counsels are practised, he resolved to apply for admission with his companions into the Order of Hospitalers, which was held in great esteem and had just received the approbation of the Holy See. He applied therefore to the superior of the house at Granada, and was readily admitted with his small community, after observing the necessary formalities. Having thus become a son of S. John of God, he studied to perfect himself in his spirit and maxims ; he regulated his hospital after the pattern of that of Granada, and strove to imitate him in all things.

All the spare time that remained to him after attending to the poor he devoted to prayer, in which exercise his fervour was so great that all who saw him wondered. He seemed to be motionless and without feeling ; deaf to all the noise that was made around him, and as if he no longer belonged to the world. He often went into ecstasies which lasted very long, and made him like a dead man who takes no part in earthly things. He was frequently seen thus in the church of the Franciscans at Xeres de la Frontera and in that of the Jesuits at Seville. On some occasions his body was raised up from the ground in the sight of all and suspended in the air for a considerable time, as though his soul which had its conversation in heaven were trying to draw his body up after it.

Xeres de la Frontera was visited with a very great drought, which had already caused great scarcity, and grave apprehensions were entertained for the future ; a general procession of the whole city was therefore made to appease the anger of God, and a miraculous image of the Blessed Virgin was carried in it. The servant of God assisted at it that he might join his prayers to those of all the inhabitants. When the procession was about to start, he knelt down on the step of the church door before the image of the Blessed Virgin and offered up a prayer so devout, so touching and so full of unction that all the people burst into tears, and uttered such sighs and groans that the voices of the singers could no longer be heard and they were obliged to stop until the noise had subsided.

As soon as the ceremony was over he returned

to the hospital, and kneeling down, prayed with such fervour that he fell into an ecstasy which lasted three entire days, during which he took no food, and showed no signs of life. His brothers, whose respect prevented them from interrupting or recalling him to his senses, watched by turns at his side all the time, being anxious to see how it would end. When he returned to himself he was much surprised at seeing many persons round him ; and wishing in some way to conceal from them what had happened to him, and not thinking it had lasted so long a time he said, " I was so tired by the procession yesterday, that I have slept till now ; I beg your pardon for the bad example I have given." He did not think it a violation of truth to speak in this manner, for his ecstasy might well have been called a sleep, since prayer is properly speaking only a sweet repose, which the soul enjoys in God whilst it forgets all earthly things. Brother Pedro Egiziaco addressed him more familiarly than the rest, and told him that on the night after the procession much rain had fallen, upon which he answered, " Yes, I know it, for our Lord shewed me a great quantity of rain and corn, but God knows who will live to eat of it." By these words he meant that a grievous pestilence would come soon afterwards, and carry off a great number of people.

When the good brother continued to ask what had passed in his ecstasy he was obliged to confess that he had said frequently to God, " Lord, if you give not bread to your poor, your servant John the Sinner will soon die," thus showing that his prayers were full of holy confidence, and that his charity resembled that of Moses, who in former times said to God, when He was angry with the Israelites for worshipping the golden calf, "Forgive them this trespass, or if Thou do not, strike me out of the book that Thou hast written." (Exod. xxiii. 32).

We have not space to relate all his other ecstasies, for they are so frequent that they would fill a whole volume ; suffice it to say that he must have had them very often, since he complained of them in some measure and desired to be freed from them, as he declared on several occasions. "Who is there who can bear the weight of God ?" he used sometimes to say, to shew the excess of the favours with which his soul was filled. Meeting one day in the streets a religious of the order of Minims, he said to him without any further explanation, "I beseech you to pray God to withdraw Himself from me." The Minim not knowing that he referred to the ecstasies which were so familiar to him, was at first astonished at such a request, but his astonishment ceased when he came to understand the real meaning of his words, namely, that he desired God not to permit him to fall into the extraordinary raptures which attracted the notice of so many persons, for he often went into ecstasies before all the people and publicly in the churches.

These great favours caused him much pain and confusion. Like the great apostle, his humility made him fear lest people should conceive too good an opinion of him, and imagine him to be different from what he thought himself. Hence when his ecstasies were over he used to punish himself, taking the discipline and chastising his body that these humiliations and sufferings might act as a counterpoise, and protect him from falling into pride.

A man who prayed with so much earnestness and recollection had doubtless much power with God, and could easily obtain any favour from His Sovereign Majesty. This was indeed the opinion of the people who came from all parts to recommend themselves to his prayers ; often married persons who had no children used to beg him to obtain this blessing for them from heaven, and in most cases their wishes were gratified, and God granted them a numerous progeny.

The devil, well knowing the power of his prayers, used all his efforts to disturb and interrupt them, and when he could not succeed by arts and stratagems he often had recourse to violence. On several occasions he beat him so cruelly that he was found by his brothers all covered with blood, and in a most pitiable condition.

The evil spirit appeared to him once under the form of a very beautiful woman that he might tempt him to sin. The horror he had of such a crime led him to do a thing which only one so full of zeal as he was ought to attempt ; he ran immediately into the kitchen and taking some hot coals spread them over the floor of his cell, lay down upon them and cried out in a loud voice, " whosoever wishes to burn me with the fire of impurity must lie down with me on this bed," and at the same time the fictitious woman disappeared and the temptation left him.

Cardinal Rodrigo de Castro, Archbishop of Seville, hearing of his great merit and eminent qualities, sent for him to his archiepiscopal palace that he might make him superior of all the hospitals in his diocese. His humility made him think this too great and honourable an employment for him, and he refused it at first ; but upon the prelate's urging him and trying to force him to accept it, he determined to consult some learned persons, and be guided by their opinion.

Every one told him that he ought to obey the command of the archbishop, and thus, in spite of himself, he became Superior of a great number of hospitals.

Our Lord, wishing to make him a perfect model of all the Christian virtues, suffered him to be loaded with injuries and calumnies, that his patience might be made known to all. He was called an impostor, a robber, and a hypocrite; his most upright intentions were misconstrued; he was accused of frequenting places of ill repute, and of keeping up improper connections. He bore these accusations with the greatest patience, not showing any signs of grief or displeasure. He did not even try to justify himself, but maintained a respectful silence concerning all the calumnies spoken against him, in imitation of the Saviour of the world, Who during His Passion would not open His mouth to refute the false accusations which were laid to His charge. But because he did not think of justifying himself, God undertook to defend him, making known his virtue and purity, by punishing in several ways, and sometimes even by frightful and tragical deaths those who had been so rash as to calumniate and speak against him in public.

It is needless to mention that his desire of assisting the poor was very great, inasmuch as his begging alms for the prisoners, and for the hospital he afterwards established sufficiently prove this; but we may add that his alms were so pleasing to God that He even sometimes worked miracles to furnish him with the means of continuing them, as in the following instance. Every year on the evening before Christmas-day, he used to give twice as much as usual in charity, in thanksgiving to God for the gift He made us of His Son, and distribute meat and bread to all the poor who came to his hospital. One year the number of the poor was so great that there was not enough for all, at which he was much grieved, for his love of the poor was so great that he could refuse nothing to those who applied to him. Our Lord, however, did not leave him long in this perplexity, for He multiplied the meat and bread that remained, so that there was sufficient for all the poor, not on Christmas-day only, but even until the Epiphany.

Angels often visited him to console and strengthen him, and sometimes united their voices with his in praising God, and formed a most sweet harmony in his cell. Many saints of paradise also appeared to him, and amongst others S. Agnes, who one day shewed him three crowns, and said—"See what God has prepared for those who devote themselves to nurse and assist the poor."

In order to exalt his virtue, and to increase his reputation in the world, our Lord bestowed on him while still on earth the gift of miracles, so that he restored health to many sick persons, who had received no relief from the ordinary remedies. One example of this will be sufficient. One day wishing to have an important deed written out, he went to a notary, who was very ill, and begged him to take his pen and write down what he dictated to him. The persons present asked him how he could think of asking the poor man to write, considering the condition he was in; but he answered with great simplicity—"I hope he will be able to write well;" and in fact he was immediately cured, and wrote out the requisite deed. He not only healed the sick, but sometimes raised the dead to life, as many witnesses have deposed. Walking one day along the streets, he met a man in great grief, who said to him—"Pray for me, I entreat you, for I am in great trouble; my wife has just died, and with her I lose everything." He first consoled him, and then said in a firm and confident tone of voice—"Weep no more; your wife is not dead." His words proved true, for the man, returning to his house, found his wife alive and in good health. On another occasion he was passing by a house from which were heard loud lamentations. Upon inquiring what the matter was, he was told that the owner had just lost his only son, and he was entreated to go in and console the family. He immediately went in, and found the body laid out, and lighted candles placed around it: he began to pray, and making the sign of the cross a moment afterwards, said to the dead man, "Arise in the Name of Jesus," and at once the young man rose up and began to walk about full of strength and vigour.

It is certain that God frequently revealed to him future events; for instance, He made known to him long beforehand all the circumstances of his own death and burial, showing him that though he had succoured so many poor persons he would himself be deserted by all, and that his body would be dragged along the streets. All this came to pass: he was attacked during the time of a severe pestilence, and it was thought proper to remove him out of his hospital to some more remote place, lest the poor patients should catch the infection. The disease was so violent and contagious, that no one dared approach and wait upon him; and thus he died deserted by all, as God had revealed to him; and after his decease, his body, according to the custom of the country on such occasions, was dragged by a cord along the streets to the burial-place in the cemetery of his hospital.

Thus died this great servant of God on the 3rd of June, 1600, at the age of fifty-three. His death caused universal grief throughout the city: it was said everywhere that the poor had lost their father and protector, and the religious of S. Francis cried out in the streets with a loud voice—"Do penance, for God has taken away from us a just man and a saint."

Our Lord suffered him to end his life in the manner we have related to humble him and to try his patience; but He soon afterwards glorified him by causing all the honours due to his memory to be paid him, and by having his body translated into a more honourable and suitable place; for extraordinary lights were seen over his grave for several nights, much to the astonishment of the brothers of his hospital, who looked upon them as a warning sent from God. They prayed and watched carefully, to see if the same thing happened again; and when they saw that it still continued, they informed their ecclesiastical superiors of it. The Vicar-General to whom they applied would not rely entirely on what they said, fearing lest out of too great affection for their beloved father, they might have imagined that they saw what did not in reality exist. He went therefore to sleep at the hospital, and after watching there for several nights, he saw the lights over the grave of the deceased. In consequence of this he ordered his holy body to be removed out of the cemetery and taken into the church. This translation was performed with great solemnity, all the officials of the city attending it; and God further manifested the sanctity of his servant by many remarkable miracles which took place during the ceremony, and are described in processes drawn up by order of the Holy See.

CHAPTER XIII. '

ON THE VIRTUES OF THE VENERABLE SERVANT OF GOD, BROTHER RODERICK DE SIGUENZA.

IT would be easy to fill a large volume with the account of the extraordinary virtues of various other children of S. John of God, many of whom were distinguished for their eminent piety; but for the sake of brevity we will speak of those only who laboured more especially in the establishment of his order. When the founder died it was simply a congregation of pious persons who had devoted themselves to the service of the poor under his guidance; and it was not until several years after his death that his community was placed in the rank of the religious orders. Brother Roderick Siguenza greatly contributed towards this by his care and forethought, and therefore it is just that he should have a place in this history.

Being descended from a noble family, of the kingdom of Arragon, he at first followed the profession of arms, in which he greatly distinguished himself for the space of twenty years, during the reign of Philip II. He held honourable posts, and most probably would have been raised to still higher, had not God called him to enter a more noble and glorious service. The desire of returning to his native country and of seeing his relations again was the reason he alleged for breaking his engagements with the army, but the real motive was his piety and love of retirement.

When he arrived in his native country, he found that his father and mother were dead, and that the affairs of his family were in so disordered a state that he had no hopes of obtaining any inheritance. This temporal misfortune served to excite in his mind a holy disgust for all earthly things, and a desire to follow seriously after virtue. He went therefore to Granada, whither God interiorly called him, and began to frequent the hospital of S. John of God. He there served and consoled the poor, worked diligently in the infirmaries, very often conversed with the brothers, and inquired into the constitutions and regulations which they observed. All this produced a great effect upon him, and detached him more and more from the world, making him desire ardently to lead a life, which he saw was so holy and so useful to his neighbour.

He opened his mind to Brother John Garcia, the Superior at Granada, and begged for the habit of the congregation. The twelve other brothers who were in the house, and with whom John Garcia conferred, readily gave their votes for his reception, knowing him to be an exemplary and pious man. Thus he was admitted to wear the habit almost as soon as he asked for it. His zeal, charity, and humility during his noviciate led them to expect great things from him; he was always the first at work, and he never spared himself in anything; he showed such kindness, patience, and gentleness towards the poor, that it was clear he loved them very tenderly. He was so obedient, not only to the Superior, but to all the other brothers, that one would have said his heart was truly humbled to the dust in the sight of God. As soon as his year of probation was ended, the office of Dispenser was given to him, in the exercise of which he showed, by his great care and attention, that he was capable of filling still higher offices. Seeing him always engaged in the infirmaries, thinking of everything and supplying all their wants, the poor generally called him their guardian angel; and he retained this name for several years, as we shall presently see.

A great war sprang up soon afterwards in the dominions of the King of Spain; for the Moors having revolted and taken up arms in several provinces, the monarch was obliged to levy troops to quell the insurrection. It would lead us too far from our subject were we to relate the particulars of this famous war; we will only remark that Roderick of Siguenza was chosen with Sebastian Arias by the Elder Brother—that is to say, by the General of the Congregation—to go and take charge of the hospital in the army of his Catholic Majesty. On this occasion his great qualities shone forth conspicuously: he quietly put everything in order; he was quick and attentive in serving the sick, skilful in dressing the wounded, and always on the watch to anticipate and satisfy their wants. He displayed on all occasions the greatest prudence, edified all by his modest and recollected air, and became a model of virtue in the midst of the camp; and the licentiousness of an army, which very often injures the piety of the most devout, could in nowise diminish his zeal, or induce him to take the slightest dispensation.

Being a perfect imitator of S. John of God, he did not confine his attention to the bodies of soldiers only, but endeavoured above all to procure the salvation of their souls; he instructed them in the principal mysteries of our religion, and often spoke to them about God; he reminded them that it was not enough to serve earthly princes with fidelity, and to obey their commands, but that they ought above all things to be faithful to God, observe His law and keep His commandments. He condemned their impious rashness in exposing their lives in battle without having first set their consciences in order and reconciled themselves with their Creator. He prepared them for confession, and brought them pious and learned confessors, as well as he could amid the confusion of a long and severe war.

When Moors were brought to his hospital to be taken care of, he successfully laboured to convert them to the Catholic faith and induce them to receive baptism; and, having gained them to Jesus Christ, he made them understand that the Gospel forbids subjects to revolt and take up arms against their sovereign, and by this means many were brought back to obedience. Thus he was esteemed not only by the Spaniards, but by the infidels also, being regarded by both as one sent from heaven to their assistance. Even the generals made much account of him, and placed very great confidence in all that he said. They invited him to their councils, and willingly followed his advice in the most important matters. They spoke of him as their angel and their guide, and looked upon him as a man of consummate experience.

The war being ended, and the Moors reduced to obedience, he took leave of the generals of the army, and returned with his companion to Granada. Hardly had he arrived there when all the brothers elected him Superior General, though he had not been in the order more than five or six years. As his reputation was very great, and every one spoke of his virtue and merit, many small communities similar to that of S. John of God, living in different parts of Spain, wished to be united to his congregation, and to have him for

their Superior; and with the approbation of the
Archbishop of Granada he took them all under his
direction, and incorporated them with his society,
whose numbers were by this means considerably
augmented.

Seeing himself in the place of S. John of God, he
strove to follow his example and imitate his admirable
qualities. He practised the same penances, and was
very careful in making mental prayer, and in keeping
himself always in the presence of God, which he
allowed nothing to make him lose sight of. He devoted the day to work and the night to prayer; he
had extraordinary zeal in the service of the poor; he
guided his brothers with as much wisdom as gentleness; he relieved widows and orphans, and secretly
helped the poor of good families; he consoled all who
came to relate their grievances to him; in short, he
was the oracle of many persons, who referred to him
their most important matters, some even disclosing
to him the secrets of their consciences.

The people, seeing in him so many virtues and excellent qualities, were in the habit of saying that
John of God had come to life again in his person, or
at least had bestowed on him an abundant portion of
his spirit, as formerly the prophet Elias did to his
servant Eliseus. He was everywhere respected,
and great honours were paid to him. His brothers
especially had so high an esteem of his merit, and
were so well satisfied with his manner of governing
them, that they continued him in the office of superior-
general for twenty-two years. He resisted indeed and
complained loudly of it, but they paid no attention to
his remonstrances, thinking that the glory of God
and their own spiritual benefit required it; for indeed

it was a great advantage to be under the guidance of so great a man.

It was in his time that the congregation of S. John of God received the great increase, of which we have spoken, by the union with it of the other small communities, and was placed in the rank of the religious orders. He was, properly speaking, the first Superior General of it ; he established in it a very exact discipline, quite in conformity with what the holy founder had begun during his life-time, and after edifying all his brothers by the example of his virtues, he died in the month of March in the year 1581, being seventy-one years old. His memory will live perpetually in his order, and he will ever be regarded as its second father, to whom it owes its formal establishment.

CHAPTER XIV.

ON THE SINGULAR MERIT OF THE VENERABLE SERVANT OF GOD, SEBASTIAN ARIAS.

This good religious did so much for the glory of S. John of God, and for his infant congregation, besides being so intimately connected with the great superior whose virtues I have just related, that it is right to speak of him also before concluding this history. The desire of making his fortune and of rising in the world led him when very young to follow the army and become a soldier; and when he heard of the riches of Peru he resolved to go with the troops which the King of Spain was sending thither, thinking he should return home a rich man for ever with immense treasures. But Divine Providence, which had other designs upon him, and destined him to be one of the chief supports of the family of S. John of God, did not permit him to succeed in the projects he had formed, but visited him with misfortune, to detach him from the world and lead him to nobler thoughts. The voyage proved unsuccessful to all who undertook it; they ran great dangers, and narrowly escaped perishing in the waves. Alarmed at his perilous condition, Sebastian began to implore the aid of Heaven and to recommend himself to the Blessed Virgin; he made a vow to serve the poor for a year in some hospital, if he had the happiness to return to Spain. God heard his prayer, the tempest subsided and all escaped the shipwreck they had deemed inevitable; their voyage became more prosperous, and thinking no more of the Indies, they sailed back to Spain, arriving there when they were least expected.

Sebastian was very careful to perform his vow, for as soon as he set foot on land he went to the hospital of S. John of God at Granada, and informing the superior of the promise he had made to God, he begged leave to fulfil it in that house. He there spent not a year only but eighteen months, serving the poor with so much devotion, assiduity and zeal that the brothers were greatly edified, and continually praised and blessed God for it.

He on his part admired them also and looked upon them as men of consummate piety; and their employment appeared to him the most holy and meritorious in the world. He ardently desired to join them and enter into their congregation, and so consecrate himself to God for ever, and be employed solely in the care of the sick poor. But his humility prevented his mentioning the subject to the superiors ; for he thought himself unworthy of living with them, and of becoming a member of their body, frequently saying to himself, "So great a sinner as I am deserves not to live in the company of these holy persons."   Still, after thinking long over the matter before God, he reflected that as this kind of life was very austere and full of mortifications, it might afford him an opportunity of doing penance, and that one object of religious congregations was to purify sinners and lead them to perfection. He thus changed his mind, and acquainted the superior with his great desire of being admitted to take the habit.   The brothers did not oblige him to remain long a postulant, for they had already received sufficient proof of his excellent qualities, and were all of them convinced that he was one of the best subjects they could receive into the house.

He did not imitate those who humble themselves and make a great show of zeal during the year of their probation, and afterwards alter their conduct and become relaxed, as soon as they think they will not be rejected and sent back into the world.   On the contrary, his fervour increased every day, he always wore the hair-cloth which he had put on when he took the habit; he was continually adding to his penances ; he was ingenious in torturing himself, and the disciplines he took were so severe that all who knew of them shuddered with horror, and could hardly comprehend how he had the strength and courage to treat his body so cruelly.   When his friends tried to moderate his great thirst for mortifications by representing to him that if he continued to practise such severities upon himself he would hasten his death, he only replied that the way of heaven was very narrow, and that in order to walk in it he must daily get rid of some of the bulk and weight of his body.

Though so very cruel and austere to himself, he was most tender and full of sweetness to others. He gave the sick everything that he thought would relieve or at least satisfy them, they were delighted with his affable manner of addressing them. He treated them with the same respect that he would have had for the sacred humanity of Jesus Christ, well knowing that the poor are the most noble of His members, and the most glorious part of His mystical Body.

It was remarked also that he advanced daily in Christian humility; the more he was exalted, the less did he think of himself; he studied to humble and lower himself in the sight of others, whilst every one else was honouring and respecting him, thereby doing exactly what the wise man recommends, "The greater thou art, the more humble thyself in all things." Out of humility he begged the superior to allow him to take his meals in the refectory with the novices, thinking himself unworthy to associate and sit at table with the professed.

On another occasion he gave a marked proof of his interior self-abasement and self-contempt. The superior had admitted a brother who was also called Sebastian, and being undecided whether he ought not to give him some other name that they might be distinguished from each other, he consulted the brothers assembled in chapter about it. When it was Sebastian's turn to speak, he said there was no occasion to change the name of the young novice, and begged the community to allow him to add to his own that of *the Sinner*, and to agree to his being called for the future Sebastian Peccador the Sinner, hoping by this means to appear vile and contemptible in the eyes of the world.

The wise man tells us that a man may be known by his look, and the thoughts of his heart, by his countenance, and if so we may truly say there never was a man more humble than Sebastian Arias, for his whole behaviour shewed that he entertained the greatest respect for every one, and that he esteemed himself inferior to all with whom he had to do. He generally observed silence, which according to the holy Fathers is a sign of a humble heart, since proud men are always seeking to attract notice and make themselves known; and when through any necessity he was obliged to speak, he did so in few words and in terms which expressed the feelings of his heart. It was also said of him, as of the publican in the Gospel, that he did not think himself worthy to lift up his eyes towards heaven, and therefore that he kept them always fixed on the ground.

The prayers which proceeded from so humble a heart were doubtless very powerful before God, and always heard with favour. The following is a striking instance of this. The inhabitants of Granada had suffered much from a long and severe drought, and the poor were reduced to the last extremity, provisions being so dear that the rich only could obtain any. Sebastian was moved at the sight of this misery, and trusting in the goodness and mercy of God he went into the middle of the public square with a crucifix in his hand, and kneeling down he entreated His divine Majesty to have pity on His people; he shed many tears and made a kind of honourable reparation to Him to appease His justice. Then the same prodigy took place as in the time of the prophet Elias, when he interceded for the Israelites who also were suffering from famine during a similar time of drought. The sky became suddenly overcast, and a very great quantity of rain fell, which fertilized the ground, whilst all men regarded the prodigy as a visible effect of his prayers. Thus people began to hold him in great esteem, and very many went to recommend to him their spiritual needs.

Like his holy founder, he knew the secrets of consciences, and God very often manifested to him the most hidden thoughts of those who conversed with him, so that sinners dared not appear before him, for fear lest he should put them to shame by manifesting their secret vices. This he did sometimes, not to bring dishonour or injury upon them, but to lead them to repentance and amendment of life, in which he was very successful. An event which occurred in the city of Granada is a striking proof of this. A man, who had lived in habitual sin for the space of ten years, passed by him one evening on his way to the scene of his debauchery. The servant of God immediately called out, "God sees thee, wretched man ; thy crime, which thou art trying to hide from the knowledge of men, is urging on His justice to punish thee. Whither art thou going ? beware lest this night be the last of thy life, and reflect that if thou diest in this state, thou wilt be cast into hell, where thou wilt burn for all eternity." These terrible words so astonished the man that he was converted on the spot, and began seriously to think of doing penance. His accomplice also profited by his example, and was converted.

We saw in the preceding chapter that he was sent

with Brother Roderick. of Siguenza to manage the hospital in the army, which was directed against the Moors by the King of Spain. He acted in perfect harmony with his illustrious colleague, shared in all his good works, and by his charity and other virtues rendered himself equally deserving of commendation. In fine, he shone as a bright light in the family of S. John of God; he edified all his brothers by his holy life, and laboured with untiring zeal for the benefit of his order, of which we will speak more fully in the following chapter.

CHAPTER XV.

THE DIFFERENT JOURNEYS HE MADE TO ROME FOR THE ESTABLISHMENT AND CONFIRMATION OF HIS ORDER.

ONE great distinction of this holy religious was his selection to go to Rome to solicit the approbation and confirmation of his order by the Pope. This alone shows him to be full of wisdom and prudence, and gifted with so high a degree of virtue and exemplary piety as to be considered a proper person to spread the good odour of his congregation in that great city, and to give the Sovereign Pontiff a favourable idea of it.

Roderick of Siguenza, as we mentioned above, had been elected superior-general on his return from the army; and it seemed to him that before all else he ought to obtain the approval of the Holy See for the institute, so that the brothers might work under its orders and protection, and by this deference to the church give additional merit to all their holy employments. He consulted Don Pedro Guerrero, Archbishop of Granada, who highly approved of his design, telling him not to delay the execution of it any longer. There could be no doubt in the minds of either of them who was the most fitting person to whom the matter might be entrusted, for Sebastian Arias possessed all the talents of nature and grace necessary for such an undertaking. To him, therefore, they entrusted a petition addressed to the Pope, containing an account of all that had happened from the commencement of the congregation. The king and all the nobles of the court gave him letters to the Pope, and to the ambassador of Spain who resided at the court of his Holiness, and he set out immediately with a companion in obedience to his superior.

When at Naples, he met Don John of Austria, who was going as it were in triumph to Rome after the famous victory of Lepanto, which he gained over the Turks. This kind and generous prince offered to introduce him to the Holy Father, to present the petition himself, and to obtain a favourable reception for it, all which he faithfully performed. S. Pius V., who then sat in the chair of S. Peter, was greatly edified by the humble and modest appearance of Sebastian Arias and his companion, and from their piety estimated that of all the children of S. John of God ; he rejoiced that in his time there should be established in the Church of Jesus Christ so holy and useful a congregation, solemnly approved of it, and issued the necessary bulls.

When Sebastian Arias had taken leave of his Holiness previous to his departure, Don John of Austria, in whose palace he had been living, wished to give him fresh marks of the affection and esteem he had for his order, and placed in his hands five thousand crowns, begging him on his way through Naples to establish a hospital there under the title of Our Lady of Victory. This establishment was very favourably received by the Neapolitans, who thought it a great advantage to have in their city the religious of S. John of God to attend to their sick poor.

Whilst the servant of God was employed in this great work, the inhabitants of Milan sent to beg him to establish a hospital in their city also. He was not able at that time to do as they wished, as he was anxious to return to Spain to give an account of what he had done, and carry with him the orders of the Pope; but he promised to bear their request in mind and to fulfil it as soon as he was able; and accordingly, on paying a visit to Rome soon afterwards on matters regarding the congregation, he founded in their city a large hospital, which up to the present day is famous for its magnificence.

Gregory XIII. having succeeded S. Pius V., Sebastian Arias made a third journey to Rome by the order of his superiors, to obtain from him the confirmation of all that the Holy See had already done in favour of their order. This great Pope again approved of it, and authentically confirmed the bulls of his predecessors. Finding also after conversing with the good religious that he possessed extraordinary merit, and was capable of the greatest undertakings, he resolved to employ him in a very important matter; namely, to go at once to the assistance of the inhabitants of Flanders who were afflicted with a pestilential disease. Many men would perhaps have hesitated before accepting an employment which would expose his life to great danger, but Sebastian undertook it readily, thinking that God was thus affording him an opportunity of making a voluntary sacrifice of his life.

He departed therefore with the blessing of the Vicar of Jesus Christ, hastened on his errand with all speed, and arrived in Flanders, when it was not thought he could have accomplished half the journey; and what is still more wonderful is that he performed it on foot, without either shoes or sandals.

It is not necessary to describe minutely all that he did for these poor people, for it may easily be imagined. He went from house to house, from town to town, and from city to city. He consoled some, attended others in their sickness, and gave food to all who were in want. He served at the same time as their physician and surgeon; he prepared the remedies himself, carried them to those for whom they were intended, and noted the effect they had upon them. He laboured not only by day but also the whole night; he watched by the worst cases, comforted those who were in their agony, buried the dead, and was to be found wherever there was work to be done.

Those who saw him thus actively engaged could hardly understand how he was able to fulfil so many different occupations. In reality his labour did surpass the ordinary strength of nature; and if charity, which is more powerful than death, had not supported him, he would have given way at the very commencement of his career, nor would he ever have been able to hold out for so long a time against such excessive and constant fatigue.

The time at last arrived when God had determined

to bestow on him the reward which his good works merited, and he passed from this life to a better. The Flemings, who were witnesses of his virtues, have always regarded him as a saint, and have frequently entreated the Holy See to complete the processes of his Beatification.

INDEX.

THE END.

R. WASHBOURNE, PRINTER, 18 PATERNOSTER ROW, LONDON.